# *Double Magic*

# Lyndon Hardy

Volume 6 of Magic by the Numbers

 Bartizan Press
Los Angeles

Version 6
Print ISBN: 978-17330950-8-2
Library of Congress Control Number: 2020918554

Other books by Lyndon Hardy

Master of the Five Magics, 2nd edition
Secret of the Sixth Magic, 2nd edition
Riddle of the Seven Realms, 2nd edition
The Archimage's Fourth Daughter
Magic Times Three

Visit Lyndon Hardy's website at: http://www.alodar.com/blog

Cover by Tom Momary http://www.tomomary.com

1. Fantasy 2. Magic 3. Adventure 4. New Adult

*To my nieces, Maria, Kate, and Star*

# Contents

The Laws of Magic     1

Map     2

Part One *Out with the Old*     3

Part Two *In with the New*     187

Author's Afterword     323

What's next?     325

Glossary     331

# Part One *Out with the Old*

1  Sylvia                         5

2  Mason                          12

3  The Presentation               18

4  Attack                         25

5  The Palace                     32

6  The Ballroom                   38

7  Enchantment                    46

8  Escape                         55

9  Mandrake Gleaning              60

10  The Carriage Factory          64

11  Lady Sylvia                   71

12  A Colony of Artists           77

13  Will-o-the-wisps and Fire Devils                85

14  Tracking Imps                                   93

15  An Election                                    100

16  A Compound of Scholars                         109

17  New Magic                                      117

18  Move and Countermove                           123

19  A Better Mousetrap                             129

20  Yterrby                                        134

21  More Alchemy                                   143

22  The Demon Queen                                149

23  A Visit with the Mayor                         155

24  Exponential Growth                             160

25  Imprisonment                                   168

26  High Stakes                                    177

## Part Two *In with the New*

1  Prediction Confirmed                     189

2  Launch                                   195

3  Realization                              202

4  Preparation for Pursuit                  211

5  Dargonel's Message                       216

6  In the Realm of Demons                   223

7  Black Pits                               229

8  Searching in Darkness                    237

9  Orbfall                                  245

10  Moonshadow                              250

11  Sylvia's Leap                           254

12  Accidentals                             262

13  Game Pawns                          271

14  Solitary Confinement                279

15  The Liturgy                         285

16  Searching                           289

17  Final Countdown                     293

18  A Matter of Gravity                 297

19  Confrontation                       301

20  An Outstretched Hand                307

21  Wrapping Up                         312

22  A New Beginning                     318

# The Laws of Magic

Thaumaturgy

The Principle of Sympathy — like produces like

The Principle of Contagion — once together, always together

Alchemy

▽

The Doctrine of Signatures — the attributes without mirror the powers within

Magic

◯

The Maxim of Persistence — perfection is eternal

Sorcery

◉

The Rule of Three — thrice spoken, once fulfilled

Wizardry

The Law of Ubiquity — flame permeates all

The Law of Dichotomy — dominance or submission

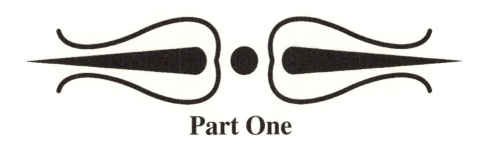

## Part One

# *Out with the Old*

# 1
# Sylvia

SYLVIA PLACED one finger on the spoon swirling around in the clay coffee mug to make it stop. She could see that the food stains were still visible on the tunic in the nearby washtub.

She rose from stooping over and stretched her back. The little aches and pains had become more persistent of late, and that had her worried. She was not all that old; in her late twenties. But the life of a do-everything servant was in no way like the pampered existence of the women living on top of the hill.

Looking down into the water in the tub, she saw a clear reflection. Midnight-black hair, wide-set blue eyes under long lashes, a button of a nose over a mouth too wide for her narrow face. She was possibly average, she told herself. Not a head-turner, but surely one of the craftsmen along the street would eventually notice — if only they would summons enough courage to visit the home of a wizard. She straightened and stretched because it felt good, but then immediately slumped. Yeah, she would be noticeable to a brave man who stood seven feet maybe. Why was she so damn tall?

"Where is my robe?" A raspy voice thundered through the curtains leading to the front room. "The one with the logos that shows clearly that I am a wizard."

"It's not ready yet," Sylvia yelled back. She resumed twirling the spoon, and the water in the washtub resumed sloshing in response. 'Like produces like.', she thought. So much easier than wrestling with the full load in the tub. "You have to put on a fresh undertunic as well. The other one is too smelly."

"They will be too distracted by the imps to notice," the wizard, Rangoth, said as he limped into the scullery. He was short and thin with loose flesh hanging like empty hammocks from seldom used arms. The skin on his pockmarked face looked like old leather that had outlived its use.

Through rheumy eyes, he scanned the room. "Thaumaturgy!" he spat, pointing at the clay mug.

"You know I do not care for the exercise of any of the other crafts here. They detract from my performances."

Sylvia sighed. "We have been over this many times, Master. The days in which all the five arts were shrouded in secrecy have long since passed. Now, even children can cast a spell or two." She waved her hand over the pile of dirty clothes still to be washed. "And without a few simple aids, a lone person such as myself cannot cater to all your needs."

"*Aids*? Wizardry is not a sling around a broken arm. It takes strength of will, a fundamental belief in oneself."

"Yes, yes," Sylvia sighed again. "Wizardry is the most elegant craft of them all. Far better than mastery of alchemy, magic, or even sorcery. All four of the others are inferior arts."

"The most elegant here in Procolon," Rangoth began repeating the patter he made Sylvia suffer through daily. "The most elegant in Procolon, Ethidor, and the other kingdoms to the south."

"And Arcadia across the great ocean," Sylvia chimed in. "Everywhere on Murdina, wizardry is best. I remember, Master. I really do."

6

"To be a great wizard, desire alone is not enough," Rangoth continued.

"No, as you always say, most important is a belief in oneself."

"Ah, the days of yore," Rangoth continued with a far-away look in his eyes. "Did I tell you of the time I summoned up not only one but two lightning djinns at the same time? One is a challenge for anyone, of course. But two, each determined to dominate my will rather than the other way around. Remarkable! The first was the stronger. He — "

"Yes, yes. Many times, Master, you have told me. Wizardry is best, and you are the best of wizards. Now, please go back and study the notes I have transcribed for you on how your presentation is to proceed. The one this afternoon could be important. A performance for no less than one of the more prominent nobles on the hill. We don't want the same thing to happen as the last time you faltered."

Rangoth mumbled something incoherent and shuffled back out of the scullery. Sylvia stared at the pile of clothing still to be washed, contemplating what to do next. She wrung out the garments and put them into a drying basket before throwing in another load of soiled clothes. It shouldn't matter, but to be sure, she emptied the mug and refilled it again from the tub.

"Once together, always together," she said to herself. "The Principle of Contagion." Finally, she voiced the simple charm that activated the spell.

Then she sat back down and twirled the spoon in the refreshed mug again. The water in the washtub swirled and swished in synchrony. Sylvia smiled with satisfaction. "Like produces like," she said as the washing resumed. "The Principle of Sympathy." Thaumaturgy was not daunting like wizardry. It was so easy.

SOMETIME LATER, Sylvia slumped into the scullery chair. Rangoth had his clean robe, and the rest of the washing was finished but there was still so much more to do. Ironing the better robe and changing the bed linens. Sweeping the cobwebs out of the ceiling corners in all the rooms. And then, after the performance, preparing an evening meal.

There were scant prospects for things to get better. She had been in Rangoth's service for almost a decade. At first, she had felt fortunate. For an orphan with only a talent for play-acting, it was a welcome alternative to a life on the street. A live-in servant to a master wizard, no less. One with a reputation for keeping his hands to himself.

But there was a reason Rangoth lived on an out of the way street. He was no longer employable at any of the great houses that ruled the land. Far too soon, his mental abilities had begun to falter. He could no longer summon demons of great power. Nor even control lesser ones to perform useful tasks. Each year, he sank deeper into dotage, able to control only the most simple of imps. There were fewer and fewer performances. And lower prices to attract more customers. What was happening could not go on much longer.

That is *why* I wrote the letter, Sylvia tried to convince herself. I had to try, right? It was rumored that in one of the southern kingdoms there was another wizard, one who was unique. Like Sylvia herself, she was a woman!

All five of the magical crafts were performed almost universally by men. Indeed, all society was male-dominated. But with a female wizard, a fairly young one at that, Sylvia thought she would be a perfect match as a servant. And who knew. Rather than a mere lackey, she might be able to learn some of the craft of wizardry —

There was a tap on the door.

The lord! Was he already here? She hadn't time to do a final thorough check on all the props. The small branches of wood that would be burned. The incense holder with the aroma the imps liked so much …

The tapping became more insistent. She brushed away the dust from her dress, straightened her hair, put a big smile on her face, and marched to the door.

"You are early, Milord, but this is perfectly —"

Sylvia stopped abruptly. There was no noble standing there. A gnome-like man with smelly clothes squinted up at her with a crooked grin. A third of his teeth were missing, and those remaining were twisted and stained. A foul odor rose from him like that of week-old garbage.

"Are you the one called Sylvia?" he asked.

"What do you want? I'm busy. Not interested in buying any hair-jumbler imp repellant today."

"If you are, then I have a letter for you. I have brought it all the way from Brythia in the south."

The little man squinted at the envelope, grimy with dirt and stains.

"From someone named 'Phoebe', it looks like. Are you interested or not?"

Phoebe! Sylvia brought her fist to her mouth to prevent herself from shouting. Phoebe, the female wizard! She had answered! Against all odds, she had answered the letter. Maybe there would be a way out of all this for her.

"Give it to me!" Sylvia reached out to snag the envelope.

"Not so fast. I had to travel many leagues and suffer outrageous hardships to get this to you."

"Didn't the wizard pay you for the transport? That is what I did to send my letter to her."

"Well, yes, but you see I have expenses that must be met and —"

"I have no more money of my own," Sylvia said.

The little man slowly examined Sylvia from head to toe. He had to crane his neck to see her hair. "Payment in kind

9

would be acceptable." He leered. "I am a reasonable man. Even a quick one would do."

"No, no quicky." she scowled. "Nothing like that. How much are we talking about here?"

"Only one gold brandel. A bargain at half the price." The little man paused a moment and then smiled. "See what I did there? Think about it. I said 'A bargain at *half* the price.' Usually, the patter goes like 'A bargain at *twice* the price.' No one ever catches on. The joke sails right by them."

"Half a brandel it is," Sylvia blurted. She was surprised at the words that had flown out of her mouth. But this was justified. The trap she was in would never end. Finally, there was a path to a better life.

The little man shuffled from foot to foot. "That was only a small joke. My clients chuckle at it when I explain to them what happened."

Sylvia scowled. "Half a brandel and that is all." She felt conflicted about the honesty of what she was doing, but at the moment, the lure of freedom was too strong. Freed from more years of drudgery yet to come. "Make up your mind now, and be off with you."

Sylvia stared at the little man, unblinking. She lost track of time. But after what felt like an eon, he spoke again.

"All right, all right. Half a brandel it is. Can you give it to me in small change?"

Sylvia did not hesitate. She opened the coin pouch hanging from a peg on the wall and extracted the payment. Quickly, the exchange was made. For a moment, she clutched the letter to her chest.

"Are they here yet?" Rangoth lumbered into the presentation room. "I thought I heard someone at the door."

Sylvia thrust the letter down the front of her smock. Damn the law that said women could not have pockets. She looked at Rangoth smiling at her, and her thoughts tumbled.

Rangoth. The aging wizard. He had been so very easy to get along with. No innuendos, no leering hints. Forgetful, of course, but never a cross word. If she left, what was going to happen to him? He was incapable of handling finances any more. And even if that was figured out somehow, in the long run, there would be no one to take care of him after she was gone. To keep track of things. Cook the meals, do the washing, make sure he was ready for the next presentation.

The next presentation! Sylvia ran to the window in the west and squinted at the sun. As near as she could estimate, it would be soon. In less than an hour, what was his name — it sounded important. Yes. Royal Impresario Lord Mason would be arriving with his three little sisters for their first glimpse at cavorting imps.

# 2
# Mason

LORD MASON Staffwielder, Royal Impresario for the Queen of Procolon, flicked the falling ash from one of his sleeves. The grey dust of the construction site might smear against his purple velvet jacket.

He touched the length of his shocking-red curls. A visit to the royal barber would be needed soon. Appearance was important for what he did. He imagined how he must look to prospective entertainers. Square jaws, cleanly shaven. A welcome smile with tiny wrinkles just beginning to show in the corners of his blue eyes. Someone you felt comfortable dealing with.

His three younger sisters, ten, twelve, and fifteen, fidgeted next to him.

"This is boring," Patience, the youngest, said.

"Worse than that, it's dirty," Althea, the middle one, joined in.

Lalage, the oldest, as always remained silent. As did the elderly matron who accompanied them.

"Yes, yes," he said. "We will be on our way to see some imps in a moment." He sighed in resignation as he examined the construction site. He had no interest in being there either. But Alpher, his eldest brother, had insisted. Check up on what Wetron, the next most senior, was up to.

He told himself for the thousandth time that the thrusts and parries of state were of no concern to him. Being the patron of the arts was far more important, a more difficult task to do well, actually. He had absolutely no interest in being the lord of a fief.

Of course, he didn't. Let his two brothers decide among themselves who was to be regarded as the most able lord. He squashed again the nagging thought that a small holding would not be all that bad, generating enough income to satisfy his tastes but not large enough to be a threat to anyone.

He craned his head upward. "Do I understand this correctly?" he said to the foreman over the roar of the nearby blast furnace. "You are going to make this tower more than three stories tall?"

"We're using the latest ideas. The heat from burning logs for the motive force rather than something mechanical." The foreman puffed out his chest. "Who knows. Five floors, maybe six."

Mason dusted more falling ash from his jacket and grimaced. He had been right. It left a smear of grey on one of the appliqués. He looked around the construction site. It was much larger than most. Bare dirt that had been roughly leveled. A pile of immense tree trunks stripped of their branches stacked in two piles on one side. A furnace so hot that the air wiggled when one squinted in its direction. And all around, dozens of workers busy with their tasks.

Some kept the furnace working, slinging shovel after shovel of coal into a fiery maw. Others loaded trunks from one of the piles into wicker baskets, then stood back as they rose upward. In a flash, they stopped at the top of a skeleton framework already the height of three tall men standing on each other's shoulders. Like busy ants, workers there hammered the lumber onto the rising structure with long, iron spikes.

"It is the thickness of the wood, its loadbearing strength,

that makes it possible to build so high." The foreman followed Mason's gaze. "It takes a lot of what the masters call energy, whatever that is, to lift the stout beams above the ground so swiftly. The heat in the furnace supplies that. No great strength is needed at all. So long as we brace and reinforce everything as we go, we can scrape the sky."

Mason did not reply. Instead, he looked up the hill toward Vendora's palace. Alpher's suspicion had been correct. He frowned at the foreman. "If you go above five stories, then the pennants on top of this 'townhouse', as my brother, Wetron, calls it, will be higher than those of the queen."

The foreman beamed. "Such is progress. One pile of logs for the framing and another to provide the energy to raise them quickly. No need for block and tackle, for thick hawsers that snap and break. The old ways fade in the glow of the new."

"Yes, I agree. There is a general feeling in the air. An excitement for change. Even the playwrights and actors have caught a whiff of it."

"It does come at a cost." The foreman shrugged. "The gondolas also raise the workers to the upper stories as well as the beams. Takes less time for them to get there. Fewer of them are needed."

"Look! Over there. A doll house," Patience shouted.

On the ground, far away from the basking heat of the furnace, stood the framework of a small, rectangular structure built of tiny, round sticks and flat, wooden spools with holes drilled around their peripheries and completely through their centers. Some of the sticks were stuck in central openings and others in those on the edges.

Next to the little structure lay a pile of unsmoothed twigs. As everyone watched, the worker attending the toy put a twig into a thimble and slowly raised it in the air. Then he stopped and moved it to touch the little structure. Out of the corner of his eye, Mason saw one of the full-sized baskets soar skyward in mimicking response.

It was clear enough to Mason what was happening. When the twig touched the uppermost story of the little house, its bigger cousin gently kissed the building under construction. The incantations to bind them together must have been spoken the first thing in the morning.

"I see," Mason said. "The twigs are from the first pile of logs. They were once together."

"Yes, when we move the twigs about," the foreman said, "the heavy timbers respond exactly in kind."

"And the heat of the burning logs from the second pile provide the motive force that is needed." Mason spoke rapidly. He did not want a mere foreman to think that he was a dotard.

"As more of this art catches on, there will be less need for the building carpenters everywhere," the foreman said. "When the furnaces arrived here, a number of the workers were let go." He slapped his knee and laughed. "They could not believe it and stood around, slack-jawed with envy at those who were lucky enough to be still employed."

Mason looked about the site. "I don't see any of them about now."

"No, Wetron sent some of his guardsmen to push them away. Now they all cluster around the palace gates shouting their chants, begging Queen Vendora to intervene."

This construction will only cause more trouble between his elder brothers. Mason frowned. If the object was to brag about a tower taller than any of the queen's, wouldn't a second one soon be started next to the first? Why couldn't the two of them just get along? They were the most powerful of all the fieflords in the land. Or even better, the thought recurred to him for the thousandth time, grant to him a portion of what they held.

Yes, by custom, a fief transferred from father to eldest son. Or, in some circumstances, it could be divided into two.

15

Vendora had managed to insist on that. She was more cunning than what one might suppose. But the result was that he ended up with nothing, a mere stipend to keep his body clothed and his belly full. An errand boy to do the bidding of both brothers. Check on the tower construction. Entertain the sisters for an afternoon …

Mason glanced at the young women fondly. Well, that part was not so bad. He had become a surrogate father for them. Alpher and Wetron neglected them so. It was a pleasure to watch them blossom into womanhood. Lalage, wise beyond her years, now already bracing herself to be a mere pawn in a strategic alliance with some other lord. Aletha, the flirt, batting her eyes at the foreman …

"You said we were going to see some imps," Patience broke through Mason's reverie.

"True," he smiled. "And tonight, I have arranged for a sorcerer, a renowned illusionist, to amuse the court. You will get to stay up past your bedtime to experience his entrancement."

"I need to go pee first," Patience said.

"Ah, you can use the outhouse over there." The foreman pointed. "Knock first to make sure."

The matron grabbed Patience's hand, and the other two sisters followed.

"Milord, you are spying for Alpher, aren't you?" the foreman said when they were alone. "You know, of course, that your brother, Wetron, is not going to like that."

Mason shrugged. "My brothers are consumed by their rivalry. They think of little else. The queen split my father's fief between them when he passed so that they would struggle against one another rather than cast eyes on the throne themselves. I try to stay neutral and concentrate on my work."

"Work? Pardon me, Milord, but besides, ah, baby-sitting, what is it that you do?"

"I am the Royal Impresario," Mason said. "I arrange all the entertainment for the court."

The foreman looked Mason up and down. He became bolder. "Ah, I see. That is the reason for the fancy dress? A velvet jacket with designs splattered over it. Leggings too tight for any possible comfort. Jowls void of hair. A frogstabber instead of a real dagger. How old are you anyway?"

Mason shrugged. "Twenty-six revolutions of the sun. And as for my dress, it is the fashion. What I have to do. I find no pleasure in engaging in the struggle between my brothers."

The foreman snorted. "You are like a gaudy snail hiding in your shell. Soon, Milord, you are going to have to stick your neck out and choose between them."

"I plan to remain neutral."

"Then *both* of them will want you dead."

# 3

# The Presentation

MASON HELPED Patience from the carriage. The livery stable smelled awful. Evidently, there was no effort spent in keeping the place clean. But the directions from the hostler were clear enough. It was only a short walk down the street to Rangoth's place.

The matron exited the coach last, and the quintet stumbled along the rutted street. They stopped at a door between two shuttered windows. Mason read aloud the faded lettering on it. "Wizard for Hire. Reasonable rates. Inquire within." He gave the door a gentle tap.

Immediately, it swung open. Mason blinked at a young woman standing there. He noticed she was taller than he. Even though her eyes sagged with fatigue, she still managed to pull a little smile onto her face. He was surprised to find her quite pretty, though her particular beauty was hard to define.

"Sorry," he said. "I am looking for Rangoth, the wizard. I am Lord Mason. My sisters and I are here for a presentation of performing imps."

"This is the place," Sylvia answered with some animation. "You're early, but no matter. Come in, and I'll summon the master."

As she hurried away, Mason smiled as he thought about

her attitude. She was probably trapped into a life of service with no real future prospects. Yet, she still managed a lively and cheerful air for the sake of impressing a paying customer.

Not so unlike himself, he realized suddenly. For the queen, he, too, smiled and praised her understanding of art and music when she made pronouncements such as 'I liked that. I liked that a lot.' Without the royal patronage, he would be out on the street, no better off than the serving wench he had just met.

He glanced around the room. It spanned the entire width of the one-story structure that was lit dimly by the twinkle of candlelight from tall, floor-mounted holders. Four small chairs faced a larger, high-backed one standing deeper within.

"Is no one else coming?" Mason asked.

"A special showing for you," the servant called back. "But if you like what you see, please tell others. We can accommodate up to a dozen." She looked back at him. "My name is Sylvia. And if you would like a refreshment, wait just a moment."

"I know little of wizardry, but wouldn't eating and drinking interfere with Rangoth's concentration?"

"He does not wrestle with djinns any longer," Sylvia said as she reentered carrying the handle of a large skillet horizontally. "And imps are easy."

The sauce in the frying pan sizzled and popped. Mason breathed deeply and inhaled an enticing aroma. He had heard that the food of the streets was more interesting than the sugar-laden fare of the court, and now he was sure of it.

"What exactly — " Mason began.

"Fried grasshoppers," Sylvia said. "Because of the summer rain, they are exceptionally big this year. Three in a serving, and for only — "

"An additional charge?" Mason asked. "Not interested." It was always like this. Everyone thought that if you were a lord, the coins in your pocket came from a bottomless pit.

He and his sisters took their seats. The matron said nothing and remained standing behind.

Sylvia sat the skillet on the floor. "It does get a bit hot in here with the windows closed. We keep it that way so non-payers can't peek inside. And if you would like something, then now is the best time — "

"I don't see any imps yet," Patience said.

"I'm hot already," Althea said. "This is boring."

As if on cue, the door in the rear reopened, and Rangoth lumbered into the room. With an unsteady hand, he settled into the high-backed chair.

"Welcome," he said in a reedy voice. "Prepare to be amazed." He looked at each of the sisters for a moment, then smiled. "Demons live in a realm different from our own. If it were not for the flame conduit, we could never interact."

He squinted at the three girls. "Haven't you ever been at a campfire at night and looked into the flickering flames? Been fascinated by them, intrigued by what might lie beyond?" Rangoth dithered for a moment and then rushed on. "What you experience when that happens is a demon beckoning to you, asking you to bring it forth."

"We are not infants," Althea said. "We know all this. Get on with the show."

Rangoth ignored the comment. "Each type of demon communicates with its own unique type of fire," he said. "The material one burns determines — "

"Jump to the imps," Sylvia whispered. She stooped to pick up a pile of sticks lying next to Rangoth's chair.

Rangoth hesitated. "The mightiest of demons we call djinns, and — "

"The imps," Sylvia said a little louder.

Rangoth stopped speaking. Even in the dimness, Mason could see the wizard had become confused. Well, what did

20

one expect for only a few brandels?

"Imps are the ones we will —" Sylvia said at full voice.

"Ah, yes. Imps are the ones we will call forth today." Rangoth got back on track. "Assistant, light the oleander fire."

"Yes, Master." Sylvia piled the sticks into a conical tent, lit a match, and thrust it into the small structure.

Almost instantly, the little branches caught fire, filling the air with an oily, pungent odor. Sylvia waved a fan to scoot the toxic air away.

"Come forth, little ones. I command you." Rangoth stared into the flame.

Nothing happened for a dozen heartbeats. Then, in a blink, more than a score of tiny lights appeared in the room. To Mason, they looked like a swarm of mosquitoes. No, bigger than that. One could make out details. Tiny squashed heads with bulging eyes over stick-figure bodies. Behind each was the flicker of rapidly vibrating wings, that filled the air with an annoying hum. And they were glowing, somehow. More like ...

"Fireflies!" Patience said. "Larger than normal to be sure, but we see those all the time. They are not imps."

"You're not witnessing mindless insects," Rangoth said. "Instead, these are intelligent *beings* — imps. Watch."

The swarm swirled to Patience's face, and she almost instantly yelled. "Ouch! My nose just got pinched."

"Yes, fireflies can't do that," Rangoth said. "What you see dancing and swooping before you are nosetweakers."

"Teehee. Teehee," a chorus of high-pitched voices filled the air. The imps darted to Althea, and she frantically tried to bat the little demons away. For a few moments, she was successful. But eventually, she yelled "Ouch" even louder than had her sister.

Lalage remained silent when it was her turn, and after an

21

even longer time, the swarm gave up and hovered unmoving in front of her.

"You're no fun at all," the imp chorus complained.

Mason squirmed in his seat. His own presentations to the queen were much more sophisticated.

"Silence," Rangoth commanded. "You are the ones who must submit to my will."

The cacophony immediately ceased.

"That's better. We have guests here, and you must perform. Show them you understand basic arithmetic. How much is two plus four?"

The buzzing resumed, and then grew louder and louder.

"It is quite simple, idiots," one imp squeaked. "You can count each number on the fingers of one hand."

"No, lamebrain," shrilled another. "Two groups of four. That's eight altogether."

"Both of you are as crazy as a gallop of gremlins," shouted a third. "Listen to me."

"Flowerbreath, you couldn't fight your way out of a bag made of fishnet."

"Oh, yeah? Where did you get that idea? Your mother must have been human."

"Come on, guys. Settle down. Let's solve this like we always do. Majority rules. The right answer gets the most votes."

Well, it was a farce, maybe, Mason decided. But certainly nothing for the queen.

The buzzing subdued but did not quite go away. Then six of the little lights aligned themselves in a vertical row. A second column joined alongside the first, followed by a third and fourth. Finally, a last row slanted across them all.

"Ta da!" the imps sang, fluttering in place.

No one else in the room spoke. The silence dragged on.

"Well, come on guys," the imps said. "This is the place where you give us thundering applause."

"Ah, I don't think five is correct," Patience said.

"Ooooh, a tough audience. Well, we don't have to put up with any more of this abuse."

In a flash, all the lights winked out. The air was clear.

Sylvia looked at Rangoth. "Master," she whispered. "You forgot to maintain control again."

"That's it?" Althea asked. "That's all we are going to see? Brother Mason, how much did you pay for this?"

"They are nosetweaker imps," Sylvia jumped in, "not mighty djinns. They are dominated and have been trained. Didn't you see?"

"Can you control any other types?" Mason asked. "Ones perhaps a bit more … impressive."

"Other types," Rangoth shook from his inattention. "There was a time when — "

"Yes, there are lots of other types," Sylvia looked directly at Mason. "But they are not appropriate for this young an audience. Hair-jumblers who snarl your curls while you are sleeping. Razor dullers who dull the blades you use to shave your legs."

She took a deep breath and continued. "Armpit gluers, panty switchers, and ah, orifice crawlers."

"Brother Mason, we've seen enough," Patience said. "Let's go back to the castle and get ready for the evening show. The one you told us about."

Mason realized this outing was a bust. He rose and reached into his purse to pay. "How much again?" he asked.

"Half a brandel each," Sylvia said. "For five, that is two and a half."

"Two and a half? There are only four of us."

"I count five," Sylvia said and pointed to the matron. She took a deep breath. "And, of course, a gratuity would be greatly appreciated. Three brandels is a good round number."

Mason grimaced. It was as he had expected. He fingered out the coins, deciding how many to hand over. As he did, the door behind him slammed open against the front wall with a loud bang.

# 4

# Attack

SYLVIA'S EYES widened. She stumbled in surprise. She could not believe what she was seeing. Four ill-clad ruffians with drawn daggers had burst into the room.

"Kill them all," the one in front yelled. "Even the children."

The intruder spotted Sylvia trying to regain her footing and rushed at her. A grin spread over his pockmarked face. "This one is mine," he said. "After I have a little sport first."

As he bent to seize her, Sylvia grabbed the skillet lying nearby with both hands and thrust it at his gut. The rogue bent double. She raised the pan and slammed it into his chin. Blood and bits of teeth sprayed forth from his mouth. Crispy grasshoppers and hot oil spattered everywhere.

Sylvia scrambled out of the way of the falling man. Still clutching her weapon, she swung it as hard as she could at the head of one of the others surrounding Mason. The brigand's skull cracked from the impact, and he slumped to the ground.

"Behind you," she screamed.

Mason twirled to face another assailant. He took a slight step to the side, avoided the knife thrust, and pinned the outstretched arm of his attacker under his own. With a deftness Sylvia could only gasp at, the lord plunged his dagger into his adversary's heart. The impresario's eyes

25

widened in surprise. Apparently, Mason was as shocked as anyone by what he had done.

The last scoundrel bolted for the door. "We will be back," he growled over his shoulder as he left. "More of us next time. You cannot escape your doom."

"Is everyone all right?" Mason immediately asked his sisters. When Patience burst into tears, he said, "Come on, let's get out of here," he said. "Big hugs and kisses later, once we are safe."

"Wait!" Sylvia shouted. "You're going to leave? What about us? They said they will be back. You heard him."

"Your struggle with street hoodlums is no concern of mine," Mason said.

"You wouldn't be standing now if not for this skillet."

Mason hesitated. He looked at the two men who had been felled behind his back and shuddered. "All right," he said. "You can accompany me. I will figure out a place where you can hide."

Sylvia shook her head. She stared at Rangoth sitting complacently in his high chair, his eyes drooping closed. "No. Not good enough. The master comes as well."

"The wizard? Look at him. He is falling asleep!"

"He nods off that way after he has finished sometimes, but we cannot leave him behind."

For a moment, no one spoke as Mason screwed up his face in thought. "All right, all right," he said at last. "What is important is to leave as swiftly as we can. If you look after the wizard, you can bring him, too. Hurry, we must go."

Sylvia roused Rangoth out of his reverie, then turned her attention back to Mason. "Why did they attack? What is it you have done?"

"Me? Nothing, of course. As I said, problems on your street —"

"You're in the thick of this," Sylvia cut him off.

"Certainly, no one would have any reason to accost an old wizard and his servant girl. There is no wealth here. What is it *you* have done?"

"I don't know. There must be a mistake."

"Okay, a discussion later. But where are we going?"

Mason frowned. "The palace," he blurted. "It is the safest place in the kingdom. No one attempts any mayhem under the eyes of the queen." He wrapped his arm around Patience, who was still sobbing. "Come along now. Everyone back to our coach."

Sylvia forced herself to calm down. She did not like rushing into strange situations without good reason. But even if no more brigands returned, when the tax collector came tomorrow, what then? She hadn't obtained the three brandels. She and Rangoth would become slaves.

What did she know about this lord of the court, anyway? Obviously, he had had at least some training about how to defend himself. Although … his shock when he dispatched the ruffian indicated that, heretofore, it all had been play. As she thought about him, a small rush of passion made her blush. His red curls were quite beguiling.

So, in for a copper, in for a brandel. She shrugged and squatted to rouse Rangoth from wherever his thoughts had taken him. "Come along, Master. We are going on a little trip."

SYLVIA SETTLED into the padded seat of the coach as it left the stable. What had happened scant moments before began to sink in. She had disabled two men, maybe even killed one of them. Left their bodies behind with no explanation. Shut and locked the door so that thieves would not …

She shuddered as sudden remorse washed over her, a feeling she had never experienced before. Two men, no matter how vile, had their lives forever altered because of what she had done. The images of the attack reverberated horribly in her mind, something she would never forget. No, she told herself; they *would* fade away. She had done no wrong. She had defended Rangoth and herself. There had been no other choice.

For a long while, no one in the carriage spoke. Only the clop of the horses' hooves made any noise. Patience's sobs quieted to a soft murmur. Her two sisters said nothing, their eyes still wide with shock. Mason tried to put his arms around all three but could not manage it.

Sylvia beckoned to Lalage. The oldest sister staggered across the space between the two facing coach benches. She curled into a ball in Sylvia's lap. The matron said nothing. She sat apart with Rangoth on a servant's bench behind the two facing rows.

"Why did this happen?" Sylvia asked Mason as the journey settled into a gentle trot. "The attack was meant for you. It has to have been."

"I don't know," Mason stammered. "I really don't." He shrugged while still managing to keep his two sisters tight to his chest. "I do not meddle in the politics of the court at all. *I* do not matter."

"It has to be related somehow to an intrigue around the queen," Sylvia said. "Why else — " She stopped and changed her tack. "And if the queen is involved, the palace is the last place you — I mean we, should be."

Mason pulled his sisters tighter. "The safest place in all Procolon is the palace. And the safest place in the palace is the queen's nursery. She has little ones of her own. When we arrive," he told the matron, "hustle these three into safety there. This is very important. Do you understand?"

"Yes, Milord," the matron answered softly. "When one is not noticed, they can go anywhere. Those strutting finery are the ones who have their motion restricted."

"What about Rangoth and me?" Sylvia asked. "Are you going to dump us at the palace gate?"

Mason shook his head slowly. "No, not there. You would not be safe. No carpenters were present at the gate when we left the palace, but by now, some might have congregated there."

"Why?"

"To shout and harass anyone who wants to pass through."

"Where will you take us?"

"I don't know!" Mason scowled. "I've said that more than once already. Give me a moment to think everything through."

The pace of the trotting horses slowed a bit. They had reached the foot of what was grandly called the "palace hill."

Sylvia heard shouting and peeked out the coach window. There *was* a noise coming from the front of the gate. She turned her head toward it and blinked. There were not only a few craftsmen there but what appeared to be over a hundred people, all agitated and angry.

Carpenters waved their measuring sticks in the air. Seamstresses brandished tambours and spools of thread. "No more machines that sew," they shouted. Bakers wearing their puffy toques lofted mixing bowls and yelled, "Hands knead with tender care. Worthy work takes time."

Yes, some workers were dissatisfied, Sylvia thought, but she did not care. She had too much to worry about on her own.

The carriage came to a halt at the rear of the crowd. Mason rapped twice on the carriage roof, poked his head out his window, and craned his head upward. "Groomsman, what can you see?"

"Please take patience, Milord," the servant replied. "A squadron of sentinels is marching down the hill from the palace itself. They will arrive shortly and force open a path

29

for us to enter."

Mason sat back down and patted his sisters clinging to him. "A few moments more, my turtledoves, and this will be a fading memory."

After what seemed like an eternity to Sylvia, with a rattle, the palace gates swung open. A herald at the fore of the troops bellowed to the crowd. "Hear ye, hear ye! The queen has spoken. Select four to enter. After the performance tonight is over, her majesty will hold an audience with you. Speak then of your displeasure. She will listen to you, but no more than four."

"Our means of livelihood," one in the crowd shouted. "The fact is simple enough. This surge of discoveries disrupts what has been the practice for generations. Ban its use. Ban it now."

"No more new magic." the crowd took up a chant. "No more new magic. Ban the new spells now."

"Do you want the audience or not?" the herald asked.

"All of us," the workers yelled. "All of us to see the queen."

The herald signaled to the troops. "Very well, then, if it is violence you desire then you shall have it."

With a precision clap, the soldiers snapped to attention, raised their shields, and drew their swords.

"Wait, wait," one in the crowd shouted. He moved to the front and turned to face the others. He extended both of his hands palms out. "Remember what we have planned. Lead with our heads, not our hearts."

The chanting continued for a few moments more, but no one else moved forward to challenge the speaker. The noise softened and then finally stopped. The crowd shuffled around. A second man and two women came to the front. "Go back to your homes," one of them said. "You will hear what happens tonight or the first thing on the morrow."

Gradually, the workers drifted away. Sylvia relaxed a bit as the path ahead became unblocked. The coach crept forward. When it reached the gate, one of the sentries poked his head through Mason's window. "Ah, Milord," he said. "It is prudent you get inside before the sun falls any lower. We may have to call out reinforcements when darkness falls."

"You suspect more trouble at night?" Mason asked.

"The queen is trying to placate them as best she can. Perhaps the audience after the enchantment will calm things down."

"The enchantment!" Mason slapped his head. "I had completely forgotten. I must speak with the sorcerer I hired immediately. This is important. I have to explain before the performance begins what he can and cannot do."

"No need, Milord," the guard said. "As Lord Wetron instructed me, I sent the master on his way when he arrived."

"There will be no enchantment at all? What entertainment instead?"

"Do not fret. Lord Wetron has procured a replacement sorcerer and is instructing him as we speak."

"That's *my* job!" Mason exploded. "*I* am the impresario of the court. I am the one who is in charge of *all* the entertainment."

"Your court function cannot be as important as what has happened," Sylvia blurted. "Focus."

The sentry shrugged. "You will have to take that up with your brother, Milord."

With both hands, Mason pushed Sylvia's words away. He scowled and tapped his fist on the roof of the carriage. "Continue to the palace," he instructed. "I will see about this."

# 5

# The Palace

THE CARRIAGE entered through the gateway arch, and Sylvia looked about. Centuries ago, the palace had been a fortress. But now, what used to be the moat had been replaced by a high wall pierced by several openings. Like welcoming arms, two curved extensions stood on either side of the original keep.

The carriage driver directed the coach toward one of the additions, away from what appeared to be a large stable on the far right. Small shops, scattered like playjacks, filled the courtyard on the left.

As she helped Rangoth to dismount, Sylvia could not believe what she had heard Mason say moments before. Like her and the others, he had almost been murdered. How could anything else be more important than that?

"This way." Mason directed the party into one of the many doors arrayed in front of them. "My apartment is one of the better ones. On the third floor, away from the more offensive smells in the levels below — closer to the sewers." After everyone had climbed the steep stairs, he motioned to the matron. "Take my sisters to the nursery."

The lord stopped. His brow furrowed. "The enchantment will begin soon. I must assess the competence of the substitute sorcerer before he acts. But with our delay in getting back here, I won't have enough time to make a proper invitation to a lady of the court as well." He eyed Sylvia, looking her up and down. "You will have to do."

"Matron, after my sisters are safe, return with one of the maids. She will assist with the proper dress."

"Assist with *what*?" Sylvia asked as the matron left.

Mason sighed. "Ritual dictates so much of court life. Some rules make no sense, but, well, they must be followed, nevertheless." He shrugged. "And one of them is that only couples can attend an entertainment. No unattached bachelors nor unescorted maidens are allowed."

"So, with you, I am to attend an actual enchantment?" Sylvia snapped her mouth shut for a moment. "No, never mind that. What about the attack? What are you going to do about that? Why is a mere entertainment so important to you?"

Mason sighed again. "I can't help it," he said. "Being the impresario is my life. Without that, I am … nothing. I can't let the queen start thinking about opening up the scheduling to others. One success might lead to another. Before one can repeat a simple charm thrice, my title, my authority, my reason for existing could be gone."

Sylvia cocked her head to the side. She still felt numb from what had happened. The images of knives and blood were too vivid. They felt like they would never go away. But the lord had defended her as well as his siblings. She could not remain silent.

"Things can't be as bad as all of that," she scrambled to say. "I am sure your sisters do not consider you to be nothing."

Mason grunted, but did not speak.

The silence did not help. There was too much to think about at once. The attack, Mason's self-doubt …

And on top of everything else, she was to watch an

entertainment orchestrated for the queen! A childhood fantasy, to be sure. Every girl on the street must have dreamed of attending such an entertainment as they cleaned the cinders from a hearth.

She felt giddy. It was all becoming too much. She grabbed the back of a chair and steadied herself.

A few moments passed, and then she remembered. As her long-departed mother had told her when she was an upset child, she should breathe slowly and deeply — a series of unhurried calming breaths.

She expanded her chest and inhaled. A semblance of peace began forming within her. She was safe here in the palace. With all the protection around the queen, she had to be. And until Mason gave her more information, all she would have to do was merely to play along. She looked down at her simple smock in need of a washing. "Are there rules about what one is — "

"Yes, yes. The matron will return with someone who can help," Mason said. "Follow her guidance. Many of the wives of outland lords need similar aid when they come. As for me, I am off to find out what I can about the substitute sorcerer."

SYLVIA EYED the maid warily when she appeared a little later, pulling a large two-wheeled cart behind her. The two women were about the same age, but by their demeanor alone, no one would mistake one for the other.

"I am Jonice," the maid said, "and, Milady, I can tell you have a prankish bent about you."

"Milady?" Sylvia said. "I am not — " She stopped for a moment and then smiled. Better to play along for a while, she thought. Until she could figure out the best thing to do. "Ah, what do you mean?"

"Your clothing. A simple cotton smock. How droll. A

statement about the over self-indulgence so common here at court, perhaps?"

"I don't —"

"Here, sit down on the stool," Jonice said as she eyed Sylvia critically. "I have brought everything we need. The dress might be a little problem because you are so tall, but that we will tackle last. The gown buttons from the back. For now, keep your smock on. It will catch any of the drips. And the coif will not be disturbed when you take it off. Sit. Sit. Hands in your lap. I will apply the ointment. It is first grade. From the best alchemist in all Ambrosia."

Sylvia sat down, slightly bewildered by the rapid rush of words. "Ointment?"

Jonice nodded as she pulled a small, short glass bottle with a wide mouth from her pocket and removed its cork. She dipped her finger into the jar and extracted a smidgen of beige-colored salve. With deft strokes, she applied the cream to Sylvia's cheeks and rubbed it in. Sylvia gasped. There was a warm tingling on her face.

"Yes, that seems to happen no matter how many times you use it." Jonice prattled on. "But, no more multiple layers: a cleanser; next the foundation; then all the rest. One application of the ointment, and the blemishes are removed, wrinkles eliminated, and no need for a blusher. Skin as new as a baby's in one easy step. The latest discovery from the alchemy factories."

She laughed. "You should see the outland women when they leave to go home. Their purses bulge with philtres and phials from the royal stores. The queen has to restock after every large entertainment such as the one tonight."

"No formula is perfect, of course," Jonice continued. "Be sure and wash thoroughly when the night is done. Otherwise, the skin on your face will stiffen and grow tight, and then there is no going back. Your last expression frozen forever in place."

Sylvia blinked. It was like so much other magic. There were great benefits but also great risks.

The maid stepped back and reviewed her work. "Perfect," she said. "Next, the coif." She grabbed a brush and began stroking Sylvia's hair. The bristles almost instantly caught a snarl and yanked Sylvia's head to the side.

"A hazard of the job." Sylvia squelched a cry of pain. "Too many hair-jumblers always about."

"Sorry. I will go more slowly. How many fancy updos do you get in a year?"

Sylvia remained silent. She did not know what to say.

"No matter," Jonice resumed speaking. "Focus on tonight. That is what is important at the moment." She untangled the snarl and then coiled a thick strand of Sylvia's hair around a small tube made of goat horn. It had tiny holes poked into it and a plunger sticking out of one end.

"Another recent invention of the alchemist," Jonice said. "Used to be that only with heat could one get a curl, and it usually lasted for maybe a single evening. These tonight will remain until they grow out and you cut them off."

Jonice pushed the plunger, and a fine mist spurted from the tiny holes into Sylvia's hair. When she was finished, Sylvia had a curl frozen in place. The maid created several more, and after she finished, piled them high on Sylvia's head. Finally, she secured the structure with satin ribbons.

"Look. This will work, right?"

Sylvia held up the small mirror offered to her. Her eyes widened in surprise at what she saw. Certainly, she was the same on the inside, but others, what would they now think?

"Now for the dress."

Jonice reached into her basket. "This is the longest I was able to find, and you are rather, ah, slim. Try it on, and we can see how it might look."

Sylvia reached for the dress, a fine brocade with intricate

lace trim. She stopped when she noticed what was draped over Jonice's arm.

"The white dress goes over the first?" Sylvia asked.

"Over —" Jonice said and then laughed. "You are indeed a riot, Milady. No, no, of course not. The silk garment is the slip for underneath."

Sylvia took the lingerie extended to her and felt another burst of surprise. It was white and clean, of course, but oh, so soft to the touch. She hurried to pull her own simple dress off over her head so she could experience how it would feel next to her skin. As she did, an envelope fluttered to the ground. With everything that had happened — was happening — she had forgotten about it. It was the letter from Phoebe, the wizard from Brythia.

Sylvia stooped and caught the missive as it hit the ground. Eagerly, she ripped the envelope open. Inside was written a single word. "Come."

# 6

# The Ballroom

MASON'S APARTMENT swirled around Sylvia. She gasped. The wizard Phoebe had accepted her appeal! It was like a rope thrown to a drowning magician. A way out of her dull life slaving in a slum. Escape from whatever intrigue she now was a part of. All she would have to do was collect what little she had and …

Her thoughts halted. How would she get to Brythia at the tip of the southern peninsula? She had no money of her own. Too dangerous to return to Rangoth's hut to collect her meager possessions, even to get a change of clothes. She looked down at the finery she wore. Well, at the moment, she again had two dresses rather than one.

Jonice was oblivious to Sylvia's thoughts, and continued her preparations. When she was almost done, Mason raced into the room. "Are you ready yet? The presentation is about to start."

His jaw dropped as he focused on Sylvia. "You're stunning!" he stammered. "By a lightning djinn's belly, you look fantastic."

"I do?"

"Here, take a look at yourself." Mason pulled back a narrow curtain on the wall. It revealed a full-length mirror. His face reddened. "I have to make sure that I show the proper image of myself from head to toe at the court."

Sylvia stared at the mirror. She had never seen herself like that! Her hair was — was magnificent. Piled so very high and dancing with curls. Two of them dipping down and framing her ears with sophistication. Her complexion radiated the smoothness of a baby, young, vibrant, and glowing.

And the dress! When she had tried it on, at first, it felt so loose around her. But whatever Jonice did with some tucks and clips in the back had done wonders. It caressed her body from top to bottom with gentle curves, not the vulgar tightness of the streetwalker nor the loose flapping and sags of one who no longer cared. Even the brocaded lace was in the right places, swirling in complex patterns that drew the eyes of men to the parts of her they most liked to study.

Mason admired Sylvia for a minute and then waved his hand in the air. He let out a deep breath. "Never mind. This is only for one evening. Nothing more will happen between us afterwards. Let's go."

"Did you find the sorcerer?" Sylvia tried to speak calmly. His focus needed to be pulled back to what was important.

"No. No, I did not. I asked everywhere, but no one told me a thing. I am still in a dither about how well he will perform. Come on. You put your hand on my arm as we enter. On the way, I will show you — "

"Not yet," Jonice said. "The dress is too short. See, it does not reach down to her ankles."

Mason glanced down and shrugged. "Not important. No one will notice."

"They most certainly will." Jonice shook her head. "Every woman there."

"Is there a hem that can be let out?" Sylvia asked.

"Not enough material," the maid said. "And these shoes." She held up Sylvia's sandals. "Jokes are one thing, Milady, but these are a bit too much."

"So, what then?" The tone of Mason's voice hardened. "Hurry up."

Jonice studied Sylvia for a moment and then regarded Mason. "Your dagger, Milord," she said.

"What has my dagger —"

"It is ceremonial, right?" the maid asked.

Mason's face darkened. "No, not such a trivial thing," he said softly. "It has a sharp blade. Today I used it to —"

"If I may, Milord." Jonice ignored Mason's words and unbuckled the weapon from his belt. She noticed the dried blood.

"Hmm, a nice touch." With a few deft moves, she attached it to Sylvia's lower leg and smiled as she rose.

"A fashion statement. Attention will be diverted from the length of the gown. Tomorrow, every lady in the court will be wearing higher hems as well."

"The shoes," Mason said. "Finally, the shoes, and we can be off." He did not protest the loss of his weapon.

"Shoes, too!" Sylvia surprised herself with where her thoughts were taking her. "Yes, of course, my elegant *slippers*. The dress, the hairdo. This is almost too much to believe."

"You are thinking of last year's fashion, Milady," Jonice said. "Now, what is in are called pumpers. The heels are as high as the width of your hand. Steady yourself on my shoulder as I slip them on. They do take a bit of getting used to."

After the high heels were in place, Sylvia tried to take a step and faltered. Her legs wobbled. "I can hardly stand in these things, let alone move. I feel like I am about to pitch over a cliff."

"You will get used to them," Jonice shrugged. "Now, I'm off to the next outland lady who discovered she did not pack smartly enough for the trip." She put what was no longer needed back into her cart, and then stopped. "I almost forgot. Here, Milady. Carry this mask with you at all times. Every attendee does. You may have cause to use it if the enchantment becomes too intense."

Sylvia took the domino mask: one covering the eyes only and held by the vertical handle on its right. "What is this dangling thread for?" she asked.

"Sometimes, a lady feels as if she is surrendering her very being to the sorcerer's will," Jonice said. "Willing to do whatever he asks. Tonight, of course, that will not happen. If it did, the conjurer would no longer find employment in any royal court. But if you do feel yourself slipping away, pull on the lid shutter. It closes the mechanical eyelids and breaks the spell for you."

Jonice paused. "Though I am told, if you do so, the headache that comes after will be quite severe. Some have had to empty their stomachs immediately, spoiling perfectly good ensembles."

"Enough delay," Mason said. "Hang on to my arm. I will *drag* you to the ballroom if need be."

SHORTLY THEREAFTER, with Sylvia stumbling along the journey, the duo came to a double door on a level below. "Watch," Mason said, holding out a finger on his left hand. "A prerequisite of the job. This ring is no less than one made by magic."

"Magic?" Sylvia asked. "I know magical objects are quite expensive. A king's ransom. They take generations of magicians performing their cryptic rituals to make one."

"Magicians have to eat, too," Mason said. "Sometimes, they wait too long for the next sale. So, they have branched out and produce less potent things, too — ones taking fewer steps to make. The powers of the ring I have are quite modest.

It is a circlet that locks and unlocks the doors before us, nothing more."

Mason touched the egress with his hand, and Sylvia heard a soft click. The lord flung one of the doors open, exposing a large, dimly-lit room. It was the largest Sylvia had ever seen. Small wall-mounted globes containing glowimps provided the only light.

There were no other decorations. Evidently, everyone's focus was to be on the presentations. Other couples, dozens of them, milled about and chatted as if nothing out of the ordinary was about to happen.

Sylvia's heart started to beat faster. It was grander than she could ever imagine. Lords and ladies at their leisure, and she was standing among them as if she were an equal.

Off to one side, she recognized the quartet of protestors who had been invited to state their case to the queen, their clothing so different from everyone else's. Mason hung back near the entrance. He pointed at a low platform along the far wall. "The queen enters from the rear with her consort," he told her softly, "and, after she arrives, the sorcerer will recite his charm. Focus on him during his entire performance. Do not look away."

"If the consequences of doing that are as great as Jonice told me, why have enchantments at all?" Sylvia asked.

"It is the thrill," Mason said. "Going to the edge of disaster, but not stepping beyond. Though she is queen, Vendora loves to take the risk."

"Stepping beyond means what?" Sylvia asked. She tried to ignore the three or four nearby women staring and pointing at her leg.

"Total enslavement," Mason said. "In the sagas of the old ages, that was what sorcerers did. By speaking their charms — thrice spoken, once fulfilled — they enchanted you entirely. You became a slave to do whatever your master desired."

"So then, why do not sorcerers rule the world?"

"Like the other crafts, sorcery has its limits. Each spell drains some of the sorcerer's life force, the more potent one is, the greater the loss. Eventually, a practitioner must stop or die in his last casting."

"And if the queen desires to experience this thrill, everyone just has to go along?"

"Yes. Whatever she decrees, no one else in the court will challenge. The reaction will be instinctive acceptance. Her word is law."

"Not so different from my lot in life," Sylvia said. She took a deep breath. Everything was happening too fast. The attack in Rangoth's hut had been startling enough. The letter from Phoebe telling her to come. And now this — fancy dress and attending a presentation to no less than the queen.

Mason shook his head. "No, very different. Sorcery is quite distinct from the art of a wizard — different from the other crafts, alchemy, thaumaturgy, and magic, as well. When enchanted, even your innermost thoughts become beyond your control."

Sylvia took another breath, trying to suppress her rising apprehension. "Everyone sees and feels the same things?"

"The more skilled sorcerers are better than that. Once an audience is under their control, they might chant different snippets to the men and women. Even intone something meant for only one person in an audience."

"But we hear all the words?"

"Yes, yes. Only you will not feel compelled to react to the ones not meant for you."

"So, what hap — "

"It is somewhat like the plate spinner I hired for last month's show. After the tenth platter twirls safely on its stick, the performer turns his attention back to the first. The image you see will fade but then renew fresher than before when you hear the words meant for you again."

"How many — "

"Enough questions. The charm will start without any preamble. Just experience and learn."

Sylvia felt like a squirrel under water. She was a stranger in a strange land. She was not sure that enchantment was something she wanted to experience at all.

The door behind the platform opened, and the buzz of conversation ceased. The queen and her consort entered and sat on two side-by-side thrones. It was the closest Sylvia had ever been to royalty. Even after several decades of rule, Vendora's beauty was still breathtaking. She brushed back the tumble of her golden blond hair with elaborate casualness. Her blue eyes mirrored the morning sea, sparkling above a slightly upturned nose and lips of apple red. Queen or not, wherever she entered, every man present would turn to look.

Her consort, Brak, however, had not aged as well. He had always disdained the fashion of the court, preferring the simple brief loin cloth of his barbaric heritage. But what had once been taut muscles now sagged with flab. His stomach protruded even more than Rangoth's.

"Lords and ladies," a loud voice boomed from the foot of the platform. "May I please have your attention." With a graceful vault, the speaker leaped up to stand next to the queen.

"Wetron," Mason said softly. "My brother always was a grandstander. Even in the council of nobles in which everyone is supposed to be treated as an equal."

Sylvia caught the resemblance, an older version of Mason. But his hair was not nicely kept. A three-day stubble covered the man's cheeks like newly planted palace grass.

The crowd hushed. Wetron brushed the side of his eye as if wiping away a tear. "As you know, my elder brother, Alpher, is a great hunter. Wild boar is his favorite game. And this morning, by a cruel twist of fate, he stumbled when his

44

cornered prey charged. The — the bleeding could not be stemmed. He died before any sweetbalm could be applied."

For a moment, the crowd remained silent, stunned. Then, like the sound of onrushing water from a failing dam, dozens spoke at once.

"Wait, wait, there is more." Wetron raised his voice over the noise. "This afternoon, I received word that Mason, my cherished younger brother … We were both so very close. Yes, Mason and all three of my little sisters were attacked and killed. I am the only one of my family who remains."

Sylvia felt the muscles in Mason's arm tighten. It made perfect sense to her what had happened. She and Rangoth were innocent bystanders in a power struggle far above her station. In the rush of things, the failure of the ruffians to carry out their part of the plan had not gotten back to Wetron yet.

"Enough sorrow for now," Mason's brother concluded. "On with the show."

# 7

# Enchantment

SYLVIA DID not have any time to react to Wetron's words. A grey-robed man who had stood next to him on the crowded floor climbed the few steps leading to the royal platform. He was skeleton-thin with skin pulled tight about his skull. Individual hairs of white radiated from the top of his head as if fleeing what lurked inside.

His eyes were deep set, piercing. For some reason, one instinctively wanted to look away. Except for that, he could be considered handsome, a simple nose over a square chin. He stood straight and erect, young and virile — as if he were a new recruit into Vendora's army. But that was not right either, Sylvia thought. More like a scholar, quick-witted, and eager to understand lectures mouthed by ancient magicians.

Sylvia looked at Mason, hoping for reassurance, but he did not pay her any attention. Like everyone else, he was focused on the platform. Without preamble, the sorcerer began to chant, his voice deep and booming. Something about the words drew Sylvia's eyes to him.

Instinctively, she placed her mask in front of her face. She heard rhythmic nonsense, but somehow what was spoken compelled her to concentrate, to think of nothing else. Except for the melodious voice of the enchanter, there were no other sounds in the room. Everyone was transfixed. Sylvia, too, was unable to resist.

After a short while, how long Sylvia could not tell, the chanting paused. The sorcerer spoke words that could be understood.

"I am Dargonel, the Master," his voice rumbled out over his audience like storm waves crashing against a shore. "Look at me. Concentrate on what I tell you. Let me reveal a hidden desire in your heart."

Dargonel's nonsense resumed. Sylvia shuddered. Put trust into a stranger's powers? That couldn't be right. It just couldn't. She should pull the mask eyelid shut before things became any worse. But she did not.

THE WORDS filling her head were alluring, intriguing. She found herself straining to hear more. A vivid vision flowered in her mind. She was in a meadow under a sun brightly shining in a clear blue sky. The scent of fresh flowers overwhelmed her sense of smell. She could almost taste the honey that the bees buzzing around would soon produce. A gentle breeze flowed over her as she ran through the grass, the remains of morning dew gently tickling her bare feet.

She laughed and looked over her shoulder. Was there a pursuer coming after her — someone familiar or maybe not quite? Was she running too fast? No, he was getting closer. Slow but sure, he was getting closer. And when he did become able to touch her, what was going to happen next? She bit her lip in anticipation.

My heart's desire, she somehow managed to muse. Is this what she truly wanted? What about wizardry? Independence? Not having to answer to anyone else? Or were the sorcerer's words planting hints in her mind with his words? At this moment, did every woman in the room feel exactly the same? Have the same image in their minds?

THE SEDUCTIVE words Sylvia was hearing suddenly changed. They became harsher, more strident, sounds she did not want to understand. The pastoral image in her mind blurred and faded.

Sylvia frowned and clenched her grip on the mask, trying to keep the scene fresh, pleasing all her senses, but she could not. She was back in the presentation room, no longer transfixed. She saw the men stiffen to attention and clutch the weapons at their sides. It was the males' turn, she realized. They, too, were entering a state of enchantment.

Sylvia twisted uncomfortably in the unsteady shoes that made the balls of her feet ache. She wanted the attention to the men to cease, wanted the soothing, seductive words back — *her* words, the ones that sharpened her senses to be so clear.

Her own image became a ghost of itself. She no longer smelled the flowers or felt the presence of the bees. Sylvia struggled to recall what she had seen, feel again the warmth that had filled her.

After what seemed like an eternity, once more she recognized the part of the chant she desired. The words of impending delight, the words of joy, of fulfillment. *Her* words, the ones she *needed* were present once more.

The colors, the sounds, the scents, they all came back, even more intensely than before. The flowers were scented primrose, sweet autumn clematis, nicotiana. The chirping of songbirds, canaries, skylarks, and nightingales joined the buzzing of the bees. She peeked over her shoulder. Yes, he was closer than before. Soon, the stranger would reach her and then ...

BUT THE stranger did not reach her soon enough. The sorcerer's voice changed, and the drab palace room crept back into view. This time the words were stranger still. Not the rumble of battle for the men, but something else, somehow more — more regal.

Sylvia saw Vendora rise clumsily from her throne. Her jaws worked as if she had bitten her tongue. Dargonel must be cycling, Sylvia decided. Now enchanting the queen as well.

"I AM Vendora, ruler of Procolon," the queen managed to slur. "What I speak is — is law."

THE CHANTING words immediately shifted to ones already familiar. They were not hers but those meant for the men. Now, in unison, they held an arm crossed over their chests as if they were brandishing shields. Sylvia's songbirds had become silent, the flower scents faint and far away. The stranger a mere outline of human form.

The muscles in her neck tightened. Her head began to throb. A headache was starting. Too much time had passed without refreshing her spell. She was falling out of the charm. No, no, not that! The tableau must finish. She had to find out what was going to happen.

AS PANIC began to bubble in her stomach, barely in time, Sylvia heard Dargonel anew. He was chanting the right words, the correct words, the ones she wanted to hear. Never mind the men, never mind paying attention to the queen.

Speak to me, speak to me only.

The scene sprang back in vibrant color. The deep crimson reds, the vibrant yellows, the luscious greens were impossibly bright. The buzz of the bees was drowned out by the birds with their melodious songs. Sylvia felt a light touch on her shoulder. She halted. He was here. Finally, he was here!

THE CHANTING for her abruptly ceased again. The words changed to those meant for the queen. The monarch spoke again. "What I say is law. I, I do not want the distraction. Hearing endless arguments by the council of nobles. About who will be best fit to serve as fiefdom master in Alpher's stead.

"I am, I am deciding now. No, I, I have already decided. Alpher's lands and chattel are hereby immediately ceded to Wetron, his only living relative. The original holding that I once cleft in two is once more whole. I am the queen, the ruler of you all, and I have spoken."

"No!" Mason shouted. Sylvia turned to look at him through her mask and saw he had closed the eyelids on his own. He clasped his jaws tight for a moment, but then convulsed and vomited onto the floor.

The image in Sylvia's head wavered like a reflection in a lake disturbed by a pebble. She did not care about the affairs of state. What was important was — are the men to be serviced next? How long until she could once more hear the seductive, soul-wrapping words meant for her? Feel her lover's arms closing around …

TWO MORE voices sounded in synchrony nearby. In unison, they started what must have been a competing chant. One not as resonant as Dargonel's, but combined, it drowned him out. Sylvia looked to her side through her mask. Two of the four workers had shed their outerwear and stood cloaked in flowing robes the same grey color as Dargonel's. The woman beside each of them held sheets of vellum that must be scripts for their companion's chanting.

"No, wait, I, I did not mean what, what I just said," Vendora stuttered. "Disregard who is to rule in place of Alpher. What is important is that, is that practice of the new magics be banned, *never* to be exercised within my realm."

Dargonel spoke louder so he could still be heard — uttering the words meant for the queen.

"We cannot have a vacuum of power," Vendora said a moment later. "Because, because — no, I mean the new practices of magic have to stop. No, not that either. I must choose. It is my duty as the monarch. I ..."

The queen faltered. She collapsed to her knees. "My head. My head. It feels like it is exploding. I can hardly think. Stop the enchantment. Stop, I say. Stop! I command it. Return me to the way I was."

The three sorcerers ignored Vendora's order. Their voices rose louder and louder, trying to dominate one another.

Sylvia's head throbbed as well. The muscles in her neck had tightened in pain. Flickering geometric lattices filled her eyes. Even though she did not wish it, without the reinforcement, her enchantment by Dargonel was coming to an unplanned end.

She glanced down at Mason sprawled at her feet, not daring to close the lids on her mask. She, too, did not like what was happening. Denying her what she so fervently desired.

The sorcerers squabbled like children, she thought — like nosetweakers trying to settle on the value of a sum. Yes, the nosetweakers. They did things in a sensible way.

"Vote on it," Sylvia yelled at the top of her lungs,

surprising herself by what she was saying. "Decide by a vote! Let the majority win."

"Yes, a vote," Vendora echoed vacantly. "Stop the dueling. Release me from the charms. End the chanting now!"

"The queen!" someone finally managed to shout. "She is in distress."

More participants fell out of their enchantments, some with little after effects, others writhing on the floor in their own spew.

"Treason," yelled one of the lords. "The sorcerers are responsible. Seize them. They must be punished for what they are doing."

Simultaneously, all three enchanters stopped speaking. Two of the men nearest the stage drew swords. Dargonel flinched backwards.

But then in an instant, he resumed his full height. He began chanting again, and this time the tone was different. Like a boulder reaching the bottom of a canyon filled with mud, the cadence slowed. The inherent tension started to wane. The sorcerer's voice softened to a whisper and faded away.

As if awakened from troublesome dreams, the charms ended. There were no more withdrawal effects for anyone in the room.

EVERYONE RETURNED to alertness. An excited babble began filling the air. Sylvia saw that Dargonel slumped. He looked like a field laborer returning to his hut after a full day harvesting a field. He reached a hand for a steadying chair that was not there.

"Call the court alchemist," someone shouted. "Get him at once. The queen has swooned and cannot be aroused."

"Vote on it?" cried another. "Vote on what? What did the queen say? What did she command?"

"What exactly does the word 'vote' mean, anyway?" puzzled a third.

"You all heard her," Wetron bellowed from the platform. "Her majesty has spoken. It is the law of the land. I am to combine my brother's fief with my own."

"No, a thousand times no," Mason tried to stagger to his feet still clutching his stomach. "The queen recanted her first statements that granted you so much. This is your doing, brother. A trick of sorcery for illicit gain and nothing more."

"Mason?" Wetron wondered aloud. "You are here — alive? What is it *you* have done?" His eyes narrowed. "How did these other two sorcerers get in here? Are you the one responsible for them?"

"I don't know," Mason said. His face was flush. He was not yet thinking clearly. "Four protesting workers entered alongside my carriage. Perhaps it was two of them."

"Ah, you admit your guilt," Wetron shot back. "He has confessed. He is the planner behind it all. Those nearest to my brother, seize him! *He* is the one who should be tried for treason." He paused. "Wait. There is no need for delay." He leaped from the platform and drew his dagger. "Stand aside. I will slay him myself!"

A path widened for him as he strode forth. Sylvia realized Mason was in no shape to defend himself. She tried to draw closer to him but stumbled and fell. She could not regain her footing.

"Damn these shoes," she exclaimed and kicked them away. Her hand fell upon the dagger strapped to her leg.

As she had acted in Rangoth's hut, she did not consciously think about what she did next. When Wetron drew close, she rose like a jack-in-the — box springing from its confinement, brandishing Mason's knife. Wetron hesitated for a moment, and when he did, with one swift swipe, Sylvia carved a deep wound in his cheek and slit open his eye.

The room froze like a painter's tableau; everyone too shocked to act on what they were witnessing.

Sylvia resheathed the knife. "Come on!" she commanded as she helped Mason regain his footing. "We have to get out of here."

Mason nodded weakly, letting Sylvia coax him through the door behind before anyone else could turn their attention to them. The two of them slammed the entrance shut, and Mason touched his ring to it. Sylvia again heard a soft click. The cold of the stone floor was painful on her bare feet.

"That will hold them until they figure out who else inside also has a magic ring," Mason said. "It might give us enough time to — "

He collapsed to the ground, putting his hands to his face. "I don't know where to go."

"I do," Sylvia exclaimed. "South. We are going to meet another wizard."

# 8
# Escape

"COME ON," Sylvia said. "The more we wait, the harder it will be to escape."

Mason clasped his face in his hands. "It is all happening so fast," he said. "I cannot decide."

"I have, for both of us," Sylvia said.

Mason was silent for a moment. "All right," he finally answered. "South. As good a direction as any." He grabbed Sylvia's hand. "There is a stairway down to the first level on the left. Let's go."

Sylvia stiffened. "No, we must go up first to get — "

"Yes, I know. We do not go anywhere without the wizard."

Shortly thereafter, the pair roused Rangoth from Mason's quarters. "What, another performance so soon?" the wizard asked.

"It is at another venue," Sylvia replied. "I will explain later. For now, just come along."

Together they all hurried back down the stairs to the first floor. As they did, the sconces lighting the corridors started to blink on and off in rapid succession. An ear-piercing wail echoed through the air. Sylvia looked upward and saw a stream of banshees flitting along overhead and emitting their mournful cries. Larger than nosetweakers, they were little more than bone. Long flowing hair, sunken cheeks, glowing eyes of red from continual weeping.

"It is a general alarm!" Mason yelled as they ran. "Part of the new magic. Copper wire in the walls connect to each of the glowimp globes. Somehow messages are sent that the specters can understand."

Sylvia could hardly think. The blinking lights hurt her eyes. No one could possibly ignore the noise. They made her shiver to her core. She tugged Rangoth's hand, urging him to keep up. "Lord Mason, where are we running to?"

"To my coach in the stables, I guess. I don't really know."

"That will be the first place they will look," Sylvia said. "There must be another way out — one that would not be thought of by — by a lord."

Mason stopped running. He rubbed his chin for a moment and then resumed his pace. "Yes, the merchant's gate," he exclaimed. "It will be the last to be secured. Wetron might not even think of it. You are right. He'll assume I will flee in my own carriage — the only means I have used for travel in years."

What Sylvia had done moments before flooded back to her. "Wetron," she said. "He will be in no condition to do anything for a long while."

"Not with the sorcerer still there in the ballroom," Mason said. "After a battle and the sweetbalm had ran out, sorcerers enchant the remaining wounded until they recover — for a fee of course."

Mason halted and looked about. "There," he exclaimed. "Behind that door are steps leading down." He placed his ring against the portal and flung it open. Cold, dense air rolled out around their feet. Water dripped from a rough-hewn ceiling onto unlit stones. "The receiving pantry abuts the river," he said. "A lot of supplies come by boat."

"We are going to row?" Sylvia asked. "Surely, that is too slow."

"Please, give me more time to think." Mason frowned and massaged his forehead. "It will depend on what we find."

After the trio had entered the stairwell, Mason relocked the door behind them. The banshee cry, although still disconcerting, softened to a whisper. The passageway was unlit. All three had to place each footstep carefully and keep a steadying hand on one of the wet walls. Ahead, a dim glow brightened the exit.

After two dozen steps, they reached level ground under an open sky. The high wall that had replaced the ancient moat loomed behind them. They were outside of the palace grounds. Sylvia saw a sleeping driver curled up in a hollowed-out firepit near some smoldering ashes.

Mason toed him gently, and the servant sprang alert. "Get the fire going again," he said as he tossed two brandels at the man's feet. "And when you are done, clutch these. They will help you when you flee. You saw or heard nothing, understand?"

The fire flickered back to life, and Sylvia made out her surroundings. They were on a rotting, wooden quay jutting into a sluggish river. No boats anchored there. A full moon cast dark shadows from trees lining the banks. They looked like a column of many-armed warriors marching to war. The air was heavy, smelling of decay. Ripped apart crates, some filled with straw, littered the ground. To her left stood three stalls for unloading horse-drawn wagons, but only one was occupied.

"Succubus' smiles," Mason said. "I was hoping for something better."

"It looks like a cabriolet," Sylvia said.

"We can't cram three of us into it. I have sent the driver away. We are going to have to walk."

"Let Rangoth and me ride inside," Sylvia said. "You can be the driver standing in the back."

Without saying more, she got Rangoth secured comfortably in the cab. She placed in his lap a bag of oats that had been lying nearby. Then, with a grunt, she twisted space for herself at the wizard's side.

"I am a lord of the realm, not a driv — " he began, but then stopped. Without another word, he climbed up onto the station at the rear of the cabriolet and flicked the reins. The horse snorted once and started slowing walking, following a path along the shoreline into the night.

MASON EXHALED deeply to gather his wits. No sound yet from the top of the stairs. He looked to the sky. The moon made it light enough that the horse could follow the riverbank trail with a sure-footed pace. He could begin to think things out in peace, come up with a well-defined plan. Not rush off with racing from one impulse to the next.

The first thing he had to do was disguise himself somehow. If he were spotted after the alarm was shouted about, his fancy courtwear would be a dead giveaway. And after a change in garb, a more practical means of transportation had to be secured.

By dawn, he needed to be well on his way to the border. That would give him time, more precious time. Time to think what to do to save his sisters. Given what has happened with Wetron, even in the palace nursery, they were in peril. They would not remain hidden forever. Ultimately, he would have to deal with his brother. At the moment, he did not know how. But these first few steps would give him more time to think things through.

And the woman. What was her name? Yes, Sylvia seemed right. She had saved his life not once but twice in the wizard's hut. What was he to do about her and the doddering master she insisted bringing along?

The air was cold and damp as expected. No one was about. The only sound the rhythmic clop of the horse. Mason felt himself settle into calm contemplation. He conjured different alternatives, examining each of them, weighing their merits without biased passion.

An hour passed and perhaps another. Rangoth stirred from time to time but did not awaken. The trail moved farther away from the sluggish river. Mason peered ahead, trying to make out the first glimmer of what he now sought. Yes! A dim glow up ahead.

"There's somebody out in that field," Sylvia called back. "A man in gaudy dress."

"Yes, a tricorn hat," Mason said. "Glow-in-the-dark lights. A warning to stay well away as he works."

"Aren't those glowsticks toys for children?" Sylvia asked.

"That, too," Mason agreed. "But no more questions for a while. I have to get off and talk to the gatherer. I was hoping that one would be about on a night like this."

"Why? Tell me what is going on. What is your plan for what to do next?"

"Ah, later," Mason said. "When we are safer, and there is more time." Without another word, he slid from the driver's post and crashed onto the muddy ground. Instinctively, he started to brush himself off, then realized how clean he was no longer mattered.

"Gatherer, hail," he called out. "Please desist from breaking open another stick. I have a proposition for you."

# 9

# Mandrake Gleaning

MASON APPROACHED the man festooned with the glowsticks and the tricorn hat. No need to startle him by a sudden movement, he thought. Or worse yet, loosen the dog straining at the rope that bound it to a stake in the ground.

"You should not be out here," the man called as he removed cotton from his ears. "I display my warnings visibly enough."

He's been muffling the death cries, Mason thought. This might turn out better than he had first surmised.

"Yes, I understand what you are about. I am interested in … in entering the trade myself."

"You'll get no help from me. There is competition enough as it is."

Mason jingled his purse. "I want to buy you out. Take everything you have here. Give you enough coin so you can rest a while and then take on another trade, perhaps take a journey down river."

He held his breath. He had chosen his words carefully. Made sure that the gatherer thought he was selling everything needed to engage in the craft, not his real purpose at all.

"Not interested," the gatherer replied. "There is little else I know how to do."

"How much?" Mason persisted. "I have little time to

dawdle. The moon will set soon enough, and I want to start gathering myself as soon as I can."

The man scowled. He batted at an insect circling his head. Mason did not move. "All right then," the gatherer said. "I want you on your way so that I can concentrate on gathering a few more stalks tonight." He took a deep breath. "I will sell to you, but for no less than forty, no, fifty brandels, of the highest quality gold. That is what it will cost you."

The man paused for a moment, then continued. "See, you are wasting — "

"Fifty indeed is too steep, but perhaps I could see my way to forty."

"Forty brandels just for my glowsticks?" The man thumped his chest. "I have worn them since moonrise. They do not have much light left."

"More than only the activated sticks you wear. The ones in your pack, too. I want everything. The mandrake spikes you have harvested tonight. Your hat, jerkin and trousers. The dog. Everything but your briefs. I want you to vanish to somewhere else." Mason stared into the gatherer's eyes. "And to honor a pledge that this transaction will remain silent. As if it never took place."

"The clothes off my back! I will freeze my tail off walking home half-naked in this gloom."

"I desire everything you have."

"Why do you want to do this? Are you daft?"

"I saw you remove the cotton from your ears." Mason shrugged as if explaining a simple incantation to a child. "You have become fond of the dog, haven't you? I want everything. I want the hound, too."

"The muffling works only somewhat," the gatherer raced to explain. "Some chest pains and stomach aches, nothing more. But after a while, they cannot be endured any longer. We return to standing farther from the plant than the dog does

61

when it is uprooted. But my cur there is the last one of the litter. Indeed, I have managed to endure things for him longer than I have for any of his siblings. I have become, well, fond of it."

"Ah, I understand your passion," Mason said. "And the mutt looks friendly enough." He rubbed his chin a few times. "All right, to seal the deal, you can keep the dog."

The gatherer beamed. He went to the fettered hound and stroked him gently. "Forty brandels, you say, right?"

Mason nodded. The gatherer stood and nodded back. Without another word, he undressed as the lord counted out the coins. When the man vanished into the gloom with his pet, Mason shed his fine garments and donned those he had purchased. He scowled in disgust. The smell was overpowering. Had they never been washed?

He built a small fire and tossed his tunic and leggings into it. For a moment, he was filled with regret about what he had done. In the palace, he had told Sylvia that without his position at court he was nothing. With his fine clothes gone, no one would treat him with any respect. He stooped and squeezed the thickness of his purse lying on the ground. Worse than that, it was half empty, and there was one more important purchase to make.

"I don't understand what happened," Sylvia said when he returned to the cabriolet.

"Hopefully, I look like a mandrake gatherer now. Everyone recognizes that the glowsticks are a sign not to come near. Those who look for a court dandy will not be able to spot me."

"What about Rangoth and me?"

"In the excitement, nobody got a good look at you in the presentation room. Even the ladies who were nearby you were focused on the dagger on your leg. All that remains is to trade the cabriolet carrying the wizard for something more befitting your apparent stature."

"Why do people stay away?" Sylva asked.

"The death cry of the mandrake."

"I haven't heard of such a thing."

Mason studied Sylvia for a moment. The wizard's hovel was north of the palace, in the middle of the slums. "You probably have never traveled outside of the city, have you?"

"No." Sylvia cast down her eyes. "No, I have not."

"Sorry, I — I didn't mean to demean you." Mason rubbed his forehead. "It is just that with everything that has happened, we are still in grave peril, and — "

"Teach me," Sylvia said. "If I were happy with being an uneducated doxie, I would not have asked."

"Well, mandrake roots are quite desired by alchemists for their formulas. To achieve their full potency, they must be harvested in the light of a full moon. And when a plant is ripped from the ground, it emits a death cry that is fatal to whomever closest hears it. Most hunters use dogs to root for them. They stay well away as the trained hound pulls the plant from the earth.

"Some, like the gatherer tonight, gamble that cotton in the ears will protect them enough. They sacrifice a dog if they can no longer stand even the muffled cry."

Mason rubbed his chin. "So far, so good," he said. He looked at Rangoth slumped in the cabriolet. "Now, if I could only figure out what to do with — "

"That is most interesting," the wizard said, suddenly wide awake and pointing skyward. "I have not seen a swarm of imps like that for many years."

"What imps?" Sylvia and Mason said together.

"Oh, you can no longer see them now. They fly so fast, probably speeding south to await the dawn."

"What *type* of imps?" Sylvia asked.

"Why, tracking imps, of course," Rangoth said. "When it is daylight, they always find what they are looking for."

# 10

# The Carriage Factory

SYLVIA KEPT alert, but she saw no more signs of tracking imps as the journey continued. She eyed Rangoth as he rearranged the blanket covering him in the cabriolet. She had learned that speaking something unexpectedly usually was a good sign. Perhaps, he was coming out of his stupor.

Rangoth arched his back and stretched. "I must commend you, Sylvia," he said. "It is a bit frigid out, but the fresh air is invigorating." He stared about and wrinkled his brow, puzzled. "But I must have forgotten. Had you already told me about an engagement for some prince? Tomorrow, a command performance? Is that it? The reason why we journey during the night?"

"No, no," Sylvia began, then thought better of it. "Ah, you are correct, Master. We are on our way to Brythia in the far south. Get some more rest while you can."

"Is what I see happening possible?" Mason asked. "Cured with a breath of fresh air?"

"His wits come and go." Sylvia shrugged. "No telling how long his clear-headedness will last."

"Keep him quiet," Mason called down from his perch. "We are not done yet with my plan." He stared for a moment for a hint of dawning sky in the east. "I want to get to the village of Carmela while it is still dark."

64

A plan? Sylvia thought. Evidently, long periods of silence were what this Lord Mason had needed to sort things out. But it would help if she were privy to it.

"Why the next village?" she asked.

"You will see."

AFTER TWO more hours of travel, the trio arrived at a portion of the river with a vertical waterwheel on the near bank, rotating slowly from the push of the current. At the right of the path was a large untended field filled with what looked like a graveyard for abandoned coaches and carriages.

Some tipped onto their sides, their axles bare of wheels. Others were erect but missing roofs, doors, or tongues. A trash pile lay nearby, filled with what looked like torn window shades and wooden panels.

"There used to be a grist mill here," Mason called out to Sylvia as they rode. "And a shaft running from the wheel in the river to power grindstones in a mill where this junkyard is now."

"What are these wagons for?" Sylvia asked.

"Originally, trade-ins," Mason said. "But now they are used for replacement parts."

"I don't understand."

"The mill was torn down, and the connection shaft removed when a new use of thaumaturgy was invented. Another of the ideas that are popping up everywhere now. See the large barn-like building a little way off on the right? That is the place that we need to get to."

"The lit doorway in the distance?"

"No, we will stop midst the collection of buggies there in the middle of the field instead. There must be more than a dozen of them there. Hopefully, no one will realize that one more has been added."

Mason directed their stolen cabriolet into the midst of the other carriages, reined in the horse and dismounted from the driver bench. He hobbled the horse and strode to the open door. Sylvia followed, and Rangoth came after the other two, saying nothing.

Trusswork and pillars supported the building's ceiling. Massive gears and squat, round cylinders of stone were propped against a far wall under a blanket of dust and cobwebs. The smell of freshly cut oak filled the air. Several smaller enclosed structures were scattered about the building's interior.

Immediately in front, a dozen or so workers managed an array of lathes and drill presses. They shaped hubs, spokes, and wheelrim segments from rough timber. Another manned bellows feeding a blistering hot furnace nearby. Close to the far wall stood what appeared to be a recently assembled carriage. It lacked only a final coat of paint to be complete.

As Sylvia watched, two lumbering giants extracted a long strip of iron from the furnace. It was still glowing red, but they appeared to be insensitive to the intense heat. Their naked arms were beefy masses of muscle, so large they could not touch their own shoulders with their fingertips. Their thighs chafed against one another with an audible scrape as they lumbered across the sawdust laden floor.

Sylvia had heard of such demons but had never seen any before. "Pinheads!" she exclaimed. "They are huge!"

Most striking was the size of their skulls. They were tiny, as small as those of baby human dolls. Both showed the smiling faces of complete innocence. And with so little brain, they were docile. Easy to dominate, easy to train, able to perform simple, repetitive tasks with minimal risk.

"Hello," Mason called out. "Anybody in charge around? You have a new customer here, one in a hurry."

A man who must have been the foreman poked his head

out of one of the enclosures. "Come back in the daytime. No salesman is here during the night."

Mason scowled. "Show some respect to one of your betters," he snapped.

The foreman eyed Mason. "You wear the hat of a gatherer. You can't be any better than me. Have you what it takes to pay for a carriage?"

Mason pointed at Sylvia. "The *lady* has the money, you dolt. I am in her employ."

The foreman glanced at Sylvia's bare feet and shrugged. "If she cannot even afford protection for her feet, I doubt she has enough to spend on a coach either."

The two men glared at each other. Sylvia could see that Mason had not thought through this part of his plan, whatever it was. She glanced at Rangoth, standing placidly at her side. A thought flashed into her mind.

"You see the flame logos here on my companion's robe, don't you?" she said to the foreman.

"Yeah. So?"

"So, you should know that Master Rangoth's temper is short. What do you think might happen with the pinheads if the instructions imprinted on their tiny minds were erased? How long do you think it would take them to reduce everything here to a chaotic shamble?"

The foreman looked at the calm expression on Rangoth's face and then at the pinheads. His eyes widened. "I beg your pardon, Master," he said. "I mean no disrespect. Please leave the pinheads to their present tasks."

"Well, indeed, this is very interesting." Rangoth stepped forward. "I have never seen an establishment such as this before. What *is* happening here?"

Sylvia groaned inwardly. What she had done might be a mistake. Once Rangoth got started down a path, he became hard to divert.

The foreman cocked his head. Sylvia could imagine the gears that were turning inside.

"What is happening here?" the foreman said after a moment. "I'm glad you asked. You see, Master, we use the latest, the very latest, ideas in magic here. You are going to find this fascinating. No need for hot tempers at all."

"I see each of your workers is using a lathe or drill press," Rangoth said. "They appear to be able to control the machinery with a feather's touch."

"Right you are, Master," the foreman said. "Rough hacking will not do. Raw power from a single shaft driving machines by belts does not work at all."

"What do the pinheads do?" Rangoth asked. "Fascinating creatures. Enormous, yet with brains of worms. I remember once, oh, it was many years ago — "

"Please, just observe Master, and you will see," Sylvia said. "No need to alter their instructions at all."

Rangoth said no more. As everyone watched, the two pinheads came closer to where the group stood. The pair gripped the ends of the still glowing iron even tighter. Their arm muscles bulged with effort, and the iron started to bow. With straining grunts, the two giants brought their hands to touch one another, creating a perfect circle of metal between them — the metal rim for a wheel.

Rangoth stroked his chin. His eyes twinkled with interest. "What then do you use instead of the power of the river to run your milling machinery?"

"But we do use the river." The foreman smiled as the threat of mayhem seemed to retreat. "The energy from the wheel in the stream is bound into a thaumaturgical spell. And as you can see, most of our milling machines are rotary; they are bound as well."

"Why work at night?" Sylvia blurted.

"Because of the pikas," the foreman said as he motioned

everyone to follow. "Look. I will show you." He led the group to another door and opened it. It was pitch black inside. He rapped the globe that housed a single glowimp. The small demon trapped inside woke and emitted a soft light.

Sylvia heard a chorus of squeaking metal scraping on metal coming from the room. As her eyes adjusted, her jaw dropped. She saw the chamber was filled with hundreds of little cages, at least a score of rows deep. Each row contained twenty or more cages, each with a single occupant, small grey animals with bushy fur and tiny dots for eyes. A few munched greens or groomed themselves, but most walked endlessly on their wheels.

"You see, the rotating wheels couple with the milling machine on the shop floor. Yes, the stream provides the power, but it is thaumaturgy that guides it to where it is needed."

"I still do not understand. Why work at night instead of the day?" Sylvia asked again.

"The pikas are nocturnal." The foreman shrugged. "Like many small beasts this size, they hide from predators during the day."

"I see you have one coach ready except for the painting. Mason reasserted himself. A clarence, right? How much is it?"

"Already purchased by another customer," the foreman said. He glanced at Rangoth's continued calmness and exhaled. "If your lady has interest, I can have one for you in a couple of days."

"Not soon enough." Mason shook his head. "When does this other buyer expect delivery?"

"Also, not for a few more days. But understand, it is prudent to keep ahead of a promised delivery date to handle the unexpected."

"What *I* understand is price," Mason said. "How much is it?"

"Forty brandels," the foreman snapped. He studied Mason up and down. "What business is that for a lady's gatherer?"

Sylvia saw Mason scowl again, but this time, the lord said nothing. Instead, he squeezed his purse with his fingers and took on a faraway look of calculation.

"You will get fifty if you paint a simple trim in plain script that reads 'Lady Sylvia' on it. There will be time enough for you to craft another. In fact, I am sure you will be able to work things so that no one else knows that our transaction ever took place. And *you* will be fifty brandels richer."

Sylvia blinked. *Lady* Sylvia, Mason had said. She looked down at her expensive dress and touched her upswept hair. In the rush, she understood what Mason's plan was all about.

He had disguised himself as a commoner, and to complete his subterfuge, he would hide as a servant to a noble lady. Clever, the lord was more than just a pretty face.

The haggling between the two men halted. The foreman rubbed his chin for a moment and then extended his hand. "Then fifty brandels it is," he said. "Done."

"Wonderful," Sylvia said. "Now, Lor — now Mason, we must move on to our next lodging. One with water service with which to wash up. My face is starting to stiffen."

# 11

# Lady Sylvia

IT WAS not yet dawn. Sylvia stood by the roadside with Rangoth and watched Mason pry the hubcaps from the cabriolet. There was no traffic in either direction, but its absence was not calming. She tried a tentative frown, then shook her head. She had not been imagining it; her face was growing stiffer. The excited rush of the escape from the palace drained out of her, replaced by a seed of panic.

"I wish the gathe — driver would hurry," she said aloud. She did not want to alarm Rangoth, but whatever the lord was doing was taking too much time. It made no sense anyway. If they had wanted to walk, they could have done that immediately after they had escaped the castle.

"No matter," Rangoth waved Sylvia's thought away. "The presentation is what is important. A command performance, you say?" He took on a faraway look. "It is not a wizard duel, is it? They are rigged from the start. Innocent practitioners lured into danger by the bait of a rich payoff."

Sylvia could not figure out how to answer. There was too much to explain. Now was not the time. She rubbed her cheek, trying to keep it supple. Rangoth needed to be distracted. "Look, Master," she said. "See what Lor — what our driver is doing."

To her, it appeared that Mason had lost his mind,

71

following some bizarre plan known only to himself. She watched him use his dagger to pry off the hubcaps from their cabriolet and remove the two wheels. He rolled them up to stack with many others lined along the wall of the barn.

"There is risk enough to summon any type of demon by oneself." Rangoth ignored what was happening outside. "Dominance or submission and all that. But with two struggling to control the same devil, the demon can play one against the other. Both could end up becoming the ones enslaved."

"A wizard duel?" Sylvia returned her attention to the wizard. "No, Master, not that. What made you think of such a thing?"

"The swarm of tracking imps," Rangoth said. "Why, I remember the time, a time when I was much younger, of course ..."

Tracking imps! The memory rushed back. Sylvia had no experience with them, but the very name sounded ominous. Could they successfully flee from Ambrosia if wizardry was involved? She wished that Mason would hurry up and finish whatever he was doing.

When the wizard finally ran completely through his recollection, he peered out the coach window. Mason continued to work without pause. He stripped the cloth coverings from the cabriolet. He slashed them to ribbons and tossed the scraps onto the trash pile. Only the naked frame remained. He dragged it aside and kicked dirt over it.

Close scrutiny would surely discover it, but Sylvia did not want to suggest it. How many hours had passed doing this, she wondered? By now, they could be much farther down the road — to somewhere where there was water, to where she could wash her face.

Mason did not appear to be as bothered. With a final brush of his hands, he ascended to the driver bench. Shortly, they were on the trail again, continuing to head south.

"How much longer until we find a place to — to freshen up?" Sylvia leaned out the window and asked.

"Yes, good," Mason answered. "Keep practicing how a noblewoman would speak. It makes your role more believable."

"I am not *practicing* anything," Sylvia snapped. "I don't know how much time I have left. These lodgings will have water available, right?"

"One last stop first," Mason said. "Carmela. It is an artist colony that sells to the nobility when they journey south."

"Stop for what?"

"To pass as a lady, you need more than a single dress."

THE HORSE clopped on. No more was said. Sylvia rubbed her face with her hands and grimaced with clown smiles, but they did little to help. Every few minutes, she poked her head out the window, trying to see signs of a settlement.

With the first rays of the next day's sun, the coach emblazoned with her name entered Carmela.

"There!" Sylvia shouted as the carriage passed a few storefronts. "Let's shop there. It advertises hair styling and making-up faces. Has to have water, right?"

"A trap for the unaware," Mason called back as he shook his head. "Very expensive. There are better-priced ones farther down the road."

Sylvia's anger flared. From the start, she had not been a willing passenger to this adventure. Necessity had made her do everything she did. This lordling was not the only one who had the right to make decisions. She had made them, too, ones in the heat of the moment. More than once, she had saved his life.

"Stop right here, driver! If you want me to continue this masquerade with you, we are going to have to figure out how we are going to work together."

Mason did not immediately answer. "All right," he said after a moment. "Paying a little more for a dress here will not make much difference."

He dismounted, and, with an elaborate bow, opened the coach for Sylvia. Rangoth stayed inside. The lord banged on the shop door. A clerk descended stairs in the back and sleepily opened it. She stared at Sylvia for a moment, noticed the carriage behind her, and curtsied. "How can I help you, Milady?" she asked.

"First, do you have a room in which I can ..." She turned to glare at Mason. "Can freshen up?"

"Oh, yes, Milady!" The clerk smiled. "Right through the curtain there."

Mason shrugged, and Sylvia went in the indicated direction. Behind the curtain, she saw a small sink and a full ewer of water on an adjacent stand. Without an instant of delay, she splashed her face and then sagged with relief. A flesh-colored paste had started dripping off of her chin and into the sink.

Her spirits lifted. She pondered the situation she was in. Mason had shown how slow and deliberate he was to act, and, she had to admit, what he did make sense. And certainly, a traveling companion to have on the road to Brythia would be good.

But, praise a succubus, he had to be shown that he could not be the only one deciding what to do. There had to be agreement before plunging onward. Yes, what she thought about things had to matter to him.

And how to show this, she mused. An argument in front of a sales clerk was not a good idea. Drawing attention to themselves might totally undo the charade Mason had put together.

In a flash, what to do to make her point came to her. She was going to enjoy this. With an impish smile, she reentered the front of the shop.

"I need a few new dresses, three or four, perhaps," she said to the clerk. "And changes of undergarments as well — a dozen or so. And, oh yes, slips. A dozen of them, too."

She spun her eyes around the shop. "Shoes!" she exclaimed. "Of course, five pairs at least. Sandals for most, but one with the highest heels you have. And, oh, a small trunk to carry everything in."

Sylvia realized that she knew nothing about the cost of anything she chose. She had managed with only two smocks for years. And pretty dresses and shoes had held no interest for her whatsoever. The objective solely was to put a reasonable enough dint into Mason's purse so that he would learn to pay proper attention to her, nothing more. She was not *his* servant to be ordered around.

"Wait," Mason whispered. "All that will be, well — expensive."

Sylvia paused. Was what she was doing the right thing? What did "expensive" mean to a nobleman? Maybe she should not be so extravagant. "The frock on the left looks interesting," she told the clerk. "Do you have it in beige?"

Later, when the pair left the shop, Sylvia said, "You see? Unexpected consequences happen when one does not share what he is thinking before he acts. It would have been quite helpful to have understood all you planned before we started. We will both fare better if I can be more than a mere slave to order about."

"*You* are the one who does not understand." Mason struggled to heft the trunk up to the top of the coach. "See the flatness of my purse? I no longer have enough for a meal and a single day's rest for the three of us at the inn the nobles use."

"Another less costly place then."

"I now have only coppers and a few silvers. There is nowhere that will take us at all, *nowhere*."

"Oh!" The vivid flush of satisfaction faded. There was no excuse for it, but Sylvia could only giggle at what she had done.

"This is *not* funny."

"How many silvers?"

"Only six or seven."

Silvia flexed her shoulders, feeling luxurious wearing one of her new dresses despite the guilt that was building within her. "Then take us to the village market. With your silvers, I will buy a small pot, some vegetables, and whip something up."

# 12

# A Colony of Artists

SYLVIA AWOKE first from the gentle tap on the carriage door. She recalled that after the skimpy morning meal, Mason had parked beside the road, and the trio had collapsed into sleep inside. Even Rangoth's snoring had not kept the other two awake.

A voice came from outside the coach window. "I beg your pardon, Milady."

Sylvia sprang alert, pulling herself erect from where she had slumped against Mason's shoulder. She studied him for a moment as a brief hint of pleasure tickled through her. Sleeping next to a man was not bad at all. Mason remained motionless; his tricorn hat pulled over his face.

She twisted the kink out of her back, but it did little to help. Her actions of the previous evening weighed upon her. She was the one who had forced this sleeping arrangement upon the other two and felt quite guilty about it. Had she more knowledge about what fine things cost, she would not have been so extravagant.

Sylvia squinted into the noontime glare. An armored soldier with a plumed helmet peered into the coach. The sky was clear. A mere hint of a breeze stirred the air.

"What is it you want?" she managed to say.

"Merely a polite inquiry to see that all's well." The soldier offered a small broadside through the window.

Sylvia felt the sudden tension melt away. Commands of nobles were treated without question by everyone else. That is what Mason had said. She had seen that behavior in Vendora's palace.

She looked at the vellum and recognized the face. Under 'Wetron' on the top was a sketch of Mason's older brother — one without the disfiguring scar. She smiled at the soldier. "I don't understand."

"At court last night, the queen was enchanted. When my squadron left this morning, she still had not recovered. The council of nobles has assumed regency until she does. Their first act was to carry out her last command as best they could."

"I still don't follow."

"Who is to be the new ruler of Alpher's fiefdom is unclear. So, the council decided to let the people therein choose." The soldier shrugged. "There is to be what is called an election. Everyone declares their preference for the new fiefholder. 'Decide by a vote!' were the last words the queen had uttered."

"And this broadside is what?"

"Not a broadside, but what is called a ballot. Text for those who can read and a picture for those who cannot. My troop has been ordered to distribute them throughout Carmela in preparation for an election."

He looked to the west. "My comrades and I have many to hand out, Milady. All through the fiefdom. I only stopped to inquire about your safety, to ensure you were not in distress."

"When is this *election* to be held?"

"Carmela's is the first. It is a test tomorrow to see that everything goes well. And after that the areas surrounding the four other towns, one by one. Now, if you will excuse me." He nodded slightly, and without another word, returned to his horse and rode off.

Mason sat up and removed his hat. "Is he gone?" he asked.

"Yes." Sylvia stretched. "Did you sleep any better than I did?"

"Probably not. I couldn't stop mulling about what to do next."

"And?"

Mason grabbed the ballot from Sylvia's hand. "Leave me alone for a while. I must think."

SYLVIA FIDGETED. Several hours had passed. Mason was still as a statue. He stared off into space.

But just when she had decided to shake him out of wherever his mind had gone, he stirred and stretched. A smile filled his face.

"The soldier's words gave me a final piece to the puzzle." Mason took a deep breath. "I have figured out what to do."

"What?" Sylvia asked.

"If I am elected the new fief lord, then Wetron will not be able to touch me. I can make sure that our sisters are not harmed. But we must hurry. Rouse your wizard from his sleep and tell him to prepare for staging a free show — after I speak to him first."

"Rangoth does not work for free!"

"This is an artist colony, Silvia. Painters, sculptors, stage actors, writers of every type. There are exhibitions and public readings all the time."

"But for *free*?"

"Put out a cup, and there will be a few donations for our next meal, and, if we are fortunate, also the fee for what else has to be done."

SYLVIA STOOD in front of the stage at the actor's compound. The ramshackle huts nestled between others for the painters, sculptors, and writers on both sides.

A crowd stood before her, one larger than what she had expected with so little advertisement about a wizard's performance. Some displayed hands clay-dust grey; others wore dirty, paint-splashed jerkins. Costumed actors mingled with both. More aloof and off to the side was a somber crew with long beards and sribepads in their hands. A few clutched ballots for Wetron. No one had offered any coins to Sylvia, but, she reasoned, everyone would wait to see if the show was worth their attendance.

As the announced time for the show to start grew closer, Sylvia's grip tightened on Mason's purse. True, she was apprehensive about how well Rangoth would perform, but that was different from how she had felt during the flight from the palace. She was no longer trying all the while to figure out what Mason was up to. After her buying spree, he had gotten the message. Before he started his conversation with Rangoth, he had patiently explained to her what he was going to try. Yes, he was indeed clever — and rather kind underneath his abruptness, too.

She had decided she would continue to help … for a while. After all, she was the one who made what they were doing now necessary. But if Mason succeeded, their paths would then part. The lord had no reason to continue to Brythia.

Rangoth stood on the jutting stage apron, hands clasped regally behind his back. He looked at the size of the crowd and smiled. "Ladies and gentlemen, freemen and women, serfs and bound servants, I welcome you all," the wizard boomed.

Sylvia blinked. The fresh air and travel indeed seemed to have had an invigorating effect on the wizard. She had never heard Rangoth speak with such confidence. But then, before she had become his servant girl, he had possessed quite a distinguished reputation. Perhaps some of that was showing itself now. But without her prompting help, could he pull this off?

"The demon realm is inhabited by many types of devils," Rangoth continued. "The more powerful ones require the greatest strength of will to control. But even lesser demons, the imps, also can be a challenge, especially if there is more than one.

"Now, I entreat you all for silence. I must concentrate to the fullest in order to succeed, to dominate not one devil, but *half a score* all at once. Watch and behold!"

Rangoth gestured to Mason, standing to the wizard's rear and still disguised as a gatherer. Without pretense about his true station, the nobleman started a small fire of cattails from the river bank and fanned them into smoldering life.

"Come forward, my pets," Rangoth rang out. "Come forward and serve your master."

It was not yet dusk, and light was fading. Nothing happened immediately, and a few in the rear of the crowd drifted away. After a few moments, almost imperceptibly at first, and then gaining form rapidly, a thin, ghost-like presence appeared. The shape was amorphous, with only hints of where a head or limbs might be. Two tiny dots of black, the eyes, twitched from side to side. To Sylvia, the demon looked like a large, square pillow that was barely present. If one stared at the being intently, the stage curtains behind it could be seen.

"A will-o-the-wisp," Rangoth said. "A water demon. Summoned by burning bullrushes. If traversing a bog alone, you do not want to encounter one. They lure you into treading onto what appears to be solid ground but is not."

An excited murmur rose from the crowd. Some threw arms across their eyes. Sylvia understood why. In all her years with Rangoth, she had never seen such a creature. Neither would have dwellers in a village as small as Carmela. They were witnessing powerful wizardry indeed.

"Fear not," Rangoth continued. "There will be no mischief done while I am in control. In fact, one such demon is not enough. I will call forth more."

The crowd crowded closer to the stage. A few hoisted children onto their shoulders. The wizard concentrated on the smoldering fire, and four more devils appeared. The crowd gasped, and Sylvia heard some spontaneous clapping as well.

"Quickly," Rangoth commanded. "Stack yourselves, one on top of another."

Rising like balloons filled with hot air, the new arrivals rose with stately slowness. They arranged themselves into a tower, one bottom squishing down onto the head of another. The structure teetered, first to one side and then the other. But when it appeared like it certainly would fall, the column stiffened into rigid stiffness. This time, all the spectators applauded. No one had ever seen such a thing; a structure that human bodies could not possibly construct.

"And now the challenge," Rangoth said. "Water is elemental." He paused for effect. "But then so is *fire*." Mason started a second small blaze next to the first, this one of lodgepole pine needles from trees lining the main road.

"Come forth, I command you," Rangoth said. "Prove to me if fire is superior to water."

With a poof of black smoke, a demon slightly larger than a will-o-the-wisp appeared next to the tower. Its skin glowed fiery red, and long horns crackling with sparks adorned its head. A caricature of a face sneered with menace. One hairy arm from its childlike body brandished a slender, glowing ember, waving it about as if it were a sword.

The fire devil did not hesitate. It poked his weapon into

the ephemeral essence of the bottom will-o-the-wisp. Steam boiled from the wound, but the water creature only trembled and did not cry out. Because of the unsteady platform, the other four above it swayed back and forth.

Sylvia saw what looked like a stream of water flow from the head of the injured water demon and up the tower to the creature at the very top, growing in volume with each being it passed through. Then, as the topmost will-o-the-wisp teetered forward, it released a large splash of liquid onto its fiery foe.

The fire devil sputtered out. Sputtered out; that was the only way Sylvia could describe it. The sword-like ember faded to black, and the demon itself huddled in dripping defeat. The tower of will-o-the-wisps regained their stability and stood as straight as a column of stone.

"That's not fair," someone in the crowd shouted. Or maybe, Sylvia thought, it was Mason still standing in the rear. "Five against one determines nothing," someone else cried.

"Yes, how about *five* against *five*? Much more interesting, wouldn't it be?" Rangoth's voice became even louder, carrying all the way to some additional passers-by in the back.

"Show us! Show us!" The crowd chanted. Some broke into more applause. "We want more."

Mason stepped forth to stand beside Rangoth. "Yes," he said. "Who wouldn't want to see ten demons fighting one another at the same time? Which indeed is the more powerful, fire or water?"

"Yes, yes!" The chanting continued until Mason put up his hand for it to stop.

"You must understand that control of the demon world takes effort and even one as proficient as Master Rangoth here must get rest. Come back tonight as the moon rises, and you will see a show you will not forget — unless ..."

"Unless what?" someone shouted.

"As you can see, the stage is not very high. Those who come early will see the most — especially if they purchase the price of admission now."

"What? How will you keep track? Do you have tickets to distribute?"

"Sadly, no," Mason said. "But we do have the very next best thing. Pay ten silvers to Lady Sylvia now, and I will anoint your head with a small dot as your receipt."

"Ten silvers! That's half a brandel."

Mason shrugged. "Master Rangoth will be gone tomorrow."

For a moment, no one moved. Then, two or three of the crowd came forward. Finally, the rest surged and jostled into a line in front of where Sylvia stood. It looked to her that the next meal was going to be a much more filling one.

"Now to see if there is enough preparation time left to carry this all the way through," Mason said quietly.

# 13

# Will-o-the-wisps and Fire Devils

WITH PURSE and stomach filled, Mason led Sylvia and Rangoth into the writer's compound. The time spent posing for an artist immediately after the performance had not taken long.

"Master," Sylvia whispered to Rangoth as the pair tried to keep up with Mason's hurried stride. "I never knew you could perform as you did earlier today. What gave you the inspiration to try such a thing?"

"The fresh air? Breaking out of the confining box in which I trapped myself? I don't know." Rangoth shrugged.

"But the fire demon looked dangerous."

"Indeed, he was."

"So …"

"It is a popular misconception that wizardry is merely lighting the proper type of fire and staring into it." Rangoth stopped for a moment and squinted into his past. "But that is the least part of what must happen. 'Dominance *or* submission' is the law. Imps and demons do not let one take control of them without resistance. If you do not demonstrate a superior force of will, you become their slave instead."

"If that happens, what do the devils make you do?"

"Belittling things, obscene acts …" Rangoth shuddered. "I'd rather not remember."

"You took on too great a challenge when you were younger, didn't you?" Sylvia blurted. "A foolish choice."

"And you always speak your honest thoughts and answer without holding back. But then, that is something I have always liked about you."

"Sorry, Master. I didn't mean to — "

"No matter." Rangoth waved Sylvia's words aside. "All who aspire to be wizards naturally want to test the limits of what they can do. Challenging demons of increasing power to ascertain where they must stop. And sometimes pride overcomes saner judgment." Rangoth's face crinkled with pain. "For two years, I suffered as the slave of a splendiferous djinn. Two humiliating years until it became complacent, and I broke free."

Sylvia looked about. They were about to enter a hut on the left that was somewhat larger than the ones near to it.

"After that, my confidence shattered," Rangoth continued. "Certainly, I will never try to summon a splendiferous devil again. But I even shied away from wrestling with a demon of lesser power, a lightning djinn, for example."

Rangoth sighed. He struggled with each word he said. "And that hesitation sowed the seed of my eventual downfall. I became over-cautious and only demonstrated what I thought was *absolutely* safe. As a result, without the practice necessary to keep a keen edge, I began to fear the mental battles more and more. The risk I took became less and less. In a downward spiral, I reduced myself to handle only nosetweakers and the like."

Sylvia smiled sympathetically. She never would have guessed. Never even would have thought to do so. She reached out and touched Rangoth's arm. "I am sorry," she said.

"A wizard who dealt only with powerless imps?" Rangoth did not acknowledge the gesture. "Who had ever heard of such a thing? My life became meaningless, without purpose.

Even being awake was not pleasant. I retreated into a world of silence and sleep. Only then could I escape from facing what I had become."

Rangoth finally smiled back at Sylvia. "And I admit, occasionally I did babble about past glories. Empty words to a servant wench who disregarded almost everything I said."

"So why did you now — "

"I don't know. Maybe, the travel did have something to do with it. Something that cracked the urn in which I had imprisoned myself. Let in some fresh air. I remember at least some of what I was before."

"Master, those things alone could not have — "

Mason looked over his shoulder. "Come along now," he said. Like a windup toy soldier marching into battle, he kept his rapid pace.

"It is the driver you hired for our journey, Sylvia." Rangoth nodded at Mason and quickened his pace. "Where did you find him? He is most persuasive. He told me that on many occasions, he had brought actors with sudden fright of the stage back from their inner terrors so they could perform. We chatted for hours, and as we did, some of my memories of bygone days returned."

Rangoth pounded his fist into his other palm and grinned. "The applause of the crowd, the feeling of success. Oh yes, the satisfaction you get when your will overwhelms that of another."

"So, you will challenge djinns again?"

"No, Sylvia. Never that. But I think I have some of my capabilities restored."

"Will-o-the-wisps and fire devils?"

"Your driver suggested it. Evidently, he has had experience in the past arranging such a presentation. What is his name again?"

"Lo — Mason. You and I can call him simply Mason."

Rangoth nodded but spoke no more. Sylvia saw him turn his thoughts inward as he had done so many times before. But this time was different. His face was not blank and staring. Instead, the wizard smiled like a cat recalling the taste of fresh, cool milk.

They were well within the compound now. She looked about. After a few more steps, Mason led her and the wizard into the next hut on the left. Inside, several of the men and women who had attended Rangoth's presentation sat on the ground in a circle. One recited from a much-worn piece of goatskin in his hand.

"Not here." Mason shook his head. "Let's try the next."

The scene in the adjacent hut was similar, except that two of the occupants were arguing. "Don't you see it, dolt? She must decline the knight's offer of marriage, remain true to her childhood love."

"So trite," answered the other. "Why do you even come, if you always ignore what the rest of us say?"

Mason pointed as they exited. "There, across the way, I see it. Every colony of writers has to have one."

The trio entered a larger structure on the right. Unlike the clutter of the huts, this one was filled with an ordered array of desks all alike. Each supported a flat tabletop and contained no drawers. The feather of a quill pen jutted from an inkwell on the left. A single sheet of fresh vellum centered upon it. Mason extracted an additional small piece of goatskin from his vest, the one he had paid the painter to decorate.

Peeking over the artist's shoulder, Sylvia had seen what it contained. At the top, the word 'Mason' appeared and beneath it his facial likeness. The image was similar to the one on Wetron's ballots but distinct enough that the two would not be mistaken for one another.

"Here is the original," Mason said as he handed the rendering he had posed for to the scribe sitting at the first desk in the nearest row.

"This will not be easy." The scribe examined the document. "Letters and words are my specialty, not bold strokes and swaths of shading. Besides, there are several others ahead of you in the queue."

"Ordinarily, it is against my nature to conclude negotiations so quickly," Mason banged his purse so that the contents jingled. "I will pay you double if you can complete it before the rise of the moon."

The scribe sighed theatrically. "Writers. Those here are so hard to deal with. 'Page seventeen is smeared.' 'Transfligafthing' is misspelled. 'Wait, I have made a few small changes.'"

"It is only a single sheet," Mason persisted. "Not hundreds of them."

"Triple the usual rate did you say?"

"Yes, yes, triple." Mason scowled. "Get on with it."

The scribe nodded and pinned Mason's vellum to his desktop. He rattled off the incantation and began tracing the lines delineating Mason's face. Instantly, a cacophony of the scrape of quill on paper filled the air.

"'Once together, always together' and 'Like produces like,'" the scribe said.

Sylvia understood immediately what was happening. It was simple thaumaturgy, no different in principle than what she used when doing the washing. Every pen in the room copied exactly what the scribe rendered. When he was done, Mason's single ballot had been replicated into a hundred.

When the ink had dried on all the copies, the scribe gathered them up and presented the stack to Mason. "Do it again, two more times," the lord said.

"Triple the usual rate once more?"

"No, you are getting enough. Think of it as a book with only three pages."

"Writers. You are all alike," the scribe growled as he sat

back down and repeated the copying process. "You pinch even coppers so tight that they begin to cry."

The scribe shrugged and began copying again.

"Now, back to the stage," Mason said a short while later when the task was finished. "We want to hand out as many as we can when Rangoth performs again."

"Won't they throw them away?" Sylvia asked. "Some will already have a ballot for your brother."

"Yes, but his reputation precedes him. I have no misdeeds blotting my past."

THE CROWD gathered to watch Rangoth as the moon cleared the horizon. The number was larger than the one for the first presentation.

A dozen conversations hummed. Word had gotten around. Sylvia collected the additional payments, and Mason's purse grew to bursting. Oiled torches provided additional light. The act started the same as it had earlier; only this time, the wizard did not stop with conjuring a single fire devil. Soon a tower of five opposed the one of the will-o'-the-wisps.

At Rangoth's signal, the demons hurled their weapons at one another. The water devils splashed liquid at their tormentors. The conflagrationers stabbed with their embers. The flames were not normal ones like those in a campfire cooking a meal. Instead, they glowed white-hot, consuming bars of metal in billowing smoke. Steam hissed and drifted away when the water struck the burning ingots. The fiery swords could not be doused with a single wave. Spontaneous betting bubbled up in the crowd. The odds for which side would win swung back and forth.

Whenever a demon could not continue, it seemed to blink out of existence. After a short while, only three will-o'-the-wisps remained to assail four fire devils. But somehow, the water demons did not evaporate away. They regained equality and then outnumbered the fiery opponents two to one. Finally, the last remaining will-o-the-wisp extinguished the fire devil at its tower base. The crowd roared its approval and satisfaction. Coinage exchanged hands to settle the bets.

Sylvia relaxed. Everything was going to turn out well after all, she assured herself. Mason's and her disguises seemed to be working perfectly. Judging from the number of ballots taken for him, he would win the vote count in Carmela. Repeat the activity in each of the four remaining towns, and he would return to Ambrosia in triumph. Become the fief lord chosen by the people as Vendora had decreed. Wetron's scheme would be foiled.

She looked at Rangoth acknowledging the praise showered onto him by the audience. He had managed to bring back at least a tiny bit of the glory of his earlier years. Now, there would be many other women willing to cater to his needs.

And herself? She would be able to travel south in comfort! A coach and enough coin to get there in style. She squeezed Mason's purse for safekeeping to her side. Of course, he would be generous with her. She had some feeling for his character now. Of course, he would.

Although her thoughts rambled on, she would miss the cranky old wizard after caring for him for so long. And Mason had not treated her as a mere servant, but, well, almost as an equal. And there was something to be said about shared experiences, no matter how brief. They bonded people together.

When it looked like nothing more was going to happen, the artisans surrounding Sylvia lost all interest in Rangoth. The show was over. In twos and threes, they wandered away. Soon only a few with tankards in their hands remained, too inebriated to notice what now was happening.

Mason vaulted from the stage to stand by Sylvia. She

smiled at him, flashing five fingers repeatedly to indicate how many of his ballots had been passed out.

Rangoth sagged to sit on the stage. Everything had gone perfectly, but she could tell that he was exhausted from the effort.

"I see them again." The wizard pointed skyward. "The tracking imps. They are back."

# 14
# Tracking Imps

LOOKING ABOUT, Sylvia saw what seemed to be a swarm of gnats — tiny creatures smaller than nosetweakers — darting about in a bubbling cauldron of confusion. The crowd was gone; the stage in front of the actor's compound empty. Only the trio remained.

"I didn't call them forth," Rangoth said. "Smoldering hornwort is needed to summon them. And you did not light such a fire, Mason, did you?" He pointed upward. "See the larger one that they all return back to? She is the queen. When she decides whoever is searched for has been identified, she dispatches one of the drones to report back to the wizard who had summoned them forth."

"They must be looking for *you*, Mason!" Sylvia said. "Twice is too much a coincidence. Master Rangoth, do something. Send them away."

"They are under the control of another wizard." Rangoth shook his head. "I've already told you that dueling for control is not pleasant."

"Mason helped you out of your melancholy," Sylvia persisted. "Don't you owe him something in return?"

The wizard sighed, stared at the center of the swarm for a moment, and then closed his eyes tightly. In only an instant, the imp queen jerked free of her drones and darted to flutter in front of him.

Sylvia held her breath. In the past, Rangoth had cautioned her not to pay close attention when he performed his spells. Especially when the number of imps involved was more than one. When a demon was present, anyone could communicate with it, mind to mind. And if the wizard's domination was not total, if he faltered for a moment, the devil could subjugate an unwitting bystander to be *its* slave. Whenever that happened, it took a lot of untangling to get everything back to what it had been.

The drones resumed their cluster around the queen, but only for a moment. In a heartbeat, the swarm broke free to hover several arm-lengths away. Rangoth, with his eyes still closed, cursed under his breath. He coiled his hands into fists and wrinkled his forehead. He sat up from his slump to sit ramrod straight. His entire body shook with tension.

A wizard duel, Sylvia realized. Whoever had conjured the trackers forth was wrestling with Rangoth for control.

"You have to stop her," Mason said. "Wetron is behind this. He has to be. If one of the drones gets back to him, he will know where to find me."

Like a fuzzy ball served over a net, the swarm zigged and zagged back and forth. Neither wizard seemed able to maintain complete control. As Sylvia watched, one drone detached from the rest. Rangoth was tiring or perhaps overmatched.

"Wait. There goes one," Mason pointed at the departing speck. Sylvia caught his panicked expression, seeing there his plan crash in ruin. She dared to focus on the imp speeding away. It suddenly stopped its flight, and she was startled at what popped into her head.

"Well, hello, wench. Want to have some fun? Stick around. I will be back shortly."

Sylvia blinked. The sensation was unlike anything she had ever felt before. The voice rasped, as if from a child with a

94

metal file in its chest. Not similar in any way to the feeling of enchantment two days ago. There was no pastoral image, no mysterious lover growing closer. Instead, she was aware of a foreign presence in her mind, not the imp itself, but something distasteful that should not be there.

"Stop!" she yelled aloud. "Stop. I — I command you."

"Well, well," the drone said. "A feisty one, eh? Perhaps I will postpone my journey for a while. It will not take much to subjugate you to my will."

Sylvia felt a surge of panic. Acid boiled up from her stomach, heartburn greater than she had ever known. What was she getting into? Everyone knew how unsafe it was to communicate with demons. 'Dominance or submission' was the law.

"I am, I am your master," she managed to say, recalling Rangoth's standard patter. "Submit to me."

The drone laughed. "It is not so easy, my pretty doxy. Do not mistake my size as an indication of my power. *You* are the one who must yield. Relax. Enjoy it. If you do, I will be gentle as we progress."

"I see no image. There is only a voice." Sylvia said the first thing she thought of, anything to distract the imp from doing … whatever it did.

"Right, only my voice. All that is, ah, necessary. Ready or not, here I come."

Sylvia tensed. For a moment, nothing more happened. Then her mind rocked as if hit by a sledgehammer. "Submit to me, wench. Submit or the consequence will be far worse than this feathery touch."

Sylvia felt the weight of the words press down upon her innermost self. She was nothing, nothing worthwhile at all. A servant girl her entire life. The lowest of the low. She had no education in the arts, no skills beyond what the slowest could learn. No one cared if she lived or died. Why should she even care herself?

She staggered and collapsed onto the grimy road. Her expensive dress smeared with mud. Her head ached, as if it were in a box, a box contracting, top and bottom and from all four sides. And when the walls met in the center, would anything be left of her at all? Wouldn't it be better to submit to the drone? Perhaps the tracker would stop the onslaught. Save at least a glimmer of what she was?

"Yes, submit, and I will save you," the imp's words rattled in her mind. "It will be so easy. Think the one simple thought, 'Yes.'"

So tempting, Sylvia reasoned. She was in a box, and the tracker imp offered a way out. All she would have to do was think …

Her hand slid down the fine silk of the dress she wore. She thought of the coif remaining in place after spending a night — not all that unpleasant — sleeping next to Mason in the coach. Her coach. *Lady* Sylvia's coach, the one that would take her to Phoebe.

Yes, the wizard Phoebe. That was her true goal, she suddenly realized. It had to be. The adventure had just begun. How it would end, she did not know. But it was not the time to give up now. She was more than an undistinguished servant wench, much more.

'Believe in yourself' Rangoth had lectured her over and over. That was the key. The merest of imps could not, would not take everything away from her. A memory of how she had swung the frying pan to fell a brigand flashed into her mind. She was not a helpless lass at all but someone to be reckoned with.

"No," she thought savagely. "No, you are the one who must — who must submit. My will is far stronger than yours."

"Okay, wench," the voice of the drone rattled in her head. "If that is the way you want it, that is what you are going to get. Say goodbye to everything you think of as part of you. Essentially, you will be as good as dead."

"No! Submit to *me*." She found new energy with which to fight back. "I am, I am, I will be a wizard, not a slave."

Sylvia breathed shallow gasps, each not enough to fill lungs beginning to starve. But as she did, she felt a change, a difference. Yes, the walls of the mental box continued their inward tracks, but now they were slower — at least a little bit.

She continued her forced breathing and concentrated on halting the advance. As she did, a few self-doubts tried to surface in her mind, but, somehow, she managed to snuff them out. Straining as hard as she could, the advance slowed even more. After what seemed like an eternity, she forced it to stop altogether.

Sylvia seized the opportunity. Not knowing quite what to do next, she impulsively cried out, "Here is a box for *your* feeble brain, insignificant one. It is so small to begin with. This will not take long."

She extemporized what the mind of an imp might look like and constructed an image of it surrounded on every side. With deliberate effort, she imagined the walls starting to shrink together. She didn't know if there was anything more to say and remained silent.

For a while, nothing more happened. Then, suddenly, the voice in her mind exploded. "Okay, okay. I submit. Please, stop this. I don't want to cease existing."

"Return to whence you came," Sylvia commanded.

"I am but a drone. My queen is still being fought over. I cannot leave her be."

"Begone, I said. Back to wherever you live. I direct you to go. There are no other choices."

As if a veil had lifted from Sylvia's eyes, the street in front of the stage flashed back into her view. The little demon was gone. Rangoth still sat on the apron, the swarm of tracking imps still hovered in front of him. One of the drunken attendees for the presentation remained, staring stupidly at what must look like a swarm of gnats. She had a

97

sudden idea and tapped him on the arm.

"Your tankard," she said. "I want to buy it. How much?"

"You should have quit when you were ahead," the man said. "The will-o-the-wisp and fire devil act was terrific." He gestured towards Rangoth's struggle. "This one is quite boring."

"How much?" Sylvia said.

"Er, I dunno. Ten silvers."

Sylvia reached into Mason's purse, still hanging from her shoulder. "Here, a brandel. Keep the change."

When the exchange had been made, she crept up to the stage. With one deft motion, she swooped the queen out of the center of the swarm into the drinking mug and slammed shut the lid. The cloud of drones descended on the tankard, their wings buzzing with anger, but they could not penetrate the confining walls of the prison. In unison, they vanished whence they came.

"Well done, Master Rangoth," she said. "Now, we can get out of here."

"No, wait!" Mason said.

"Why?"

"It is part of my plan. If I win here, we will know that it works. Then we garner the next elections in the same way, and *I* will become the new fiefholder. My brother's plot will be thwarted. We have to stay through tomorrow in order to find out."

"We have recovered what money I wasted," Sylvia held out her bulging purse for inspection. "If we leave early tomorrow morning, by nightfall, we will be a full day closer to my goal."

She inhaled deeply and rushed on. "Stay if you must, but Rangoth and I have no interest in fiefdoms and warring lords."

"What about the tracking imps?" Mason said. "Do you

think that the pursuit is only for me? We were lucky this time, but what about the next? I don't think that Wetron will stop sending the demons merely because of a single defeat."

"Why do you care about us?"

"There will be elections in the four more towns of the fief, and I don't know how to conjure up water sprites and fire imps on my own."

Sylvia opened her mouth to speak again, then immediately snapped it shut. Rangoth was the one that Mason needed, not herself. She was only a serving wench. To be honest with herself, the trip south accompanied only by an old wizard was frightening. Now that she had experienced a little of it, there was so much she did not know about the world. To think that she had once contemplated such a journey entirely on her own was the height of naivete.

"All right," she said at last. "Rangoth and I will stay until we get the election results. Then we will decide what to do next."

# 15

# An Election

MASON PACED in a circle. His room at *Travelers Rest* was sparsely furnished but far more elegant than most along the southern road. His bed was wide enough to sleep two comfortably. Two cushioned chairs surrounded a small, round table near a ceiling-high window. The owners knew quite well what attracted the nobility vacationing in Carmela.

For the dozenth time, he estimated how many ballots Sylvia had handed out, but he could not be sure. There was no way around it. He was going to have to risk being spotted and observe how the voting was going tomorrow. In front of the mayor's dwelling, starting at noon, ending at sundown, he had learned. That was still many hours away.

There was a soft knock on the door. "Can I come in?" he heard Sylvia ask.

"Of course." He opened the door. "What is it you wa — "

She blushed as she entered. "It is this dress," she said. "Like all the others, it buttons in the back. I don't know how to get out of it."

"And underneath …" Mason stumbled.

"A simple shift. I suppose that would be all right if you were to see me thus. It is the circumstance we are in that makes it necessary."

Unbidden, a vivid image flashed in Mason's mind. Sylvia

wearing only a shift. A mere single layer of cloth covering the mysteries lying beneath. He shook his head to make his thoughts dissolve.

"Ah, that will not be necessary. Go down to the lobby. Ask for the assistance of a maid. She will return to your room and take care of everything. Even have the dress cleaned during the night from the dust of the day."

Sylvia nodded. "Thank you." Without saying another word, she left to descend the stairs. When she was gone, the image of her in her shift returned in Mason's mind. It did not go away. Despite his fatigue, he felt a hint of rising lust. Sylvia. Sylvia. He rolled the sound of her name around in his mind. A servant girl …

No, that is not right, he told himself. Much more than a mere wench. Certainly, to him, anyway. Not once, but twice she had saved his life. Captured the tracking imp queen. With no experience, she was pulling off the image of a noble lady of the court without a misstep.

He smiled as he thought about her. There was the incident in the dress shop. But that was well-reasoned and justified on her part. She deserved to be treated in a better light. He had been too blind to see that. And tomorrow …

A kaleidoscope of more adventures to come tumbled into his mind. After Carmela, there were four more towns in the fiefdom. He, no *they* need to find out which city will be next. There would be stress, of course, and he needed Rangoth. But through it all, Sylvia could be there with him, too. He must convince her not to leave for the south just yet. More relaxed since learning of Wetron's treachery, Mason threw himself onto his bed. In minutes, he was fast asleep.

THERE WAS a knock again, this time louder and more urgent. What time was it? Mason stood up, stumbled to the door, and opened it. It was Sylvia in another of her new dresses.

"A line is already forming in front of the mayor's house," she said as she entered. "It is high noon."

Mason rubbed the sleep from his eyes. "I want to see what happens as up close as I dare."

"I figured you would, so I bought you these."

Mason frowned at what Sylvia was handing him. "What is this thing?"

"Sun blockers. The clerk in the inn store said they were the rage with the noble visitors during the summer months. One of the products of the new magic. No need for old fashioned alchemical formulas. Only add dark pigment to molten glass. Slip the curved ends over your ears and center your nose in the middle."

Mason complied. "I can hardly see anything with these."

"I was told that outside in the sun, they work better. But the important thing is that others will not be able to see your entire face." She reached up and ran a finger along his jaw. "With your gatherer's hat, the sun blockers, and a few days without shaving, your disguise will be complete."

Mason blinked in surprise, then smiled. The feeling of her finger along his cheek lingered.

FOR A moment, Mason squinted through his sun blockers. Gradually, his eyes adjusted to the bright sunlight. He glanced at Sylvia. She was wearing sun blockers, too. From the inn, other nobles had joined the pair. They were similarly adorned and awaiting the unusual spectacle. Only Rangoth, standing apart from the others. squinted into the glare.

"One who deals with demons must not have his sight diminished by any means," he had said.

The mayor's house was grander than those on either side,

but not by much. A drab single story with neither door nor windows facing the street. In the very front stood a black kettle. A large lid was visible leaning on its rear side.

Even though the day was half done, a group of writers formed the front of the line. Either they had stayed up all night, or this was earlier than normal for them to be awake. Behind them stood painters, sculptors, and other types of craftsmen. In the huts down the street, more men-at-arms were rousting them out of their slumbers. If someone did not already have a ballot in hand, a soldier handed them one.

A ballot with Wetron's image, Mason thought. The confidence in his plan wavered a bit. Of course, there were many in the village who never attended Rangoth's performance. Wetron would be their only choice.

Mason examined the voters closest to the kettle. He counted off ten and estimated how many he recognized from the night before. From where he had stood at the back of the stage, he could not be sure. But any guess, no matter how approximate, was better than none.

Three of the ten, he did not recognize at all. Their clothing was quite different — toques on their heads, white coats and whiffs of flour. Bakers and such. More sensible types not inclined to spend time on entertainments. The others he could not tell for certain, but maybe a half-dozen might have watched the wizard's show.

The dislike for Wetron was well known throughout Alpher's fief. Certainly, no one would vote for him, Mason tried to convince himself. Yes, those six votes would be for him. Had to be. Perhaps, Wetron would be defeated by a margin of six to four!

As he studied the next ten in line, the creak of cartwheels coming from the edge of town caught his attention. He removed his sun blockers. The wagon contained serfs and other workers from the farms surrounding Carmela. Wetron was smarter than he had thought. His brother was garnering every vote he could in order to be sure.

Mason's high spirits started to crumble. His brilliant plan might not work after all. He reached down and squeezed Sylvia's hand. "A single performance by Rangoth might have been insufficient," he whispered. "I forgot about the people in the outlying areas."

Sylvia's eyes widened at Mason's touch, but she did not withdraw her hand. There was something about it, something different in its gentleness. She leaned closer and said softly, "That is why I gave a few coins to some of those attending the performance who looked the most trustworthy. Their task this morning was to fan out and distribute the remaining ballots for you."

The line moved swiftly. There was no ceremony or oath-taking of any sort. One approached the kettle, folded their ballot,fief and dropped it in. In less than an hour, no voter remained in line.

"As directed by the council of nobles, I shall remain here until sundown," the mayor finally said. "At that time, I will place the lid on the kettle and keep it in my house overnight. Tomorrow at noon, a dignitary from Vendora's court will come here and count the ballots."

"Are the votes from all the villages cumulative?" one of the nearby spectators shouted.

"As I understand it, no," the mayor answered. "Alpher's domain has been divided into five areas, one around each of the towns in his fief. There will be a single winner for each. Whoever has the most victories of the five will become the next fiefholder."

Mason released Sylvia's hand. He realized he had been squeezing it too hard. He took a deep breath, knowing he dare not descend into a spiral of doom. Use what skills he had to come out the victor. Think and think fast.

But as he felt the muscles in his chest loosen, another cart of voters appeared at the end of the street. "Wetron! Wetron!

We want Wetron," the soldiers accompanying it shouted.

AS THE sun peaked the next day, Sylvia and Mason stood on the street alongside the other nobles. Rangoth did not join them. "I have some practice exercises to perform," the wizard had said. "I must not let my skills slip away again."

A coach decorated with the heraldry of the queen arrived in front of the mayor's house. Waddling as he had the day before, the mayor brought forth the kettle and set it on the ground. With a flourish, he removed the lid and set it aside. "Safe and untouched," he said as he bowed to the noble dismounting from the coach.

The lord wore a brocaded vest, embroidered slacks and shoes with silver buckles. Two lackeys, better dressed than most, followed. Their tunics and leggings were clean and evidently been tailored to fit. One stood beside the cauldron. The other unfolded a chair for the officiant and turned to face the crowd.

Sylvia glanced at Mason. She remembered how impressed she had been when he had come to Rangoth's hovel. His purple velvet jacket, form-fitting leggings, and freshly-shaven chin. He was the same person on the inside now, of course, but his gatherer tricorn and baggy shirt gave no hint. And even if he were dressed as she remembered, he would be a mere shadow to the newly-arrived lord.

The first lackey dipped into the cauldron, unfolded a ballot, and handed it to the counter. The noble glanced at it, then added a mark to a piece of vellum attached to the back of the second lackey. Finally, he stuffed the vote into a satchel placed at his feet.

There were hundreds of ballots to tally. After the first twenty, Sylvia decided to stop counting. What difference did the total make? It was who had the most that mattered.

The counting took most of an hour. When the last had been tallied, the noble stood and cleared his throat. All the watchers, nobles, and townsfolk alike fell silent. Some cupped their ears to be sure of catching what was to be said.

"Lord Wetron — 137 votes," the noble said.

Sylvia held her breath. She had given out more ballots than that. She was sure of it.

But the noble did not speak further. She could not stand the silence. "How many for Lord Mason," she blurted. "There are more to be counted."

The noble shrugged and instructed the lackey with the tally sheet on his back to turn away from the crowd. Sylvia gasped. Yes, there were marks grouped in collections of five under the name Wetron. They did look like they summed close to the total announced. But there were no other name nor marks at all.

"Ballots for Lord Wetron were the only ones in the kettle," the noble said. "It is official. Lord Wetron wins the election in Carmela. The next will be in Oxbridge to the west."

"That cannot be!" Sylvia shouted, ignoring Mason's sudden hand on her arm.

"See for yourself," the mayor said. With a grunt, he pushed the kettle onto its side, showing it was empty.

"I know for a fact — " Sylvia started, but Mason's increasing grip forced her to stop.

"The mayor must have removed them during the night," he whispered. "Wetron is no simpleton. He has reacted to the council's announcement in a way that furthers his own desires."

"But, but — "

"This election business is so new. No one at court anticipated that the ballots could be tampered with after they were cast."

106

"Yes, your plan was clever, but — " Sylvia said.

"Let's get out of here before we draw any more attention," Mason said. "I must have some time to think."

Sylvia scanned about. Mason was right. The crowd had almost totally vanished. Nobody wanted to be the last one remaining there. She let him guide her from the street, back toward the inn where they had been hiding.

"No matter how many ballots we prepare," Mason said as they walked, "Wetron's minions will disregard them. Bribe mayors to open ballot boxes early and discard votes not wanted. My brother will jig to victory in all five of the elections."

Sylvia studied Mason's expression as they walked. The rush to escape from Ambrosia was catching up with him. There was resignation in his voice. Being tired was part of it, of course. They both were. Probably Rangoth, too. Even two good night's sleep was not enough after all the stress they had endured during their escape from the castle.

Sylvia glanced back at the mayor's house. He was handing out small pieces of vellums to a row of the men-at-arms who had assembled in front of him. Because of the distance, she could not be sure, but the sheets looked like the ballots that Mason had created. The soldiers fanned out, stopping everyone they met and showing them the image. Some mounted their horses and galloped off, presumably to Oxbridge, the next town with the election scheduled.

"Even with your costuming, milling about in the open is dangerous," Sylvia said. "Eventually, that will result in capture."

She recalled wistfully what she was thinking about before the appearance of the tracking imps. Journey to the south. Apprentice to a wizard … The carriage with 'Lady Sylvia' emblazoned on it was ready. A coachman had been procured. The horse was rested, too. All that remained would be to explain things to Rangoth, say goodbye to Mason, perhaps even with a kiss … But could she do it? Had any of her feelings from before changed?

"I don't know what to do!" Mason said. "I need, I need the advice of someone who thinks more wildly than even I."

Sylvia looked at Mason and sighed. He was intelligent, yes, someone who strove to get things done, good-looking with his curly red hair. But so slow to act in an emergency. With Wetron interfering with the elections and actively searching for him, he would be like chum dangled in front of a shark.

"Even more wildly," she found herself repeating instead. "What do you mean? Who would that be?"

"There is an initiate magician named Albert living on the road inland from here that I have met once before. Well, he used to be an initiate before he could not pass his exams. He lives on the outskirts of Oxbridge with other misfits like himself. He is a little odd, but I may as well visit him."

"Odd?"

"Yes, quite odd."

She sighed again. She could not abandon Mason when he was at his nadir like this. So, perhaps, one more town, just one more. Get him a fresh slate, tied in the count, one to one. By then, she would be more comfortable with the idea of parting from Rangoth, more at ease in her role as a lady traveling south by herself. Yes, after one more town, *then*she would follow her own path.

"Tell me now," she said. "Exactly how is Albert odd?"

# 16

# A Compound of Scholars

MASON HALTED the carriage and leaped to the ground. He extended his hand to assist Sylvia as she exited. Rangoth followed, looking alert and curious. The journey had taken almost a full day. The sun would be setting soon.

Sylvia looked at the structure in front of her. It reminded her of the artisan compounds in Carmela — a cracked and sagging outer wall extending over a large expanse of ground. A crudely lettered sign over a doorway proclaimed: 'Welcome to greater Oxbridge where what goes up does not always come down.' Visible over the top of the wall and in the interior, a slapped-together wooden tower poked into the sky. The walls did little to muffle the sounds of pounding and sawing that filled the air. Occasionally, loud clangs and shrieks of metal on metal added to the mix. She wished she had some earwax enhancers so that she could think clearly.

"Will there be beds we can use?" she asked. "I enjoyed the stay in the Carmela inn much more than the hard coach bench. And do the rooms have thick enough walls?"

"I don't think so," Mason said. "Inns are in the center of town, not out here. These explorers seek patronage rather than paying guests."

"Explorers?"

"They call themselves that. Dropout students from the

five crafts. Ones who did not meet the requirements to become masters. Some are quite old by now, like Albert."

Mason banged on a ring clapper attached to the rough wooden door. Eventually, the entrance swung open.

Inside, the cacophony was louder. Sylvia felt amazement at the beehive of activity causing it. Near the tower, a man wearing the brown robe of thaumaturgy, barked out orders. Four minions pulled a rope basket filled with large rocks toward the top. While they did, another worker at the apex rolled two of the boulders to the edge so that they fell back to the ground.

"No difference," another worker cried out as they landed. "The one weighing three stones arrived at the same time as the one that weighs six." The leader nearby recorded the results in a big journal propped in front of him.

Another cry caught Sylvia's attention. "The angle of twist is three times what it was before." She turned to see two more massive stones strapped to the walls of a wooden frame. Between them, suspended at the ends of a horizontal beam were fluffs of cotton. The beam itself hung from a thick rope attached to the top of the structure.

"Ready, begin!" shouted yet another worker nearby a set of swings. It held seats for five in a row, and all were occupied. The worker who had alerted the riders dragged the leftmost chain of the first swing to the side. Then he released it so that the occupant swung back toward the center, crashing into the next swing in line. When it did, the next rider barely moved. Likewise, the next two vibrated a bit but remained in place. The last, however, sailed to the side almost as swiftly as the first had approached.

A sudden glow of flame erupted from what must be a foundry off to the left. Immediately after, the clang of a dozen hammers filled the air. Smiths, Sylvia surmised, shaping hot metal before it grew cold.

She was agog. What was the point of all this activity?

Rangoth appeared enraptured, greedily taking in all that he witnessed. "Like a convention called by a demon prince," he said. She glanced at Mason, but he did not seem perturbed by what he saw.

"Things have been laid out differently since the last time I was here," he said. "Many factions, each with their own ideas. Pay them no heed." He held out a copper and waved it at one of the minions as he passed. "You there. Can you direct me to the explorer named Albert — a small man with a far-away look all the time?"

"Albert? Do you mean *One tankard*? That is what we call him here."

Mason scowled in irritation. "Yes, yes, of course. I forget. Where is One tankard?"

"I dunno. Look for him in his hut."

"One tankard?" Sylvia asked. "Why is this Albert called that?"

"After finishing a single mug, he goes off to somewhere in his head," the workman replied. "No one, not even our most erudite explorer, can grasp what he jabbers about after that."

"We will have to search a bit until we find Albert's hut in this chaos," Mason said loudly. "He does not work with any equipment, so he gets relocated quite a bit."

But before a single step was taken, a loud gong sounded over the din. Everyone ceased what they were doing. The compound became silent. "A patron," the nearby workman marveled. "One not scheduled to appear has come."

The explorers and their helpers ceased their activities. They marched to the foot of a stage jutting out from the rear compound wall. Sylvia and her companions followed, mingling with the rest.

The curtains parted, and Sylvia gasped. Wetron strode forward, and a respectable pace behind came Dargonel, the sorcerer. At the palace, his face looked smooth. Now, the blush of youth was gone. Rather than match the lord's confident step, he shuffled behind. Both were dressed wearing the same garments they wore in Vendora's presentation room. Wetron had a patch over his damaged eye, but to Sylvia's mind, his swagger remained undiminished. She wondered why the sorcerer was there. Shouldn't he be under suspicion for what had happened to the queen?

"By now, you have learned of the unfortunate demise of my dear brother, Alpher," Wetron orated. "And I presume you are also quite aware of the extent to which he funded these little games you play. Well, henceforth, that is part of the past. Once the silliness of the election is finished, *I* will be the new lord of this fief."

Wetron paused for a moment as if waiting for a pebble to sink to the bottom of a pond. "The important thing for all of you is that I will be the one who controls the largess coming to this place. I have pondered and reached conclusions that make quite good sense." He waved his arm over the large courtyard. "The unguided patronage of my brother will no longer be given."

"No, no, let us keep exploring," some shouted from the crowd. "We are getting closer to new discoveries. For a certainty, we are."

Wetron extended his hand palm down for silence. "I am the one who is speaking," he said. "Do you want to hear all I have to say or not?"

The protesting died away. Wetron scanned from side to side like a hawk looking for prey. Finding no targets, he said, "*Unguided* patronage will be no more. It is so very inefficient."

Several in the audience hissed. Others gasped.

"Pay attention to my words." Wetron waved a hand back and forth. "When it becomes official, and I am the legal lord of this fief, patronage for your efforts will *not* go away."

A collective sigh filled the air. One or two of the explorers clapped their hands.

"Pay attention, I said. This is important. Yes, patronage will continue, but only for those efforts I deem worthy."

"Which efforts?" someone shouted. "What will persist?"

"That I will decide after careful review of everything," Wetron said. "I am … leaning to give greater support to Isaac, Oldpound you call him, and to the foundry. Great work is going in both of those areas."

"The foundry?" several of the robed journeymen cried in unison. "There is nothing original going on there," called out one older than the rest of his cohorts. "Those workers are only a support group, building the apparatuses we explorers desire."

"Everything will become clear in the fullness of time," Wetron shook his head. "Document in detail for me the status of your efforts to date — the benefit you hope to achieve. Perform this task carefully. The more promise your petitions hold, the more favor they will garner."

The lord said no more. He and Dargonel left through the rear curtains. The crowd dispersed, talking in groups of twos and threes. Gradually, they returned to what they were doing before. But, Sylvia noticed, with far less enthusiasm.

Wetron was cunning, she thought, and with all his resources, he was a force to be reckoned with. How was Mason ever going to win? The trip to Brythia receded further into the future.

AFTER MUCH searching, Mason spotted Albert's hut, centermost in a scramble of others. It towered over its neighbors, looking like a damaged, two-story carton thrown from a wagon and covered with pieces of rotting cowhide. To Sylvia, the swirl of the resumed activities and loud noises seemed to batter it from every side.

Mason pushed against one of the flapping pieces of cover and vanished inside. The other two followed.

Little light filtered through the gaps in the cowhide. It took a while for Sylvia's eyes to adjust. When they did, she saw half a dozen large slabs of slate held upright in vertical frames. Symbols written in chalk covered them from top to bottom. She recognized none of them.

As best she remembered, she had taught herself how to read as a youngster with no outside help. Listening to her parents speak signage on the streets as they passed by had been enough. But the characters drawn on the slates must be in some foreign tongue.

In the center of the shack stood a smaller structure half the size of a full-grown man, its every angle square and true. Rather than cowhide, more pieces of slate covered every side. There were no visible gaps between the frame and its panels.

Mason tapped on one of the framing struts. "Albert, are you in there? Come out. You have visitors."

Nothing happened. Mason tried a second time with the same result. Then he grabbed the cube and with a grunt, rolled it onto its side. What was now the topmost panel slid away, and a gnome of a man emerged. His face was a map of wrinkles, and his small eyes squinted like those of a mole emerging from its hole. To Sylvia, most striking was his bushy, white hair. It reminded her of Dargonel's, although not standing straight upwards toward the sky.

"Why do you go in there?" Sylvia could not help asking.

"So, I can do my best, my lady. It smothers almost all the noise. Quiet enough that I can reason in peace. Haven't you heard of the term *thinking inside the box?*"

Before either Mason or Sylvia answered, Albert's eyes clouded over. He stood as motionless as a rock. He looked as if he were outside, staring at the stars.

Suddenly, he shouted, "Of course, that's it!" He hobbled to one of the slate boards and with his sleeve erased two rows of symbols. He then scribbled with chalk to fill the vacated spaces. Running out of room, he scooted to another slate and squeezed in more writing appended by an arrow pointing back to the board he had just abandoned.

"There, that should do it," he announced as he sat back down on a flimsy chair. "A paradox resolved."

Another brown-robed journeyman entered the hut. He looked as old as Albert but had put more effort into his personal appearance. His robe was clean and fresh. No patches on the sleeves. Had combed hair and was cleanly shaven.

"Isaac, what is it?" Albert growled. "I am entertaining a patron of mine who has been a faithful contributor for many years. No time now for you to wax about your latest approximations."

"You haven't heard, have you?" Isaac said. "Well, you may as well pack up your belongings now. It has already been decided."

"What do you mean?"

"What's his name, Dargonel, pulled me aside as he exited the rear of the stage. He had heard of my work, and we had a private chat. He became quite excited about what I have done — what more I can do. Fits in with, ah, Wetron's own plans nicely. Not something to spread about yet, the sorcerer told me, but I cannot resist. Albert, you are the first to know."

Isaac thrust out his chest. "I was assured that with the reallocation of funds, I will have no concerns. I will receive enough coin to guide the work of not one or two lackeys, but the efforts of a *dozen*!"

"You swallow whole the words of a mere sorcerer?" Albert scowled at the news.

"I have told you several times that my formulas were accurate enough, but you never agreed. Soon, the mantra will be spoken everywhere. 'Gravity is not just a good idea; it is the *law*.'"

"I do not need lackeys to do my work." Albert ignored Isaac's words. He tapped his forehead with his hand. "All my effort is spent here. I need workers only to cook my meals and freshen my …"

Albert closed his eyes for a moment and then resumed erasing and entering more symbols on his slates.

"You better start learning how to do such things yourself, old man," Isaac said. "It will be only days before you find yourself expelled to the road with an empty stomach and nowhere to go."

Albert did not react, but instead continued scribbling. With a swish to gather his robe tighter about himself, Isaac exited the hut.

"Ah, this might not be the best time to ask," Mason said. "I — we have a problem. Maybe you could do a little more of that thinking inside the box?"

# 17
# New Magic

ALBERT IGNORED Mason's question. He studied the new symbol he had written and shook his head. With his sleeve, he tried to erase the entire line, but the chalk was not disturbed. His robe was saturated with it. He waddled to a side table and pulled a small white tissue that peeked into the air from a box sitting there.

"Fauxvellum," he said to no one. "A failed attempt by a local paper mill to be part of the new magic. True vellum is quite expensive. Not enough calfskin to go around. And the millers could not produce a substitute substantial enough to accept ink."

Sylvia was intrigued. "When you pulled the one sheet out of the box, another one immediately appeared. Is the box magic? It never becomes empty?"

Albert returned to study the slate with the smeared symbols for a moment. He scanned over its entire area. "This is all wrong," he muttered. With sudden vigor, he began wiping the writing away.

"About the box," Sylvia persisted.

"Oh, um, what?" Albert continued wiping for a moment, then turned to address her. "Yes, the box is magic, but not in the way you probably think." He wagged one of his hands. "The ring I wear seals and releases the bottom. That is the only magic involved. An extremely short ritual creates the binding. It is like the band Lord Mason here wears — for opening and shutting a door somewhere, nothing more. I manually refill the box from the bottom whenever the last one is retrieved."

Albert smiled. He seemed to have forgotten what he had been doing. "The hard part is folding a stack of the fauxvellums correctly. Once that is done, they pop up, one after another until they are gone. And, well, I must confess, I sometimes also use them to blow my nose."

"What do these symbols on the slates mean?" Mason asked. "Exactly, *what* is it you study?"

Albert answered immediately. "I seek to understand the fundamental laws of the new magic," he said. "Nothing more and nothing less."

"Fundamental laws?" Rangoth came alive. "Things like 'What goes up cannot stay up' and 'Toast falling from a table always lands butter side down on the floor.' Those are laws, aren't they? Isn't that what Isaac proclaims? A new law?"

Albert shook his head again. "Indeed, your two examples are true, but they can be *derived* from truths far more basic. Just as 'Like produces like' is fundamental to thaumaturgy. 'Rub a wart with a rag and bury it will make the wart go away' is a mere consequence of it." He waved at his slates. "Isaac claims *he* has discovered a fundamental law of new magic, but his is only an approximation."

Before more could be said, a workman ducked into the hut. "Albert, it is already starting," he panted. "Lord Wetron has decreed. Each practitioner must pay four brandels on every new moon to stay in the compound. If one cannot, he must leave."

"By what authority can he do this?" Albert snorted. "I have heard nothing of a final decree from the council of nobles."

"Nevertheless, he has assembled his men-at-arms. They

are going from hut to hut demanding payment."

"Isaac was *right*." Albert slumped. "I must prepare to go."

"No, wait," Mason said. "Here, take these coins. I can spare them. Think of it as advanced payment for helping me solve the problem I have sought your counsel for."

In a flash, Sylvia came up with an idea. She felt a swell of pride. She had thought of it first. "Give him the brandels," she said. "Not as advance payment but for the final one."

"We haven't even told him yet what our problem is," Mason said.

"Yet, Albert has come up with what to do anyway."

"What?"

"He can change the fauxvellum box to be controlled by the ring you have, Mason, rather than his. The slit on top makes it perfect."

"We don't need something that dispenses paper."

"Yes, we do. Well, almost. But rather than taking slips out, we use it as something to put slips in."

SYLVIA STRETCHED, trying to loosen the knots in her back caused by spending another night in the coach on the side of the road. She looked out the window. The outlines of the first houses of Oxbridge were sharpening in the distance.

It was early morning. The perfect time to arrive, Mason had explained. Most nobles timed their entrances to when they would be the center of attention. After the start of work at sunrise, but before the heat of the day. Time enough to confront the mayor, get more ballots drawn, and for Rangoth to stage his shows in the evening.

Sylvia grimaced. Part of her wished that she had not been so quick to seize upon the first solution that occurred to her back in Albert's hut. Yes, the only person able to open the box was the one with the magic ring. No one else would be able to remove any ballots before the royal counter showed up the next day. And when he did, the crowd that watched would ensure that the totals were correct.

She fingered Mason's ring. It was surprisingly heavy. The fact it was magic was patently clear. It had sent tingles through her hand and partway up her arm as soon as she had touched it.

The ring. That was the part she had not thought all the way through — who would be the one wearing the ring? Sylvia had blinked when Mason had offered it to her.

"It will not do for a mere gatherer to inform the mayor that he must use a box he had never seen before as the receptacle for the ballots," he had said.

She had her doubts about the optimistic conclusion. As in Carmela, soldiers of the crown probably would have already arrived before them, instructed the mayor, and announced the voting the next day throughout the town. They would be questioning everyone if they had seen anybody looking like Mason.

Posing for the benefit of shop clerks when buying dresses and sunblockers had been one thing. Easy enough to carry out when there was money to exchange hands. But convincing a mayor to use a different receptacle than his own. How was she going to manage that?

As the coach drew closer and closer to the center of town, the soreness of the muscles in her back receded. The tumult rising in her stomach grew.

SYLVIA EYED the mayor of Oxbridge with what she hoped was enough haughtiness. Unlike Carmela's official, he was tall and bone-thin, sallow-faced. and frowning.

"The men-at-arms mentioned nothing of this when they

arrived yesterday evening," he said. "I was told I could use whatever container I wanted."

Sylvia raised her chin a fraction higher and half-closed her eyes. She wanted to look behind her to where Mason and Rangoth were standing in rigid attention beside her coach, but she did not turn around. 'Her coach', she mused. A few days ago, who would have guessed?

"And I am telling you that the noble council has changed its mind. There were … irregularities in the Carmela voting. This box will ensure that no ballots are removed once they are placed within it tomorrow."

"How do we get them back out so they can be counted?"

"Simple layman." Sylvia's voice dripped with all the scorn she could muster. "Were you not listening moments before? Do I need to report to the council the impediments you are placing in the way?"

"No … no, Milady," the mayor stammered. "It is that you said only you could open the box after the ballots had been cast. I see no keyhole or seam in any of the sides."

"Here, touch my hand," Sylvia commanded. "You will be able to tell your grandchildren you have done so. Go on, touch it."

The mayor reluctantly complied. His eyes opened in surprise when he did. "Magic," he said softly. "The ring is the key. I have heard stories but never been close to any such thing before."

"Yes, the tingle is the proof. I will be here when the official counter comes to do his duty. The one to open the box for him, ensuring that there was no tampering. Now, will you obey?"

"Certainly, Milady. Please forgive me. I merely wanted to make sure."

"Good enough," Sylvia said as she handed the mayor the box and turned away. "I will not mention your name in my report to the council."

She wanted to race but instead forced herself to walk regally back to the coach. "You know, now that I have tried it, I kind of like this role," she said to Mason as he helped her back inside.

"There is more to do," he said as she entered. "I will have to find another scribe here in Oxbridge to render a new set of ballots with my image."

"Is there a writer's colony here, too?" Sylvia asked.

"Every town has writers, hundreds of them."

As they chatted, none of the three noticed the mayor calling to one of the youths playing diskgoal in the street. "Here is a copper," he said. "Tell the man-at-arms who was here earlier that I have something to tell him."

# 18
# Move and Countermove

IT WAS noon the next day. Mason paced back and forth on the other side of the road from the Oxbridge mayor's house. He felt more vulnerable this time. There was no cluster of nobles and attendants to hide among. Only Sylvia and Rangoth stood at his side.

Still, both of the wizard's presentations the day before had gone as planned, even smoother than in Carmela. Everyone who received a ballot also accepted the identifying mark on their forehead. In fact, today, he could tell that the first ten voters clutched ballots with his name and image upon it.

As the eleventh townsman approached the ballot box, Sylvia's grip on Mason's arm tightened. "Look," she said. "The next voter is holding more than one ballot."

Mason stared. She was right. It looked like a dozen pieces of vellum, and the carrier's forehead was clean. No mark acquired from Rangoth's presentation.

Sylvia let go of Mason's arm and strode unsteadily across the road. Mason grimaced as he watched her navigate the ruts in her ridiculous shoes. Any lady of the court would be well-acquainted with how to walk with stateliness no matter what was underfoot.

"Hold on a moment," Sylvia called out to the mayor. "One ballot per person. That is what an election is all about."

The mayor shook his head. "I received no such instruction when the man-at-arms told me what to do yesterday." He frowned. "With all due respect, Milady, we are using *your* collection box rather than my washbasin. Isn't that enough?"

The townsman stuffed his votes into the box and walked away. Behind him was another who also carried a handful of ballots. Mason realized what was going to happen. The mayor would watch the box all through the night, just as what was done in Carmela. But this time, not only was there no way to remove ballots bearing his name, there was no way to remove any at all. Tomorrow, when the royal counter arrived, the result would be the same as it was before. Wetron would win again. The score will become two to none.

"Here, let me touch the box with my ring," Sylvia blurted. "Give it to me."

She was angry, Mason thought. As angry as when he planned to leave Rangoth and her alone at the wizard's hut after the attack of the brigands.

"The bottom will become unlatched," Sylvia said. "Scoop out the ballots so far and put them in your washbasin. Give me back my container. There is no need to continue this charade."

"She is feisty when aroused," Rangoth said softly to Mason when she joined them.

"Indeed." Mason nodded. "And a bold spirit is not what is most needed now."

He stopped speaking abruptly. He had spotted a man-at-arms walking toward Rangoth. He ducked behind the wizard as Sylvia returned to stand beside him.

"Excuse me, Milady," the soldier said as he approached. "I notice that the images on some of the ballots bear a resemblance to Lord Wetron's traitorous younger brother. Here is one which appeared in Carmela a few days ago. Have you caught sight of this brigand in your journeys?"

Sylvia glanced for a moment at the offering, then stared

the man in the eye. "Traitorous? Of course not. I have no dealings with such. What should I do if I happen to spot him on my travels?"

"Report to any man-at-arms bearing the heraldry of the queen. We will be visiting Ytterby next and after that, each polling place in the fief that has not yet voted. Every one of us has instructions to track this man down."

Mason held his breath as the soldier walked back to the line of voters. Methodically, the man-at-arms compared the ballot he held with the ones carried by each in line. Some clutched a stack of them, obviously all in favor of Wetron, and shook their heads. Others nodded when they displayed the ones they held.

"We have failed again," Mason whispered. "We have to get out of here — now! Soon enough, someone in line will point out Rangoth standing here, and the soldier will return."

"Form a sandwich," Sylvia said.

"Sandwich?" Mason did not understand.

"I used to do it when I was a girl," Sylvia said. "A trick to play with my friends. March between Rangoth and me as we return to the coach. When we do, all that will be seen is Rangoth's back."

"All right. Better than nothing. But where will we go?" Mason's thoughts churned. Like at the palace presentation, events were evolving too fast. He needed time to think things out. He always did.

"I agree," Rangoth said. "Perhaps another visit to this Albert friend of yours. I find the things he contemplates most interesting."

"Wait!" Sylvia said. "Maybe now is the time for …"

Her words trailed off. Going back to the river road would go right by Albert's compound anyway. Stopping for a little longer probably would not hurt. Finally, she said, "Mason, your determination is admirable. Yes, a brief stop at Albert's hut. Let's get that part of the journey over with."

A SHORT time later, Sylvia's coach again approached the explorer's compound. For Mason, the return was none too soon. Despite Sylvia's words of praise, his spirits had sunk even lower. The departure from central Oxbridge had been successful; they had not been caught. But neither had the desired outcome been achieved.

And even if Albert did figure out a way to prevent ballot stuffing, there would be no way to strut on a stage to orate Rangoth's presentation in Yterrby. He would be discovered almost at once. Wetron would win the next of the five elections, and that would be enough. He would have a majority no matter what was done thereafter. He would triumph as the new lord of Alpher's fief.

Deep in thought, from his driver's bench, Mason did not immediately notice that the scene before him had changed. Now there were more than a dozen huts spaced along the road opposite the compound. A banner was stretched from poles at either end of the group. It proclaimed "New Magic — Learn About It Here. Only five coppers to see every exhibit." In the middle, above Albert's, stood a smaller sign proclaiming: "Isaac's Law is not exact."

Mason was puzzled. 'New magic' 'Not exact' Why would anyone care about any of that? He reined in the horse. Apparently, the drop-out magician did not spend the money given him on rent.

The trio decoached and entered the old man's hut. The slates were crammed with strange chalk markings as before. Mason could not tell if any changes had been made to them or not.

"You're not returning the box, are you?" Albert asked when they entered. "It's magic. Works exactly as it is supposed to, each and every time. The Maxim of Persistence states that 'Perfection is Eternal.'"

"No, not that." Mason shook his head. "But it wasn't enough. We should have told you more about my problem the first time we were here."

"*Our* problem," Sylvia added.

"You stated before that what Isaac has done is only an approximation to a true law," Rangoth said. "Now, you announce it to the world. Why?"

"The formula *is* useful, true," Albert said. "It can predict how far a ballista's bolt will travel. Determine in advance the march of the wandering stars across the sky. No need for epicycles. Those things I don't deny."

Albert screwed up his face. "But the true law, expressed correctly, predicts strange effects that even I find hard to believe. Holes in existence. Great forces that rip apart anything approaching. Falling into nothingness, never to return."

"Does anything of what you profess have any practical value?" Rangoth asked. He arched his eyebrows. "Something in which even a wizard might find merit?"

"Probably not," Albert shrugged. "The pursuit of truth is sufficient reason for me."

"But apparently Wetron does have interest in what Isaac is doing," Sylvia said. "Why do you think that is? Increased accuracy with weapons, forecasting fortunes from the motions of the wanderers ..."

Albert's eyes lit up. "Ah, so much can change in a day, Milady. Dargonel, Wetron's factotum, has visited me, too. We spent a long time together, and I think I have convinced him. Or maybe, he sought me out deliberately. No matter. Now, he shows interest in my work. Perhaps even to the extent that Wetron will no longer care about the dropping of stones from towers or predicting when the next eclipse will occur."

127

"Then why is your hut out here on the side of the road rather than inside the compound?" Mason asked.

"A tactical move," Albert said. He smiled impishly at Sylvia. "One I am sure you are familiar with, Milady. It is called 'Playing hard to get', right?"

Mason sighed. "You are so out of touch, Albert. Haven't you heard of 'Out of sight, out of mind?'"

"I rather subscribe to 'Absence makes the heart grow fonder,'" Albert said. He blushed. "Not that I am actually saying anything like that to anyone, but the contradiction seemed to me …"

"This is getting us nowhere," Mason scowled. "What I — we need, Albert, is a way to ensure each individual can cast one and only one ballot into your magic box. And also, a method for handing them out without my presence being obvious."

He faced Rangoth. "And please, Master, perhaps we can keep focused on the task at hand."

Albert approached his slates and studied them one by one. He selected one and muttered, "This part is rock-solid enough — easily rederived. I will commit it to memory." It took both sleeves to wipe the slate clean, but soon he was filling it again with script. This time with letters Mason recognized. It gave him little satisfaction. Even with a perfect ballot box, how could he prevent Wetron from winning the third election?

# 19

# A Better Mousetrap

IT TOOK several more hours for Albert to finish his scribbling. "Now what?" Mason asked.

"I have *derived* the ritual," Albert said. "Now, we must *perform* it. Objects of magic are not built the same way one constructs a carriage."

"The words on the slate read like a list of steps," Rangoth said. "Is it their execution that produces magical rings and such?"

"Exactly!" Albert smiled at the wizard. "Perform them perfectly and get perfect results. For simple objects like boxes, even novices learn how to do them."

"How does one know the correct steps?" Rangoth continued. "Did you go into some sort of trance — like a sorcerer would to discover what they are?"

Albert shook his head. "No trances, merely deep, logical thought." He waved an arm at the slates. "Building one result on top of another in a methodical fashion. The symbols for magic boxes are simple — layman instructions that even you can understand. But they result from the same kind of thinking I do for my more interesting inquiries."

"So, now what?" Mason asked.

"We perform the ritual," Albert said. "Each of you will have a part. Listen carefully as I explain what you must do.

Your actions must be precise."

MASON FELT foolish. He found it difficult to stand on one leg, bend his other knee as far back as possible, and grasp his ankle in his hand. Wasn't this something his sisters did when they were younger? And his neck was cramping. He wasn't sure he could hold the orange Albert had placed under his chin and not drop it.

"Begin as soon as I strike the gong," Albert said. "Hop in sequence into each of the chalk squares I have marked on the floor. Use both feet for the two in the middle. Then, grasp your other foot before you continue to the end. When you get there, turn around and repeat the process in reverse."

Albert hit the gong with a small hammer, and Mason began jumping. As he did, the orange slipped. He tried to strengthen his grip on it but could not. The fruit fell to the floor with a splat.

"I only have three oranges here," Albert said. A hint of annoyance wrapped around his words. "Each one can be used only once. They have to be virgin. Pay attention and perform the step correctly."

Mason scowled. Albert was a washed-out initiate magician, not a member of the nobility. He himself was a lord and should be addressed with respect, even if he did look like a mandrake gatherer. He opened his mouth to protest, then slammed it shut again. An image of Sylvia forcing the Oxbridge mayor to use Albert's box flashed in his mind. She was not highborn, either, yet …

"I will manage this time," he said as he brought his thoughts back under control. "I think the key is to secure the orange first before balancing on one leg."

He spoke no more. Clearing his head, he finished his journey along the grid without error. Albert nodded, satisfied, and struck the gong a second time. Sylvia sprang to attention and closed in on Mason. She lifted her chin high and cocked her head, trying to transfer the orange from his neck to hers.

Mason stood as still as he could, not letting go of the fruit until he was sure Sylvia was in the proper position. She held her hands clasped behind her back and pressed forward to keep close. As she did, he felt the curves of her body against him. He smelled an alluring scent mingling with the aroma of orange blossoms. Her lips were so near. He relaxed his chin so that Sylvia would be in a better position ... The orange slipped to the floor.

"Amateurs," Albert growled. "Don't they teach you *anything* outside of magic castles?"

Mason took a deep breath and relaxed. He looked at Sylvia as she backed away. Was he imagining things, or did her face betray the hint of a blush? He pushed the thought aside. Before he could overthink what he had to do, he raced through his part of the ritual for the third time. Sylvia did better as well. With the orange safely in her grip, she walked slowly to where Rangoth sat on Albert's stool. She raised her chin slightly and dropped the little sphere squarely into the wizard's lap.

Albert tossed the gong aside and scooped up the fruit from Rangoth and flung it to the ground. He smashed it under his heel and then in a flurry, played a small flute and danced a spirited jig. This performance continued for a very long time. Mason did not know what else to do. Like the others, he stood silently and watched.

Finally, Albert, gasping for breath, collapsed to sit on Rangoth's lap. "It is done," he said.

Mason hurried to the ballot box resting on a tripod in the corner. "It looks no different," he said.

"But it is," Albert said. "Notice how much narrower the slit in the top is now. Only one ballot can be entered at a time."

"That solves nothing," Mason said. "My brother's minions would merely take longer to cast each of the stacks they held."

"Not so. Someone with a ballot in his hand has to place his other palm onto the end of the box in order for the slit to open. Open to accept the next ballot. That contact renders a unique impression. The box remembers. After one vote has been received, no more would be accepted from the same person."

"Are all magic rituals like this?" Rangoth asked. "What we did seemed quite, well, unimpressive."

"That is because the result *is* unimpressive," Albert said. "If you want something of true worth, like a sword that never dulls, or armor that can withstand the breath of a dragon …"

Albert trailed off, a distant look in his eye. "If you want one of those rare and costly things, the steps to be performed are elaborate and time-consuming. Things most rare can take hundreds of years to complete and involve scores of initiates. That is why magical objects are so rare and costly."

"Thank you — I guess," Mason said. "But what you have done solves only part of our problem. We still must find a way to provide the patter needed for Rangoth's presentations. Wetron has been alerted. Even with my gatherer clothes, I am sure to be recognized prancing on the stage. Too close to where ballots are being distributed with my likeness on them."

"You do not need me to help with that." Albert shook his head again. "You have the answer right before you."

"What do you mean?"

"Put Lady Sylvia on the stage."

"Yes!" Sylvia blurted. "Yes, indeed. I think I could well manage that."

"But the vellums themselves," Mason protested. "With my visage on them, Wetron's men would know I was in the

132

area. I would be hunted out."

"I agree," Albert said. "Your image should *not* be on the ballots."

"Whose then?"

"Why, Lady Sylvia's of course."

# 20
# Yterrby

MASON SAT alone with his thoughts on the coach's driver bench. He shrugged. He could think of no other way. Albert's logic was sound. Sylvia's name on the ballot rather than his own.

But why was she doing this? There was no reason for her to remain involved. Yes, she had convinced him to take her and Rangoth along when he fled the slaughter at the wizard's hovel, and perhaps felt she owed him something for that. But his subsequent fight was not hers at all. He had no hold over her. If she struck out on her own now, he had no argument for her to stay.

Yet she did remain, and he realized he was afraid to ask why.

No matter what happened with the elections, he would miss her if she left. She was unlike any other woman he had ever met. She had none of the affectations of all the women of Vendora's court, none. Well, she acted them out splendidly, but they were all only part of an act.

The real Sylvia was refreshingly different. Clever, sharp as a dragon's tooth. Working tirelessly to help him do what he had to in order to get his sisters to safety. Always upbeat, ready to try again whenever they failed.

And ultimately, if he did somehow gain control of the fief

in the eyes of the rest of the nobility, the final result would be the same — a parting of the ways.

SYLVIA NOTICED the smell when the town of Ytterby was barely visible on the horizon. Not a perfume or mere odor, definitely a stink. The closest she could relate it to was the spray of a frightened skunk, but that was not correct either.

She studied Rangoth sitting at her side. He was silent as he often was, but his eyes were alert and his brow furrowed. He reminded her of Albert trying to think his way through a difficult problem. She decided not to interrupt the wizard's thoughts and leaned out of the window to call up to Mason, "How much longer?"

Mason did not immediately answer. "Does it matter?" he said after a moment.

He's thinking through the implications of Albert's suggestion, Sylvia realized. Suppose they did get more ballots produced, and this time with her image upon it rather than his. Enough so they could win the election. The logical next step would be to repeat the process in the remaining two towns. If she triumphed in those, she would be the overall victor, not Wetron. Mason's brother's scheme to seize control of Alpher's fiefdom would be thwarted.

But was that really a victory? Could a serving wench assume control of a fief with no blood connections to the nobility at all? Wouldn't the council declare the entire effort void? Or worse, would she become a mere puppet? Somehow obligated to follow everything Mason commanded from the shadow of her skirt?

So, only one more town, she thought, and that would be the last before she left for the south … She shook her head. She was kidding herself. She was in too deep now. In for a copper, in for a brandel. Convincing another mayor to accept an improved ballot box. Standing on a stage to keep a crowd engaged in Rangoth's wizardry. She could not turn back. Not until Wetron was defeated in Yterrby and the last two towns. Until she was declared the victor. She knew she had no real desire for the responsibilities of governing so she would cede the fiefdom to Mason to do with as he wished and continue her own journey.

Her thoughts twisted. She frowned. Continuing south would mean leaving Mason's company, probably forever. It was hard for her to admit, but she felt … she was becoming fond of him. Shared adversities bonded people together, it was said. And she had to admit, it was true. He was resourceful, quite knowledgeable about the world of privilege and wealth. And after the rough start, he treated her with courtesy. As if she indeed were a lady. She sighed. He could not possibly have any interest in journeying to the far south with a serving wench.

MASON SAT on the coach's driver bench, hoping for Sylvia to say more. To ask another question that he could answer better. Add another brick to the weight of his worth in her eyes. In *her* eyes? As he pondered, he blinked where his thoughts were taking him. Suppose 'Lady' Sylvia did win the election in Ytterby — and the remaining two that followed.

If her pretense was accepted, and Alpher's fief became legally hers, what would happen to *him*? Would she accept the largess thrust upon her and cast him aside? He would have no base of wealth. He tugged at the gatherer hat he wore. Would fate consign him to the life he had inadvertently chosen to hide in?

He remembered the warmth of her body against his own in Albert's hut. No, Sylvia would not behave that way, he reassured himself. Nothing would change, but somehow, they would manage to share the future they were crafting together — wouldn't they?

The horse pulling their coach suddenly stopped and whinnied. A gust of air brought more of the pungent smell their way. Mason dismounted. He retrieved some oats from the bag they had taken from the palace in Ambrosia and gave them to the steed. But the bribe did not work. The horse would go no farther.

Mason coughed. He did not blame the gelding. Squinting into the distance, he saw a cluster of farmhouses. Maybe they could at least get that far. He removed the horse from the traces and hobbled him nearby. "I will get help," he called to Sylvia and began walking down the road.

The stench increased with each step he took. Several times he halted and endured a spasm of coughs. The first farmhouse he came to appeared more distressed than others nearer to the town. He could not contemplate the prospect of continuing. With a weak knock, he announced his presence in front of the door.

An older man, his face furrowed like a newly-plowed field, opened the door and examined Mason up and down. "Not from around here, I see."

"My lady's coach —" Mason whispered. He could not continue speaking.

"Yes, yes. Only idiots venture out when the factories are operating at full tilt. Come in, come in. I have some lozenges I can sell to you for three coppers each. Here, suck on a sample."

Mason grabbed the offered tablet and shoved it onto his tongue. Almost immediately, the gag reflex vanished. He fumbled for coins in his purse. "I have heard of these in Ambrosia, but never had the, ah, opportunity to try one."

"Yes, they work well enough. It was the least the alchemists could do. Well, they should do more. Give them away instead of charging. Some of the townspeople cannot even afford the going rate — a single copper for each. They wear face masks and get used to it as best they can."

"I guess having to use them is because of the new magic, right?" Mason asked.

"Right as a queen's reign. The alchemists are no longer producing potions and creams one bottle at a time. Instead, they brew large batches and store the output in huge vats and tanks. Use new formulas that do not need transcription in order to activate. Create new, unheard-of substances. 'Chemicals' they are called."

"Lady Sylvia's carriage is a way down the road. Her horse has balked at coming any closer."

"A sensible beast, unlike most who live around here. The lozenges work on livestock, too. Although it is a bit tricky sometimes to stop them from spitting them back out before they start to work."

"So then, could I buy more from you and — "

"I have an extra bucket of them to use in case of an emergency. Everyone does. I can give you some for only three coppers each."

"You said that they only cost a single copper."

"Do you want relief or not?"

Mason looked closely at the bucket standing next to the old man's feet. There were hundreds of lozenges there, maybe the better part of a thousand. Their own party would need some, of course. There was no doubt about that. But how many, he could only guess.

"I will give you ten brandels for the entire lot," he said after a moment.

"That would be less than three coppers each," the farmer protested.

"Old man, you can continue to buy lozenges for one copper each, and then sell them for three for the rest of your life. With all of these, so will your son and his own son, too. I

138

offer you an instant profit right now. Think of what you could do if you possessed ten coins of gold."

The farmer frowned as if digesting Mason's words, one by one. "Deal," he finally said.

SYLVIA SUCKED on the lozenge Mason had given her upon his return. The taste was cloyingly sweet, but she welcomed anything to combat the stench. When she decoached with Rangoth in Yterrby a short time later, she saw hazy, brown air in every direction.

It was as if the entire town had been shrouded under an old threadbare blanket. Beggars in rags, masked so that only their eyes showed, slowly shuffled down the main street. They assailed more well-to-do travelers for spare lozenges or coins.

Most of the buildings reminded Sylvia of the alchemist shops in Ambrosia. Narrow doors stood between panes of isinglass on both sides. Phials and philtres, dusty with age, filled the displays behind the windows. Only shadows of the price labels remained. Spiderweb-like cracks covered the walls. Some even tilted slightly to the side.

There was activity around the others, the ones belching smoke and tainted air. From them, gutters gushed full of waste-water and sludge. Wagons queued at their doors, and workmen carried pallets of bottles and jars to load them in haste.

Sylvia noticed that the waste matter congealed into a playground for children at the end of the street. It was almost completely covered with juvenile messages. "Gandar loves Myra." "Mutrone is a banshee fart." "Why did the colossal djinn and the tracking imp get married? — Because they had to."

Three of the shops were strikingly different. There were

no doors or window displays at all. Old cracks and seams were only dimly visible, covered by freshly applied paint. From one, the water gushing to the curb was red-tinted as if mixed with blood. Evidently, wealthy customers entered from the rear.

"It is the fickleness of the clientele," Rangoth said. "Like performance wizardry, the rage for the latest potion sweeps aside what was the most desirable a mere month before. Those peddling the out-of-fashion decline; those offering the new thrive."

"With this miasmic air, it is no wonder that no one walks the streets," Sylvia said. "How will we find the mayor? We have to get the ballot box switched before the voting starts." She frowned. "Will there even be anybody who will vote?"

"Let's circle to the back and start with the more prosperous-looking shops," Mason said. "Where there is wealth, the concern is greater about what the edicts from authorities might be."

In the rear alleyway, the first freshly painted shop showed the same façade as the other two. A wall with no displays surrounded a single windowless door without a latch or handle. 'Gibbon glue' was written on it in a fancy script. Mason pounded on the door, but got no answer. He tried a second time with greater force.

"Coming, coming," a faint voice called from inside, and then swung open. "You are early. There is nothing to show you yet. Remember, I said ..."

The voice trailed off. The man standing there had a wide smile that looked as if it might break into a thousand pieces. He was bald on the top of his head but had let the hair from his temples grow almost to his waist. The nose was shocking. Only a stub of it remained. Over the years, he must have inhaled too many drugs.

He wore what once probably had been a vivid white robe with the inverted black triangles signifying a master alchemist. Now, the icons barely stood out against a dingy grey background.

"You are not Dargonel," the alchemist said. "What is it you want?"

Mason started to speak, then stopped when Sylvia poked him gently in his ribs with her elbow. "I am Lady Sylvia," she said. "I am looking for the mayor. Do you know where I can find him?"

"The mayor? Well, yes, we have one. A person to talk with royal auditors whenever they come to visit and is smart enough to mind his own business otherwise."

He studied Sylvia for a moment, then bowed. "I am sorry, Milady. Please excuse my preoccupation. The next few steps in the brew I am working on will be tricky. Even with the best formulas of alchemy, it has only one chance in ten of succeeding. Our basic law, 'The attributes without mirror the powers within' guides us, but is silent on the chances of success. I *can* take your order, but all my time until the end of the month has been pledged to fulfill a request for Lord Wetron. Can you imagine? Not a petite bottle, but a barrel of the stuff. A full barrel of Gibbon Glue!"

"Why does your shop not face the street?" Sylvia blurted. "The building arrangement seems quite strange."

"Well, you, too, would turn away from accepting coppers when real gold is being offered at the rear by nobles who are cautious. But please note that I am not like the practitioners of the other two farther down the street. I don't dabble with the new magic. No, I make my product the old-fashioned way. Small batches, many steps, and most likely meager results every time I try. It is only by repetition that I will produce in a month how much Lord Wetron has asked for. I only opened the door to you because I thought you were Dargonel, his factotum."

"Why would Lord Wetron want a barrel of the stuff?" Mason asked. "Gibbon glue is for repairing chipped vases and such, right?"

"Yes, that is true. I do not know why the lord desires so much. Nor do I care." The alchemist turned his attention back to Sylvia. "But I am a merchant. After this month is over, the next will come. I am happy to take your order now for delivery then, Milady."

"You don't know how to find the mayor, do you?" Sylvia asked again.

"Alas, I do not. And if you are not going to do business with me, I must return to the vat of flaxseed I am reducing." With that, the alchemist shut the door, muttering about unwanted distractions.

"What is my brother up to?" Mason stared at the closed door.

"It won't matter if we — I win the remaining elections," Sylvia said. "It won't matter at all."

"Producing Gibbon Glue indeed is work of an alchemist," Rangoth said. "But, mark you, Dargonel is a *sorcerer*." He shook his head. "Practitioners of one craft seldom communicate with those of another. They fear revealing their own secrets in the exchange. This is most interesting. I, for one, want to find out more."

# 21
# More Alchemy

RANGOTH SLID past Mason and knocked on the next rear-facing door. He brushed the dust from his robe and smoothed his beard. Neither Sylvia nor Mason noticed. Instead, they tried to make sense of the sounds coming from the other side of the entrance. A cacophony of hissing, screeching, sneezing, and whimpering.

The door opened, and another alchemist appeared. This one was younger and better groomed than the maker of Gibbon Glue. His face was plain and smooth, and his hair cut to the collar. Most striking were his eyes. They appeared to twinkle, radiating kindness and care. Wrapped over his shoulder was a silver ferret. Another chocolate-colored one he let move back and forth from one of his hands to the other.

Behind him, Sylvia saw a dozen cages stacked on top of one another. Each contained an additional ferret. All the small creatures were animated, creating the noise. One in particular caught her interest. It was not caged and stared into a dark hole on the floor. A glass globe with two hoses attached encased its head. One connected to a frost-encrusted crate, the other to a bubbling vat. A third tube ran from the vat back to the coffer.

Rangoth thrust his head forward, eagerly peering at the crate. "There is a Maxwell's demon in there. I can sense it. What are you using him for?"

The alchemist blinked. "How did you know I — " The glance at the flame logo on Rangoth's robe cut him short. "Of course, a wizard. You have experience with such creatures."

"Indeed," Rangoth said. "I am intrigued. To what purpose would you put such a demon?"

The alchemist ignored Sylvia and Mason. "Please let me introduce myself. My name is Avagadro. Who are you, and what brings you here? I had almost made up my mind to ask Wetron's factota to procure services from one such as you."

"I accept!" Rangoth said. "My, ah, command performances in the south can wait. I am at your disposal. What help do you need?"

"Master!" Sylvia exclaimed. "What are you saying? There is an election we have to campaign for here. We have no time for this. Either this alchemist can lead us to the mayor or he cannot. And if not, let us be off to ask another."

"Um, yes, Sylvia. But perhaps that will happen in the goodness of time." He waved her words away as if he were sweeping a rug. He kept focusing on the alchemist. "Let me guess, everything is fine at first, and then there is a drop-off in performance. The output to the cold side of the chest is less than it was originally."

"Exactly!" Avagadro said.

"Yes. Maxwell's demons are noted for becoming bored easily. After all, how exciting can it be to continually bat tiny pieces of air in one direction or the other, depending on how fast it is travelling? Dominance is easy, but you must create challenges and rewards for success, too." Rangoth paused to catch his breath. "Why is it you need to collect so much cold air anyway?"

"Not any kind of air. Dargonel is interested in the one my fellow alchemists — the ones exploring the new magic — have discovered. Air is not merely a single substance but composed of many types. It is the one they have named 'oxygen' that is the important one."

Sylvia's impatience grew. She did not like what she was hearing. "Wetron!" Sylvia blurted. "Is he your patron, too?"

"Not a patron, no. Nothing long term. Dargonel has given me a request — a well-paying one — to deliver a crate of *frozen* oxygen to him by month's end."

"Why does he want something like that?" Mason asked. "Has my brother gone daft?"

"*Your* brother?" Avagadro frowned for a moment. "I don't know," he said at last. He rushed back to the table with the englobed ferret. "See William here? Breathing good air from the crate of oxygen as he needs, he can explore deep into the earth. That is the reason I was told anyway."

"Your pet has to exhale, too," Sylvia said, despite herself. "How does he get rid of the bad air he makes?"

"Why, with my invention here. I am an alchemist, after all. In addition to using *old* magic to garner the oxygen, I employ *new* magic to dispose of the bad. No need for repetitions. No uncertainty in the results. Do things one time, and you are done."

"Excuse my pedantry," Avagadro continued. "We practitioners of the new magic call the bad gas 'carbon dioxide.' I run it over quick lime. The bad air is captured as limestone while releasing new oxygen to be refrozen, and the cycle can repeat."

"But why ferrets?" Sylvia asked. She grimaced at what she had said. There was nothing of interest to be learned here. She had to be more like Mason, she told herself. Think before speaking.

"I am not the only one who needs them. I provide a supply to the other alchemists, too. Well, to the ones practicing the new magic, at least. They have complex machinery with many pipes and tubes. Over time, these acquire unwanted coatings on the inside that must be removed. Otherwise, their reactions work at lower and lower efficiencies.

Avagadro scratched the ferret he was holding under the chin. "Hear that? It is *dooking* now, a sign that I am giving her pleasure." His voice shifted to a higher register. "Yes, you are a cute one, yes, you are. I love you, too. I do. I do."

"Ah, maybe I should not have asked," Mason said. "We are distracting you."

Avagadro stopped his petting. "Oh, right," he said. "Where was I. Um, yes. Dismantling, scrubbing the inside of pipes with brushes, and then reassembling is too time-consuming. Far more efficient is to place a ferret into an apparatus and let its fur do the job as it explores the pipes."

"This is, of course, interesting," Sylvia said. "But I have to ask. How do we find Yterrby's mayor?"

"Ask at the end of the row." Avagadro shrugged. "Justus might know better."

"All right then," Mason said. "Let's move along." He eyed the wizard. "Master Rangoth, maybe there will be some time to return here later."

"I will stay with this young man, Avagadro, is it?" Rangoth said. "There is much I can teach — and learn — from him."

"If you want to learn more about the wizardry we use here, go talk to Justus," Avagadro said. "What you find out there will literally knock your boots off."

THE TRIO walked down the alley behind the row of alchemist shops. Mason glanced at Sylvia. He could tell from her expression that she too was growing increasingly impatient. They did not come to these shops merely to seek lessons in the crafts.

When they came to the end of the row, he raised his fist to knock. The door was freshly repainted and sported a new latch and hinges. But before he acted, banshees began wailing on the roof of the shop. A warning! There were more of them than had been in the palace in Ambrosia. Instinctively, Mason drew Sylvia to him and held her close. She did not resist. The cries were loud. The eerie sounds pierced their souls.

Mason found his voice and started to say something reassuring. But before he could, the sky erupted with a brilliant flash. It jammed his eyes completely closed. He staggered. Then, a thunderous clap rang in his ears; a wave of pressure pushed against him. He tripped to the side, and still holding Sylvia closely, fell to the ground. The building behind him swayed from the impact. Fresh cracks emerged in what must have been a freshly-repainted wall.

"What *was* that?" Sylvia asked. She held on to Mason tightly.

"I, I don't know." Mason tried to pull both of them back to standing, but his legs were weak from the shock. "It can't have been lightning. The flash was the wrong color."

"Amazing, absolutely amazing," Rangoth came running up. "I never thought I would witness such a thing." He took a deep breath, then continued to ramble. "Titanic djinns. That's what they are, has to be."

"You understand what just happened?" Mason asked.

"Yes, yes. A part of wizard lore since before I was a beginner. Before I connected with the demon world for the first time."

"Slow down, Master," Sylvia said. "If you know what happened, please explain."

Rangoth took another breath. "It's quite simple, really. We communicate to the realm of devils through flame, right? And each species of demon is attached to only a single type of fire."

"Yes, yes. We know that much," Mason said. "Almost everyone does."

"But suppose there is a type of demon, a rare one, who can only communicate through the most exotic of fires — a tremendous explosion."

"Master, you didn't cause this, did you?" Sylvia pushed on Mason's shoulder and managed to regain her footing.

"No, no, of course not. I have no knowledge of how to create such a flame."

"Then, some great demon is walking among us now?" Mason managed to stand as well.

"No, no, there is no danger. Not one but two titanic djinns are in our realm. I can sense them, and they are quite docile. Like pinheads. Pinheads with wings, and with almost no brains at all."

"Who is controlling them?" Mason persisted. "Is there going to be another wizard battle between you and him?"

"Not at all. They have submitted to the wizard within the shop behind you." Rangoth shrugged. "A beginner. A nobody. I can tell."

"Then, why the banshees?" Sylvia asked.

"Probably a precaution." Rangoth shrugged. "The trouble with playing with explosives is that one does not know how strong they will be."

"I don't think that this experimentation should be going on." Mason frowned. "Toxic fumes, enormous demons, new magic … it needs to be under responsible control."

"The fiefholder can demand that," Sylvia said. "And that means — "

"Yes," Mason agreed. "These practices of new magic must be restricted. But for now, we must keep focused. There is an election that we have to win."

# 22

# The Demon Queen

MASON KNOCKED on the entrance to the last of the three prosperous shops. "Master Justus, we have a question for you." Sylvia and Rangoth clustered beside him.

Nothing happened for several moments. Mason prepared to knock again when the door opened. An alchemist stood there; two heads shorter than Sylvia. Jowls hung low from both sides of his face. His robe bulged in front and on both sides. His hands and arms stained yellow up to his elbows like dirty rags. An odor like that from rotting eggs hung heavy in the air. From an open drain gurgling on the floor came the red-tinted water escaping to the gutter behind the other end of the shop.

"Yes, come in, come in. It was grand, was it not? Are you the observers employed by Dargonel? You saw it. Surely, you must be pleased."

Behind the alchemist, the shop was crammed full of vats connected by an array of pipes and pumps. Under some, small flames heated their contents. Others were bathed by cooling streams of water. Sylvia's eyes darted from place to place, taking in all the marvels.

"Impressive, isn't it? And all with new magic only. No need for the old." He shrugged. "I admit that the sureness of the result every time could make one dispense with caution,

149

but I am careful. No explosions from my products until they are needed."

"We are looking for the mayor," Sylvia said. "Tell us where he is." Each time she had to do this, she realized, she was slipping into her role as a lady more and more easily. She sighed. But now to suffer through another lecture.

Justus' eyes narrowed. "Why do you need to see him?"

"It is about the election. I brought the new ballot box that must be used — by order of the council of nobles."

"The election starts tomorrow at sunrise. I am sure that right now the mayor is a busy man."

"Sunrise!" Mason blurted.

Sylvia stepped on Mason's foot. She frowned, hoping he would understand to be quiet.

"Nevertheless ..." She turned her attention back to Justus. "I don't know where he is. You will have to track him down."

Track him down? Another unplanned delay! Her impatience blossomed into a barb of panic. Sunrise. Would there be enough time? They had to find the mayor, convince him to substitute boxes, have Sylvia pose for an artist — Mason had agreed it would be her face this time, not his, locate a scribe who could replicate the ballots from the sketch, have Rangoth perform not one but two of his acts ...

Sylvia took a deep breath. First things first. Track the mayor down. How could that be accomplished quickly? Track him down ... Tracking imps! They were still imprisoned in the tankard! It was fortunate that she had decided to hang on to it. While Mason was off finding a scribe, Rangoth needed to wrestle control of them. After that ...

Planning ahead was too complicated to figure out now, Sylvia realized. She understood better why Mason took so long to construct his plans.

"The mayor. Describe him," she commanded Justus.

150

"I dunno," the alchemist shrugged. "Tall. Thin. Well-trimmed, short beard. Wears the mayor's medallion around his neck."

"Yes, that may be enough. Come, Master Rangoth. Let's go back to my coach."

"I'm staying," Rangoth said. "I have something to offer."

"I handle my craft expertly. Dargonel needs no more alchemists."

"I am a wizard with experience," Rangoth said. "Did you not look at my robe. How much of my craft does this Dargonel employ?"

"One, as far as I know."

"One wizard only? With my own eyes, I have seen two titanic djinns being brought into our realm. Is that prudent?"

Justus scratched his chin and pondered. "I will ask," he said.

"Master, what are you doing?" Sylvia asked.

"Titanic djinns, Sylvia. The chance of a lifetime. This Dargonel is on to something fantastic. I was right. There is a reason why he seeks help from all the realms. I must find out more. Here is where I desire to be."

SYLVIA AND Mason exited the shop. The door slammed shut behind them. She was stunned. No amount of pleading with Rangoth had made any difference. Just like that. After everything she had done over the years. Rangoth tossed her aside like a worn-out dishrag. She looked at Mason and saw his face sag with defeat. He did not take another step.

She shook her head rapidly back and forth, trying to snuff out a growing sense of failure. Like a drowning fisherman impulsively clutching at wind-blown flotsam, she took a deep breath, grabbed him behind his neck, and kissed him.

Mason's head jerked back in surprise. I'm making a fool of myself, Sylvia thought in a rush. But in the next instance, he relaxed and wrapped his arms around her, drawing her close. His lips sought hers and the second embrace was a long, satisfying one.

Sylvia blurted, "We can still go south, Mason, the two of us," she said. "South. That was my original idea. Remember?"

Mason disengaged. He shook his head. "I have seen too much," he said. "Everything happening here. A fief is not merely a gift, Sylvia. The holder has a responsibility to protect his subjects, help them prosper. Do more than merely fend for himself. I mean for myself — or for, for you. No, I will not slink away. I need you at my side to help me, Sylvia. Wetron cannot be allowed to win here."

"Then we continue," Sylvia said. "Do what almost worked before. The two of us together. Win the election here in Ytterby and two more after that."

Mason sighed. "I understand what has to be done. That has not changed. But we are caught between a waking griffin and a cliff crumbling behind us. We only have half a day." He grimaced. "And without a complete plan."

"So, we do the best we can. I will find the mayor and press Albert's box upon him. You locate an artist to render a likeness of me and a scribe who can create some more ballots."

"But without Rangoth's performances …"

"You will think of something," she said. "I know you will. For now, we return to the coach. You drive me to the center of the town. Our targets are most likely to be there anyway."

Sylvia's thoughts bubbled. New feelings swept the despair away. Mason and her together. Somehow they would find a way. And afterward? Not something to think about now. There was work to be done.

SYLVIA PUT another lozenge into her mouth as her coach jogged along. On the driver's bench, Mason flicked the reins sparingly, coaxing their horse to keep plodding. An idea struck her.

She began rummaging through the detritus of their travel piled up next to where Rangoth sat?—used to sit?

Her idea was simple enough. Take control of the tracking queen imprisoned in the tankard. It was around somewhere. Impart the description of the mayor, however that was done. Then, release the imps to fan out and locate where he was.

But with Rangoth gone, she saw no way around that she had to do this *herself*. Her encounter with one of the drone imps had been scary enough. She had barely managed to avoid being the one dominated. Surely, the queen would be a much greater challenge.

But, in for a copper, in for a brandel, she told herself as she spotted the tankard and picked it up. Believe in oneself. That was the key. No communicating flame with the realm of demons was needed, she reasoned. The queen was already here. Like with the drone, she should only have to quiet her mind and reach out ...

"Help me, please help me," she heard as a thought exploded in her head. "My drones are too many. There is no way for me to stop the breeding."

Sylvia's eyes widened. She nearly dropped the tankard. "Help you how?" she asked aloud.

"Like most of you creatures, my minions are of two sexes, and they have become restless. They have nothing else to do. No mission to fulfill. And now is that time in their cycle when their lust runs hot. I have tried to command them to stop, but even the words of a queen have not proven enough."

Sylvia was confused. "So, you are running out of food or

something. Where does the, ah, substance that makes up the new drones come from?"

"Transmuted out of the air. But as more and more are created, what remains becomes less. Two make two more, and then there are four, eight, sixteen … Soon, we all will suffocate or be crushed together into a gooey pulp."

"What about the two of us?" Sylvia asked. "How do we decide dominance or submission?"

"I submit. I submit. I will do whatever you want and command my drones to follow. Open the lid of the tankard. Please, open it now."

Sylvia remembered tales of childhood. Ones about wily demons who duped mortals into doing foolish things. Maybe, this was an example of exactly that. She should be more careful, she told herself, but there was little time for that.

The voice had sounded so sincere. Sure, escape was the queen's goal. Would she actually comply with what she said she would do? "You will have to track down someone for me.

His description is not very specific."

"Yes, yes, my drones will do it. I have so many now that we will do it quickly. Let us out. Please hurry before our numbers increase any more."

Sylvia understood she had to decide and decide now. Without another thought, she released the lid holding shut the tankard.

The air in front of Sylvia filled with buzzing drones. Like bees disturbed from a giant, low-hanging nest, they swirled around her. She cast her arm over her eyes but felt no stings.

After a moment, she lowered her guard and said slowly and distinctly, "Tall. Thin. Well-trimmed, short beard. Wears the mayor's medallion around his neck."

# 23

# A Visit with the Mayor

SYLVIA LOOKED out the window. The carriage was approaching what looked like the center of town. They had been lucky. Shortly after starting, Mason had spotted the sign for a portrait artist. The likeness he drew of Sylvia was crude, simple lines and little shading. She was certain that she did not look like that.

She peered into the flagon. It was empty. None of the tracking imps were to be seen. What was it like, she wondered? Trapped with no way to escape. Every moment twice as bad as the one before …

A new thought hit her like a slap from a djinn. It was insane, but given the pressure of time, it might work. "Mason," she cried out the window. "Stop the carriage. There is something I have to give you. Something more to add to the ballots you are preparing."

"What?" Mason halted the coach. "Every moment is precious."

"I know. I know." Sylvia rummaged through their baggage for her purse. She extracted a quill and a small bottle of ink from it. Digging more, she found a scrap of vellum and started writing.

"Add these instructions to every ballot," she said when she was done. "They may not be followed by everyone, but it

155

cannot hurt."

Mason examined the fragment. "What's this 'surprise gift?'" he asked.

"I haven't figured out that part yet."

"But suppose you can't?"

"Not now, Mason!"

Without another word, Sylvia walked away, the magical ballot box in her hand.

"Wait!" Mason shouted. "How will you find me again?"

"Gatherer's hat, red hair and not bad looking," Sylvia winked and called back.

Mason waited a moment and then shrugged. She was impetuous as ever. His job was to perform his part of the task. Continue the search for a many-copy scribe.

SYLVIA TRAVELED only a single block in a random direction before the tracking imp queen buzzed in her face.

"Two blocks to the left, second door," the tiny demon said. "What is your next command?"

"I don't have any," Sylvia said. "I release you."

"It's not that simple." The queen fluttered closer until she hovered immediately in front of Sylvia's nose. "The only way that I am released is if I go back to my realm through the proper flame."

"No time to find the correct plant." Sylvia shook her head. "Take a break."

"Break? Break what? My drones and I are too small to damage anything in your realm. If we could have done so, the tankard would have been shattered long ago."

"Then just hover out of human sight. When I need more help, I will let you know."

The imps vanished, and soon Sylvia was standing in front

of the indicated door. She stepped back into her shoes and smoothed her dress. By now, her coif was looser than at first, but she reasoned, it still looked good enough. She knocked once, and almost immediately, a serving man opened the door. "I am here to see the mayor," she said. "I bear a command from the council of nobles."

"Mayor Hadlon is indisposed with another guest at the moment," the servant said. "Whom shall I say is calling?"

"Lady Sylvia — with, as I have just said, a command from the council." Sylvia glowered. "It is urgent."

The servant averted his gaze. "Please wait here, Milady. I will check."

Sylvia waited for what felt to her too long a time, but eventually, the serving-man returned.

"Mayor Hadlon will see you now," he said.

SYLVIA'S CONVERSATION with the mayor of Yterrby went much the same as with the mayor of Oxbridge. The only difference was that the man facing her this time was tall, slender, and much more richly dressed. His tunic shimmered in the morning light; a spiral of pearls decorated both arms. In the end, Hadlon accepted the ballot box, assuring Sylvia that it would be used on the morrow.

Sylvia felt as if a great weight had been removed from her chest. If Mason succeeded in getting enough ballots printed, they still had a chance. There might be enough time left today to distribute them to villagers so that they would vote for her tomorrow. The nagging thought that, unlike Mason, she was totally unknown in Ytterby, she pushed aside.

"I would like to introduce you to another visitor from the Queen'a court," Hadlon said. "It might be you know each other."

"No, I doubt that," Sylvia said, coming out of her reverie.

"Seldom, I am there. I — "

"Then, I shall introduce you. Here he comes now. Lady Sylvia, please meet Lord Wetron."

Sylvia froze. She almost stumbled out of her shoes. It was Mason's brother, all right. There was no mistaking him. A jeweled eye patch covered the slash she had made — what was it now — almost a week ago. As best she could remember, he wore the same clothing as before. Brocaded tunic, embroidered leggings, and a crimson cape with a collar that cradled his head up to his ears.

Wetron cocked his head to the side. "Forgive me, Milady. As you well know, there are hundreds of us who come and go to Vendora's court all the time." He scratched the stubble on his chin. "You look familiar. I am sure that I have seen you there before, although I cannot remember the occasion."

Sylvia was not sure exactly what to do. She tipped her head slightly and curtsied. "Milord," she mumbled.

"Ah, you are a new one, I can tell. But please, do not be shy. I do not bite." He looked Sylvia up and down critically as if he were examining a slab of beef freshly slaughtered. "Are you here to observe the election, and, dare I say it, the congratulatory festivities to follow?"

Sylvia's thoughts raced. The quicker she could leave, the better. But certainly, Wetron would be curious about the new ballot box and why he had heard nothing about it. Would it be better to leave the matter to Haldon, whose second-hand explanation might create suspicion, or brazen it out herself to keep the lord unsuspecting?

"I come as a messenger from the noble council," she said at last.

Wetron's eyebrow shot up. "Indeed, the council? I have just come from there myself and heard of no new messages."

"Ah, as well you should not," Sylvia said. She hoped what sprang into her mind would work. "I am sure you understand the delicacy of the matter. You are a candidate to become the new legal fiefholder, are you not?"

"But of course! There is only me and my traitorous brother."

"And suspicions of irregularities at the elections so far?"

Wetron puffed out his chest. "All that is rumors and lies. I have won the elections from both Carmela and Oxbridge. A victory here at Yterrby as I expect, and it will all be over. I will be the legal fief lord as the queen wanted — the most popular representative of the people."

"The council, in their wisdom, desire that there be no question about that. There is enough discontent about the abuses of the new magic as it is." Sylvia took a deep breath and stared at Wetron. "They decided to ensure the results by means of special ballot boxes — ones that none of the candidates knew anything about. That is why you have not heard of them."

Wetron squinted at Sylvia with his good eye. His stare lingered for longer than she wished. "And you are sure, you say, that we have not somehow met before?"

Sylvia could withstand the tension no longer, no matter how bad it might look. "Excuse me, Milord. It has been a, a pleasure meeting you. Now, I must go."

She rushed out the door, removed her shoes, and scampered away. As she did, the last of her lozenge melted in her mouth. Immediately, she began coughing and almost could not stop. This was additional stress that she did not need. With her free hand, she fumbled in her purse for another tablet.

In an instant, her coughing stopped, and the stink went away. Sylvia smiled. The last puzzle piece fell into place.

"Are you still there?" she asked the gnat-like cloud hovering nearby. "Gatherer's hat, red hair, and not bad looking."

# 24
# Exponential Growth

DAWN OF the next day took far too long to arrive. Although the sun was barely up, the smoke from the alchemist shops was already making it difficult to breathe. Sylvia gently removed Mason's arm from around her so he could sleep a bit longer while she stretched. With Rangoth gone, they both could have had an entire coach bench for themselves. But without saying anything, she sat next to him after he had selected one. Nor did she protest when he wrapped his arm around her shoulder as they grew cozy. The day's objectives had been met. She had done what she said she would, and so had he. His arms had been comforting. They were a team striving together toward a common goal.

"Did you sleep well?" Mason asked as he roused. His arm started to slip away from her.

Before she answered, Sylvia pushed it back to where it had been before. She liked his gentle touch more than she had imagined. "Yes, and you?"

She blushed, then turned her head so he would not see and scowled at herself. Amateur, she thought. Was that the best she could come up with? He was a lord, familiar with many sophisticated ladies of the court. Who knew, maybe there were even some he had known quite well. What could he see in her? A serving wench putting on airs and nothing more.

"The best on this journey by far." Mason smiled. "I, I liked the feeling of you nestled next to me. I hope that you did not think me, ah, too forward."

Sylvia could not help herself smiling back, but no more words came. She did not want to spoil the moment. Mason, too, was silent, looking intently at her.

Finally, he roused. His voice became all business. "If Wetron is here, we will need some protection," he said. "He would see through my disguise at once if he spotted me. But not all of the men at arms here will be his. Some serve the queen directly." He slapped his purse. "A brandel might be enough for each of them."

Sylvia nodded, accepted the gold coins he offered, and put them into her bag. The moment had been nice while it lasted, but now it was over. Back to business. She stuffed in the ballots with her picture on them and found room for the special surprises, too. The latter were fewer than the vellums — small bundles bound in colored cloth and cinched with decorative bows. But she had counted them twice. Based on the turnout for the previous two elections, they would be enough.

As she decoached, she saw the mayor standing in the middle of the street and in front of the alchemist shops. Every few moments, he reached out to touch the magic ballot box on a table nearby. Already a short queue of voters was there, each holding what could only be ballots for Mason's brother.

Sylvia smiled. At most, a score of people were there. Of course, she reasoned. Wetron must have thought there was no need to get a hundred people involved when only ten had sufficed at Oxbridge.

"About last night," Mason said when he joined her on the ground. "I hope you understand that you could have refused my touch."

"Yes, *you* are a *lord*. I do understand." Sylvia paused. "And *I* am a *lady*. I had as much choice in the matter as did

161

you." She blushed at her boldness, then felt relief when Mason did not take offense.

"I will take five ballots farther up the street, nearer to the artist who drew your likeness," Mason said. "Let's hope I will find enough people there to get the pump primed."

Sylvia nodded. After she could no longer see him in the distance, she procured the services of three men-at-arms standing nearby. Each bore Queen Vendora's escutcheon on their surcoats. Word about the first two outcomes must have reached the noble council. The group probably wanted to ensure the legitimacy of the remaining elections with their own observers.

It might have felt better if Rangoth were there to help, she thought. But three helpers aiding were probably better than only one. She took up a position only a few steps away from the voting and waited.

As before, the first voter arrived with a thick stack of ballots with Wetron's picture on them. After failing to stuff in the wad at once because the slit was so narrow, the townsman managed to insert only one. Subsequent tries were unsuccessful, and the voting line grew longer. Finally, the mayor had no choice but to order the man to move along and make room for the next.

The scenario repeated a score of times. Eventually, one of the voters not in the original queue reached the front of the line. He hesitated a moment before placing his ballot in the box. Sylvia held her breath. It was one of hers; she could tell by the color that was slightly off.

After the townsman had voted, he stepped away from the ballot box and stared at Sylvia. "Excuse me," he coughed. "Are you the lady on my ballot?"

"Yes, I am." Sylvia smiled and handed him one of the small packages. "Here is your special surprise."

The voter pulled the confining ribbon and examined the contents. "A lozenge!" he exclaimed and immediately broke

162

into a coughing fit. Despite his efforts, he could not bring himself back under control. With obvious reluctance, he put the tablet on his tongue, and the spasms vanished.

"I had hoped to save this lozenge for a better time," the man said. "But, I am grateful, Milady, nevertheless."

Sylvia smiled. The townsman had reacted as suspected. The air was so foul here that any relief, even if only for a little while, was worth its weight in gold to one who was too poor to buy many at all.

"Do you remember everything written on the ballot?" she asked.

The townsman frowned for a moment. "Remember all the instructions? I think so." He inhaled with pleasure and rattled off more:

"Ask for the lady.

-She will give you your surprise and hand you two more ballots.

-Give them to two of your friends.

-Show up with them as they vote, and you will get two more gifts for yourself."

"Wait a moment," the voter continued. "If I do this, I end up with *three* tablets in all?"

"That is correct!" Sylvia smiled.

"But I can return with these two vellums and vote again."

Sylvia shook her head. "Only ballots successfully placed in the box will count. The box will remember. You can only vote once."

The townsman nodded and grabbed the two ballots offered. He raced back down the road deeper into town.

IT DID not take long for the explosion of voters to occur. The first voter for Sylvia returned with two of his friends. They received their lozenges and scampered off to find more balloters. As it had for the tracking queen, two became four, and then eight and sixteen ... Soon, the line waiting to stuff their ballot in the box stretched beyond the last shop on the street.

There was some pushing and shoving. But the men-at-arms Sylvia had hired kept reasonable order near where the ballot box stood. More importantly, they held the eager voters straining for lozenges into a second, well-mannered line. She had enough space to hand out the gifts. Enough time to make clear to them what was to be done next in order to get more.

After a little while, Sylvia stopped counting. The outcome was obvious. The vote is going to end up overwhelmingly for me, she thought. I am going to win!

She took a deep breath. The implications of what the victory would mean were too mind-bending to contemplate. Those thoughts were for later. For now, she would savor the anticipation.

AT NOON, the line stretched around a curve in the road and out of sight. How many ballots did Mason replicate? Sylvia asked herself. He had produced far more than enough.

Abruptly, the mayor grabbed the ballot box in his arms and pulled it from the table. "I have seen enough," he said. "There is no need for more. The poll is now closed. Everyone remaining can disperse."

Ugly shouts rang out from the people still remaining in line. Other men-at-arms appeared to maintain order; Wetron's minions, she could tell from the crest on their surcoats. She did not know what to do with the three she had hired, but a confrontation probably was not wise. She paid them and let them go.

To help calm things down, she dispensed lozenges to

whomever waved ballots with her image on them but had been denied casting them. It did not take long until the bucket containing the tablets Mason had purchased was empty. Hundreds more townspeople remained unsatisfied.

"I want my lozenges," one of the unfortunate ones near Sylvia said. "I deserve them as well as anyone, noble or not."

He headed for her, but the soldiers blocked his passage. Sylvia reached into her purse. There were two or three more tablets there, not nearly enough, but maybe the gesture would …

The line dissolved and reformed, clustering around Sylvia, surrounding her on all sides. The lozenges had become a symbol, she realized. Unwittingly, she had provided a touchstone for the malcontent. It was as if they had been waiting for an excuse to assemble and express their displeasure.

There were whispers for a moment. Another chant rang forth. "Throw the first torch, Lady Sylvia. Throw the very first one."

Sylvia blinked. What! What was the crowd saying?

Nothing happened for a moment more, and then a pathway opened to her. A townsman approached, holding a burning firebrand high. She shook her head and pushed out both of her hands, but the torchbearer kept coming.

"Wait!" She shouted. "What are you doing?"

"The alchemists are the ones responsible for our dirty air," the townsman shouted. "The least they could have done was to produce unlimited lozenges for whomever wanted them."

The torch sailed through the air and hit one of the older shops. The rotting forewall burst into flame. Sylvia was stunned. From nowhere, several more torches had been lit. They launched in a coordinated salvo.

"Stop," she cried. "When I, when I win as fiefholder, we

can, we can sit down and talk together — "

It was too late. The missiles landed against more of the nearest walls. Fine wooden paneling smoldered for only an instant before roaring out of control. Rocks crashed through windows. A nearby log became a battering ram and thundered against one of the shops having the entrance in the back.

More people lured by the mayhem poured in from side streets to join in the riot. More men-at-arms appeared, but they were too few. Overwhelmed by the rising fury, they fell back.

This was not her doing, Sylvia tried to reason with herself. Oppression had smoldered for years. Her line of denied voters for an election was merely the fuse that set everything off.

The fire along the row of alchemy shops grew into an inferno. Everyone had to retreat from the flames because of the heat. For a long while, everyone watched silently. Then Sylvia heard the snap of a whip and saw two frightened horses pulling a wagon onto the street from the path to the rear. 'Gibbon Glue' a sign on two large vats proclaimed as the caisson clopped past, not avoiding anyone who chanced in the way.

Another wagon followed stacked with cages. The ferrets, Sylvia realized. As the dray rumbled past, she recognized several chests frosted and cold on all sides. Jumbled with them were bags of quicklime crystals spilling their contents as they jostled by.

Three more wagons appeared, one after another. On the first were stacked large, unmarked wooden crates. On the second were smaller, open frames inside of which tiny boxes were suspended by springs. Their motions back and forth absorbed the jolts of the road.

The last wagon was the longest of all, barely able to turn onto the street. On it, lying prone and looking fast asleep were two impossibly large demons. They rested upon folded wings, each three times the height of a man. They held clasped hands upon their chests. Except for the overall size, they resembled the pinheads at the coach shop Sylvia had seen before. Titanic djinns, she decided. Rangoth had been right.

Finally, two horsemen emerged trailing the fleeing wagons. Sylvia recognized them both. One was Dargonel, the sorcerer, and the other Rangoth, her employer for so many years.

Dargonel looked more exhausted than when she had last seen him, but that did not matter. What was importan was that she could no longer deny it. Rangoth had abandoned her.

One of the storefronts suddenly exploded, probably from reagents inside. Several of the mob cried in pain as sharp splinters thrust into their flesh.

Sylvia looked about, not sure where to turn. Where was Mason? She had to find him. She scanned down the road, and her heart stopped.

Wetron was approaching with men-at-arms on either side. Worse, next to him, hands in shackles and head downcast, Mason was being prodded by a baton pointed at his back.

Before Sylvia could move, Wetron's troop approached her.

"I knew I had seen you before. Now, I remember where."

# 25

# Imprisonment

SYLVIA PACED back and forth in her tiny cell. She was alone. Three days had passed since Wetron's men-at-arms had whisked her and Mason away to the Yterrby jail. For the thousandth time, she surveyed her surroundings. She had failed to discover any means of escape. Her thoughts were so muddled. Her chamber was mostly underground. A small barred window near the top of one of the walls let in light — but only for a small fraction of each day. The prison walls reminded her of the alchemy shops that were now only smoldering shells. On all four sides, paint was faded and peeling. Roots from surrounding shrubs pierced every crack and meandered to the floor in their quest for water.

Rotting planks in the dugout stairs outside squeaked. Someone was coming. Maybe Mason — he was a legitimate lord after all — had been able to argue his own release and was going to rescue her. Sylvia instinctively smoothed down her gown, grimy with dust from sleeping on a dirt floor. She checked her hair. The coif still maintained its curls.

Sylvia held her breath as a key rattled in the lock and swung open. Her smile died before it could get started. It was Wetron, not Mason, as she had hoped.

"I have news," the lord said as he entered. Two men-at-arms followed. "For a while, your fate was uncertain. My brother, of course, as befits his station, will be beheaded and his body buried. But what to do about *Lady* Sylvia is a different matter."

Wetron wiped his hand on his vest. "It took some time, of course, for the royal heralds to check all the records, but they did it twice to make sure." He extracted a short scroll from a pocket next to the dagger on his belt. He unfurled it and began to read. "Ahem. Be it known to whomever it concerns, this document bearing the royal seal affirms without equivocation, that there is not, nor has there ever been, any personage of noble blood bearing the name 'Lady Sylvia.'"

Wetron rolled the scroll back up and thrust it away. "It seems my impetuous younger brother was remiss. He did not inform you of the risk associated with undertaking the role you did."

"What difference does that make now?" Sylvia shot back. She was tired. Sleeping on a cold, unyielding floor had done little for her disposition. She did not know which was worse; Wetron's treachery from the start, or his lording over her now and rubbing it in. She sighed, struggling to maintain her composure.

"A difference? Oh, it is a very big one. Mason's de ... Mason's death," Wetron faltered for an instant. He shook his head and scowled as if trying to vanquish an unpleasant thought. "His death will be swift and only painful for a moment. Yours will last longer, much, much longer."

"Get to the point."

"You see, my lass, there is a severe penalty for impersonating a noble. There would be utter chaos in society if such practice were allowed to happen unchecked. And so ... as presumed fiefholder elect, I hereby inform you that you are to be burned at the stake. The entire town will attend and watch."

Despite herself, Sylvia gasped. She withdrew into herself. Like almost every child, she had heard the scary stories. How the ordeal was not short. Possibly hours of increasing pain

169

while the victim roasted. How a scorched and swollen tongue would allow only strange, muffled pleas for mercy.

"Ah, your reaction is precious," Wetron said. "I knew I had to witness it."

Almost as if she were a titanic djinn, Sylvia pulled herself back together with a heave of mental effort. This swine would not get any of the satisfaction he craved. She spat in his face.

Wetron blinked, surprised by the gesture. "How — what," he stammered. The spittle ran down his cheek, but he did not appear to notice. "My brother," he cried. "I do not want to." He grasped Sylvia's hands and squeezed them. "It is said that you are a wizard," he croaked. "Help me."

Sylvia frowned. She was puzzled by Wetron's actions. What was going on with him? Almost as rapidly as his demeanor had changed, it reverted back to the savagery she had seen in the queen's palace. The lord said nothing for a moment. He turned, colliding with one of the men-at-arms behind him. With a sidestep, he skirted by and exited the cell. The soldiers followed, and soon Sylvia was alone again.

Any try was better than doing nothing, she thought. Muddled thoughts were no excuse. She had managed to subdue a tracking drone and dominate his queen. What would happen if she tried again? It could not be any worse than what Wetron had planned for her. With determination, she surveyed the plant roots covering the walls of her cell.

THE NEXT morning, Sylvia again heard the tromp of boots. They were coming for her quite early. Her heart raced, and she sucked in air until she felt lightheaded. After filling her lungs twice more, she abruptly stopped. That would not do. Her salvation lay in clear thinking, being alert to any opportunity presenting itself. Her plan was a feeble one, but she had not been able to think of anything better.

Wetron was accompanied by the same two soldiers as before. The men-at-arms said nothing as they positioned her arms behind her back. Two quick loops of cord bound them together. She held both of her fists tightly closed. If they pried her fingers open and saw what was inside, everything would be lost.

As a last step, one of the soldiers found her heels discarded in a corner of the cell. One man-at-arms held her, while the other raised her legs one at a time and inserted her feet into them. Sylvia grimaced. It made no difference, but wobbling to the stake was not the image she relished being remembered by.

She blinked as she emerged into the light of day. In the near distance, a raised platform had been constructed. It stood on top of some of the ruins of the alchemists' shops. Hundreds of townspeople were arrayed around it. Some still jostled to get better views of what was to come.

As she drew closer, the crowd quietened. They needed no prodding to part so she could climb the three steps to the stage unimpeded. Wetron stood there the same as he had at Dargonel's presentation. The escutcheon of his heritage brightly embroidered his vest.

And next to him, there was Mason, hands bound behind like hers, but unlike her, he stooped and his head was bowed. His chin rested uncomfortably on a square block stained blood-red. His eyes were closed, as he waited patiently for the inevitable.

Sylvia was positioned in front of a stout pole erected in the center of the platform. It stood amidst a bed of broken twigs and kindling scattered over larger branches. One man-at-arms cut the cord binding her wrists. Then the other looped her arms around the stake and secured them again. Finally, several turns of rope coiled around her. Evidently, the idea was that she would have room in which to strain and twitch.

She glanced down at the kindling sprinkled around her

feet. Most of it was rather green, some still oozing sap. It was as the old tales related. The point was not to build a fire that roared from the start. But instead, it should be a struggling one that could take hours to become a crackling flame.

When the men-at-arms had finished their preparations, they left the stage and vanished into a side alley. Wetron raised his arms upward, signaling the crowd to become silent and pay attention.

"Observe closely what happens here," he bellowed. "See first-hand the fate of those who dare to rise above their station." He lit a torch and used it as a pointer. "Note well also, that even one of noble birth can be punished for transgressing."

"What transgression?" someone in the crowd shouted. He stepped forward boldly. His sleeves were ragged and soiled. A dark stain blotched the tunic's chest. "Even though the count has not yet become official, we all know Lady Sylvia won the election. One could tell by the number favoring her who stood in line. She is the choice of Ytterby."

"She is *not* of noble birth," Wetron yelled back.

"Noble enough for me," another joined in. "I don't recall you, or even Alpher, for that matter, dispensing lozenges to those who could not afford them."

"They cost only a single copper," Wetron answered. "It takes that much to make one. There is no profit." A hint of irritation tinged his voice.

Sylvia felt a ray of hope. Things were happening as she envisioned. The nobles and the alchemists had to be unpopular with the townspeople. And if enough of them acted together, as happened four days before, they might riot again.

"Do you notice how fresh the air smells today?" she called out as loud as she could. "Don't let the same folly be thrust upon you again. All five elections have not yet been completed."

"Lady Sylvia. Free her. Free her now!" someone cried. In

an instant, it was repeated. Like a battering ram pounding against the portcullis of a castle, it sounded again and again, each yell louder than the one before.

Wetron started to say more, but he was drowned out. No one could hear him above the din. He scowled, hesitated for a moment, and then waved his torch high overhead as a signal. Immediately, horns from the side alley echoed in reply. A troop of soldiers marching in cadence poured onto the street, shields at the ready and swords drawn.

The chanting ceased, and the townspeople froze in position. The troop strode forward into their first rank, and with the hilts of their swords, banged on the heads of those in front of them.

The second row turned to flee but was blocked by those behind. Like a wave breaking onto a rocky beach, the assembly dissolved into an incoherent mass. Everyone rushed to disperse, shoving those aside in front. Some unlucky ones tripped and fell, only to be trampled over by those who came after.

The men-at-arms pursued relentlessly, using their shields to plow townspeople aside. Bodies piled two and three deep but did not slow the men-at-arms. Still in step, they trod on the fallen, breaking limbs and cracking skulls. After the soldiers passed over them, the injured staggered to their feet, completely disoriented. In twos and threes, they limped to wherever there was an opening between buildings, trying to vanish.

In mere moments, the street was empty. Only Sylvia, Mason, and Wetron remained. Wetron did not seem to care. He smiled and walked menacingly toward Sylvia, waving the torch back and forth. Looking her directly in the eye, he touched it to the tinder at her feet. The dry brush steamed for a moment and then began to smolder.

"You see how unpopular your decision was," Mason yelled at his back. "Release us now, before something worse than the last riot ignites the entire town."

"I am no dunce," Wetron said. "Another show of allegiance to you, I prepared for. Ten times the men that were here four days ago. The buildup of anger at least partially sated. There is no one who will dare come and aid you. They all will be too busy saving their own lives."

Sylvia grimaced. She had hoped for better. An uprising that resulted in her and Mason's freedom. But there was nothing to be gained by ruing what did not work out. The other thing to try was exceedingly risky, but she had not been able to think of anything else.

"Not so smart." Sylvia stared back at Wetron as boldly as she could. Being rescued by the crowd had been the key element of her plan. But she refused to give up. May as well perform the other steps that remained. Who knew what would happen? "You didn't even think that the fire must be started on all sides," she said.

"Easily enough remedied." He walked around Sylvia and started the brush behind her to burn. "Here's a final tip, wench. You should think of the consequences of your words before you speak."

Wetron stepped back to admire his handiwork. He spotted Mason, who had stood up in the confusion and was looking about.

"And you are no better," Wetron said. "Right now might have been a moment when you could have stumbled away."

"I will not abandon Sylvia," Mason said. "Our fates have become intertwined."

"You were always like that, Brother," Wetron said. "A tilter against balloons even when we were little — "

He stopped speaking and choked for a moment. A tear appeared in one of his eyes. "We were both so innocent, you and I, the duo, standing as one against Alpher when he tried to mistreat — "

174

Wetron grabbed Mason by the arm with his free hand. "I do not want to do this, Brother," he said. "Help me. Help me, please."

Mason managed to free himself from Wetron's grip. But rather than retreat, with his arms still bound behind him, he crashed into his brother. Together they tumbled onto the platform floor. Mason kicked for leverage in order to propel himself on top. The torch skittered away.

Sylvia sucked in her breath. The soles of her shoes were starting to get hot. She pivoted her toes upward and rested herself only on her high heels. But that would work only for a while. She was getting hot, sweating from every pore. Her eyes were stinging from the smoke. The smell of burning wood clogged her nose. There was no longer a crowd to help her, but if she was going to attempt anything at all, she had to do it now while Wetron is distracted.

She opened her fists and flung their contents onto the ground. She couldn't see what she had accomplished, but hopefully, enough would also catch fire. Bits of oleander root might not work the same as the leaves, but she had not thought of anything else to try. She calmed herself as best she could and closed her eyes.

Nothing more happened for a moment, and then, "Hey, what happened to the old guy?" she heard in her mind. "You're not Rangoth. You're his serving wench, right?"

Sylvia squirmed, trying to concentrate. She felt the heat coursing into her from every direction.

"Nosetweaker, I am your master," she commanded as sternly as she could. "You must submit."

"No dice, girly," the imp answered. "We don't work for just anybody. We have standards."

"Yeah, we have standards," another imp joined in. "They are low, but even we have standards."

"Fetch me bullrushes," Sylvia said. "From the river running by Carmela."

"Girly, that's a long flight from here and back. It will take a whole bunch of us to carry even a single stalk."

"I don't care how you do it. Get it done quickly. Can't you see, I am burning up here."

"Yeah, and we're dying up on stage here, too. If you are going to be the dominant one, you have to give us some material to work with."

"See the two men wrestling in front of us?"

"Yeah, so? As an opener, we've seen better."

"The older one. Give him everything you got."

"Which one? You humans all look alike."

"The one with the vest and a dagger at his waist."

"*Everything*? Our full repertoire? Why didn't you say so? Stand back and watch."

"No, wait, the bullrushes first, then your act."

"We'll do both! Use the ol' one-two. Half of us to get the bullthingys. The other to start the attack."

The soles of Sylvia's shoes grew almost unbearable. Instinctively, she started to kick them off but then halted. Exposed bare feet would be even worse. Her mind began to wander. It was so hot — getting difficult to think. To remember what to do next.

# 26
# High Stakes

MASON DID not know what to do. With his hands tied behind his back, there was no way he could get to the dagger at his brother's waist. He saw Sylvia struggling against her restraints. Somehow, he had to reach her.

There was a buzzing sound in his ear and then a blur in front of his face.

"Ow!" Wetron shouted. "What was that?"

Wetron swatted at his nose. Two more imps appeared, one on each side of Wetron's head. They yanked his earlobes and sped away tittering with each other. Soon a cloud surrounded him. Like a swarm of worker bees adding pollen to a honeycomb, they darted in and out, each trip causing a sudden nip of pain.

Wetron released his grip on Mason. He flailed at his assailants and began thrashing on the ground. More and more imps erupted from around the stake and joined in the fray. Soon the pulsating shroud around Wetron's head became impossible to see through. He opened his mouth to yell for help, but then slammed it back closed. In only an instant, his tongue had bulged a fiery red from the swelling.

Mason continued to hold his brother down with his body as the barrage persisted. He only dimly realized that he received no tweaks himself. He looked up at Sylvia with longing eyes. He had to get free somehow before it was too late.

The attack did not abate. Imp after imp dove at Wetron and pinched. The lord swatted furiously, but it did little good. By the dozens, the nosetweakers continued their harassment.

Mason lost track of time. His exertions tired him out. Could he possibly keep Wetron down? He glanced again at Sylvia. And what purpose did that serve?

Finally, Mason noticed a difference. It was subtle at first. Wetron's flailing changed. Mason felt his brother's heart still beating fiercely beneath his own. But, surprisingly, not as rapidly as at first. Rather than gulping air at an increasing pace, Wetron's breathing grew calmer and calmer. He let go of Mason and pushed him off.

"Yes, the distraction," Wetron said as he panted on the ground. "That is what I need to break free of the enchantment."

Mason scrambled upward as best he could. "Your dagger!" he shouted. "Cut her loose!"

Wetron shook his head. "Dargonel still has some control over my thoughts. They have been weakening, but to purge him, I must confess first. I must tell you. You have to know."

"I don't care about anything you might say. Release Sylvia. Release her now."

"When Alpher died," Wetron ignored the plea, "I grieved. I truly grieved. You must believe me. The sorcerer, Dargonel, told me he could help. All I had to do was to relax into his enchantment. The two of them, my grief and the spell, would dissolve and vanish together."

Mason whirled away from Wetron. He backed into his brother, trying to grab the dagger off his belt. Wetron slapped Mason's arm aside and kept talking — as if he were a child revealing to a parent about a hidden theft.

"The plan was none of my doing, none." Wetron's voice

rose with pleading. "For some reason, the sorcerer needed things that could be made only with the new magic. He also knew Alpher would not have allowed it. But with me enchanted and our two fiefdoms combined back into one …"

"Sylvia!" Mason shouted. The kindling was burning in earnest now. The large branches would ignite any second. The hem of her dress would be next.

"Don't you see," Wetron continued. Like a boulder rolling downhill, he could not stop. "Dargonel was behind all of this. Combine the two fiefs. Ensure I won to rule over both. I am innocent. You must believe me. I never meant you any harm."

Mason plowed into Wetron a second time, sending both men sprawling. He crashed his own head into the back of Wetron's skull, but his brother kept talking.

"Yes, I feel it now. The sorcerer's control is weaker. His power over me is waning. I can feel it. The imps were the first step I needed in order to start breaking free. An overwhelming distraction."

There was a sudden splash behind the two brothers. Both men turned to see what had happened. A will-o-the-wisp balanced on top of the stake. Sylvia and the ground underneath were soaked. The fire was out.

"Bullrushes for water sprites, right?" Sylvia said. "I used the oleander to summon the nosetweakers, them to get what I needed to command a bigger demon."

"Enough," Mason commanded. "Untie me. Release me now."

Wetron cut Mason's bonds with his dagger and handed his blade to his brother. Mason ran to Sylvia and freed her as well. The pair collapsed into each other's arms.

"Are you all right?" Mason asked. "The thought of losing you was the foremost thing in my mind."

"In mine as well," Sylvia answered. She blinked,

surprised at where her thoughts were taking her. She sighed and did not say more, enjoying the comfort of Mason's surrounding arms instead.

"*You* can rule this fief, Mason. It rightfully is your due. I never coveted it in the first place. That was all Dargonel's doing. Now, order can be restored. All this bad dream will be gone."

Mason studied his brother for a moment, then shook his head. He filled his chest with air and smiled at Sylvia, drawing her tighter. "It is an ending worthy of the sagas," he said. "No more running. No more pursuit. All's well that ends well."

"No, that could not be more wrong," a new voice rang out. "I have come as quickly as I was able."

The trio whirled to see a man approaching on a road-weary horse. It was Rangoth, the wizard.

THE QUARTET munched on fruits provided by Yterrby's mayor. Everyone but Rangoth sagged with exhaustion. "You are correct about Dargonel's original plot," the wizard explained. He paced back and forth impatiently as he kept talking. "But having an election slowed it. His recovery plan, of course, was to have Wetron, while still under his control, win in at least three of the towns. That way, his plan would go on uninterrupted. It was only the riot and fire that forced the sorcerer to flee with whatever he was able to salvage."

"Why are you here?" Mason asked. "Everyone saw you leaving Yterrby with Dargonel."

Rangoth sighed. "Yes, even an old man can succumb to the pull of his ego and self-importance. All I can say is that a mistake corrected is better than one that is not."

"What made you change your mind?" Sylvia asked.

"Underneath it all, Dargonel is a cautious planner, not so

different from you, Mason." Rangoth pulled at his beard. "Have two of everything when one will do — what he called 'backups.' That also applied to wizards." He sighed. "How interesting it might have been. Domination of a titanic djinn."

"You did not answer my question," Sylvia persisted.

Rangoth looked at her and smiled. "Yes, my young lady. You show the necessary drive and focus. My decision to return indeed was the correct one. You and your — excuse me, I do not know what your arrangement is with this young lord, and I do not mean to pry."

"She is asking why you came back," Wetron said.

"To get help. Dargonel must be stopped. You have troops here, Wetron. We must send them to Oxbridge at once. That is where the sorcerer has gone. Don't you want some measure of revenge?"

"I am free of the man," Wetron shook his head. "I want no more dealings with him. You must understand. The chance of being enchanted again is too horrible to contemplate. For me, even Oxbridge is not far enough away."

"I am here to tell you that the stakes are much higher than deciding who is to be the lord over a petty fiefdom."

"What then?" Sylvia asked. "What could be more important than that? Is the throne of all Procolon in jeopardy?"

Rangoth sighed again. "Far more than Procolon. Far more than all the kingdoms to the south, all those across the sea, and even the islands in the great ocean. Far more than even other orbs like the one on which the Archimage's daughter dwells."

"How do you know any of this?" Sylvia asked. "Are you under Dargonel's control, too."

Rangoth shook his head. "No, he needs a clear-headed wizard to aid him, not one whose mind is fogged. He had to explain things to me just as I am telling you now."

"I repeat," Sylvia said. "What then is at stake?"

"Everything," Rangoth said. "Unless we manage to stop him, Dargonel will bring about the end."

"The end of what?" Wetron asked. "I am getting tired of riddles."

Rangoth sighed for the third time. "The end of the Murdina, the end of the sun, of all the stars in the sky. The end of *everything*."

Wetron scowled at Rangoth with distaste. "Your hyperbole does not impress me, wizard. How can one mere sorcerer do as you say?" He looked at Mason and Sylvia for affirmation of his view. "The end of everything. What does that mean?"

Rangoth nodded slightly. "I admit I do not understand all of it, myself. When it comes to the rituals and equations of magicians, I am as uncomfortable as a farm laborer. Never could I predict eclipses of the moon."

"Time is of the essence," the wizard continued. "Every tick of the clock takes the sorcerer further towards his goal. You must believe me, Lord Wetron. Dispatch your men-at-arms to capture him."

"To Oxbridge?" Wetron shook his head. "I don't think so. Mason is to be the fiefholder. He is the one with the responsibility to stifle internal unrest, to assemble men-at-arms to enforce peace. And, of course, to provide their pay. I will vacate north as I have said I would."

"Despite how dire a picture I paint?" Rangoth persisted.

"I understand none of your arm waving, wizard. Leave me be."

Rangoth slumped. "Then it will have to be the two of you." He pointed at the pair. "We will have to win by fortitude and guile rather than by force of arms. Exactly what you have shown me already over and over again. Will the two of you rise and accept the challenge?"

"If this is so dire, then why not inform the Archimage?" Mason asked.

"You know as well as I that he has vanished on some mysterious quest. No one has seen him in months. He is not here to help prevent the end."

Sylvia tried to clear her head. At the very least, she was confused. The one thing that had kept her centered from the very beginning was the journey to the south. To study under a female wizard. Hopefully, to become one herself.

She glanced at Mason and blushed. Now, there was a new feeling competing for her focus. A new path even more rewarding than the first.

"For me, the most important thing is what Mason decides to do," Sylvia said. "His path is clear to legally become holder of this fief."

She stared at Wetron, daring him to deny the words he had spoken moments before. She wanted to make the choice clear. She sucked in her breath after she had spoken. Wait, perhaps, maybe she did not.

Wetron averted his gaze. "Despite the image you have of me, I am a man of my word. Yes, my brother, Lord Mason shall become the holder. I have no objection and will so inform the Queen."

"She still has not recovered," Rangoth said. "Dargonel told me as much. She remains under his control."

"No matter. I will act starting now as if the transfer of stewardship from Alpher to Mason has already taken place. Withdraw my men-at-arms. Let my brother do with this fief as he will."

So, just like that, Sylvia thought. It was settled. Mason would assume his new responsibility. She and Rangoth, well, perhaps Rangoth, would continue to the south. Although … another thought crashed into her mind. Rangoth had spoken highly of her. She had shown, what was it, yes, the necessary drive and purpose. She had dominated a tracking queen, nosetweakers, and a will-o-the-wisp. Perhaps *Rangoth* could be her mentor. There might be no need to journey any farther.

She studied the wizard in silence. Would that really work? She knew so much about the old man — too much. How he had to be reminded to bathe because of how ripe he had become. The soiled undergarments she had to clean over and over again. Would she feel the full respect that the pupil should show her teacher, knowing the man as she did?

"Excuse me," Mason said. "Sylvia states my path is clear to become the legal fiefholder. My brother, Wetron, says for me to do with the province as I will. Don't *I* have any say in this?"

"Yes, of course," Rangoth interrupted. "By all means. But as I have said, there is only one course that any person of honor and passion would pursue. Now it is of utmost importance that you focus on Dargonel and — "

"Sylvia," Mason interrupted. "What is it *you* want to happen?"

"Do you care?" Sylvia could not believe the words she was saying. He was a lord with a large fiefdom almost in his grasp. Despite everything that had transpired, she was still a mere serving wench. Well, one who did show some talent, but still …

"What do you want?" Mason repeated.

His words finally sunk in. What do *I* want. He must care for me. He must. He must.

Like a tidal wave reaching shore, a flood of emotion coursed over Sylvia. Perhaps, it was fatigue. Perhaps it was a mere rebound from a narrow escape from death. But damn it, 'why' did not matter anymore. Whatever came next, she knew whom she wanted to share the future with. Her trip to the south could wait until … until who knew how long. Or perhaps even never.

"What do I want," she blurted. "You! I want you." She rushed at Mason, and they embraced as they had after her

184

rescue from the flames.

A dozen heartbeats passed while the two luxuriated in their embrace. Wetron cleared his throat. After another dozen, Rangoth said, "Now that is settled, let's focus on what must be done."

"Exactly what are you asking us to do?" Sylvia finally disengaged and regained her composure.

"Capture the sorcerer. Subdue him. Disrupt his plan."

"Well, we did find a way to win the election," Mason said. He intertwined his fingers with Sylvia's. Together they swung them to and fro.

"And a way to save your lives using self-taught wizardry," Rangoth added.

There was silence for a moment. Then Mason asked, "How long would this take?"

"It will all be over in a day or two, either way," Rangoth said.

"And I will keep order here in Yterrby until you return," Wetron added.

Mason smiled at Sylvia. She smiled back. They both nodded, intoxicated with each other.

"Right now, we feel invincible," Mason said.

"What is the first step?" Sylvia asked.

"Dargonel is making his final preparations. If we hurry, we can thwart him before he departs."

"And if we stop him, *everything* does not end after all?" Possibilities abounded. She no longer looked forward to an impossible choice: Mason or one of the five crafts. She could have both. Instruction in wizardry from a master. Paired to a fief-holding lord. A lady in more than name.

Sylvia shook her head. She was tired from all the chasing, the perils. It would be wonderful to relax and enjoy life for a while. But then, she never remembered Rangoth speaking so forcefully before. There must be truth in what he was saying.

What point would there be to have bliss for only a few days and after that … nothing?

"You claim that if we do this, we will save the world, right?"

"More than one mere world. The sagas are full of fanciful tales of heroes who have done such as that. It is as I have said. Yes, Murdina, but also all the stars in the sky and the orbs that revolve around them."

"And if we don't?"

"As I have said, nothing will matter thereafter at all. Everything will be gone. At least, you have to try, Sylvia. You must."

## Part Two

# *In with the New*

# 1
## Prediction Confirmed

AS THE coach jogged along the road back to Oxbridge, the trio were silent. The wizard was alert, but he stared off into the distance. Sylvia could not fully comprehend what Rangoth had told her. Neither could Mason. But at least, they had the outline of a plan.

Rangoth would duel with Dargonel's wizard for control of the titanic djinns. She would distract the sorcerer's minions with nosetweakers and will-o-the-wisps. Mason would physically subdue him. Maybe when they arrived and observed what was happening, more would become clear.

The coach stopped, and Sylvia looked out. The ramshackle group of little huts across the road from the walled compound was gone. Evidently, now everyone had been welcomed back inside. The trio decoached, and Mason banged the ring clapper. As before, nothing happened for a while. But eventually, the grate of a bar sliding along its supports sounded, and the door opened.

Sylvia took a few tentative steps. She saw immediately that much had changed inside. There were as many occupants as before, but they had divided themselves into two clusters, each around a newly-erected stage.

"Good," Rangoth said. "We are not too late. Dargonel has not yet left."

"Bad," Mason said. "This place has been completely transformed. The hubbub of disconnected activities is gone. It looks as if the sorcerer is in complete control."

"He must be in the foundry," Rangoth said. "Let's hasten there at once."

"No," Mason said. "The more we learn first, the better we will fare."

Sylvia grimaced. Of course, on reflection, her lover would not like this situation one bit. Charging blindly ahead with no idea of what to do.

She stood on tiptoe, but even with her height, she saw no evidence of the sorcerer. The stage to the left was filled by a half-dozen magician acolytes. Each sat at a desk and stared blankly at the commotion all around them.

"Dargonel's doing," Rangoth whispered. "His enchantment has shut down most of their minds. All that is left is the part that does computation."

"Why has he done that?" Mason whispered back.

"I don't know."

"Then we should watch. What happens here might give us a clue on how to attack."

"Last challenge," a magician initiate over the crowd assembled around the stage. "These are the final six. The winner will be the one chosen."

"One hundred brandels," someone near to Sylvia called out to a nearby companion. "Can you believe it? One hundred. Merely for calculating the results of sample computations that Isaac has prepared."

"Yes, one hundred guaranteed, but only upon return," came the reply. "That part of the bargain, and I do not like it. There is risk involved."

"Here are the inputs," the moderator on stage continued. "A is thirty-four. B ninety-two, C four-hundred-thirty-seven divided by a thousand thousands."

The crowd quieted; no one spoke. The hush continued for what Sylvia thought was a very long time. Then, one of the participants stood up and shouted, "Veer four degrees of a circle to the right."

The moderator checked a vellum in his hand and then shook his head. "Remember. Foremost, the answer must be correct. Speed is important but secondar — "

"Veer three and *one half* degrees to the right," a second voice yelled.

The moderator nodded. "Yes, we have a winner. Please proceed to the foundry and prepare to board." He waved his hand out over the assembled spectators for attention. "We have finished earlier than expected. If you have completed the tasks you have been assigned, you can watch the initiates compete next."

"This is proceeding far too quickly for my liking," Rangoth said. "The foundry is where we should be."

"The other stage first," Mason insisted.

Sylvia was not surprised. Mason was acting as he had from the beginning. Caution first. Assemble information at the start. Then after careful consideration, create the best possible plan. And what about herself? Was she fully convinced either? All either of them had to go on were the words of a man who, for a few brief days, had awoken from long-standing senility. She thrust the thoughts away. Mason was right. Observe and learn.

In twos and threes, the spectators surrounding the stage on the left joined the throng on the right. Most of everyone's pockets jingled with coins. Evidently, Dargonel had secured attention to his needs using what was in his purse, as well as what was in his mind. The sorcerer did not have a few minions loyal to him, but what looked like over a hundred.

Sylvia recognized what she saw on the rightmost stage. It had been here in the compound at both her previous visits. Two massive stones were strapped to the walls of a wooden frame. Between them, suspended at both ends of a horizontal beam, were fluffs of cotton. The beam itself hung from a thick rope attached to the top.

Another of the initiates climbed onto the platform. He squinted at a needle that pierced the rope suspending the bar. It pointed at a curved strip of metal scored with calibrated lines. "The angle of twist is three marks, what it has always been," he called out. "All is in order. Let the competition begin."

The first contestant climbed onto the short set of steps leading up to the platform. Clutching two medium-sized stones, he wobbled as he ascended.

"Nothing of substantial mass." The initiate waved the contestant away and beckoned the next. "You know the rules."

A succession of other initiates mounted the stage, some with exotic lash-ups of springs and gears. Each performed what looked to Sylvia's untrained eye to be a badly choreographed dance. After each performance, the gauge was checked, but there was no change. Finally, the last candidate came forth.

"Isaac," Mason said. "I recognize him from before. He was the one whose formula Albert kept insisting was only an approximation."

On a far corner of the stage, Isaac erected a mirror glass and pointed it in the direction of the large stones. The reflector was not flat but curved into a deep dish instead. On the mirror's centerline, he placed what looked like a tiny icosahedron with porous sides all around and open at the top. While Isaac recited nonsense syllables, he dribbled iron filings into the geometric structure. After it was full, he banged together two small cymbals he had brought. Finally, the magician began rubbing his stomach while patting the top of his head.

"Now, for the tricky part," Isaac called out. "I am going to reverse what I am doing: pat my stomach while rubbing my crown."

He did so and smiled at the crowd. "Did you catch that? Notice what I did? When most practitioners executing this mini-ritual reverse what they are doing, they also change the position of their hands. The one that was rubbing the stomach becomes the one rubbing the head. It took me a long time to figure out how to do the next step correctly. But once I did, the rest of the ritual became easy to derive."

Using elastic bands, Isaac slipped the cymbals onto his legs. Then he marched in a circle, banging them together with every other step.

"Surprisingly simple, once you figure out what to do," he said. "Now, moderator, call out the twist of the rope."

The other initiate rose from where he had taken a seat and approached the gauge. His eyes widened with disbelief. "Oh, my stars, Isaac. You have done it. Not three marks exactly, but three and a smidgen more. There can be no other explanation. The cotton is attracted to the large stones more strongly than before. The force of gravity has been increased."

"Well, only locally," Isaac said. "But even Albert now has to be impressed." He picked up his equipment and dismounted the stage. With a smile of triumph, he marched off toward the foundry. "I have the proof," he said. "Wetron's factotum, Dargonel, will be so pleased."

Everyone else in the compound followed. "Quickly!" Rangoth grabbed Mason by the arm. "See what is happening? Dargonel must be leaving soon. We have to stop him now."

"We still don't know the details of what Dargonel plans to do," Mason protested. "If this is as dire as you portray, then I first must think things through."

"But at each of the elections, the two of you always came up with something. And without knowing for certain what would happen. Somehow, you improvised as the situations demanded."

"Actually, Master, it was Albert who came up with the ideas surrounding the ballot box," Sylvia said. "And even with our planning, we failed at the first two elections anyway."

"All right, all right," Rangoth said. "We are making a scene. Some of the initiates are turning to look. We will go to the foundry and find out what we can learn there. Then when we see the first opportunity, we must act."

# 2
# Launch

THE FOUNDRY'S chicken-coop fencing surrounded a much larger area than that of either presentation stage, but only the two furnaces blocked a small portion of the view inside. The crowd around the perimeter became only a single person deep. The trio stood side by side with views as good as everyone else's.

"Dargonel told me about these," Rangoth said. "The foundry has completed its fabrication. He must be almost ready to leave," Rangoth repeated. "We have to do something now."

"I don't see the sorcerer anywhere," Sylvia said. "We can't subdue someone who is not here."

"Keep on the lookout," Mason said. "I am going to learn what more I can."

He scanned the interior of the foundry methodically. Like flotsam in an angry sea, discarded fabrications of rusting iron were scattered everywhere. Webs of pulleys hung from more than a dozen frames. Inclined slopes and heavy wheeled carts were everywhere.

Mason focused on the two huge metal cylinders resting on their sides in the center of the yard. In both, a large rectangular hole had been cut, revealing that they were hollow inside. His brow wrinkled. He had never seen anything like them ever before. What possible use can these things have for the sorcerer?

The one on the right rested open to the air. A sheet of isinglass, inserted and caulked, filled the opening of the one on the left. Dense crimson gas inside obscured the view through the window. Two fairly large sprites, each the size of a human child, vigorously exercised a handpump connected to both the cylinder and a large barrel standing nearby. Their wings were strapped tightly to their backs. They panted to keep the crank wheel turning.

"Faster, crawling scum, faster," a thaumaturge, almost as short as the sprites, commanded from nearby. "The pressure inside must be much greater so we can be sure."

Mason focused on the cylinder with the unobstructed view. A flat horizontal shelf extended along the wall, vanishing out of sight on both sides. Beneath it, a second one supported three chairs facing the curved, blank rear wall. Near each seat, vertical compartments on the top shelf were crammed with books and ledgers.

"A leak! I see a leak," the thaumaturge yelled and pointed to the bottom of the isinglass.

Mason followed the master's pointed direction. A thin spray of redness was spurting into the air midway along the bottom isinglass seal. A foundry worker scurried out from wherever he had been hiding, carrying a bucket and brush. He lavished the opening with two quick swipes and stood aside to admire his handiwork. The spray weakened and then fizzled altogether. An excited buzz rose from the spectators. "Hooray for gibbon glue," someone down the line from Mason shouted.

The pumping continued for a while longer, but no more leaks appeared. The reversing lever on the handpump was thrown. Gradually, the obscuring red faded into nothingness. One could see into the isinglass clad cylinder. Now, except for the window of mica, the two cylinders looked the same.

196

Airtight, Mason deduced. The structure was as leakproof as it had been before the opening had been cut. It looked polished, complete. Mason's pulse quickened. Perhaps, Rangoth might be right. Dargonel could appear here soon.

"There!" Rangoth pointed. "See them lying behind the cylinders. They are almost the same size themselves. The titanic djinns."

"Are they awake or what?" Sylvia asked. "They aren't moving. Master, can you detect their thoughts?"

"Strange," Rangoth said. "The wizard, wherever he is, has induced them to sleep. But when they arouse …"

"Can you detect when that happens?" Mason asked.

"I … I think so," Rangoth said. "You have to understand. These djinns are so very different."

Mason sighed with frustration. They still had no idea of what to do. "Then it won't hurt to do some more data gathering," he said.

He strode along the boundary fence to get better views of the ends of the cylinders. The one on the right was completely bare on one end. At its other, a faint outline of a closed accessway could be seen. The structure on the left was different. Isaac was there, calling out orders.

"No, no," the magician yelled. "Symmetry is important. It must be mounted perfectly in the center. At the cross-mark, I have inscribed. The location of the manipulator-arms has a greater tolerance. For them, you do not have to be as careful."

Mason studied Isaac's actions. The magician was directing the mounting of a mirror arrangement similar to the one he had used for his demonstration a short time earlier. Similar, but much larger, as wide across as the cylinder itself.

A commotion started at the other end of the structure. Mason shifted his position, walking rapidly behind the line of onlookers. The doorway at the other end sprang open. A queue of alchemists began carrying their products into the

197

interior.

Mason recognized two of them, Dalton and Justus. Each was accompanied by several of their novices. Dalton's carried a frost encrusted chest, presumably filled with liquid air. Another rolled a barrel of quicklime from Dalton's shop. One of Justus' minions struggled with a large, rectangular carton filled with his explosive. He tripped, and his cargo flung from his hands and crashed to the ground. Several of those standing nearby instinctively cringed, but nothing happened.

"Careful, you lout," Justus called to his second factota. His package was much smaller. "If you had been the one who tripped, we would still be searching for where your limbs were flung."

Next came the initiate who had won the other contest on the stage — the dim-eyed one who calculated rapidly.

"I feel them arousing!" Rangoth shouted. "Dargonel must be planning to leave almost immediately. Hurry now. What should we do?"

Mason's chest constricted. He felt as he had when Wetron had charged at him in Vendora's palace. Like then, there was no time to react effectively. And now was not the same. There was no assailant. They were at a foundry. His thoughts ricocheted in his mind. Yes, a foundry. But different … than the one at the coach shop.

"Start dueling for control of the djinns," he yelled. "The demons here are like the pinheads, remember? Only much larger. Yes, they are here because of the cylinders. They could move them about with ease."

He blinked. Where did that idea come from? No matter. He hurried back to where Sylvia and Rangoth had been standing. The wizard had sunk to one knee, and he was perspiring.

"So different," Rangoth gasped. "I hardly know where to begin."

A large veined wing of one of the demons twitched. With

a jiggery tremor, it flailed about. Foundry dust fowled the air as if blown in by an ocean storm. Sylvia clutched at the fence to steady her balance. The behemoth arched its back and stretched, arms thrust forward and legs twitching. Its twin remained quiet and unmoving.

"Perhaps, only one is needed," Rangoth said. "They are as tall as these fabrications are long."

"One sounds good," Mason said. "Better than both. Can you wrestle its control from the other wizard?"

"It is not a matter of strength of will," Rangoth said. Resignation crept into his voice. "I feel no resistance to attack. There is little to try and dominate."

"Can I help, Master?" Sylvia asked. "Certainly, two against one would be better."

"I ... I don't know."

The giant rose to his knees and forearms. Shouts of wonder escaped from the crowd.

"There! I can see him," Sylvia cried. "It is Dargonel. He is coming — marching toward the accessway."

For a moment, Mason felt paralyzed by his indecision. He did not want to leave Sylvia anywhere near the awakening demon. But if Dargonel was to be stopped, it looked like these few brief moments would be their only chance.

He slapped his cheek hard, feeling the sting penetrate deep. With his head as clear as could be expected, he ran toward the doorway on the cylinder's end.

"Aaargh," Rangoth cried, collapsing to the ground. "It seems to take only a feather touch," he said, "but I could not find where to tickle the mind of the djinn."

Slowly, the demon rotated his torso to vertical and drew an enormous breath. Flying insects were sucked into his mouth. Turning his head to the side, he stood and made a first, cautious step closer to the cylinder.

"Do something, Master," Sylvia yelled. "I cannot fathom

any way that I can help."

Everyone's eyes were on the giant. Each footstep reverberated through the ground. Like a baby attempting its first walk, he tottered from side to side. Out of the corner of his eye, Mason saw Dargonel march into the cylinder and slam shut the door behind him with a clang. The lord heard what sounded like a wheel inside, twisting the seal tight.

Almost immediately after, two long parallel doors on the top of the prone column rotated open. More cranking noise accompanied a scissor lift slowly cranking upward. The djinn reached the rising platform when it was about waist high and carefully rolled his torso onto it, extending his feet and arms in front and back.

The direction of the lift reversed, and in a few moments the demon was deposited on the top of the cylinder. The lift vanished back inside and the parallel doors closed. When they did, the djinn straddled the rear of the structure with its legs and cradled the front with his arms.

Dargonel was inside, safe from anything either Sylvia or he could do, Mason realized. He looked back at Rangoth sprawling on the ground. What could one expect? he thought ruefully. We never actually had a plan.

The djinn opened his wings and beat them against the air. The dust on the foundry floor rose and billowed. Through the dirt and rusted grime, the cylinder rose from the ground. Impossible, Mason thought. Nothing could lift such a heavy load.

But the titanic djinn had. With one powerful stroke after another, he pulled the — what, Mason thought. What should it be called? It was not mere welding of metal and mineral but a ship. Yes, a ship meant for an ocean far above the sky. With everyone else, he watched it gain altitude to become a mere speck barely able to be seen.

As the ship faded from view, there was a flash of light, one like what the trio had seen outside of Justus' shop. Then,

200

heartbeats later, the sharp crack of explosion. Dargonel had disappeared into the vastness of space — the space between the orbs and stars.

"What now?" Mason asked as he staggered back to Sylvia and Rangoth. Knowing what had been explained to him before, he felt a defeat far deeper than the one of losing an election in a small town.

"Now?" Rangoth echoed as he and Sylvia approached. "I don't know."

"Albert then," Mason said. "Maybe he can tell us what to do."

# 3

# Realization

AS THE trio made their way from the foundry, they were surrounded by an excited crowd. Everyone was buzzing about what they had seen.

Sylvia was troubled. She had no idea what would happen next, what the true consequences were of the agreement she had made with Mason in a swell of emotion. "Master Rangoth, I don't understand what we just saw happen."

"As we witnessed before in Yterrby, the explosion ripped open a portal into the realm of demons," Rangoth said. "The titanic djinn shoved Dargonel's ship through it. So much metal in the thing," he marveled. "Only great strength could accomplish such a feat."

"Yes, a ship," Mason said. "That describes the craft well. But I am puzzled by what you have concluded. How could anything built by mortals survive in what must be a completely alien place?"

"At first, when I met Dargonel, I was excited," Rangoth said. "The chance to control a demon of such might was invigorating. And the sorcerer immediately accepted my offer to join his adventure with open arms. He seemed so anxious, so driven to follow the path he had created for himself."

The initiates and acolytes flowing around the wizard bumped and jostled, but he did not seem to notice as he kept talking. "All my life, I have honed the craft of delving into the minds of devils, probing for weaknesses I could exploit. Find the leverage to bring them under my control. Close examination of an alien mind is what we wizards are trained to do."

"I have interacted with a few sorcerers in my day," Rangoth smiled wistfully. "But even so, Dargonel was different. I detected it from the very first. Rather than a fierce stare, he carried a faraway look in his eyes. There was no menace of enchantment there. Instead, they betrayed an internal rage, one boiling relentlessly to surface."

"I do not remember him that way," Sylvia said. "I was under one of his enchantments back in Ambrosia."

Rangoth shrugged. "When I met Dargonel, the man did not seem quite right. But other than that, there was no additional clue. Initially, I was somewhat suspicious and suggested we toast one another in honor of our new partnership. Make plans for an introduction to the other wizard. The one who already must be engaged to manage the titanic djinns. While I sipped one cup, Dargonel polished off three. He became talkative and told me some of the details of what he was about. Despite everything else, he is brilliant in his own way. He talked about how to construct his ship and procure everything to go within it — every idea was his own."

"But a ship such as we saw had to be more than merely an airtight chamber," Mason said.

"What about the air to breathe?" Sylvia asked.

"The chest of liquid oxygen and the barrel of quick lime from the alchemist, remember?" Rangoth said. "The two of them can regenerate the air for a very long time."

"Food? Water? Waste Disposal?" Sylvia pressed on. "Ah, probably in some of the other crates brought on board, right?"

"The sky is so vast," Mason interrupted. "Whatever the destination, how would Dargonel know which way to go?"

"In our cosmos, star sightings and calculations point the

way," Rangoth said. "I conjecture that is the reason why the enchanted calculator became a member of the crew. Rapidly generating commands to arrive at their destinations when they were needed." The wizard paused. "Although, traveling into the realm of demons is a surprise. Dargonel did not mention that."

"To *what* destination?" Mason persisted.

"As I think about it, I am now unsure," Rangoth sighed, "Perhaps the magician, Albert, can shed some more light."

ALBERT'S HUT was in a new location within the compound, but eventually, the trio found it. As before, the walls were filled with drawing boards. There was a cot, a few chairs, and very little else. The magician inside was busy scribbling and erasing his slates when they entered.

"Have you heard?" Sylvia asked without preamble. "Dargonel has escaped." She nervously smoothed her dress and licked her lips. Uncertainty continued to unsettle her. How could she and Mason proceed with so little to go on?

Albert put down his chalk and sighed. "I already have tried to explain to the wizard here. Dargonel's goal is thousands of lifetimes away. He is a good riddance, nothing more."

Sylvia shook her head. Good riddance? That was not so clear. "The ship is pushed by a titanic djinn," she said. "Who knows how swiftly one can fly."

"Not swiftly enough," Albert said. "It could take millennia even for a beam of light to reach where Dargonel wants to go."

"Suppose the djinn could race even faster," Sylvia asked.

"No, it could not. Nothing can."

"Why are you so sure?" Sylvia persisted.

"Because it is one of the laws of the new magic. A fundamental characteristic of our cosmos. Nothing made of matter can travel faster than the speed of light coursing between the stars." Albert smiled. "I am the one who postulated it."

"Isaac accompanied the sorcerer," Sylvia said. "Why would he do that?" She felt the beginning of frustration and set her jaw. There were more questions than answers bubbling in her mind. She resolved to keep digging until everything became clear.

"Not to worry," Albert scowled. "As I just said, they will not be able to reach their goal in their lifetimes."

"What goal?"

Albert shook his head and sighed. "I am as guilty as the next with my lack of constraint. I should not have been bothered about Isaac's boasting of his so-called law of gravity." He waved at his slates filled with chalk. "I teased him about its shortcomings and derived a much deeper result — the correct one. And in my hubris, I assumed my discovery had no more impact than the one I established about the speed of light. Let the passage of centuries of time restrain any misuse."

"But Isaac's demonstration was a success," Sylvia said. "Surely, that is important somehow." She felt like a barrister arguing before the queen.

Albert shrugged. "As I have just told you, Isaac came up with an approximation to predict the force of gravitational attraction between two objects — any two. It was quite simple. With it, he is able to calculate to a fair degree of accuracy the motions of orbs about our sun."

"And your solution?" Sylvia asked. She struggled to remain patient.

"My theory looks at gravity in a different way. Not a force like electricity or magnetism, as Isaac assumed. It allows the existence of the bizarre objects I alluded to when you were here before. Ones I call 'black pits.' For them, the pull of gravity is so strong that anything getting too close can never escape, not even fleet-footed light. *Everything* close is consumed."

"So, should we stay away from such things?" Sylvia asked.

"Indeed. There are several concentric spheres around the center of a pit, well not physical ones, merely mathematical notions. Nobody should dare to get closer than the radius of the outermost one."

Albert waved his hand over his sketch. "I have derived equations for the sizes of the radii, all of them. They are proportional to the strength of gravity. The stronger gravity is, the larger is the sphere. The largest I call the innermost stable one."

"There are other shapes as well." Albert shook his head slightly. "Thin rings and bloated pillows. And I have shown my results to Isaac. Explained the true difference between his so-called law and mine."

"Dargonel is the one who desires to get close," Rangoth said. "Isaac is no more than one of his enchanted tools."

"To do what?" Sylvia asked. She felt slightly better. She might be getting somewhere and was gaining a better appreciation for how Mason operated. Decisions were much easier when one had all the facts.

Yes, she felt better but not yet calm. The thought that she and Mason had naively agreed with Rangoth's plea still felt like a cactus thorn in her palm.

Albert scratched his head. "To do what? Probably more than merely explore. The equation for the sizes of the spheres also depends on what is the 'gravitational strength.' The larger the value, the bigger the spheres. Once inside the sphere of instability, one would be drawn into even smaller globes, ones of absolutely no return."

"Isaac's demonstration," Mason exclaimed. "Using the

old magic, he has a way of making the strength greater."

Albert smiled at Mason. "Very good," he said. "I have not taken on an acolyte in many years, but you might make — "

"So Dargonel takes Isaac close to a black pit," Mason rushed on. "The magician changes the gravitational strength while near there, and the distance to avoid becomes larger. But why?"

"Dargonel is unhinged," Rangoth said. "Some time ago, a lover ended their relationship, rejected his attentions. A sorceress. One strong enough to resist his enchantments if he tried to use them on her."

"A spurned advance?" Mason asked. "Not the first time such a thing has happened between a man and a woman."

"Evidently, Dargonel's revenge is more than dealing only with the one he desires," Rangoth answered. "In revenge, he plans to destroy everybody else in addition. There will be no one left to remain aware of his pain."

"I still don't understand how," Sylvia said. Her patience had grown as thin as a soap bubble's film.

"Well, it is just theory, mind you," Albert said, "Dargonel gets Isaac close to a black pit. Not so close as to get bombarded by other matter or sucked more inward, but near enough so that the gravitational strength inside the pit can be increased."

"Isaac makes the change happen," Albert's head shakes intensified. "As a result, the sphere of instability expands. Dargonel retreats a bit, and Isaac repeats the process. The sphere grows in size again. This continues until the boundary not to cross reaches all the way back to where we ourselves float in the cosmos. Inexorably, everything we know of would be ripped apart, continue inward, and then finally vanish completely."

"What about Dargonel himself?" Mason asked.

Albert shrugged. "It depends on what the sorcerer does.

Long before being pulled within the sphere of instability, gravity would be intense enough to wreak havoc on everything surrounding the darkness. But as long as Dargonel was cautious and did not get too close, he could stay safe and still expand the shell around the pit. He ends up destroying everything."

"But wouldn't doing such a thing take a tremendous amount of, what do you call it, energy?" Mason persisted.

"Yes, a tremendous amount," Albert said. "More than any of you could imagine."

"So, where does Dargonel and Isaac get that?" Sylvia said. "From where does it come?"

"It is true that in the *new* magic, energy is conserved," Albert said. "As it is with thaumaturgy as well. But the workings of the other four crafts have no such restraint. Think about it. How does a sorcerer influence the mind of another at great distances? What about alchemy makes some formulas more likely to succeed than others? Where do demons get the where with all to journey to and from our realm?

"We magicians forge objects that last forever. According to the new magic, great amounts of energy would be needed to create such things. But sometimes very simple rituals produce the result desired with little effort."

"As I have forewarned you." Rangoth looked intently at Mason and Sylvia.

"And as *I* have explained," Albert said, "Isaac has to get close enough to a black pit first. His magic does not work far away. And as far as our stargazers can tell, there are no black pits anywhere near enough to us to visit in thousands of lifetimes. We have nothing to fear."

"You see," Albert spoke as if lecturing children. "As I have repeatedly told anyone who would listen, Isaac's mixing the two magics is an example of what can happen. The old magic has no concept of black pits; the new one is silent about rituals that modify the gravitational strength. It is the confluence of the two that has brought upon us the possibility of new evils."

"But isn't that how progress *is* made?" Sylvia asked. "Do what the initiates are attempting here. Make accurate observations and deduce from them fundamental laws. Discover which is more basic, the old magic or the new. Or maybe they are both only layers derivable from something more fundamental than either one."

"We are not mature enough to handle such a process so rapidly." Albert shook his head. "It lets us march too quickly. Our culture, our society, our wisdom. They do not have a chance to grow first and moderate what is discovered. Too much, too soon with no thought of the consequences."

Albert took a deep breath. "Even my postulate about the speed of light has dangerous implications. Thaumaturgists use energy to provide the motive force for their spells. And except when gravity is involved, energy can be transformed but neither created nor destroyed. That's a part of the old magic and has been so for many years.

"But when you add the constancy of the speed of light," Albert continued, "strange consequences are predicted. The most alarming is that all the substances around us, the air, the rivers, the rocks and stones — everything we call matter is another form of energy, too. A potent one, so powerful that it is hard to imagine what would happen if it were transformed. Fortunately, it probably will take centuries to figure out how to unlock it — a very good thing, indeed."

"But Dargonel is mixing the two magics in more ways than one," Rangoth persisted. "The titanic djinns are not attempting to propel the sorcerer between the stars in our cosmos. Instead, he has vanished into the realm of demons."

"Why does the realm of demons have anything to do with this?" Albert asked.

"Who knows exactly how our two realms are connected," Rangoth said. "I doubt we could merely walk along paths parallel to one another and end up traveling the same distance. With blisters and cavities along the boundary between the realms, the journey in one could be quite different than in the other. If we pop into where demons dwell, march a league down a road, and then return, where will we then be — also exactly a league farther here?" The wizard shrugged. "No one even knows if there are even such things as roads there."

"Worse than that." Rangoth frowned. "A journey in our realm of ten thousand lifetimes might be possible among the demons in only a few heartbeats. If one knew what he was doing, he could dip into another realm for a mere instant and then return back here at a desired destination."

Albert's jaw dropped. "That is what Dargonel has done? Gone into another cosmos, one different than our own? That is a place of which I know nothing." He slumped into a chair. Several moments passed before he could speak more. Finally, he stirred and looked about his hut. "I have some brandy here somewhere. We may as well enjoy it while we can."

# 4
# Preparation for Pursuit

LIKE A fire dampened by a soaked blanket, the mood in Albert's hut struggled to continue with life. No one spoke. Rangoth jiggled his empty cup, and Albert refreshed all the drinks. Everyone drank more slowly this second time around. They savored each sip because they all understood that it might be their last.

"How long?" Sylvia asked, finally. "How much time do we have?" She reached out and drew Mason close.

Rangoth growled. He dashed his cup against one of Albert's slates. It splattered its contents and smeared the chalk as it dripped toward the floor.

"My equations!" Albert shouted and grabbed a cloth to blot away what damage he could. In a frenzy, he oscillated between absorbing the leading rivulets and attempting to build a crude dam protecting the lines at the slate's bottom. Then, he stopped. "Silly," he said. "These no longer matter, do they?"

Sylvia watched Albert struggle and finally surrender. A part of her wanted to deny what was happening, to ponder instead with other thoughts.

"Maybe it is not so easy to return as Dargonel expects," she said. "How can he know precisely where to come back? Rangoth, what is it like in the demon realm?"

"I know very little," Rangoth said. "From incidental chatter I have heard over the years, it is mostly void. A huge, dark volume, but with a definite sense of up and down. Scattered everywhere are lairs of many sizes. Some with imprisoned glowimps to mark their location. Others hidden in the blackness."

"No roads or signposts?" Mason asked.

Rangoth shrugged. "None that I know of. Domination of a demon is a challenge. One does not engage in small talk with them. There is no 'Now that I have seen your place, come and visit mine.'"

"So, there may be time?" Sylvia asked. "Time enough for Dargonel to be thwarted."

"Thwarted?" Rangoth snorted. He waved his arm around the hut. "How? Once the flame is extinguished and we allow a demon to return to its own domain, it is no longer under the sway of anyone here."

"Even if, as a dominator, you went after?"

"I don't know if —"

"The second ship!" Mason interrupted. "Dargonel's 'backup' as you called it, Rangoth. If one can travel into the demon realm, why not the other?"

"It did not look as complete," Rangoth said. "It does not have Isaac's device mounted on one side."

"We do not need such a contraption!" Sylvia said. "We have no idea how it works, anyway."

Rangoth pondered for a moment, then his cheeks lifted with the hint of a smile. "My instincts appear to have been right after all. Yes, Sylvia and Mason. The two of you should pursue."

"Not only us." Mason shook his head. "We will need a wizard, surely." He turned, looked at Albert, and pointed to the slates. "And also, your understanding of what we might encounter if we return somewhere else — near to, what did

212

you call it, the sphere of something or another."

"I am a man of thought," Albert protested. "Not some hero from the sagas striding forth with his trusty sword and shield."

"Incorrect." Sylvia waved at the slates. "Your mind is our sword, and these scribbles are our protection shields."

THE FLURRY around the foundry was even more frenzied than it had been under Dargonel's direction. Albert's words had carried much weight among the other initiates and acolytes. Many hands placed an isinglass window into the second cylinder and tested it for leaks. More equipped the interior with duplicates of the supplies laded into the first.

Sylvia and the others in the volunteer party stood out of the way so they would not be a distraction. Including Algeran, the initiate who had finished second in the rapid mathematics competition, there were five of them. Only five in all, she thought. Five of us with the task of saving everything in the known cosmos.

What were they getting into here? she thought. It was one thing to outwit locals in a procedure as simple as an election. But going into the realm of demons was quite another. It sounded so ominous. They might never return. Or they could die in unimaginable agonies as the playthings of powerful devils.

She remembered the stories from the sagas her parents had told her to make her behave when she was a little girl. They were so scary and rightfully so. Powerful djinns who enslaved you far more completely than could any human sorcerer. And the agonies of the submission, so horrible that Rangoth did not wish to speak of them.

But Dargonel had to be thwarted. There was no question about that. Thanks to Albert's explanations, everyone in the compound understood. But was each member of their group of five the best choice? Less than a fortnight ago, she was a serving wench. No education. No special talent. One swept up by circumstances far outside of any experience that mattered. Well, there were her dabbles into wizardry, but did they contribute, really? Rangoth was a true master, one who could battle whatever powerful demons they encountered. And wouldn't a sorcerer be a better selection than her? Or, for that matter, a master thaumaturge or alchemist.

Sylvia looked at Mason concentrating intently on the loading process. He would make sure nothing was forgotten. She sighed. If he was going on this trip from which there might be no return, then that, too, is where she wanted to be.

MASON CHECKED off another item on the provisioning list one of the acolytes had found as the next was loaded. There had to have been such a document, the lord had reasoned; Dargonel was too detailed a planner to leave anything to chance.

There was even a hint of admiration as Mason thought of the sorcerer. Except for the horrible goal Dargonel strived for, the planning was perfect. Could he even measure up to such a standard himself? In fact, what was he good for at all? A third son, one kept away from the experience of managing a fiefdom by two competing brothers. Untested in dealing with surprises such as the failure of crops or worker unrest. Totally ignorant of the machinations of the nobles at the court. An impresario at best.

Careful planning might indeed be a necessary ingredient for successful outcomes, he reasoned. But by no means sufficient. Sometimes, decisions had to be made quickly — selecting not the best, but the good enough.

Even so, this path of action had been decided upon much

too quickly. There had been no true deliberation at all. If he had not been so moonstruck at the time …

He glanced at Sylvia and could not help smiling. She had taught him so much. How she came up with the things she did was a mystery. Impetuous, wonderfully impetuous. Dashing into things with no hint of a plan, only the hint of solutions. A recipe for eventual disaster. But together, he grinned even more, they were like a mortar and pestle. Separately, they could fail. Together, they had ground into submission every challenge they faced. Whatever was going to happen, he wanted nothing else than to share it with her.

"Hey, buddy," a high-pitched voice sounded in Mason's ear. "Are you the guy in charge here?"

Mason instinctively brushed the air away from the side of his head. A talking mosquito? Where had he heard such a high-pitched tone before? Oh, right, a nosetweaker.

"I haven't got all day," the imp said. "Gotta get back to home base and get my reward."

"I've no time for you now." Mason tried to bat the little demon away.

"Suit yourself, but Dargonel said you guys might want to hear this."

# 5
# Dargonel's Message

MASON STARED at the nosetweaker for a moment, shocked by its presence. "What message?" he finally managed to ask. Sylvia and the others clustered around him.

The imp shook its head. "I saw the extent of the crowd when I flew in. Everyone needs to hear this. Somehow, when you humans repeat things, the message gets garbled and twisted."

"I have exactly what is needed," one of the nearby initiates said. "A perfect use for my new invention. Wait a moment while I get it set up." He ran off to his hut and dragged a cabinet on wheels back to the foundry. On the top of the cupboard was a thin, erect diaphragm. Its rear side connected to a tube that disappeared into the top of the box. Behind the membrane, what looked like a large blooming flower made of metal pointed to the side.

He opened the door of the cabinet. "See the microhead imps inside? The four of them pump on the bellows compressing the air. The draft flows through a valve modulated by the speech captured by the diaphragm. The air carrying the sound waves comes out through this trumpet on the top."

"More mixing of the new with the old." Albert scowled. "This contraption wouldn't be possible without almost

216

brainless imps providing the power."

"I have to get back," the nosetweaker said. "I was told so much to remember, and it's starting to slip away."

"I am ready," the initiate said. "Speak normally into the intake."

The nosetweaker fluttered to hover directly in front of the membrane. Mason heard the wheezing of the bellows from inside the box.

"I speak for Dargo —" the imp began, but then stopped, startled at how loud he sounded.

"Go on, go on," the initiate coached.

"My voice doesn't sound right."

"Never mind that," Rangoth said. "Do as you have been told."

"I speak for Dargonel, the annihilator of the cosmos. By now, you must have heard what the traitorous wizard, Rangoth, has told you. Despite his treachery to me, his words are true. Everything will be destroyed. Destroyed by me, and destroyed soon. Spend what little time you have left venting your wrath on iniquitous Hel, the sorceress, Hel, the imperious one. She is responsible for what will befall you. And be warn —"

The nosetweaker faltered. "Just a moment. I will have to recall the rest."

"Everything destroyed? We will see about that," Rangoth growled. "Shortly, we will be in pursuit."

Mason stirred uncomfortably. Everything was moving too fast. Not every detail had been explored.

"Wait, Master," Sylvia shouted. "In our haste, we have not thought everything through."

"Exactly as I feared," Mason said. "What?"

"Once we have thwarted Dargonel in the demon realm, how do we get back?"

Mason smiled. "Exactly! This is not a suicide mission. I

217

am not sacrificing my entire future for some greater good." He beamed at Sylvia. "There is much more for me to live for after we are done."

"The barrier between the realms is pierced only by fire." Rangoth shook his head. "And there can be no flame in the demon realm itself." He shrugged. "Even beginning wizards are aware of that. Dargonel is trapped there and cannot return."

"But if he cannot," Sylvia said, "how did the wizard on Dargonel's ship command this nosetweaker here?"

"Through burning what you humans call oleander," the imp said. "Even beginners know how to do it."

"Who set the fire here on our own globe?" Sylvia persisted.

"I dunno. Dargonel or his wizard."

"He must have some way to get fires lit in our own cosmos. How else will he get Isaac close enough to the dark pit to change the law of gravity?"

"Right!" Mason exclaimed. "We have to capture Dargonel, not merely destroy him. Ours will not be a one-way trip. We will find out from him how to come back."

"Ah, I remember the rest of the speech now." The nosetweaker buzzed closer to the diaphragm.

"And be warned. Pursuing after me in the second cylinder will not work. The ship has a flaw in it and will not survive the journey."

Without saying more, the nosetweaker flittered away and vanished.

"See, this is an example of what I have been telling everyone all along," Mason shouted. "We have to cover every possibility first. Let's begin by searching every part of the ship in order to find its defect."

"We don't know how long Dargonel will take to complete his task," Rangoth replied equally as loud. "We must leave now before it is too late."

Almost everyone began voicing their own opinion about what to do, drowning out one another.

Sylvia put her hands over her ears. The bickering could go on forever, she thought. She looked at Mason and winced. The frustration in his face was evident. Both his and Rangoth's arguments had merit, but if they continued arguing, they would never find out who was more correct.

So, if it were up to her, what would *she* do? She concentrated as hard as she could but fathomed no solid answer. The uncertainty was too great — as great as that a master wizard might face when challenging a new unknown demon for the first time. She cocked her head to the side. Then, what did a truly great wizard do?

The answer was upon her in a flash. Action, of course. The great wizards always had a bias for action.

Sylvia looked again at Mason and smiled at him weakly. Mason, dear Mason. She could not fully understand it, but she loved him deeply. Their experience together had bonded their souls forever. But he and Rangoth would both argue for as long as they both could speak. She looked at Albert and shook her head. His words were respected, but he was no leader. There was no one she could think of who …

She took a deep breath and ran to the soundbox. "Enough!" her words boomed, and everyone was stunned into silence. "It has been decided." She inhaled deeply. "*I*, Lady Sylvia have decided. We will board the ship *now* and prepare to leave."

Mason's jaw dropped. As did Rangoth's. Sylvia hesitated no longer. She flicked off her shoes and strode to the cylinder's hatchway as regally as she could.

She was uncomfortable about the role she had thrust upon herself. Was this what it felt like to be the lord or lady ruling over a fief? She scowled and pushed the last of her self-doubt aside. There was no other way. Rapid decisions might be required with no time to put them to a discussion and committee vote.

"Mason, is there anything else that needs to be loaded?"

"Ah, no, my love. It is only that —"

"Rangoth, are you ready?"

The wizard blinked. "Why, yes, Sylvia, of course." He studied her for a moment. "You have come a long way from how once you were."

Sylvia was not sure if the wizard's words were a compliment or not, but that did not matter.

"Albert? Algeran?"

"Yes, my lady," Albert answered. "Ah, you *are* a noble lady, right?"

Algeran had no questions. He marched immediately to the hatch at the end of the cylinder and boarded. Silently, the other four followed. The mood had grown somber. There was no more time for second thoughts.

Sylvia looked about. In the ceiling, she saw what looked like the faint outlines of circular portals all tightly shut. Extending to the isinglass window in the center, the interior walls of the ship were covered with sheets of slate. Albert halted at the first he encountered and started writing.

Sylvia slid by and pushed against the edge of the next chalkboard. The slate moved on rollers and revealed double-decked sleeping silks and furs. Two alcoves on each side, she calculated. The ship accommodated eight in total. Dargonel and seven minions. Was that how many they would be up against?

She looked down the central corridor past where the window let in ambient light. A telescoping metal arm controlled by a crank and chain lay there. Nearby, ready to ride out to the end of the arm on a platform also geared by the crank, sat a large barrel of explosives. Next to it was a smaller keg, probably containing the trigger powder.

Somehow, Mason had managed to store everything they needed in cabinets on either side — the breathing equipment, water, food, explosives, and weapons. Overhead, glowimps danced in tiny prison globes, shedding a feeble light.

The structure was so simple, Sylvia thought. What had Dargonel meant when he said the ship was flawed? Was it merely a bluff to discourage anyone following? Or did he choose the ship he did because of a discovery made during the foundry casting?

She shrugged. Mason probably never would be satisfied that every possibility had been explored. The pig knuckles had been cast.

She climbed the small ladder bolted to the alcove enclosure and settled with her back to the rear wall. There was barely enough headroom for her beneath the curved ceiling. But when the titanic djinn started to propel the ship, one had to have a firm surface behind their back.

At the last moment, after Mason had enbunked below her, she secured the slate from sliding back and forth. "Are we ready?" her voice echoed in the volume containing her.

Then she remembered what they had agreed upon to do when they were set. Because of the slates, voices did not carry far from their cocoons. Her code was one knock repeated over and over. Mason's was two, close together. Albert's and Algeran's were more complicated. There was an established order, and she was the first to bang a small hammer against the wall.

It took three times to get all the way through the sequence without interfering with one another. After the last, from where he sat strapped into one of the chairs at the cylinder's center, Rangoth started giving commands to the titanic djinn.

The ship rocked from side to side for a moment, and then with a lurch, lifted from the ground. Sylvia felt each surge of strength of the djinn's wings as they rose higher. Was it her imagination, or could she hear through the vibrating metal the

221

rumbled breathing of the demon as it labored?

She imagined what Rangoth had to be doing. There had been no way to practice before they left, but the steps seemed simple enough. Open the forward hatchway and extend the telescoping arm as far as it would go. When it was in place, move the barrel of the explosives out to the very end and follow that with the trigger keg. Finally, take a deep breath and fire a crossbow bolt into the trigger.

Before she pictured more, the hatch struggled open against the on-rushing air. Turbulence clattered the slates against their tracks, and whistling noise made it impossible for anyone to speak. Then, sharp bolts of light flashed into Sylvia's bunk from around the edges of the slates. Almost immediately after came a thundering roar. Then, most disconcerting of all, she felt pressed tightly against the wall behind her.

And after that — nothing. Darkness. No sound. A faint lizard-like smell that she could not place. Sylvia shuddered. They now must be in the realm of demons, and she was the one in command.

# 6

# In the Realm of Demons

SYLVIA PUSHED the slate aside and climbed down from her bunk. The floor was cold, and there was only feeble light emanating from the glowimps. Evidently, the sudden acceleration had knocked the little creatures silly. With hands stretched out in front of her, she moved toward the center of the cylinder. As she did, she found it tricky to maintain balance. With each step, she bounded upward, almost knocking her head against the ceiling. She heard others stirring from their bunks, but did not call out to anyone. Excitement was bubbling within her. What did the demon realm look like?

Sylvia reached the isinglass window before anyone else and peered outside. The massive arm of the titanic djinn wrapped securely around the vessel at one edge of the glass. The other was encircled by an even more gigantic leg. But between them, there was nothing much to see. Except for an occasional dot of light here and there in the distance, the vista was totally black.

For a moment, Sylvia watched the meager twinkle of lights. Some of the little glowing dots appeared to be traveling horizontally from left to right; others did not move at all. No, they were all stationary, she decided after a moment; the cylinder was what was in motion, not the lights. Some were just far, far away.

Algeran emerged from his confinement and took a position beside Sylvia. He held some sort of sighting device in one hand and squinted through it. "The lights farthest away will mark where we are," he said. "I will record the angles so that we can find our way back."

Sylvia nodded and looked down the corridor toward the metal arm. It was retracted. The hatch beyond it closed. She glanced again at the lights, and a balloon of panic mingled with the excitement within her. She had ridden in a carriage only a few times in her entire life. The bounce of the road and sway of the cabriolet somehow had been reassuring. At any moment, she could always poke her head out and see what was ahead. But this was different. She felt disoriented. She could not see where they were going. There might be a collision with something at any time. Or would the titanic djinn alter their course? *Could* it change their course?

"Isn't this all so very interesting?" Rangoth asked as he took a position on the other side of Sylvia from Algeran. "No wonder demons are so eager to come to our own realm. They were always complaining that there was little to do in their own."

Mason appeared and slid his arm around Sylvia's waist from behind. He kissed her on the nape of her neck.

"No, not now." She disengaged. "Master Rangoth. Open the front hatch again. We must see if we are about to collide with something."

"I am not sure if that is wise." Albert joined the group. "We have no idea of the pressure of the outside air, or even if there *is* outside air. What we have around us might rush out in a burst."

Sylvia took a deep breath. She remembered how she had insisted they all embark. Everyone had complied. It had been established that she was the leader, hadn't it? And that meant everyone had to do as she commanded. "I said, 'Open the front hatch.'"

No one moved. Sylvia blinked, not sure what to do next.

"Sweetheart," Mason said. "This situation is not the same as before. Your words at Oxbridge spurred everyone to action when they indeed were needed. But no true leader is absolute. He — or she — has to earn continually the right to be followed."

"By caving into everyone's wishes?"

"No, by acting with prudence and, well, gaining a reputation for guessing right most of the time."

Sylvia breathed deeply again. Being a leader required much more than a piece of paper or a heartfelt plea.

"I fear we might crash before we even get started," she said as calmly as she could. "How do we make sure we do not?"

"I can command the titanic djinn to stop," Rangoth said. "Rotate us, so this window faces the direction we are traveling."

As Sylvia pondered what to do, something outside caught her eye. "Wait! What's that?"

As a huge complex structure came into view from the left, everyone looked. The structure was huge. Sylvia had no real way to determine the scale. To her, it seemed as if it were the length of hundreds of men lying head to heel in a row. From delicately carved windows, fierce beacons blasted the evidence that whatever demon resided there basked in grandeur. Matter retrieved from other realms had been transmuted into stunning works of art. Etchings of gossamer wings. Landscapes capturing the serenity of deep caldera lakes. Fused stalactite and stalagmite columns barring the entrance to hidden caves.

"I have figured out how to contact the titanic djinn," Rangoth said. "He tells me that we are witnessing the palace of Elezar, the Golden. One of the mightiest devils of the realm. What should we do?"

"We stop," Sylvia blurted. "Maybe we will learn something we can use."

As she spoke, a flurry of wings burst from the highest towers of the palace and sped toward them. "Lightning djinns," Rangoth said, "the outer guard."

There were a dozen of them, flying in formation. Large, yellow beasts wearing fierce growls. What looked like tiny bolts of electrical energy sparked from limb to limb. Their wings were covered with dark veins of black. Each of their powerful strokes drew them closer and closer. The group fanned out, and half of them disappeared from view on both sides.

"That was a mistake!" Algeran cried out. "Look at them! They are surrounding us. We are going to die!"

Both Albert and Rangoth turned their eyes to Sylvia. They had the same question, even if no words were said. She sucked in her breath. Another lesson. If a crew had an opinion, they voiced it vociferously. If they did not, they expected the leader to tell them what to do.

"Rangoth, convey a message back through the titanic djinn," Sylvia said. "Tell them to inform this Elezar that we come in peace." Her thoughts raced on. "That we seek another ship like our own. Has there been any sightings of it here?"

Rangoth nodded and shut his eyes. His brow knitted. At the very top of the window, Sylvia saw the djinn's wings unfurl. For a moment, nothing more happened. Then abruptly, everyone felt a sudden impulse to stumble closer toward the front hatch. Sylvia hung on to Mason as he spread his stance for balance.

The lightning djinns — at least the ones Sylvia still saw — halted their approach. Like ice skaters on a smooth pond, they came to an effortless stop and hovered. With only occasional beats of their wings, they formed a fence through which it was clear that Sylvia and the others dared not pass.

"How many more of your kind are coming?" Rangoth translated.

Despite herself, Sylvia smiled. More of your kind? This might turn out okay. Dargonel must have come this way, too! All they would have to do was increase their speed somehow, and the sorcerer would be overtaken.

"How many more?" Rangoth repeated.

"Tell them none, of course," Sylvia said. "Our goal is to capture those who have transgressed here and return them home."

After the message was relayed, one of the lightning djinns broke from the line and flew back to the palace. As it ducked into the tower from which it had originally emerged, from almost every other opening, what looked like a flamboyance of flamingos fluttered into the void.

There were hundreds of smaller demons of all sizes and descriptions flying to see the strange intruder. Some were cautious and remained behind the lightning djinn's perimeter. Others continued forward landing on the cylinder itself. The boldest converged on the isinglass window, and with hands cupping their eyes, peered inside.

Sylvia recognized some of the types: nosetweakers, water wisps, and fire devils. A couple of what must be banshees plastered their lips on the isinglass, making it vibrate with their mournful wails. The interior of the ship filled with a cacophony of ricocheting echoes.

She guessed at the identity of a few others from the tales told to her when she was young and had misbehaved. Drink dribblers, hairjumblers, gargoyles, and gremlins. There were many more for which she had no clue. Long, slender ones with limbs looking like they might break. Others squat with arms bulging with muscle and legs so tiny that they seemed useless.

Rangoth put his hands to his ears. "Such a racket in my head. I can't focus."

"Why are these devils here?" Sylvia asked.

"Satisfying their curiosity releases some of the ennui," the wizard said. "I don't think they mean harm. Look, some are getting bored again already."

Sylvia looked to where Rangoth was pointing. Several of the smaller imps had disengaged from the window. They scooted into the armpit of the titanic djinn, tittering all the while. The huge demon twitched and let out a deep rumbling laugh that vibrated the cylinder. He was being tickled, she realized in alarm.

The huge demon spasmed a second time, releasing its grip on their ship with a kick. Everyone inside slammed onto the floor, flailing to regain their footing. Sylvia saw Elezar's palace flash by. Shortly after, it appeared again, this time a little farther away.

They were spinning out of control in a vast, alien realm.

# 7

# Black Pits

SYLVIA HELD on to the back of one of the chairs as best she could. "Rangoth, command the djinn to regrip us and stop the spinning."

She looked at the jumble of people around her. Everyone seemed unhurt.

"Measurements, I must make more measurements," Algeran said as the titanic djinn remounted and halted the spin.

"Why is that so important?" Sylvia asked.

"The distant lights are the only navigation aids we have here. They are like our fixed stars back home." He made a few more sightings and wrote the results in his log. "Yes, we are a little to the, I will call it east, of where we were, but at the same height as before."

"On the same track as Dargonel," Sylvia said. "Excellent. Now, let's turn to face the way we are traveling as I wanted to before. Have the djinn push us from behind with his hands. Then, we can see where we are going."

"We may be able to avoid the likes of another structure like Elezar's," Albert said. "But with no ambient light, not the sorcerer's cylinder. It will be as dark as the realm itself."

"Then, we need to illuminate what is immediately in front of us."

Mason jumped up and pushed against the nearest ceiling portal. The little door hinged open. He grabbed the glowimp globe nearest and jammed it up the opening. "This may be enough," he said.

No one said anything more. After their ship had been rotated, everyone settled in to watch for their quarry.

HOURS PASSED in silence. Except for Elezar's palace, the scene before them appeared the same as it had on the side. Small dots of light scattered in the distance, nothing more. Some of the five pursuers tried to get comfortable, sitting on the chairs and swiveling them to look out the window. The rest sprawled between them on the floor. Mason thought of the battle sagas he had read as a youth. They were filled with action and excitement, nothing like what he was experiencing now.

"Albert, tell us more about these black pits," he said. "Exactly, what is Dargonel looking for? What would one see as he drew closer?"

The magician struggled to his feet and moved to the front of the nearest slate. He studied it for a minute and began drawing. First, he drew a circle in freehand. Holding a piece of chalk in the middle, he smudged a band of grey around it.

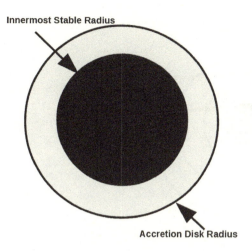

Innermost Stable Radius

Accretion Disk Radius

"The black pit is in the middle, right?" Mason asked as everyone crowded behind the magician. "You told us before that nothing could escape from it. But you said nothing about a ring of grey surrounding it. What's that?"

"The smudged chalk represents what I have named an "accretion disk," Albert said. "An accumulation of matter that the black pit has pulled around it. The material there rotates rapidly and is extremely hot. I doubt if Dargonel would venture into such a place."

Mason's brow wrinkled. "But if he were to get to the interior edge of the disk, he would fall into the pit, right?"

Albert shook his head. "No, that is a neophyte's mistake in thinking. The actual radius of the pit is even smaller. If it is not rotating, it is only a third as far across as my sketch illustrates."

He started drawing again. "Here's what is actually happening."

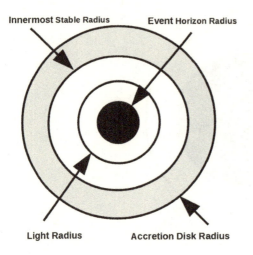

Innermost Stable Radius    Event Horizon Radius

Light Radius    Accretion Disk Radius

"I call the edge of the pit the 'event horizon,'" he said when he was finished.

"Shouldn't we then see stars that are behind? Ones shining between the inner edge of the accretion disk, what you call the innermost stable radius, and the boundary of the pit?"

"It is complicated, Mason," Albert said. "Light not yet swallowed is also bent by the intense pull of gravity. When we look towards the pit, we also see the back of it. What is on the other side appears as a ring around the side nearer to us. Yes, the backside also is featureless, but if you have a means of propulsion, theoretically you could maneuver closer. Into what I call the light radius."

"Master, is the djinn pushing us more comfortable now?" Sylvia interrupted.

"Yes, I believe so," Rangoth replied. "He is propelling us faster than when he straddled our ship."

"So, when will we catch up with Dargonel?" Sylvia

asked.

Everyone looked blank. No one immediately answered.

"Approximately, what would be another twelfth of a day in our own realm," Algeran blurted after a moment.

"What!" Mason exclaimed. "How do you know that?"

"I noted the position of the sun, both when Dargonel left and when we did on the following day. It is my habit to keep track of such things. Assuming the sorcerer's course and speed are the same as ours when we first arrived, that clocks tick the same in both realms, and measuring how the fixed stars seem to move — "

"Twelfth of a day?" Sylvia asked. "Are you saying that in only a few more hours, we will see the other ship?"

"Please understand my result is approximate. There, of course, was some error when we realigned after our spin. The error between our two headings means our paths diverge more and more as time goes on — "

"What is our plan for confrontation?" Mason asked. "The sorcerer is not going to surrender meekly because we ask him to." He stomped his foot on the cylinder's floor. "Damn it. I knew we rushed out too soon without thinking everything all the way through."

"We start thinking now," Sylvia said. "We have two hours to decide what to do."

TWO HOURS passed and then a third. The only sound was Albert's ceaseless scratching on his slates. There had been no sign of Dargonel's ship. And it was just as well, Sylvia thought.

Yes, they had come up with part of a plan. The first thing that must happen is that the other titanic djinn had to be subdued. The two huge demons would be commanded to fight each other. While Sylvia directed their own, Rangoth would struggle to dominate the other one. Hopefully, the distraction of the mental duel between the two masters would mean the other demon would lose the combat.

Then, with no means for propulsion, the two cylinders could be abutted end to end. Despite his protesting, Mason did have the foresight to include swords and shields when their craft was loaded. And he probably had more military training than anyone else on either of the two crafts.

But how to get the other cylinder open? More time was needed to think of a means.

"Tell our djinn to stop pushing," Sylvia decided at last. "Because of the measurement errors, it looks like continuing on this course will not work."

"I never claimed my prediction had no uncertainty," Algeran protested. "My calculations were estimates — the best prediction that could be made, but estimates, nonetheless."

"It's all right, Algeran. I understand you did the best you could. Now, we will have to try something else. In the meantime, we can continue to refine the boarding plan."

"Something else, like what?" Algeran asked.

"Well … I have had a little experience with tracking imps before. Perhaps, they can help us once more."

"Tracking imps?"

"Shush, Algeran. I have to concentrate."

Sylvia closed her eyes and made her mind as blank as she was able to. What she was attempting was something she had never tried before. But she had witnessed Rangoth controlling the titanic djinn within the realm of demons without any flame to make the connection. Perhaps fire was only used to bridge. Something closing the gap between different realms.

She thought of her previous encounter with the tracking imp queen. What the feeling was like, how the voice in her mind had been. For a moment, nothing happened, but then, in an instant, her head felt as if it were exploding. She heard the chatter of thousands of voices, some shrill like a piccolo's, others deep like the basest of drums. Only snatches of words she comprehended. They were jumbled, making no sense at all.

Sylvia clenched her fists, struggling to remember what the tracking imp queen looked like. How she sounded when they had interacted before. The voice had been regal, one used to respect. A queen's voice rather than that of a serving wench washing clothes.

She pushed aside memories of when Rangoth dottered. When she had had no aspirations higher than to finish filling a clothesline and afterward preparing an evening meal. She was more than that now, far more experienced in the ways of the world. Regarded by many as a lady of breeding, as one worthy of the love of a lord. Yes, she was important, one who could rightfully command the service of even a demon queen.

"Where are you?" a voice louder and more clear than the rest sounded in her mind. "I have not forgotten the kindness you showed me and my minions. Do you have another request? Our debt has not been totally repaid."

Sylvia gasped, reining in the feeling of triumph of what she had done. "You found some smoldering hornwort and were able to return, didn't you? I need assistance," she formed the words in her mind. "Can you locate where I am?"

"I am a queen of tracking imps, Lady Sylvia," the voice chuckled. "My minions and I can find anything."

"Then, travel to where I am located in your realm. I am in a moving cylinder of metal but will halt our motion until you arrive where we are." Sylvia took a deep breath and rattled on before the unbelievability of what she was doing sunk in. "Study my vessel well. I seek a second ship looking almost exactly the same. I need to be led to where it is."

"Of course," the queen said. "Tracking in our own realm

235

is far easier than in yours. And when this is done, perhaps there will be time in which we can chat and catch up on things."

# 8

# Searching in Darkness

SYLVIA FELT a tap on her shoulder. She sighed and stood up to stretch. Algeran bumped her aside and sat in the chair. Her anger flared, but she clamped her mouth shut. The counting metronome indicated it was the navigator's turn now. The two other swaps were also made without incident.

Three long, boring days had gone by. Well, approximately, she thought. Three cycles of sleep, anyway. Sleep, eat, stand, or sit. There was nothing else to do. And through it all, no word from the tracking queen that Dargonel's ship had been found.

"I did not expect this to take so long." Mason stood next to Sylvia and squeezed her hand. "Had I known, I would have laded more food and water on board."

"How long will our supplies last?"

"We are half-way done. If we do not find Dargonel within three more cycles …"

Sylvia grimaced. Another problem. Obviously, things were not going well. Everyone was approaching a breaking point.

"Enough! Enough!" Algeran bolted up. "What we are doing is madness. This realm is too big. More vast than our entire orb back home. We must turn around and return to the palace we saw when we first arrived. Ask for help to get out of here."

He pulled out the sextant he always carried with him on his belt. "Turn around. Turn around. I can guide us back. I know I can."

Mason put a hand on Algeran's arm, but the navigator brushed it aside. "We are going to die," he shouted. "Don't the rest of you understand? This quest is hopeless. Yes, Dargonel is going to end everything anyway, but at least we can have a few days of comfort before that happens."

Algeran started convulsing. Foam appeared around his mouth. Rangoth jostled behind him and pinched a nerve in the navigator's neck. Algeran's eyes rolled backward and he collapsed. Mason and the wizard settled him to the floor of the cylinder as gently as they were able.

"Master, what did you do?" Sylvia asked.

"I did not wear this robe from the instant I was born," Rangoth said. "As a young man, I was a bouncer for a carnival until I found my true calling." He waved his hand back and forth a few times as if to make his words vanish. "Way before you were born, Sylvia, way before."

Sylvia studied Algeran's twitching form on the floor. "If we had some sweetbalm with us, we could make him comfortable, at least." She looked at Mason expectantly.

"We do not!" Mason growled. "We were in such a hurry, remember. How could I think of everything?"

"What about our *air*?" Albert asked. "Do we have enough to continue onward?"

Mason took a long, deep breath and calmed. "Enough to last a very long time." He pointed at one of the storage bins. "See the blue-white brick there? We are breathing what melts from it while it is replenished from what we exhale."

"It is warm enough in here. What prevents the brick from melting away?"

"A Maxwell's demon," Rangoth said. "Maybe several of

them. They bat aside warm particles of the circulating air and keep the cold ones."

"Wait!" Sylvia interrupted. "I am hearing a message from the tracking queen."

Everyone stopped speaking and turned to look at her. The inner voice she heard carried an unexpected tone.

"I am sorry," the imp said. "Never in my existence has such a thing happened to me and my brood."

"What happened?" Sylvia formed the thought.

"Our realm is vast. But not so vast that we have not been able to explore every part of it."

There was silence for a moment.

"Yes. Go on."

"The object you seek is nowhere here. We have checked twice to be sure. Nowhere in our realm at all."

Sylvia relayed the words to the others. No one else spoke for a long time.

"Isn't our working hypothesis that a return is not so easily accomplished?" Albert asked finally. "Let's not jump to a conclusion not warranted without more proof."

"Right," Mason said. "This thought just came to me. Master Rangoth, do Maxwell's demons have any cousins, others with similar capabilities?"

"Well, I have never conjured up one myself, but I have been told there are many varieties, each with its own specialty."

"So, rather than particles of air, there might be ones who play with light instead?"

"Yes, probably so."

"Then, how about this?" Mason rummaged through one of the drawers near the chairs. He pulled out a vellum and commenced drawing. When he was finished, he passed it from hand to hand.

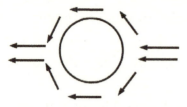

"What does this explain?" Rangoth asked.

"Say a light beam approaches Dargonel's cylinder from the right. A demon hovering nearby deflects its path so it travels to one of his swarm-mates nearby. That one, in turn, routes it to another. And so on around the circumference of the craft until the last sends it on its way in its original direction. With enough imps to guard every angle, the sorcerer's craft is invisible to everyone who searched for it."

"Highly speculative." Rangoth shook his head.

"Nevertheless, my lad," Albert said. "I am impressed. Have you ever considered the possibility of becoming a magician's acolyte? You show skill in thinking beyond the moat."

"Yes," Mason said. "We need to probe with some other type of demon, ones that could overwhelm —" The lord halted in mid-thought.

"Banshees," he blurted. "Their cries disturb whatever passes for air in this place. Waves of sound. And a wave is composed of many particles moving together. Master Rangoth, can you bring some of these howlers under our control?"

"I don't know," Rangoth said. "I have never tried."

"Then, try," Mason said. "If we cannot locate Dargonel, we will have no way of stopping him." He looked from Algeran's slumbering form to the other stress-twisted faces. "And we have little time to do it."

SYLVIA PATTED Mason's arm around her waist but paid him

scant attention. After Mason's pronouncement, no one else had spoken for what seemed to her like hours more.

Her thoughts whirled. There must be a way to confront Dargonel. But even if they were able to locate him, they still were faced with the problem of gaining entry into his ship. And that was essential. They had to capture him not only to thwart his plans but also to learn the method by which they would return home.

Carefully, she reviewed what Rangoth had told her about the sorcerer's grand design. Get close enough to a black pit so the strength of gravity could be increased. But the nearest was too far away to travel to being carried by a djinn, no matter how fast it was.

And that meant periodically popping from the demon realm back into ours. Making measurements for where they were. Returning to resume traveling in the correct direction. What would take lifetimes in her universe could be only a few wingbeats where the devils dwelled.

Yes, Sylvia realized, return to their universe, perhaps many times. That was the weakness of Dargonel's plan! Her heart began to race as the idea blossomed. Back in more familiar surroundings, they might have a better chance against the sorcerer. And he could be attacked more than a single time. The trick was to get to these measuring points, too.

"Master Rangoth," Sylvia said. "Explain to me again how Dargonel can travel back and forth between our realm and this one."

"I do not know for sure," Rangoth roused out of the chair into which he had reoccupied. "A titanic djinn has to transition through flame no differently than any other demon. For one of such great size, a powerful explosion is needed, no simple fire of burning twigs."

"So, Dargonel's cylinder was laden the same as ours. Enough unstable material so there could be many

241

explosions." Sylvia grimaced as the next thought hit her. "Maybe the reason the tracking queen did not find his ship was that he indeed was no longer here." She patted Mason's arm again. "No need to postulate the existence of demons who bend light."

"Exploding something here would be quite foolish." Rangoth shook his head. "That would puncture the integrity of the realm's boundary. It would deflate into who knows what. The ruling princes all decree that no fire is allowed here. Every imp or devil with which I have dealt has emphasized that to me over and over again."

Sylvia's chest tightened. "How do *we* get back ourselves if Dargonel perishes? What could his secret be?"

"I have pondered the question at length," Rangoth said. "The only thing I can think of is that he must have help from our side — from an explosion in our realm."

"That would only bring him back to our orb." Sylvia frowned. "How does the sorcerer make any progress toward his goal?"

"Explosions on other orbs, ones closer to the dark pit." Rangoth shrugged.

"How?" Sylvia persisted. "Not any kind of explosion, right? They must be from substances linked to the passage of titanic djinns." She rubbed her chin for a moment and then continued thinking. "The one lighting the explosive is on one side of the barrier between our realms. The explosive itself is on the other …"

The monotony of their silent passage through the almost featureless nothingness continued. Although there was little room to maneuver, Sylvia removed Mason's arm from around her and began pacing. Her thoughts trickled from her lips. "Besides the titanic djinns, the only demon Dargonel has had any traffic with was a nosetweaker imp — the one who recited his gloating — "

"Nosetweakers!" She halted abruptly. "Master, you have

242

had a lot of experience with them. Could *they* carry anything as they journey to our realm."

Rangoth rubbed his chin. "I suppose. But not much. And such is not their nature. They have no need."

"'Not much' repeated many times can add up to a lot." Sylvia stopped pacing. "Yes, that's how he does it! Dargonel commands nosetweakers to transfer the explosive material across the barrier. A small amount at a time — as much as they can carry on each trip. Once enough has accumulated, the imp sets it off. The titanic djinn pushes the sorcerer's ship through the opening."

"Highly speculative," Mason said. "No better than my idea about deflecting light."

"Maybe Dargonel does both," Sylvia said. "What is important, we now have another way to track where he is."

"How?" Mason and Rangoth asked together.

"Master, send out your thoughts. Search for the imps wherever one might be."

"Wouldn't they be on our orb?" Mason asked.

"Yes, there certainly, but perhaps somewhere else, too. On any orb on which oleander naturally grew."

"Or something similar enough to it," Albert chimed in. "There probably are many orbs with conditions conducive to life such as ours."

"How does a nosetweaker get to somewhere else in the first place?" Mason asked. "For the very first time. He would only be able to appear there through an oleander flame. Who would set that?"

"Perhaps burning a forest fire caused by lightning," Rangoth said. "According to our legends, that is how demons challenged our minds in the distant past."

"So, reach out and try to make contact, Master," Sylvia said. "This does seem unlikely, but if you touch the mind of a nosetweaker who isn't either in this realm or visiting our own orb — then that may mean we have caught up with Dargonel."

Sylvia felt elated. She was more than merely a woman. More than eye candy. She inhaled deeply. Yes, much more than that. A leader. She was a leader. And one with brains.

# 9
# Orbfall

"THIS IS absolutely no fun," the nosetweaker complained. "We have much better things to do than haul powders into your own realm. Why didn't you leave them there in the first place?"

Sylvia sighed. Rangoth had been successful. Found a nosetweaker idling outside of the demon realm, but not on their home orb. But even with her help, he was having difficulty in convincing all the imps they had assembled to work together. There were over two dozen of them, divided into squads of four. Each group grasped a small sack of primer or a brick of explosive wrapped with twine and vanished out of the realm. Mason directed Algeran to loop the bricks and Albert to fill the sacks carefully.

"Enough," Mason finally shouted. "One load of primer and a dozen bricks. The same ratio used to get us into this realm."

"Enough!" the one who was the imp-leader said. "Enough for what? We've transported enough to curl one's wart hairs. You humans are so crazy. Not civilized like we Wabangis or our benefactors, the ones we call the gnomes."

"Didn't someone else already use you to perform this task before?" Sylvia asked.

"Well, yeah, I guess so. But we are to get a special reward

later if we promised not to talk about it."

"What kind of special reward?"

"You mean you will reward us, too?"

"Not if you don't tell me what it is first."

"Well, you see, we are a curious lot. Can't help ourselves."

"Go on."

"Over the eons, we have been able to witness many strange customs, but some of the sights seem to be forbidden to watch. Apparently, we are not allowed to witness them."

Sylvia frowned. She did not like where this might be going. "Like what?" she asked.

"Well, I know this is incredible even to imagine, but it has been said by others in our realm, that there are times when …"

"When what?"

"When two humans actually press their lips together!" the nosetweaker rushed on. "I know, I know. It sounds disgusting. But I can't help getting excited thinking about the possibility of seeing it actually happen."

Sylvia laughed. She glanced at Mason. He was supervising the cleanup of spilled power, unused string, and sacks littering the cylinder's floor. "I think a glimpse of that can be arranged," she said.

SYLVIA BRACED herself against the walls of her alcove as she had done before. The nosetweakers knew nothing about how explosives were set off, so they were given an additional incentive. Drop the largest stone they were able to carry onto the primer themselves. For doing so, they would get to view not one buss between her and Mason but three of them.

"They are releasing it now," Rangoth's muffled voice

filtered into Sylvia's ears.

Before she thought of more, she was slammed against the wall. The titanic djinn was pushing their ship through the opening between the realms.

This transition was not like it had been the first time. The demon realm projected some sense of up and down in one's mind. But as far as Albert or any of the others could tell, there was no pull of gravity there at all. It had taken some effort to get used to the sense of always falling, but everyone in their cylinder had managed to cope.

Now, Sylvia heard the whistling of air around their ship as the djinn slowed its descent. With a jolt, it crashed onto the ground. A few of the cabinet doors jarred open, and some of their contents fell to the floor.

Sylvia wiggled her upper back. Some of the built-up tension dissolved. They had returned. Admittedly, on an orb who knew how far from home, but they were back from a realm she did not care for in any way.

Mason tapped on the door that sealed her sleeping alcove. "The air outside tests good," he called. "Let's go and look around."

Everyone exited their bunks. Rangoth and Algeran smoothed their robes. Albert did not seem to care about his. It was as wrinkled and torn as on the day when Sylvia had first met him. Mason strapped on a sword at his waist. "We don't know what sort of beast we might meet," he said.

"Wait a moment!" Sylvia's tension roared back like a lion. "Do you hear it? It sounds like a faint hiss."

Everyone quietened. Mason slowly walked the length of the cylinder and then back. He stopped midway and pulled open one of the high cabinet doors.

"There!" he shouted. "I see a small crack."

"It is our air escaping, isn't it?" Albert asked. "The pressure here is higher than outside."

"The flaw," Mason growled. "Dargonel said something about that when he left. Why he chose the cylinder he did over this one. The two explosions we have experienced, or perhaps even our landing has enlarged it."

"Then open the hatch," Albert said. "Outside must be breathable or else Dargonel would not be here. When the pressures equilibrate, we will lose no more."

"How will we get back?" Algeran exclaimed. "We have been traveling in the demon realm for days. Even if we subdue the sorcerer, it will take three more to retrace our course in the demon realm."

The navigator collapsed to the floor and started to sob. "I knew something would happen. I just knew it. We should have returned when we could. We are all trapped here, trapped. We are going to die."

"One thing at a time," Sylvia shouted before anyone else could. "Remember our mission. First, we must overcome Dargonel. Then we can figure out what to do next."

"But don't you see — " Algeran tried to continue.

"Make yourself useful," Sylvia snapped. "Focus on the here and now. Our first task is to exit and explore."

Mason nodded. He twirled open the latch at the rear end of the cylinder and pushed his shoulder against the door. It did not budge.

"Evidently, we have sunk into the soil a bit," Albert speculated.

"More muscle," Mason said. "Algeran, give me a hand."

"A moment," the navigator sighed, and then answered, "I must load up my gear first."

Sylvia held her breath. She was surprised by herself. There could be danger here, but that was not her primary concern. It was more a sense of expectation, of wonder. What did a different orb look like? What would they find here? Was Dargonel nearby?

Algeran jostled to the door next to Mason. Three sextants and two telescopes hung from his back. On both arms were strapped protractors, quills, ink, and vellums. He looked like a large fish, barnacled on all sides.

Together, the two men strained against the door. It dragged open, and with a rush of air out of the cylinder, the pressure equilibrated. A sliver of hot outside air mixed with that inside. It was hot and muggy with the scent of rotting fruit.

Mason and Algeran shoved again. This time, the door scraped over the top of a small stone and swung open.

Sylvia and everyone else strained around each other to get clear views. She blinked at what she saw. Their view was blocked by two bipeds, both taller than any of their crew. Each carried a long spear with a flint arrowhead bound to the end. They wore no clothing but instead were covered head to foot with long stringy hair.

Their pelts were blond but dirty, like soiled rags. Here and there, patches of lichen blooms snarled the strands. On the closer being, obviously a female, there was even a small swarm of insects buzzing about a mud-daubed nest. She wore a belt made of vines. On it hung a short knife, wooden cup, a two-pronged fork, a spoon, and a small box of shiny metal. Only the faces of the natives were bare, angry pink skin peeling in the strong, blue light of an overhead sun.

The second creature, a male, shouldered the first aside with a growl. For a moment, the two struggled to be the one closer to the hatch. Finally, the woman pointed to the metal box. She pressed a button on the top and continued snarling.

"We will not be deceived this time," a perfectly understandable voice sounded out of the box. "I am called Wakona. My mate, Wabi. You are the prisoners of our tribe, the Wabangi, but we will not revert totally to our primitive ways. Behave, and you will not be flayed first before we cook and eat you."

# 10

# Moonshadow

MASON'S FIRST instinct was to reach for his sword, but he managed not to do so. This was no time for haste. Yes, there were only two adversaries, and he did have a superior weapon, one that slashed as well as stabbed. But he was not an experienced warrior. Acting alone, he was not sure he would prevail.

Better to follow the command until everyone had exited their ship. Then somehow communicate in secret to formulate a coordinated plan. Break free and overcome Wabi and Wakona before they were herded into a village. A place where they surely would be hopelessly outnumbered. On the trek to wherever, even one helper might be enough. But which one?

Mason studied Algeran first. The navigator had calmed down some, but now his face showed anger. He must be upset at his loss of status with the others. And there were his swings in mood, the outbursts they all had witnessed. Mason shook his head. No, not Algeran.

Rangoth would fight sensibly. He claimed he was a carnival bouncer in his youth. Must have had some experience with the physical. Mason glanced at the wizard and sighed. No, he was too old, too slow. His best years had passed.

And Sylvia? Of course, not Sylvia! She had to be protected at all costs. That left only Albert. A little man, quiet, muttering the formulas ricocheting in his mind all the time. It would have to be him. Perhaps he was wiry enough. Probably the best choice of the four. If he could only get a few moments to alert him, so he would know what to do when he drew his sword.

Mason raised his hands over his head and marched out of the cylinder, eyes alert and appraising. Except for the translator box, these creatures look quite primitive, he thought. They might not even know what is in my scabbard.

Reluctantly, the others imitated Mason and followed. One by one, hands high, they exited.

"Look!" Algeran pointed upward. A ragged band of stars stretched across the sky from horizon to horizon. "Crystal blues, fiery reds, and violent yellows. In broad daylight. I have never seen anything like that."

"Dargonel has been lucky with his first probe back into our realm," Albert said. "He is much closer to the black pit than when he started."

Mason stared upward with the rest. He shielded his eyes. One side of the starry band was hidden by an even brighter light, the local sun shining fiercely. On the other, the background chaos was blotted out by a second disk, one of black, about the same size as the local star.

"It is a moon," Algeran said. "Like our own orb, this place also has a moon."

Wakona prodded Algeran to keep moving, but he brushed the spear aside as if it were a toy. He unbuckled some of his gear and let it crash to the ground.

"Move along," the translator voice boomed with an edge of insistence.

"A moment, a mere moment," Algeran said. He started sighting and jotting down measurements, first of the sun and then the moon.

Wakona looked at Wabi, but he only shrugged. Strange, Mason thought. Shrugging. Was that action common across the cosmos? Were the spears merely for show? He decided to test and find out.

"We mean you no harm," Algeran said. "Why the spears?"

"We have been peaceful for many years. For thousands of cycles around our sun, our only contacts have been with the gnomes. They are the ones who occasionally appear through a sacred portal.

"From them, we Wabangi learned to curtail our ceaseless wandering. Our symbolic cannibalism of captured enemies. Plan crops for unlucky times rather than rely solely on hunting large beasts to stave off hunger. How to use a simple device like the voice-speaker they gave to me, Wakona."

"If you don't eat mortal flesh," Rangoth asked, "why threaten us with becoming one of your meals?" Rangoth asked. He pulled himself up to stand as tall as he could.

"Normally, we would not. Exchange with the gnomes has proven to be beneficial to both sides. So, of course, we welcome other beings like yourself when they appear."

"The most recent did not behave as you expected, did they?" Sylvia asked.

"They did not. The one whose hair stands on end tried to force himself on another of our women in a way she did not expect. We fought, and three of our kind speak no more. Then the bad visitors vanished within the portal."

Wakona thrust her spear at Algeran to stop what he was doing and start moving.

"We, too, have great power," the navigator said as he gathered up his gear. "Power that could forever change your world."

"What do you mean?"

"Be warned!" Algeran said. "We can make your sun

vanish from the sky. Have a great black beast consume it whole. You will be plunged into darkness. Your only light will be the glow from the fiery wreath. Do not dare to toy with us."

Wakona said nothing and turned off the translator. She and Wabi retreated and conversed rapidly in their own language.

"What are you talking about?" Mason scowled at Algeran. "We will fare better if we deal honestly with these people."

"It turns out we are lucky." Algeran shook his head. "The black sphere is their moon, right?"

"Yes. So?"

"My measurements don't lie. On this particular transit, the moon will pass directly in front of their sun. A solar eclipse. Nighttime darkness. They will be frightened out of their woolies. We will say we can save them if they let us go."

"The native is coming back from her conference." Rangoth pointed.

Wakona approached and pressed the translator button.

"We will take advantage of your suggestion," she said.

"Not eat us, right?" Algeran asked.

"Oh, no. We still plan to do that. But we will wait until after the eclipse is over."

# 11
# Sylvia's Leap

THE LITTLE band walked single file through lush vegetation. Wakona led, walking backward to keep her eye on them. Wabi marched at the rear. Even though she was not looking, Wakona slid easily around bright red and blue leaves as large as elephant ears dangling onto the trail. They swished back to slap Algeran, who was next in line, in his face.

Sylvia strode second, and Mason was third. It was hot, oppressively hot. His tunic was soaked with sweat. He batted at swarms of tiny insects determined to get into his ears. Off in the distance, the cackle of raucous birds made it hard to think.

Mason slowed his pace and let Rangoth pass. Soon, he was close enough to Albert bringing up the rear so that they could talk as they walked.

"Albert, you must get in front of Rangoth and get Sylvia to pass her dagger to you."

Silence.

"Albert, can you hear me?"

"I have no slates," the magician mumbled. "It is so hard to hold all the equations in my head at once."

"Not now, Albert. Musing about the laws of new magic can come later. We have to escape while we have only two Wabangi to deal with."

254

"Don't these transitions strike you as odd, Mason? Think about it. We move from one part of a multiverse into another, and yet there are no velocity corrections needed."

"What do you mean?"

"We cruised in the demon realm at a certain speed and direction. Went through a gap back into our own space with no guidance maneuvers at all. We landed on some foreign orb. It, in turn, is slave to a star racing around a dark pit with high velocity. We touched down with only a small bump and walked out as if we were leaving a dwelling."

"A tremendous change," Albert continued. "Modifications in speed and direction compensated for as if we were piloting with precision. How is this possible? What is the mechanism for this to happen? Nothing to do with the new magic for sure."

"I don't know, Albert, but this is not the time for new fundamental discoveries. We have a mission, remember? One on which the fate of our entire world rests."

"It appeared to me when we were in the demon realm. At least *some* of the laws of the new magic apply just as they do here. Well, there is the problem of how the demon lairs manage to float themselves. But nature is telling us something important. How things work at the most fundamental level."

Mason grew irritated. "Albert, our mission. I need you to arm yourself."

"I do not come up with my theories out of nothing, Mason. I am no mere scribbler of fantasies. Like any good magician, I am guided by observation. It is experimental results that led me to formulate my three great laws. From them, in our realm, everything else can be derived."

"Albert, the seven laws of what you call old magic are not mere appendages to your three."

"No, not yet. As things stand now, old and new magic are different. There are many laws of old magic, but only seven can function at any one time. Old magic has metalaws, and

255

'Seven Exactly' is one."

Albert took a deep breath and, as if lecturing a sluggish student, raced on. "The new magic has a metalaw as well, more of a guiding principle, actually. Reductionism, it is called. Always strive to reduce the number of laws to the lowest possible number. And I have done so. There are only three fundamental forces of the new magic, and I have found all three."

"Have you? Have you really?" Mason felt his exasperation boil over. "Does everyone agree with them? What about Isaac and what he calls his law of gravity?"

"Well, yes, most of my colleagues initially did disagree with my conclusions. They promulgated a plethora of apparent paradoxes. Which twin is older? Does the speeding carriage fall into a crevasse? What about falling into an impossibly small crack? What happens when an object sails past a long, open window?"

Albert puffed out his chest. "But my theories have produced answers for them all. The challenge now is to explain how our realm and that of the demons actually couple."

Mason racked his mind for what to say to the magician. Focus him to help on the urgent task they all had agreed upon. The very *existence* of their realm was at stake. Who cared what the detailed rules were for how it interacted with another? If their group failed to thwart Dargonel, there would be no one left to applaud Albert's brilliant mind.

Mason heard chattering ahead and looked farther up the trail. His heart sank. He had been too late to get Albert to act. Ahead was a tall palisade wall made of timber with a large gate swung open in the middle. They had arrived at the Wabangi village.

SYLVIA GASPED as she entered the compound. She was reeling from fatigue. With each step she took, the angry sun drained her energy like a sponge. The chance to stop was a relief. She wiped the salt from her eyes and scanned about. The sprawl of huts made from tall grass swards bound together was everywhere. To the right, near the rear part of the palisade, lay Dargonel's cylinder.

Was he still here? she thought. Could they attack the cylinder and end the quest? Could ...

No, the sorcerer was not here. She sighed. Wabi had already told them that. The bad ones had journeyed to the gnomes through something called a portal. Focus. First, learn what else she could about this place.

To the left, a small stream meandered through the village grounds. Directly in front stood a large, chest-high cauldron of rusted iron. One that could easily hold all their crew at once.

She swung her head around to take in the rest of the scene. Except for children, no one else was about. They played what looked like a complicated version of tag. When one was caught by two others, he had to toss a small rock into a person-sized hole in the ground nearby. Sylvia heard one stone skitter down what sounded like a metal pipe. Then, a resonant foghorn answered before it became quiet.

Like cattle being prepared for slaughter, the crew was directed into one of the huts. With only one doorway and no windows, it was dark inside. Sylvia plopped to the ground, and Mason joined her. The other three arranged themselves on the dusty floor as best they could.

Wakona and Wabi stood guard at the hut's entrance. They barked orders to other natives living in the village. Peering at the activity behind the pair, Sylvia saw a burst of activity. Men dragged splintered logs to the cauldron and thrust them between the vessel's feet. Women staggered under large clay pots propped on their shoulders and dumped their contents into the big pot.

Many trips were needed to fill the cauldron to the brim. When that was accomplished, several more women approached, each carrying a cup similar to the one on Wakona's belt. In unison, they dipped them into the cauldron and extracted a cupful of liquid.

Wakona stuck her head into the hut. "It is part of our tradition," she said. "Each of you will be given what we call a 'last cup' to savor before you are tossed into the cooker. You see, we are not so barbaric as we have been in the ancient past."

IT TOOK a while for the kindling to catch the logs on fire, but once that happened the heat of the flame made the air dance. Hot waves blasted relentlessly from them into the hut.

The darkness of the eclipse came and went, but Sylvia hardly noticed. Even though she moved as far away from the hut opening as she could, the smell of burning wood tormented her. Her heart spasmed. In a flash, the memory of being tied to a stake had rushed back to fill her mind. That water was involved this time did not matter. She was going to die a heat death after all. Shouldn't facing that once in a lifetime be enough?

Her thoughts tumbled out of control. After everything that had happened, all the challenges, would this be the end? Visiting the realm of demons, winning the election in Ytterby, escaping the pursuit from Vendora's palace, surviving the attack of the brigands at Rangoth's hovel. Everything was for naught?

Many hours passed waiting for the cauldron to boil. The sun started its dip below the horizon. "What do we do now?" Sylvia asked Mason as dusk deepened. "Have you thought of anything? Speak up. They can't understand us while the translator is off."

"I don't know." Mason answered. "Nothing that is sure to work."

Sylvia sighed. She had been around her loved one to recognize what was happening. He was paralyzed with indecision, not impulsive the way she herself was. She looked at Rangoth and the others and saw only panic in their eyes. Confronting Dargonel with violence had never become real for them; that there could be bloodshed along the way.

If anyone were going to come up with something, it would have to be her to …

A thought seared through Sylvia like a sharpened knife. But she had to make the attempt. She did not have time to consider anything else. Wakona entered the hut with a dozen more armed men. One by one, the crew was prodded out into the open to stand in a line before the cauldron that finally had begun to simmer.

Wabi raised his spear into the air and pumped it up and down as if he were stabbing the stomach of a passing dragon.

"We will not be able to exact vengeance on those who wronged us though we did them no harm." His words echoed through the translator. "They have gone to visit the gnomes, perhaps never to return."

He pointed to the box at Wakona's waist. "No matter. Devices such as this, the intensifiers, the projectors, the dampers, and all the rest are not for us. Our lives are simple, and we should be content."

"But as you can see," the native continued, "here are more of their kind. They have come to make a payment with their lives in exchange for those we have lost."

"There are five of us." Sylvia surprised herself by blurting. "You said you only lost three."

The native frowned at Wakona but did not direct her to turn the translator off.

"First, we will send the necessary offering. It is that time of year. The gnomes deserve recompense for what they have done for us. Despite their evil machines that lessen rather than strengthen, they have pulled us up from savagery."

Wabi pointed at a primitive two-wheeled wagon. High slatted sides surrounded a balloon stitched together from hides and oozing water from many leaks. "The gnomes' orb has little water of its own. It is our one possession they desire most, and faithful to our oaths, we shall provide it. To the portal. Let the gift be on its way."

Sylvia shifted on her feet, impatiently. Angry bubbles of steam rose like erupted lava in the cauldron behind Wakona's mate, brother, father, or whatever he was. She shook her head. She had to keep her mind clear.

Concentrating, she was only dimly aware of what was happening on the left. Let the warriors who pushed the cart return to be close by first, she thought. But then her focus sharpened on what was happening.

The cart was near the hole in the ground that the children had been playing by earlier. Could it be? Was it that simple?

It seemed like an eternity for the natives who had towed the cart to return and cluster around the crew. Wakona, with help from four others, offered the 'last drink' to them.

Sylvia dipped her finger into the cup of water offered her and started to swirl it back and forth. The incantation came back to her effortlessly. She had recited it so many times before. The words were nonsense, of course. Only a few of them mattered, hidden in all the rest. But 'once together, always together' and 'like produces like' were two of the laws of magic and could not be denied.

The water in the cauldron exploded from its confines. The warriors standing in front of it were bathed in its chaotic rush. Dropping spears, they ran in circles trying to shake off the hot water scalding their backs.

Sylvia took advantage of the chaos. "Follow me," she

260

shouted to the four men. "There is no need for us to choose sides." In the confusion, she bolted across the ground.

"Wait!" Mason shouted. "What are you doing? You are leading us deeper into their encampment."

Sylvia did not answer. She headed directly for the hole yawning open in the dirt, jumped into its blackness, and disappeared from view.

# 12
# Accidentals

SYLVIA FELT a wave of disorientation. Her senses rampaged like a boiling cauldron. Flashes of light across the spectrum burst into her eyes. She heard a cacophony of tinkling bells, croaking bullfrogs, and the rumble of earthquakes. The smell of lavender mixed with the putridness of cesspools. Her arms erupted with goosebumps while her legs felt as if they were blistering. She was falling, falling …

Then, as abruptly as they had begun, every sensation ceased. She had no sensory input at all. No light, no sound, no orientation. She tried to reach out with her hand, but discovered she could not move it, even tell where her arm was pointing. She was unsure if her heart still beat. There was no way to measure the passage of time. Despite her best efforts to stop where her thoughts were taking her, panic started to fester. What had she done? How could she have been so impulsive?

She remembered when she was a child and had been sent to bed without supper. What had worked then? Lie still. Well, perhaps she was already doing that. Think of how things would be better in the morning. What morning? How long would this night last?

She longed for Mason to wrap his arms around her. Mason. Had he and the others followed her into the hole? Were they to be separated forever? Did she truly jump into a portal leading to where the Gnomes dwelt?

A soft click brought her thoughts back into focus. A sliver of dim light appeared to her right. Right side? Sylvia could not be sure. She blinked as the slit widened. Was she holding her breath? She could not tell.

"We got another one." She heard a soft, gravelly voice announce. Praise the singularity. It is different from that of the Wabangi. "And it looks like four more are coming after."

The slit widened into a door. A gnarled hand thrust forward. Spindly fingers with nails longer than Sylvia's thumb beckoned her to exit the portal. Feelings coursed back into her body. She regained awareness of the positioning of her limbs. Tentatively, she stepped through the portal into another strange place.

"Look!" the voice said. "I have never seen one like it before."

Sylvia looked about. Two short humanoids stared back at her. They had faces like wrinkled and tossed aside overaged prunes. Rheumy eyes dripped onto cheeks thick with what must be the dried trails of previous seepages. Ears sprouted tufts of hair hugely out of place on their tiny heads.

They were clothed similarly to Rangoth, long flowing robes covered with arcane symbols. One was deepest black, the other looked like it had been left out in a spring shower of multicolored droplets. Oranges, reds, and occasional blues swirled together in chaos. Thick leather belts held translator boxes and other devices at their waists.

To Sylvia, they looked like gnomes from a child's book of sagas, creatures who never smiled. Gnomes, she thought. Of course, that was the translator's doing.

"More are coming." One studied a console in front of the other. "Four more in all."

Sylvia nodded to herself. Mason, Rangoth, Albert, and Algeran. They all had escaped.

AFTER THE last of their crew had exited the portal, no effort was made to search any of them for weapons. And neither of the two escorting gnomes seemed to be armed. Instead, the crew was led along a narrow hallway into a slightly larger room. Recessed lighting made the volume brighter than that at the portal exit, but only barely.

Sylvia felt drained. The transport through the portal had been bad enough. When she looked around her, the advanced culture of these small people was obvious in every direction. Polished walls that fit together perfectly. Air fresh and cool blowing from vents along the way.

Although their party towered over their escorts, they showed no apprehension. Like livestock herdsmen, they were carrying out a normal day-to-day task. To the gnomes, she and the others were no more challenging than the primitives on the orb they had traveled from. Domesticated cattle to be handled as was fitting.

She glanced at Mason. It was obvious he was experiencing the same feelings. Bravado had been replaced by apprehension. What had they got themselves into?

After her eyes had adjusted, Sylvia realized that the room divided into two distinct halves. On one side, the walls, ceiling, and floor reflected nothing, the same whiteness as the robe of one of her captors. The other half mimicked the motley swirl of dyes worn by the second. There were no windows. Although the crew of five clustered in the center of the room, each gnome was careful to stand in only the portion colored the same as his garment.

A painting hung on the colored wall. It showed an ebony circular disk surrounded by a halo of pigments that were the same as those on the attending escort. The being noticed her squint. False color," he said. "It allows us to imagine what we cannot see."

"Falseness is contagious," the other gnome rebutted. "It must not be encouraged. The image on my side is the correct one to contemplate."

Sylvia's eyes followed to where the gnome's hand pointed to a second picture frame. In it, the image was entirely pitch-dark, oppressive. No features at all. Sylvia looked about the room for a second time. The dimness did little to lift an overriding feeling of gloom. It felt to her as if she were in a tomb.

"Five is an odd number, Bask," the black-clad gnome said. "That will make it harder to choose."

"I know that, Mush," the other shot back. "As always, you have the bad sense to waste time on the obvious. I bid one hundred on the one with long hair. I see some hints of sharpness in her eyes."

"A hundred? A full one hundred? Is this some sort of trick? Do you think me daft?"

"You already know my answer to that. Are you going to bid?"

Before there was an answer, a deep rumble sounded around them. The entire room rocked back and forth for a few moments before quieting down. A sharp crack sounded in the air immediately after. Sylvia was not sure, but to her, it felt as if the floor had acquired a small, permanent tilt. She was growing more uncomfortable with each passing moment.

"Closer," sighed Bask. "Every day, we get closer and closer. It will not be long before we fall to within the accretion disk that — "

"And every time we suffer a small collision with a meteor of some size, you sing the same lament," Mush said. "None of us has tried to leave through a portal for longer than any who remains can remember. It has been decided. This is our home. This is the way the great singularity wants it. We accept. We are content. Get over it, Bask, and prepare to play the games."

"An accretion disk?" Albert asked. "Accretion disk! That

is something I would love to see. Can you take me to the surface of your orb?"

"No point to," Mush answered. "There is nothing to witness. Up there, every particle of light has so much energy that its vibrations are far faster than any of our eyes can register."

Albert waved his arm around the room containing them. "So, you live far underground to avoid the bombardment."

"We do. At least ten thousand strides deep of solid rock everywhere. Even so, enough high-energy light penetrates to age us prematurely from what we would normally enjoy. There are only a few more than a thousand of us left to play the games." He bowed his head slightly. "It is what the singularity wants for us."

"Why not tunnel deeper?" Algeran asked.

"No brain in this one." Bask pointed and laughed. "Let me have the female for one hundred, and you can have the idiot for ten."

"He *might* be worth about ten," Mush rubbed his cheek in thought for a moment. "Serve as a debris disposer." He looked at Algeran and spoke slowly. "Pay attention. We don't want to get too deep. Do you understand? The showering light warms the rock through which it travels. That heat is a minor source of our energy for other things."

"Excuse me," Sylvia spoke up. They were here on a mission. And these two looked harmless enough. There was no time for absorbing local culture. "This is important. By any chance have you seen other beings who look the same as us?"

"Hard to tell, Longlocks," Mush said. "Hard to tell. We get accidentals like you falling into our portals all the time, and to us, you look pretty much the same."

"Accidentals?" Mason was coming out of his torpor, too, Sylvia realized.

"Like Mush said. All the time," Bask answered. "It should be clear enough. We have no nourishing sunlight here. No fertile soil. No water other than what we get as offerings. Everything we need we acquire from strange beings like yourselves in exchange for trinkets you go gaga over." The alien raised his shoulders in what Sylvia took to be a shrug. "And occasionally, one of you falls into one of our portals."

"You don't like that?" Sylvia asked.

"On the contrary, your arrivals are what adds fresh blood to our games." Bask waved his arm around the room. "Without you, life would become like this reception room, rather dreary."

"And you are much better to deal with than the rocks some of your neighbors toss through the portals," Mush added. "Those stones mean nothing but potty duty for us. It is a drudgery to keep things clean. Why do you keep doing that?"

"Why not go through a portal yourselves?" Sylvia asked. "To the orb of the Wabangis or perhaps even another." She looked about again at the overwhelming walls of gloom. "Surely, almost anywhere else would be better than remaining like this. Why do you put up with it?"

"Your question borders on sacrilege, but because of your ignorance you will not be punished — immediately. Long ago, we had many factions, each with their own beliefs. Now there are only two. Guided by our faith in the singularity, we dug into the ground to protect ourselves while the others fought and eventually exterminated themselves. By the grace of the singularity, we are all that remain. We will not make the mistake of not adhering to our fundamental beliefs."

"But, but — "

"Enough chatter," Bask said. "I said one hundred for the female. If nothing else, she can serve as a symbol turner in the Wheel of Destiny game."

Mush studied Sylvia up and down. "For a hundred, you

can have her. That is way more than *I* would spend."

"You said ten for the ignorant one, right?" Bask asked.

"Yes, yes. Now, you have only four hundred remaining to my four-ninety."

"What are you doing?" Sylvia blurted. "We are not cattle to be auctioned off."

"As a matter of fact, you *are*," Bask said. "In each bidding cycle, every new accidental becomes the property of the higher bidder."

Mason drew his sword. "There are only two of you and five of us. We will not become your slaves."

"Ah, a warrior," Mush said. "It has been a while since we have had one." He stuck out his tongue at Bask. "I bid ninety for him. He might prove to be useful."

"Let us be," Mason growled. "We have done you no harm." He stepped in front of Mush and placed the tip of his blade at the gnome's throat.

Mush did not blink. He touched one of the devices on his belt. Instantly, he was surrounded head to foot by a shimmering, transparent cylinder that extended high overhead. "Look about you. See the evidence of our understanding of the four forces of nature. For millennia, we have exploited them all."

Mason poked his sword tip at the cylinder wall, but it did not penetrate. In frustration, he hauled back and swatted at it with all his strength. The blade skittered aside with a high-pitched shriek. While Mush smiled, safe within his barrier, the lord circled behind and continued his onslaught.

Finally, chest heaving from the effort, Mason halted. "All right," he said. "For the moment, we will wait and watch. Watch for an opportunity to — "

"Wait! What did you say?" Albert interrupted. "There are only *two* types of forces — gravity and electromagnetism."

"An intellect!" Bask clapped his hands. "Splendid. One

hundred for him as well."

"Two hundred."

"Three."

Mush rubbed his chin. "You have only one hundred left now. You cannot stop me from garnering the robed one. He will be mine for only one hundred and one."

"That is not right," Rangoth suddenly spoke. "*I* am a *master* of wizardry." He stood as tall as he could. "Give me the wherewithal to perform, and you will see. 'Flame permeates all.'"

Sylvia's eyes widened in surprise. In all her years with Rangoth, she had never seen him act this way. Did the passage through the portal unlock a hidden vanity within him that had been secreted away?

Both Bask and Mush convulsed with laughter. "A shaman. No less than a native shaman," they said simultaneously. "When was the last time we had one of those?"

"I can perform great magic," Rangoth rumbled. "Give me the makings of flame, and you will bc amazed."

"Look around you, shaman," Bask said. "We have no need for primitive superstition here. We survive within the chaos of an accretion disk because of the solid foundation on which our civilization is built. We call it *science*, not the mumbo-jumbo of old-wives' tales."

"And you can have him, Mush," he continued. "Bid one hundred and one, and he is yours." He teased, "I have to admit. This time, you are the craftier one. Well played. Well played."

"I don't have to do that! Take him. I have no interest in an unsophisticated native at all. I will save my units for whoever is the next to visit through the portal."

Bask shook his head. "My bid is zero, not a single unit more."

"Then, so is mine."

Sylvia felt her anxiousness grow. Time was ticking away. Dargonel must be here somewhere. The Wabangis at the other end of the portal said so. And if these captors were only a thousand or so …

"We can assign him to the portal potty task along with the other." Bask pointed at Rangoth and Algeran. "Neither one is going to survive the games and, if not those, the cleansing at the end of the cycle anyway, no matter what tasks they are given. If things go as they do most of the time, the other three will not survive as well."

"Cleansing. What do you mean?" Sylvia asked.

"We have only enough resources of air, water, and the rest for the 1012 of us to survive for the long term," Bask said. "But we are not witless savages as some of you are.

"Accidentals are divided between our two factions. You are taught the skills to perform the more menial tasks among us. At the end of each cycle, *everyone* including Mush, myself, and all the rest of us are ranked according to the contribution we make toward the common good. The atoms of those who do not make the cut at 506, half of 1012, for either faction are put to better use the next time around. But enough of that now. It is time to prepare for the games."

# 13
# Game Pawns

"HAVE YOU seen him?" Sylvia asked Bask for the dozenth time as they moved down a long, motley-colored corridor. She winced with a misstep. It was hard to think and walk at the same time. Being barefooted, she did not mind. But if she did not move forward at the correct pace and in the right direction, a painful shock would zap her insole.

"Think about it," she managed to say. "Even for an alien like one of us, he had distinctive features." She remembered Dargonel's bizarre appearance at Vendora's ball. Red hair standing on end at the top of his head.

"I recall no one as you describe," Bask said. Even with the translator working perfectly, it was sometimes hard for Sylvia to understand him over the squeak of his rubber shoes.

"And, as Faction Master," the gnome continued, "I am the only one who also serves as a collector. Now, pay attention to the cadence I have programmed for you and move along to your seat."

"Are you sure?" Sylvia persisted, but Bask said no more. She preceded Albert onto the balcony of a vault much larger than the reception room they had just been in.

"It is called the competition chamber," Bask said. As before, the walls were black on one side and colored on the other. Lights in the high ceiling provided the only

271

illumination. A gentle breeze stirred the air. It was cool, but not unbearably cold.

Sylvia was the second of a trio to enter the row. The other being, the first of the three, was a humanoid she had never seen before. Not covered with hair like a Wabangi, he looked thin and willowy like a living tree. The top of his head bulged over his eyes. They had a far-away look to them as if he were contemplating deep truths of nature. They reminded Sylvia of how Albert's seemed sometimes.

She paused for a moment to compare the two and immediately grimaced. The shocks of pain in her bare feet continued relentlessly. Only by continuing to move as directed did the incessant reminders cease.

The balcony door behind her quietly closed with a click as Sylvia took the middle seat in a single row. Looking down, she saw that on both the left and right of the floor stood audience areas facing the center. Those nearest all wore garments of color. Those farther away were clad in black. Each section contained about 500 of the small, wizened people who lived here. Was that all? Every single one was present?

High on each of the walls behind the groups were two rows of glowing symbols, both looking the same. The central floor level below her was grey and filled with a scattered array of machinery. Some silent, others hummed with energy.

Sylvia felt the muscles in her neck tighten. These natives were so advanced. The clean elegance of the chamber spoke volumes about their abilities. And force of arms was not going to get them to help. Mason had already demonstrated that. They didn't even bother to remove her dagger. She looked across to a second balcony parallel to hers and spotted four occupants there. Another humanoid was first; Rangoth next, slumped low in his chair. Algeran was third, and finally, Mason. All were subdued.

She fidgeted in her seat. Every moment spent watching

this ceremony a waste of time. She scanned the other occupants again but did not see Dargonel. Yet, the sorcerer had to be here somewhere. He had to be, didn't he?

"Mush, this time, you begin," Bask stood up from the first audience row on the right. Somehow, he had descended to the floor quickly. His voice boomed.

"Fire away," Mush answered. "What is the challenge?"

Bask nodded and motioned to his followers. Several stood, and, one by one, tottered to the central area carrying large smooth rocks in their hands. They dumped them on the floor in front of the machinery and returned to their chairs. The last one dragged a sack and flung it on top of the pile of stones.

"Over two hundred items in all," Bask said, "and each with a numerical value inscribed on it. There is only one container to put them in. The problem is the sack is not large enough to hold them all. What is the highest score possible that can be achieved — the sum of all the item values in the sack?

How does one achieve that? It is not as obvious as it might seem. Maybe the value of two smaller rocks is greater than that of a single larger one. Which will you pick in order to maximize the result?"

"That is not fair! *You* don't know the answer to this puzzle either!"

Bask pointed to the alien in the balcony seat between Sylvia and Albert. "I have a solution provided by one of the accidentals. It might not be the best, but you will have to equal it at least. I have set our score to its value. Do you forfeit the round or wish to compete?"

"Very well," Mush replied. He snapped his fingers, and a dozen of his comrades rose and rushed to the machinery in the center of the chamber.

In a flurry, lathes, milling machines, and drill presses began producing metal parts. They were assembled into more specialized machinery, some outfitted with wheels. Soon, an array of hardware optimized to the task at hand was in operation.

Carriers scurried off and returned with irregular rocks and small boulders. These were fed to grinders tailoring them into multiple replicas of the stones Bask's followers had brought forth. Others were sewing machines stitching together sacks waiting to be stuffed.

Immobile machines, newly created for this one job, plucked stones from the nearby piles. There were dozens of them. They stuffed as many as they could into sacks until they were unable to hold more. Then they dumped them back out and tried again with different selections. From time to time, the lower symbol row on each of the walls showed an updated result.

Sylvia was amazed at what was being accomplished. She had accepted that there would be advanced civilizations encountered in their travels. Ones far more advanced than the one on her home, but this was amazing.

"Brute force!" Bask laughed. "You are resorting to brute force to find the best solution haphazardly. No mathematics to guide you. Only trial and error. Fill a sack, dump it, and try again. Is that all you got?"

"It does not have to be the best," Mush said. "Merely equal or better than the one your maxi-brain has come up with."

After a time long enough for Sylvia to begin squirming in her seat, a gong sounded from somewhere. The construction and stuffing activity stopped.

"We win, we win!" Mush pointed at the symbol rows. "Look at the total score for ours. It is the greater. Quantity overwhelms quality, every time. One hundred points to us, the victors."

Mush smiled broadly. His satisfaction was clear to Sylvia, even though it was on an alien face. "And now the penalty," he gloated. With a dramatic flourish, he pressed a key in the top of a pedestal at his side.

The floor underneath the alien sitting between Albert and Sylvia suddenly opened. The chair tipped, and with a startled cry, the occupant fell toward the floor below. Before he hit, a panel slid to the side so that he fell through. It did not close soon enough to cover the sound of grinding flesh and bone.

AS MUSH conferred with his nearest neighbors, Sylvia grew more and more agitated. She squirmed in her seat. Sweat stuck her clothes to the chairback. It was obvious that one of Bask's contestants would have to answer next. Suppose they failed. Would she or Albert be the one to pay the penalty?

Sylvia looked across the hall to the other side. She could see that Mason and the others were not faring any better. Mason, Rangoth, and Algeran all leaned forward with their backs stiff. Their faces pulled tightly.

Mush tapped on a small button on his robe. Pops and crackles filled the air. "You all can hear me clearly, right?" he asked. "Even the two of you in the balcony."

"That doesn't matter," Bask said. "Get on with it."

"Oh, but it does," Mush said. "You used the intellect of one of your accidentals in your last challenge."

"So?"

"So, the precedent has been set. They are part of your faction. Our challenge will be to another one of them."

Sylvia sucked in her breath. She did not fully understand what the last challenge was about. How could she …

"Describe the interior of a *rotating* black hole," Mush said. "Not a stationary one. That's easy. Everyone knows about them. I choose the one with the ebony hair to answer."

Sylvia's chest constricted as if she had been struck by a

mortal blow. She squeezed her eyes shut. Albert had sketched something about black pits when they met in his hut. What were the words? 'Innermost Stable Something' It was too long ago. She should have paid more attention.

"Well?" Mush said. "We are waiting."

Sylvia took a deep breath. She was Lady Sylvia. What would a lady such as she do? In an instant, a possibility came to her.

"That, too, is so easy," Sylvia blurted. "I am surprised you even pose it." She pointed at Albert. "Child's play. I will prove it to you. I defer to my assistant on the right."

"You can't do that!" Mush exclaimed. "I explicitly chose you."

"And it looks like another precedent has been set," Bask interrupted. "Let the learner try his hand at it."

"But, but —"

Albert leaped to his feet. "There are only three characteristics a black pit can have: mass, angular momentum, and charge."

"Charge is unlikely," the magician rushed on. "If a pit had an excess, either plus or minus, it would consume enough matter of opposite sign to balance it out."

Albert stopped for a moment and scowled. "I wish I had access to a slate so I can explain things better. It took me several years after I had postulated the theory of gravity with no rotation to get a solution for a pit with angular momentum."

Bask motioned to one of his faction in the first row. The factotum jumped up and disappeared. Shortly he was at the balcony level and thrusting a display pad into Albert's hand.

The magician studied it for a moment and then started drawing with a stylus. The image was reproduced on the chamber walls below the counters.

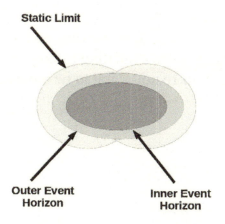

Static Limit

Outer Event
Horizon

Inner Event
Horizon

"Looked at from the equator," Albert resumed, "a rotating black pit has two event horizons rather than one. The outmost curve shows what I call the static limit. The region inside I have named the ergosphere. Theoretically, one could travel there, get energy from the dark pit, and escape from the pull and return."

Sylvia surprised herself with where her thoughts were taking her. Dargonel could be closer to the black pit event horizon than even here in the accretion disk! Was he there now?

"Enough, enough," Mush said. "I concede the round. We are tied at one hundred points each when we resume after the launch."

"Agreed," Bask said. He squinted up at Sylvia and shook his head slightly. "Don't get your hopes up," he said. "We can get away with that trick only once." He turned to look at Albert. "But you, my erudite one, you might survive for many rounds. I feel lucky that I won the auction for you."

"Rounds?" Sylvia yelled down to Bask. Her apprehension had been replaced by anger. "How many must one endure?

You act as if you are civilized, yet this game, as you call it, is barbaric."

"How many?" Bask answered. "Easy enough to compute the expected value. Let's see. At a fifty percent chance of surviving play of the game, the odds of getting through ten is less than one in a thousand. You're not going to be around all that long."

# 14
# Solitary Confinement

SYLVIA STUMBLE-STEPPED out of the balcony. The electric jolts kept her moving despite how much she wanted not to. She and Albert followed Bask through several corridors. Each was almost identical to the last, shiny, mottled stone with no other features.

They reached one that was different — a long hallway lined with doors on both sides. In each was an eye-high slit, and below it touching the floor a smaller hatch for the transfer of food.

A matron, looking much the same as Bask, hurried forward. She was smaller and older with matchstick limbs of sagging flesh.

"Put her in any of them," Bask directed. "I don't think she has any skills that will help her to last long. But make sure she does not hunger-strike and retains enough of her wits about her when the game resumes."

"Yes, Faction Master." The matron dipped her head as she pulled a handheld device from her belt. She punched a few buttons, and one of the doors swung open.

The shocks in her feet led Sylvia inside. The last she glimpsed of Albert as the door swiveled shut with a soft click was Bask leading the magician away.

For a moment, she felt like pounding on the door and

demanding to be let out, but the feeling soon evaporated. That would accomplish nothing. She was alone. Where was Mason? What was going to happen to him? And Rangoth and Algeran? Would their little team ever be together again?

The built-up stress overwhelmed her. The entire mission was folly from the start. She had to admit that now. This was not an adventure for the sagas. What chance did they have against a master sorcerer? One who must have planned for every contingency before he even set out.

Sylvia fell to the floor, wrapped her arms around her knees, and withdrew into herself. The gnomes here could not be thwarted. She and the others were mere gnats flitting aimlessly about. Waiting for the swatter that would end their misery.

IT FELT to Sylvia that an entire day might have passed. She roused from her fetal position and looked about. She made use of the small commode in the back corner of the cell. There was no window. No bed. Nothing on any of the walls. Except for the eye slit and the transfer door near the floor, there was nothing else to notice at all. She rubbed her arms briskly. It was cold. Not impossibly frigid, but cold enough that her energy was sapped.

She stood up and bent a little at the knees. She was too tall to see out of the slit without stooping. The corridor outside was empty, the same as she remembered it from when she arrived. Her stomach growled. How long had she been this way?

Maybe a full day, maybe more. Since entering the realm of demons and then coming here, she had lost all sense of the passage of time.

More hours passed, and then yet still more. Now, hopelessness began pressing down upon her. Her thoughts became repetitive, wagon wheels of iron making deep ruts in the roadbed of her mind. She ran her tongue over the inside of her cheeks. She was thirsty, increasingly thirsty.

She thought again of the others, especially Mason. How was he faring? Would she ever see him again? Would they have a future together?

Despite herself, she let out one weak sob. In frustration, she banged her fist on the door. Let her get back to the competition room. Even falling into a meat grinder would be better …

There was a squeak in the small door near where she slumped. Like a vanishing sheet of smoke, it slid upward into the door interior. A wizened hand quickly thrust a small packet through it to flop onto the floor.

Instinctively, Sylvia knew what it was. Food wrapped in some sort of transparent sack. Like a tropical tigercat, she ripped the bindings apart. With her fingers, she stuffed a gooey paste into her mouth. It was not only tasty but moist. Her feeling of thirst faded.

She twisted some of the wrappings between her fingers and brought them to her nose. They smelled of sweetness and spice. Without thinking any further, she wadded them up and wolfed them down.

Sylvia took a half-dozen deep breaths. She felt a little better now. Not much, but at least a little. Her thoughts wandered. Mason. Where was he? How did he fare? Was he feeling as helpless as she?

She remembered their first meeting. The ruffians crashing into Rangoth's hut, intent on murder. How she had helped, swinging a frying pan as if it were a lethal weapon. And later, when her skin started to blister as the flames around her grew higher. He had done more than merely return the favor. Together, they had survived, one helping the other.

Sylvia looked around her sparse confinement. Oppressive? Yes, but surely not as bad as what she had already endured. However small any chance remained, then, somehow, she had to take it. Her brow knitted as she tried to focus. A chance. What could that be?

SYLVIA WAITED for what her body told her was approximately another day back home. She pressed her back against the door, ready to pounce.

Again, she heard the warning squeak and saw the little door rise. The matron inserted her arm with the food packet, and Sylvia seized it. As if she were sizing kindling, she grabbed it with both hands and broke the small, slender bone.

The matron cried and tried to withdraw, but Sylvia did not let go. "Open the door and let me out."

The little gnome did not respond, so Sylvia gave the limb a savage twist. She grimaced at what she was doing, what she had become.

There was an immediate click, and the door unlatched. Still holding the matron's arm, Sylvia scooted the door open. She pushed her would-be captor ahead of her on the smooth floor. Then moving rapidly, she extended her other arm around the door frame and grabbed the other woman's neck with her free hand.

"These controls," she said. "How do I use them?"

The matron whimpered and passed out. Sylvia removed the handheld and the translator from the gnome's belt and inspected them. Along one side of the handheld was a series of visual touchpads, their meanings clear enough to interpret. She selected the one that unlocked all the doors simultaneously. There was an immediate reaction.

Humanoids of every size and description exited their cells. Some had heads on stalks, others short and protected with shells like a turtle. Still more with impossibly thin limbs like huge praying matisses flailing the air. Like stampeding prey escaping a carnivore, they thundered away down the hall in a chaotic mass. Only one unopened door remained. Sylvia pushed the matron into her own cell and locked it. She walked closer to the last door and squinted at the eye slit. Whatever was inside returned the stare, but did not push open the door. She felt a sudden queasiness.

Later, Sylvia tore her attention away, something to investigate later. Her task now was to find Mason and the others. This last prisoner would have to fend for itself.

SYLVIA HURRIED down one empty corridor after another. They all looked alike, and worse, were empty. Maybe the gnomes were in the competition room having another contest. The one Mush had called, what was it, a 'launch.' If so, that is where her shipmates could also be. She was still weak from her imprisonment. She did not know what she would do when she got there, but she hurried her pace as much as she could.

Sylvia began to flag. One meal in what must have been several days was not enough — even for a hero from the sagas. Think twice and then act once, she told herself. She studied the handheld again, this time more closely.

A few of the buttons had symbols that were almost worn away. Others looked pristine — ones that the matron had no real use for. Yes, she thought excitedly, buttons for getting directions.

Shortly thereafter, Sylvia stood in front of a familiar-looking doorway. She pushed it open quietly. The scene was much the same as before. Two seating areas on either side of the large central aisle, every one filled with gnomes. Colored robes on one side, black ones on the opposite. She scanned the balconies but was disappointed. They were empty. No sign of Mason or the others.

The center looked different as well. No longer was it

occupied by a mélange of small machinery. Instead only a single empty dais stood there. Sylvia scanned the walls. Multiple scenes were displayed. Several showed different side views of two massive cylinders aligned vertically. The one on top was a short, featureless disk, its diameter five times the height of a gnome. The bottom one, long and imposing. A cluster of deep, empty bowls attached to its rear, opening downward. Hundreds of smaller cones protruded from its sides. The two were connected by a complex of springs, clamps, and tubes.

Another display aimed upwards from the smaller cylinder of the two, the disk. The two were in a snug tube that seemed to carry on forever. At the other end was a scattering of pin-point lights. Thick bands of what looked like giant rings of copper spaced to the top.

Sylvia checked the symbolic displays. On all of them, the left-most symbol in the row changed at a heartbeat frequency. When the first one Sylvia noticed repeated, the one next to it advanced once. Counters, she realized. All the displays were counting either up or down to something.

No one looked her way. Every eye on the floor studied either one of the displays or focused on the images of the cylinders.

Sylvia heard a scraping noise behind her. She whirled and was startled by what she saw. It was another human, what else could it be? Long hair, wide hips, and a chest curve beneath a robe dotted with the all-seeing eyes. One foot dragged behind the other. Her face was deeply lined, her eyes tired, as if she no longer wanted to see the evils of the world.

Instinctively, Sylvia threw her arm across her eyes to shield them. A sorceress. What was she doing here?

"I am Hel," the woman said. "The one Dargonel wants as a mate."

# 15

# The Liturgy

SYLVIA'S JAW dropped. "How did you get here?" she whispered.

"In one of the boxes Dargonel packed into his cylinder." Hel shook her head. "No, it was not sorcery. He drugged me instead."

"Keep your voice down." Sylvia raised hers slightly. "Bask insisted he knew nothing of any other recent visitors but us."

"*Us*? More than only yourself? Good. There is hope."

"If Dargonel is here, why did Bask deny it?"

"Use your brain, woman." Hel swished her robe. "See the logos? He is a sorcerer, after all."

"But the gnomes here are so advanced. Surely, one from our orb, no matter how skilled, could not — "

"The more advanced people are, the easier it is to enchant them. They reek an air of false superiority. 'No way your magic could be better than mine,' they think. But they are wrong."

"How did you end up in a cell?" Sylvia's thoughts raced on. "What happened to your leg?"

"I woke up there. Clearly, Dargonel did not want me walking around, telling everyone what he was up to." Hel looked down at her hem. "Born with it. The reason I was attracted to sorcery in the first place. A way to get into the minds of others, the unkind ones, and make them pay."

"But you also can perform spells, right?" Sylvia asked.

Hel shook her head. "One must be strong, and I am weak." The sorceress pointed at the chamber floor. "What's going on there, anyway?"

"I don't know," Sylvia said. She scanned about. There was nothing to duck behind. What was the phrase back home — sitting geese? All it would take was a single glance their way, and she and Hel would be detected.

But everyone in the chamber was intent on what was happening on the screens. All the gnomes were here except perhaps for a matron or two. The humanoids might wander around in the corridors without any notice for a while. If she and Hel kept quiet enough, the two of them might learn something that could help.

After a few more moments, a gnome, more bowed and stooped than any other Sylvia had seen, walked onto the central aisle from another entrance somewhere. His robe was neither black nor colored, but grey. He arched both arms skyward and prepared to speak into a small device dangling down from the roof.

"It is time for the blessing of the singularity," the gnome intoned. It sounded solemn through the translator Sylvia clutched. "Everyone, take control of your attention. Focus. Gird yourself to speak joyfully what you must say. We must reaffirm we are grateful."

"We are grateful," the assembled gnomes shouted back as one. "Grateful to the singularity. The one that provides the bounty of energy from the ergosphere for our needs."

"Even though we are far away?" the leader asked.

"Even though," the rest of the gnomes answered. "Even though we are far away from the ergosphere. Far away even from the globe of no return. Far away even from the accretion disk."

"Ergosphere? What's that?" Hel whispered.

"I don't know, really," Sylvia answered back quietly. "A region closer to a black pit than here."

"Closer!" Hel spoke louder, then clamped her hand over her mouth.

Sylvia scanned the audience, holding her breath, but no one appeared to have noticed.

"That's it," Hel continued more softly. "The cylinders must be some kind of ship that can travel through space. Like Dargonel's but bigger. That's where he must be now. How he plans to get even closer to his goal. So that Isaac's ritual will be more effective."

"May this bounty never cease," the leader shouted.

"May this bounty never cease," echoed off the stone walls.

Sylvia grimaced. Like being at a circus, it was hard to keep track of everything going on. She studied one of the counters on the wall. The one on the far left still clicked rapidly, about once every heartbeat. The one next to it updated after every ten. She studied for a moment and deduced what the symbol for zero must be. Most of the ones on the right showed zero as well. Only two in the middle indicated something else.

She gasped. Ten multiplied by ten two times was only a thousand. A thousand heartbeats in all. There was little time left to stop the madman.

"Let us recite both parables in unison," the grey-robed leader said. "All of us, colored and black together."

"Yes, we recite the parables. The fallacy of witnessing all the eternal fall. The bounty of the ergosphere."

"First is the eternal fall," the leader said.

"The eternal fall. Yes, the eternal fall is misunderstood by many."

Sylvia punched buttons on the handheld. "I see the

competition chamber." She punched a few more. "Yes, one of the countdowns on the wall. Perfect." She experimented some more. "This looks like a list of sources and sounds for the device. Maybe if I click on … Yes, I think I have connected. We can see *and* hear what is happening while we get to the cylinders before they are launched.

# 16
# Searching

SYLVIA AND Hel crept out of the competition chamber. The ceremony inside droned on.

"What do *we* witness if someone gets closer and closer to the singularity?" the leader asked.

"We witness that, for the traveler, time seems to pass more slowly." The audience responded.

"Is this slowness constant, like that of a faulty chronometer?"

"*No.* As the traveler falls, the difference in rate between us and him grows greater and greater."

"When will the fall end? For us, how long will it take?"

"For us, forever. The traveler reaches the horizon of events at the very end of time as we know it."

Sylvia punched buttons on the handheld. It flashed views of other parts of the underground complex one after another. She was getting more proficient by the moment. One of the images presented was a schematic of the spaceship. It appeared there was a side entrance to the lower cylinder near its top. Perhaps a pilot cabin. That is where Dargonel was most likely to be. She and Hel would have to climb six flights of stairs to get to it. There would be little time to explore anything else first.

The pair reached the nearest stairwell, and Sylvia started

to climb. The dearth of food made her feel lightheaded, but she willed herself on. After one flight, she did not hear Hel to be immediately behind her. Looking down the stairs, she saw the sorceress' face contorted in pain as she negotiated each step.

"Sorry, I forgot," Sylvia said. She glanced at the competition chamber image on the handheld. "There is still enough time. When you get to this level, let's put our arms around each other and go forward together."

"What does that mean?" the voice of the leader came through the translator. "Our skies to become increasingly cluttered forever with images of foolish explorers?"

"*No*, that is the fallacy. Even light itself is in the grasp of the singularity. Just as with clocks, the frequency of vibration slows."

"And that means what?"

"The color of all light changes. From violets to blues, then yellows and reds. Finally, to frequencies we cannot see with our eyes. Long before they cease to be, all travelers toward the singularity fade from view …"

Hel reached the landing, sucking in gulps of air. Sylvia tried to hide her concern with a small smile, but she was conflicted. Traveling together, they might not reach Dargonel before the space ship lifted off. But certainly, two challengers of the sorcerer were better than one.

Almost immediately, she decided. She put her arm around Hel. No time for contemplation. Together they puffed up the stairs.

SYLVIA HAD not looked at the counter during the entire climb. But when they reached their target level, she could no longer resist. Only about 500 heartbeats left. Three-quarters of the time before departure was gone.

The pair exited the stairwell. They both panted. "Wouldn't a culture this advanced have something better for changing levels than stairs?" Hel asked. "A little room or something that moves between floors with a push of a button like on the handhold."

"I don't know," Sylvia shot back, irritated. "Focus." She eyed Hel critically. Were all sorcerers like Dargonel — at least slightly insane?

"A handheld!" One of the escaped prisoners yelled from down the hallway. "See her? That one. She has the gizmo that opens doors. Grab it so we can get to the portal and out of here."

A group of four sprinted towards the pair. All humanoid in shape, but each had differences. Sylvia grasped the handheld to her chest and scanned about. The doorway leading to the ship cabin was around here somewhere. If she and Hel could get to it soon enough …

Too late. The four acted as one, plowing the two women to the ground. One was tall and covered with barbed fur everywhere. It grabbed the handheld and strained to tear it away. Two other shorter ones climbed on Sylvia's legs, holding her down. The fourth wedged between her and Hel, keeping them apart.

Sylvia strained as hard as she could, but did not have the strength. Slowly, painfully, her fingers were pried off, one by one. She had to let go. The handheld crashed to the ground. Barbed-fur grunted and stood.

He reached into the tangle of arms and legs and grabbed for the device. One of the short ones kicked it out of his reach. It spun across the floor like an elongated puck. Sylvia staggered to her knees and smothered it under her torso. Barbed-fur growled in frustration and kicked Sylvia in the side.

"Klaatu, berada, nicto. Klaatu, berada, nicto. Klaatu, berada, nicto."

Sylvia blinked. Hel was speaking. The handheld on the ground — was it broken?

The four assailants froze in their tracks.

"Emergency sorcery." Hel shrugged. "We don't like using it much except in emergencies — such as when under physical attack. But like any charm, it follows the law. 'Thrice spoken, once fulfilled.'"

Sylvia shook the handheld and heard no rattle. It still functioned. She looked at the counter being displayed and slumped. Now, at most only a couple of hundred heartbeats remained.

# 17
# Final Countdown

SYLVIA OPENED the door in front of her. "Down one more hallway, and we will be there."

"Go on without me." Hel panted. "Even with your help, I can't keep up."

"No, I need you." Sylvia shook her head. She crouched down. "Here, climb up. I will carry you piggy-back."

"You said we had only minutes more. I will slow you down."

"Climb on, damn it, or I will drag you by your hair."

AT THE far end of the hallway, Sylvia released the sorceress. She collapsed to sitting, breathing deeply. She studied the door in front of her. It was different from all the others she had seen. It was made of metal, curved at left and right to fit snugly into the side of a vertical cylinder that disappeared into both the floor and ceiling. Near the top of the door was a small window honeycombed with wire-reinforcing glass.

"We have reached the spaceship," Sylvia gasped.

She struggled to stand and peered through the window. Her eyes widened. She recognized who were inside, Isaac and Dargonel! She had found them. Isaac looked very much the same as when she had seen him last. Dargonel looked changed. Loose skin sunk from heavy jowls. Most of his white hair was gone. He was an old man.

In front of the pair, two golems sat in front of a bank of switches and displays. The wall in front of the nearer one was colored; the one on the other was black. An identical door, also black, was directly across. Both mechanical men were busy sliding levers and adjusting knobs.

The sorcerer and magician were in an animated conversation. They ignored the console of flashing lights and activity in front of them. Dargonel watched Isaac flail his arms. With effort, he managed to shake his head with a smug look on his face.

It took Sylvia a few moments, but she was able to channel the translator to get its feed from inside the ship. The first thing she heard was more of the litany from the competition chamber. It was piped into the cockpit, too.

"The bounty of the ergosphere," the leader intoned through the translator. "What does the singularity in its wisdom give us?"

"*Energy*," was the immediate response. "The singularity shares with us a portion of itself. Energy so that, even in this cold, cold cavern, we continue to survive."

"How is this done?"

"We make an offering to the singularity."

"And how is *that* done?"

"The smaller of our two ships is the offering."

"How so?"

"It is blasted from the larger toward the horizon of events. It is consumed. But, by the grace of the singularity, our larger vessel returns. Comes back with more energy than when it accelerated away from us."

Isaac began shouting over the chanting in the background. His body shook. "This one time only, Master. After that, we stop."

"I can make you perform your rituals while enchanted," Dargonel growled back. "Not all of my lifeforce has vanished yet. Is that what you want?"

"It is the transits through the demon realm. I do not like repeating them over and over. I do not like that at all."

"Haven't you been paying attention?" Dargonel snapped. "These gnomes have portals everywhere. We use them to travel precisely from one spot to the next."

The voice of the litany leader sounded again. "And so, the larger ship returns with our bounty?"

"Ah, but not immediately," the audiences responded.

"Why not?" the leader asked.

"It is because of the dilation of time. The ship we launch in moments will not return for thousands of our cycles around our sun."

"But we rejoice, do we not?"

"We rejoice. Soon, the ship we sent forward many sun cycles before will again be close."

Sylvia had heard enough. She didn't know what she should do next, but she had to do something. She yanked on the door latch. With a hiss, it opened a crack. An alarm immediately went off. Both Dargonel and Isaac turned to look.

The door at the other end of the corridor sprang open as well. A dozen golems wheeled into view. Sylvia pulled on the heavy door in front, but it was too heavy for her to move by herself.

"Help me, Hel," she cried. "Help me get inside. Maybe you can stand off Dargonel while I tackle Isaac."

The sorceress wobbled to her feet, but it was too late. The golems whooshed down the corridor and scooped up the two women. Kicking and scratching did nothing to stop the process. In an instant, they were beyond the other door and it,

295

too, was sealed shut.

The lights dimmed, and the entire complex shuddered slightly downward. The ship carrying Dargonel and Isaac to the ergosphere had been launched. No one had been able to stop it.

# 18

# A Matter of Gravity

AS SOON as the ship had departed, the golems dropped Sylvia and Hel back onto the floor. Then they scurried away and disappeared. Sylvia raced back to the door they had just passed through, but it would not open. Not locked perhaps, but with the ship gone, the air pressure on the other side must have dropped to zero.

Maybe if she got around to where the walls were not colored but black, their party could reunite and then ...

Hel stirred, but did not stand. "It is strange that he left after all."

"What do you mean?"

"You heard the chanting. Time will pass more slowly on the ship than it does for us."

"I can't make any sense of anything like that." Sylvia shook her head as if trying to dispel an ache. "Does it matter?"

"Dargonel is doing this only to get back at me because I spurned him. To make me regret my actions."

"Well, according to what the liturgy said, Dargonel won't return until — "

"What? What are you thinking?"

"We did not actually see him and Isaac depart." Sylvia rubbed her chin. "Maybe they did not. The security golems grabbed us right before then. Suppose that at the last moment, they abandoned the craft through the cabin door opposite the one I looked through."

Sylvia discovered the handheld lying nearby on the floor. It had fallen from her hand during the struggle with the golems. "They must have been programmed only for security during the launch. Didn't care about anything else."

"Then all of Dargonel's journey is for naught." Hel stood and wobbled while trying to balance on her good leg. "From the little I know of his scheme, the black pit is still too far away from here. The magician's ritual would not have any effect."

Sylvia started pacing. "Yes, yes. Too far away. Not enough strength in the magic. I do not fully understand that either." She closed her eyes, trying to pull out what her mind was trying to tell her.

"I remember seeing Isaac's ritual at the compound near Ytterby," she said at last. "It was fairly simple. He performed it himself without needing any assistance. Even a golem could —"

The golems! Sylvia felt a rush of excitement. "Isaac is no longer essential to Dargonel's plans. He could program golems to go through the steps. Yes! I see a method in his madness now."

"What? What do you understand?"

"Suppose that rather than one golem, Dargonel uses a hundred. Or maybe even a thousand, all synchronized and acting together. I am no magician, but wouldn't the effect be a hundred or a thousand times stronger? And once the ritual completed, start it again. The golems can perform it untiringly over and over."

"Golems can't do magic!"

"No, of course not. But they are no different than any other piece of equipment a magician uses when he performs a ritual. All that matters is that s step be done, not how it is implemented."

"Then you have hit upon it," Hel agreed. "Dargonel can increase the strength of gravity from right here! He would not have to travel any closer to the dark pit. Not get involved with the strange workings of time."

"We have lost after all!" For a moment, Sylvia's heart plunged.

Then, just as suddenly, she remembered. "Wait! There is a limit. At some point, Dargonel will have to stop what he is doing."

"Why so?"

"Before our pursuit, Albert explained that increasing the strength of gravity also means that the distance of closest safe approach expands as well. There is a limit to how near one can get safely."

"So?" Hel shook her head. She frowned with frustration.

"Picture it," Sylvia said. "The golems repeat the ritual over and over until this very orb is at the-what did Albert call it — the innermost stable radius. The strength of the dark pit could not be increased any more, or we all would be trapped, Dargonel included."

"So," Hel stood as tall as she could. She rebutted like a lawyer arguing before a high court. "Dargonel stops just before that happens. He then transports all the golems through a portal and repeats the process somewhere else. Sure, this idea was not part of his original plan. But once he learned what was happening here, he seized upon it. Yes, that is what he will do. I know the man."

"Ouch!" Hel suddenly stumbled to the ground.

"What happened? Are you okay?"

"I don't know. My leg doesn't feel quite right. Like it has grown heavier."

Sylvia swung one of her arms out in a testing arc. Was Hel correct? Was she imagining things herself? Did her limb seem to be weighing more?

Albert, she thought. He was a magician. Maybe he would know what to do. Her thumb and fingers flew over the handheld for several minutes, but she found nothing that indicated where Albert might be.

She sighed. Probably in a room that had slates and chalk, completely absorbed by a calculation. Mason and the rest, then. They would likely be in cells on the other side of the color-divide, positioned in a symmetric spot to where she had been imprisoned. Yes, that is what to do. Find where Mason and the rest were held.

But as she pondered, she felt herself growing heavier, moment by moment. Taking a single step became no longer second nature. How much time did she have?

"Hel, let me help you up," Sylvia said. "We have even farther to go."

"No." The sorceress shook her head. "I slowed you down too much already. Go on. I will follow as best I can."

Sylvia hesitated for a single heartbeat, but no more. She keyed new directions into the handheld and plunged down the corridor.

# 19
# Confrontation

MASON FELT a rumble, a deep vibration that shook the walls of his cell and woke him from a stupor. He looked anxiously about, expecting to see cracks and fissures, but there were none. Then as abruptly as it had begun, the grumble stopped. Silence returned.

It was the almost total absence of any noise that had gotten to him the most. Except for the slide of metal on metal at the bottom of the door, there was nothing to measure the passage of time. How long had he been here? How much longer would he have to stay? What was happening to Sylvia? What could he possibly do to save her? He had to come up with a rescue plan, but there was nothing in his thoughts that he could build upon.

Suddenly, he heard his cell door click. How long that was after the rumble he had no way of estimating, but it seemed more than a short while. He tried to spring up from his curled stupor and found that he could not. His limbs felt heavy and unresponsive. Too little food, he reasoned. He was slowly starving to death.

Steadying himself with one arm on the wall, he kicked his door open. He stumbled out into the hallway and blinked in surprise. Rangoth was there, a fist-full of his robe clutched in one hand by … Isaac!

Isaac! Was he hallucinating? It couldn't be. He glanced at Rangoth and saw the astonished expression on the wizard's face as well. The magician left with Dargonel on his cylinder. Mason was sure of it. He had seen the ship lift off the ground by the titanic djinn and then vanish into a hole in the sky. How did Isaac get here?

Mason pulled on Algeran's door, and it was unlocked, too. He flung it wide and peered in. The navigator huddled in a corner with his thumb in his mouth. Behind Mason, other humanoids relished their freedom and scampered away.

"Wizard, I recognize you from Yterrby." Isaac waved a handheld in his free hand back and forth spasmodically. "A stroke of luck to be sure. I unlocked these doors to find any help I could. Never mind. I don't care how you got here. What is important is whether Albert is present, too. Did he travel here with you?"

"He did come with us," Rangoth said. "But where he is now, I don't know."

"I don't want to have any part of this anymore," Isaac rushed on. "At first was the intellectual challenge to see if I could do it. But now, no more. Dargonel is deranged, utterly deranged. I am sure of it.

"He forced me out of the gnome's spaceship moments before it took off. Something he heard in the litany disturbed him. He, he enchanted me. I guess that is what happened. Forced me into some sort of exoskeleton to perform my ritual. Have it recorded somehow. Afterwards, he started hundreds of golems duplicating it."

"But you're not enchanted now, are you?"

"No, no. It wore off quickly," Isaac answered. "I think Dargonel might be getting weaker, but that does not matter. Gravity is getting stronger. Can't you feel it? Where is Albert? Maybe he can make the sorcerer stop. If he does not, the radius of the last stable orbit will keep expanding. Albert had tried to explain such a thing to me in one of our intellectual battles, but I had refused to listen. I am unsure what he portends will happen, but the risk is too great."

Mason sucked in a deep breath. He remembered some of what Albert had sketched in the hut. If the strength of gravity increased, then so also would the demarking radius inside of which one would ever return. What happened to this orb of gnomes after it was consumed might take who knew how long? But no matter what, no one would get back out alive.

"Where is Dargonel?" Mason asked. "How do we stop what the sorcerer has started?"

"He has connected a handheld to a master power switch," Isaac answered. "One button click and the golems stop performing the ritual. But the problem is not *how* but *when*."

"What do you mean?"

"I told Dargonel as much as I understood about Albert's theories. I think I convinced him, but I am not sure. He wants me to compute exactly *when* he should halt the golems. The last possible moment before we cross the boundary into the accretion belt. I tried to reason with him. Explain that my knowledge is only qualitative. That I don't even know what the formulas for the radii are. Albert is the one who does. I have no — where is Albert?"

"Ah, there you are." Dargonel's voice cut through Isaac's chatter. He shuffled forward slowly from a doorway on the left, neighter foot clearing the floor. His shoulders stooped and his brow shown with droplets of sweat

Isaac placed his arms over his face and cringed. "This place is vast. How, how did you find me?"

"I am a sorcerer, remember?"

"But I do not feel sluggish," Isaac said. "I am able to think freely."

"Of course, you do, dolt," Dargonel snapped. "Your brain is worth little to me if it is not functioning at a high level. I merely left a tiny afterthought in your head as part of your

303

first enchantment, one you are unconscious of. You can think of it as a beacon. One that I can detect."

The sorcerer waved his handheld in front of the magician's face. "Now, tell me exactly when I am to press the button."

Mason shuffled to the side as unobtrusively as he could. He glanced in Rangoth's direction, trying to catch the wizard's attention. Moving slowly, he grasped the hilt of his sword.

"I, I cannot, Master," Isaac said. "My formula does not speak of black pits at all. Albert has convinced me that mine is only an approximation."

"Who is this Albert?"

"You met him once back at the compound near Ytterby."

Dargonel grunted. "I remember now. Little man. Shock of unruly hair. Always muttering about symbols and such."

"The very one." Isaac pointed at Rangoth. "The wizard here says that he is somewhere among the gnomes."

Mason knew that this was his moment. He started to pull his sword from its sheath and frowned. He was surprised he could not whip it out, at how heavy it felt.

Dargonel smiled at him with dismissal. "Klaatu, berada, nicto," he intoned.

The words bore into Mason's brain. He felt himself begin to freeze. No, that was not quite right. There was nothing cold about what was happening. It was more as if he was being dipped into a pool of cooling lava, not so hot as to burn, but warm enough to congeal.

Dargonel repeated the words twice more, and the chant was complete. Mason could not move. His eyes seemed cemented in place. Even his eyelids no longer blinked. He saw that Rangoth and Isaac were frozen as well.

"Now, wizard," Dargonel said. "I will release you ever so slightly. Enough so that your mouth and tongue can move.

Tell me where is the one named Albert hiding?"

"I, I do not know." Rangoth struggled to speak. "Somewhere on the other side. Among the colored gnomes, not the black."

Dargonel sagged to one knee. "I will handle the three of you later. First, I will find out where this Albert is hiding."

The sorcerer removed a knife from his waist and managed to wave it in the air. "My sorcery is quite effective. But it is even more so when I add sharp slashes as part of convincing someone to act as I deem fit."

Mason strained against the mental constraint that bound him. He tried to pull his sword the rest of the way out of the sheath, but he could not. He felt his flesh sag around his bones. Even if free, he was not sure if he could maneuver. It was clear that Dargonel now focused on the other half of the gnomes' dwellings, the side where Sylvia must be.

All Mason had left was hope. She would have to be the one who would stop what was happening.

SYLVIA CAUGHT her breath. Now, there was absolutely no doubt about it. Each step was a challenge. Every single one a struggle. It was as if Hel were still on her back. She placed a hand along a wall to steady herself and continued forward.

There was a path connecting the two sides of the gnomes' dwelling. It detoured around the competition chamber. She took it, not reflecting on her good fortune that it existed. She had to get help without interference of the gnomes and soon.

Two dozen more steps and the effort became even harder. Her handheld slipped and clattered to the floor. Steadying herself with one hand on the wall, she stooped and wrapped her other around the device. But her leg muscles quivered from the effort when she tried to return to standing. She was unable to do so. She sighed as she collapsed to the floor.

Sylvia tried to get up twice more, but each effort was less successful than the one before. Finally, she pulled the hem of her dress as high as she could. On hands and knees, she continued crawling forward.

The colored walls changed to black. She peered into the increased dimness. There was someone else in the corridor creeping toward her. Two sounds marked the progress, each of ringing metal. Sylvia waited, gathering her strength. After what seemed like an eon, she was able to tell who approached. It was Dargonel pushing a handheld with one hand along the and sliding a knife with the other.

# 20
# An Outstretched Hand

SYLVIA TENSED. Even being on hands and knees was tiring. Her skin protested with itching aches wherever they had scraped against the floor.

Dargonel crawled up to face her. He panted from the effort. For a moment, she was back in Vendora's ballroom participating in the entertainment. She saw the same skin pulled tight over his skull, white hair standing on end. Only the eyes looked different. They were deeper, more sinister, but not quite well focused as she had remembered. They darted from side to side like those of a frog looking for an insect to snare.

"Where is Albert, the magician?" Dargonel demanded. "I must find him and quickly." He waved the handheld he had slid along the floor. "He is to tell me the precise time to click this button to stop the rituals and the growing strength of gravity."

"I, I do not know," Sylvia stammered.

"Liar!" Dargonel shouted. "Your expression gives you away. You are like the others. Trying to deceive me. To stop me from what I am destined to do."

Stop the rituals, Sylvia thought. Yes, her surmise had been right. Stop all the replications. As soon as possible. Otherwise, the force of gravity would keep increasing. After some point, no one would be able to prevent what would happen.

"Press the button now, Dargonel, before it is too late. Don't you realize the peril that all of us are in?"

Sylvia's thoughts raced. She shook her head, trying to rid herself of extraneous thought. She would not reach Mason and the others in time. That was clear now. It was up to her and only her to stop this madman.

She lowered herself to her elbows and leaned against the wall. The tendons in her arm shrieked with pain as her weight transferred to her left side. Clamping her mouth shut so she would not cry out, she reached her other arm slowly down the side of her leg. The dagger in its sheath was only inches out of reach.

"Stop that!" Dargonel commanded. "I am a master sorcerer, not an idiot. I see what you are doing. Klaatu — "

Sylvia recognized the words. She slammed shut her eyes and drew her free arm up to cover her right ear. The other she pressed against the wall, hoping the sound would be deadened enough.

"Very well then." Dargonel understood what Sylvia was doing. He seethed. "You will wish dearly you had not done that — for every *remaining* moment of your life."

He wiggled his knife. "See this blade? You will get to know it well."

Sylvia stared at the blade. Dargonel had stopped speaking. Cautiously, she uncovered her ears.

"It is one thing to dissolve into a lilting charm," Dargonel continued. "It is what we sorcerers do for those who possess gold like a queen. But not all charms lull one into pleasant dreams. Others intensify, increase senses to agonizing heights."

Dargonel stared into Sylvia's eyes. "Yes, I shall enchant you. Have each twist of the knife I will thrust into your gut be amplified a hundredfold with each jerk I make."

The sorcerer started speaking the words Sylvia knew would seal her doom. A growing relentlessness began pouring into her head. She knew that she could not manage to seal her ears again. A voice confining her, twisting her thoughts where she did not want them to go. It felt like losing the battle for domination with a powerful demon …

No, that was not quite right. This was different than engaging with a being from another realm to see who had the stronger will. And not every encounter was a fight. Her interaction with the tracking imp queen had not been like that at all. She had found common ground on which a friendship was built.

So, where did that lead her? A battle with a sorcerer is not the same as a struggle with a demon. How did the old adage go — know your enemy? There was a clue here, but what was it?

A sorcerer's exterior was cold and hard as iron, she reasoned. It had to be. Everyone shunned them, avoided them as much as they could.

From an early age when he showed the first proficiency in the craft, Dargonel must have been ostracized. Reduced to begging for meals and coppers from those brave enough to experience his mental paintings.

Dargonel's drone halted for a moment. Instinctively, Sylvia somehow understood that the first time through his charm had been completed. The second and third recitals would be more difficult for him to finish.

Feeling alone and isolated, she continued cranking through her reasoning. Okay, shunned by everyone. Such was a sorcerer's lot. What weakness does that understanding reveal?

That a futile resistance to Dargonel's charm was not the thing to try. Instead, focus on her antagonist, on what she could learn of him as his words buffeted her soul.

Yes, that was it! The thought suddenly shouted in her head. What was it that someone who was a sorcerer would desire more than anything else? But so risky. If she were wrong, then it definitely would be all over for her. Sylvia hesitated.

The second recital of the charm concluded. Only one more remained. The aches in Sylvia's limbs from the pull of gravity intensified — grew far more than dull pains. Her skin chafed from the weight of her dress. The air felt wetter and more humid than she had noticed before. Through it all, she saw Dargonel creep closer, scraping his knife along the ground, practicing how he would twist it once it was in her gut.

The third recital began. Could she bring herself to do this? Did it have any chance of working? What were the consequences if it did? Sylvia breathed as deeply as she could. She had no other choice.

The words formed in her head. She had to spit them out slowly, one at a time.

"Dargonel," she said, "I want to be your *friend*."

The sorcerer hesitated. He exhaled, startled, as if he had received a blow. There was no turning back. Dargonel was in her head. She had to convince him of her resolve.

"I understand," she rushed on. "I really do. It must have been horrible for all your life. Shunned since you were a child. No partners, no pals going to the tavern for a late-night ale."

Dargonel stopped chanting. "Hel," he said softly. "I thought that with her I had a chance. She also practiced the craft. If anyone could comprehend my loneliness, she would be the one."

The sorcerer looked at Sylvia with a crooked grin and shrugged. "*You* could serve as well."

The pressure on Sylvia's thoughts began to dissolve. For the briefest instance, she wondered what she had done.

"Hel, Hel, Hel," Dargonel repeated and craned his head upward. "You have come. After everything that has happened, you have come."

Sylvia turned her head to the side and blinked. It was the sorceress! And she was standing! How could that be? She felt a tug on her leg and glanced to her side. Hel had lifted her dagger from the sheath.

Dargonel's eyes widened. He let go of the knife and grabbed Hel's hand, straining against her thrust. Sylvia decided what she must do.

"Dargonel, let a friend help you," she said.

The sorcerer glanced at Sylvia and hesitated a second time. In a flash, she strained against the relentless pull and raised both her hands to clasp around Hel's. Together, they plunged the blade into Dargonel's heart.

# 21
# Wrapping Up

SYLVIA LOOKED at Dargonel's crumpled body sprawled in front of her. She managed to press the button that stopped the golems from repeating Isaac's ritual, then turned her attention to Hel, who had collapsed beside her.

"How did you manage to follow me?" Sylvia began.

"I self-enchanted myself," Hel answered. "Something to completely block the pain. A moment, please."

Hel started a chant that Sylvia could not follow. It had no effect on her at all. In a moment, the sorceress had completed it. But before Sylvia could speak again …

"I feel it everywhere," Hel shrieked. "On all my limbs. I pushed too hard, too fast. I feel what has happened. Tendons have been ripped from my bones. The gravity is too strong. Oh, the pain, the pain. I must enchant myself agai —"

The sorcerer spoke no more. She slumped to the floor. Sylvia slid an arm towards her, fearing the worst. There was no reaction. Hel was gone.

IT TOOK some while for Sylvia to compose herself, but somehow she managed to do so. Slowly, with many rests, she slid herself along the corridor from which Dargonel had come. The fact that she would find out the fate of Mason and the others kept her going. She lost track of time but repeated to herself over and over that it did not matter as long as he had survived.

Eventually, she reached the corridor that looked familiar, one with prison cells like the one in which she had been confined. Her heart leaped with what she saw. Mason was there, alive! And so was Isaac, Rangoth, and Algeran.

"We have to reverse what has happened," she cried out. "Doesn't every magical spell have a reversal?"

Isaac answered. "Indeed, there usually is. Finding one that we can perform with the limitations we are under is a challenge. None of us can stand. But I almost have the derivation completed. Less than an hour more."

Mason crawled to Sylvia. They both extended their outstretched hands until they touched.

THE HOUR promised by Isaac stretched to several more but eventually, he figured out what to do. With everyone taking a role in performing the ritual, the strength of gravity was restored to what it had been before. Everyone stood and stretched. No one applauded or slapped one another on their back. The next task was to get out of this place and return home as quickly as they could.

The gnomes were only too happy to help. None of them spoke about the relative merits of either of the two factions. All were eager to send their visitors away as soon as they could. The members of both crews were located and assembled, Dargonel's and the one that pursued him. One by one, they plunged into the portal that took them back to the realm of the primitives.

"WE WISH to leave in peace," Sylvia held out her upraised palm to stop the Wabangi warriors who assembled upon their arrival.

The natives halted a respectable distance away and talked among themselves with no translator turned on. After what seemed like hours, Wakona approached and said, "It has been decided. Take your strange devices and go. You disrupt our way of life too much."

"One of our cylinders is damaged," Sylvia explained. "It will no longer stand the strains of a departure." She looked over her shoulder at the doubled group of travelers. How were they all going to fit? "The one that we leave is made of metal. It melts more easily than the iron you use to fashion your cauldrons. A resource. Surely, you can find uses for that."

Another conference took most of a day, but eventually the Wabangis reached a consensus. With spears lowered, they led the travelers to Dargonel's cylinder, and everyone squeezed on board. Even with two boarders tucked into the accommodations originally meant for one, several of Dargonel's original crew had to be left to lie outside in the central corridor when the blast that would thrust them back into the realm of demons came.

The titanic djinns were found a short distance away, sleeping with thumbs in their mouths, oblivious to the world. Rangoth and Dargonel's wizard roused both and prepared them for what they were to do. The natives were warned to stay far away when all the preparations had been finished. Finally, with an explosion that Sylvia was sure to find its place in the Wabangi legends, the ship was hurled back into the realm of demons.

WITH TWO titanic djinns providing the propulsion, the speed in the realm of demons was twice as swift as it had been before. Algeran kept busy with his sightings, guiding the ship back to near where it had originally entered the realm.

"We should stop for a moment when we near the palace of Elezar, the prince," Rangoth advised. "Despite the fact that he has powerful djinns under his control, we must advise him that journeys like ours will no longer occur."

"How can we guarantee that?" Sylvia asked.

"We can't." Rangoth shrugged. "With the advances of the new magic, who knows what will be discovered next."

"In our own realm, no one will believe what we will tell."

"They will, Sylvia. They will. Tracking imps and nosetweakers will blabber and embellish the tale whenever they are summoned by wizards. Word will get around."

THE OLEANDER fire tended by some of Dargonel's minions still burned. Through the connection between the realms, Rangoth instructed another explosion that enabled the crowded ship to pass back into the human realm. A final blast enabled the two titanic djinns to return home.

The travel from there back to Ytterby was a slow one. Rangoth had been right. Some wag with a way with words, probably an up and coming sorcerer, coined the word 'demonaut.' Beside the clarence with 'Lady Sylvia' as its trim, three more carriages stood in line to carry everyone else back to Ytterby.

At the edge of the city, the procession was waved to a stop by dignitaries from the two remaining towns in the fief. With all the pomp they could muster, they presented to Sylvia the results of their elections. She was now too famous and had won in both. Even if Wetron still coveted the fief, he would have lost, three to two.

With an impressive escort, Mason hurried the results to the capital, Ambrosia. Vendora, the queen, was no better, and the council of nobles acted quickly, certifying the results, making them official. Sylvia was the holder of the fief.

Mason retrieved his sisters and hurried back to Ytterby with them.

"I am not going to call her 'Mother,'" Patience said. "No matter what."

"Of course not," Mason replied. He smiled at them, Lalage in particular. "You'll see. Sylvia will be a friend you will welcome to have now that you are on the cusp of, ah, womanhood."

He was not entirely sure about how things would go between Sylvia and his siblings, but he decided to hope.

"I CALL it time dilation, Isaac," Albert said. "I know it is difficult, so out of all of our experiences, but it is a consequence of the laws I have proposed. Even if we erroneously assume that your law of gravity is the fundamental one, the speed of light in a vacuum is still the same for everyone, no matter how fast they move themselves."

"Then because of our trip, we should be younger than those around us, right?" Isaac asked.

"Yes, yes." Albert exhaled with a slight hint of impatience, then caught himself. "But we were gone for such a short time, there has been little effect on us. Look, let me diagram it again."

He began erasing a slate, then realized that he did not have to. The new 'Center for Advanced Studies', given to him and Isaac by expectant merchants, had so many that it would take days to fill them all. And some interesting experimental results were coming from examination of microscopic phenomena. Isaac seemed to have a flair for obtaining credible observations that would be important to understand.

"YES, I am giving up performance wizardry," Rangoth explained to Sylvia. "Here, take one of these cards. It has the particulars on how to get in touch. I got the idea from a colony of writers."

"But why?"

"First of all, I have had my fill of world-changing adventures. I am too old now for more of that. More importantly, there is no money in it anymore. People are jaded. Well, certainly in the big cities like Ambrosia where all the wealth is." The wizard smiled. "But you knew all about that very well, didn't you, Sylvia?"

Sylvia examined the rectangular scrap and frowned. "So, you will do what, exactly?"

"I will be a tutor. Teach the craft of wizardry."

"And you can earn enough by doing this?"

"Not at first, of course. Have to build a reputation. In the meantime, I have talked with a carnival owner to be his bouncer again. Use irritating nosetweakers instead of muscle. Not something desirable, but it will keep my stomach full as my new calling gains traction."

Rangoth raised an eyebrow. "And you?"

Sylvia smiled. "I will miss you, Mast — Rangoth. You taught me well. Wizardry is the best. And you are the best of the wizards."

Rangoth voice cracked. "And I will miss you as well, Sylvia. To an old wizard, you are a queen."

No more was said. They clasped in one long, final hug.

# 22

# A New Beginning

THE MUSCLES in Sylvia's neck tightened. It was to be her first meeting with representatives of the fief, and she wanted to make a good impression. She blew on the ink in the note she had finished, folded it, and applied the wax.

More than a note had been sealed, she thought. Her path had been altered permanently. She would no longer pursue what had driven her. Along with everyone else, the wizard Phoebe also needed to know.

Throughout it all, she *had* aged, matured considerably. From a serving wench to one who acted, faced perils, commanded others, decided what to do. She had changed. Believed far more deeply in herself, in what she was capable of doing.

"They have assembled, milady," the attendant poked her head through the doorway. Sylvia nodded. "I am almost ready. Only a few moments more."

Mason would be arriving shortly. His decision had surprised her. She had not seen it coming.

"I am no fiefholder," he had protested. "I'm a man of arts, not of state, have always been. I feel a sense of accomplishment when one of my productions is enjoyed by many. On the other hand, you, Sylvia, you are the one who has demonstrated without a doubt the mettle that is needed.

You will live forever in the sagas, the one who saved not only Murdina but the rest of the cosmos as well. Immediately, you were accepted as the new fiefholder. No one shouted discontent."

Mason was right about himself. He did not have the slightest notion about what lay ahead. People were starving, not only here but in every fief in Procolon. Bounties of food, but no means with which to pay for it. The new magic was changing everything too swiftly. There was not enough time to sample cautiously and adjust.

She frowned. But what should she do? Was Albert right? He thought that the old magic accelerated the growth of the new too swiftly. Made it easy to experiment and explore the minute details as well as the overwhelming facts with little effort. Should compounds of scholars like the 'Advanced Center' be allowed? All the Alberts and Isaacs of the world held by a tight leash? Perhaps the study of the new completely banned?

I am so impulsive, she thought. How will I get the patience to find the right possibility rather than only the first? She took a deep breath. No, it won't be as bad as all that. She will have Mason at her side. Slow and methodical, weighing all options. Together, they will select the best choices.

"Sweetheart," Mason bounced into the room. "I have just returned from the council of nobles. You will never guess what they are saying."

Sylvia's neck tightened even more. "They don't accept that I, a woman, can become a fiefholder? Wetron is having second thoughts?"

"No, no. Far better than that. Vendora is still recovering from her enchantment. The lines in her face grow deeper by the day. Speculation runs rampant that she does not have much longer to live."

"No children!" Sylvia nodded. "And no legal successor. The nobles are already jockeying for position and choosing up sides. Don't those busybodies understand? Now is not the time for a civil war."

"They *do* understand, my love. They do. And the sentiment is growing. More and more see merit in the idea. Someone neutral. A hero, well, heroine, who, when the time comes, will be accepted by all."

"Neutral? Who?"

"You, you silly goose! The mortar is already setting. Sylvia, when Vendora passes, you will be the ruler of all Procolon, the next queen!"

Sylvia slumped to a chair. "You are sure of this?"

"Yes, yes, absolutely."

"And then, you will be the ki —"

"No, no. Obviously, that would be a complete sham. But, my dear, as long as I am with you, 'consort' is a title I would happily accept."

"But the fief?"

"Give it back to Wetron when the time comes. He could run it well enough."

The strain on Sylvia's neck increased. It felt as if bands of steel were pressing her forehead into her skull. Become the queen? Would she have sufficient power then to ban the new magic? Was it ethical she do so? How would a serving wench fathom the best path to take? And perhaps even more important, she was no great heroine to be immortalized in the sagas. Dargonel had not been dispatched in fair combat but by deceit. Trickery. A lie.

Sylvia shook her head violently. She needed to channel her thoughts elsewhere. Take her mind off of what loomed ahead. She studied Mason for a moment and decided.

"Take off your tunic," she said.

"You mean now?" His eyes brightened. "You and me? Only moments before the meeting?"

"No, not that! Just give it to me, and please go. I must

compose myself."

Mason shed his tunic and left. Carrying it on her arm, Sylvia filled the tub against the far wall with water. She thrust in the garment and began rubbing it back and forth over the scrubbing board. Each stroke removed a little more of a small stain.

Sylvia sighed. The rhythm soothed her. The tension in her neck relaxed. Her efforts brought back fond memories. She was glad she had thought to have simple washing tools brought to her quarters.

Accomplish a simple task well, she thought. A full stomach and a roof to deflect the rain. Taking care of a doddering old man who kept his hands to himself. Such a life had not been a bad thing after all.

She recalled her plans to leave, journey south to begin a new life that would open the world for her. And by a different path, she had done that. A few tastes of wizardry and a trip even into the realm of demons. But that had been enough. Perhaps the mysteries of magic were glorified in the sagas a bit too much.

And now, the responsibility for other people. The looming threat of new magic destroying a traditional way of life. A future even more challenging in the offing.

"Milady, the assembled workers are growing restless." The attendant entered the room and whispered. "They are anxious to hear what you are going to do."

Sylvia stopped her scrubbing and held the tunic up for inspection. Yes, perfect. The stain was gone. She hung it on a peg over the hearth and took a moment to admire what she had accomplished. Yes, a simple job but one that was done. Perfect in every respect. Satisfying. Complete.

Sylvia sighed again. What had she gotten herself into? She looked at the soapy water in the washtub. Well, if she needed a confidence boost, she would always be able to find a task that she was sure she would complete correctly.

# Author's Afterword

Did you enjoy *Double Magic*?

Do you know others who might like it, too?

Why not contact them right now?

Do it now, while *Double Magic* is fresh in your mind. It will take only a few minutes.

Just send an email to one or more of your friends, telling them what you liked about my book. Word-of-mouth is the most powerful form of promotion. It will help me a lot!

To get a small appreciation gift for your effort, just point your browser at the link below. It will take you to where you can download *The Joy of Kiteflying*, a short science piece I have written.

Thanks for your help!

http://www.alodar.com/blog/kfd

# What's next?

If you want to start at the beginning, read *Master of the Five Magics* first. You will meet Alodar, the struggling journeyman thaumaturge under siege in a frontier fortress. He is smitten by Queen Vendora, a ravishing beauty for whom all the nobles in the land strive. His quest for the Fair Lady takes him on a journey to explore alchemy, sorcery, wizardry and true magic.

Order Master of the Five Magics
now
http://www.alodar.com/blog/mfm

In *Master of the Five Magics* we learn that there are five crafts governed by seven magic laws. Is seven all? The title of the second book, *Secret of the Sixth Magic* might lead you to think so, but (spoiler alert!) that merely was a marketing ploy when the book was first published years ago. The situation is much more complex.

The cover depicts what one might see if trapped inside a transparent cube, but (spoiler alert two!) the problem is that the dimensions of the cube are shrinking, and there does not seem to be any way to get out.

Order Secret of the Sixth Magic
now
http://www.alodar.com/blog/ssm

The first two books in the series, and this one, too, can be read in any order. Each of the three have their own independent set of characters. In *Riddle of the Seven Realms* you will meet, Astron, the one who walks—a denizen of the realm of demons with a congenital birth defect. His wings are shriveled and he cannot fly.

The cover of the book depicts an event that takes place in the palace of Elezar, a demon prince. Most of the realm of demons is a featureless void. It is hard to transport solid matter there from other places, and it is extremely valuable. The utmost ecstasy for a lightning djinn is to blast something of beauty into a scatter of individual atoms.

Order Riddle of the Seven Realms
now
http://www.alodar.com/blog/rsr

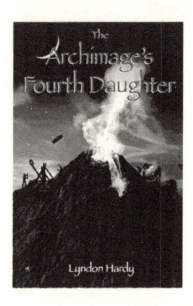

Briana is the youngest daughter of Alodar, the Archimage. Rather than wed a nobleman, she desires to go on adventures as did her famous father. She uses a magic portal to take her to another world. Her first task is to figure out what is going on in this strange, unfamiliar place.

The cover depicts some of the bad guys catapulting cylinders of a sulfuric gas into an active volcano. Why would anyone want to do that? Briana is determined to find out.

Can stepping on a butterfly in the Jurassic change human history? Might denizens of the realm of demons have something to do with it?

Read *Magic Times Three* to see if Fig and Briana find out.

From Chapter 2:
Fig stumbled a step backward. No towering devil stood before him as he had imagined … and feared. Instead, he gazed at a female about the same height as himself. The face more alluring than any artist's rendering of beauty could be.

"I am Lilith, what you on Earth call a succubus. Kiss me. That will be but a first hint of what delights await when you submit your will to mine."

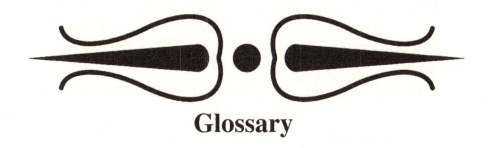

# Glossary

**Accretion Disk**

Matter circulating a central body due to force of gravity. Became part of our collective conscious with the publication of the first image of a black hole in 2019.

Wikipedia: https://en.wikipedia.org/wiki/Accretion_disk

See also the glossary entry: False Color

**The Archimage's Fourth Daughter**

Fourth book in the *Magic by the Numbers* series.

**Alchemy**

On earth, the root of the word comes from the Greek for transmutation. In the Middle Ages, alchemy focused on changing baser metals into gold, finding an elixir of life and a universal solvent. Some alchemical practices ultimately became the basis for modern chemistry.

In *Master of the Five Magics* and its sequels, alchemical procedures were described by formulas of arcane symbols kept in grimoires. Formula success was governed by probability; the more potent the result the less likely it was to succeed.

On earth, the most similar craft is that of a chemist.

Wikipedia: http://en.wikipedia.org/wiki/Alchemy

## Banshee

On the earth, an Irish folk legend about the harbringer's of death in the family. In *Double Magic*, there is not such a connection. Instead, banshees merely like to cry out because they think they are making beautiful music. Used as alert sirens by the nobility.

Wikipedia: https://en.wikipedia.org/wiki/Banshee

## Black Hole Image

The publication of what a black hole looks like caught everyone's imagination when it was published in 2019. With the addition of a couple of interlopers, it even appears on the cover of this book!

We saw a black center surrounded by a glowing asymmetrical ring. Without exploring further, it was easy to identify the boundary between the black center and the asymmetric band of color as being the event horizon, the radius smaller than which no one could ever return. Likewise, the band of color was the glowing accretion disk.

Well, that's not quite right

For me, a good explanation of what is really going on can be found in this YouTube video — one made even before the image was first shown! Be sure and check it out.

YouTube: https://www.youtube.com/watch?v=zUyH3XhpLTo

See also: Accretion Disk in this glossary.

## Bullrushes

A standard trope of adventure fiction — hiding in the bullrushes. Bullrushes are also called cattails.

Wikipedia: https://en.wikipedia.org/wiki/Bulrush

## Burning at the stake

According to references, it is quite painful. And evidently the intent of the stake-builders was to build not too big of a fire. They did not want things to get over with quickly.

Quora: https://www.quora.com/How-long-does-someone-burned-alive-at-the-stake-feel-pain-How-long-are-they-conscious-after-the-pain-stops

## Cabriolet

A two-wheeled, horse-drawn carriage. Room for seating two, with a driver standing in back on the outside.

Wikipedia:
https://en.wikipedia.org/wiki/Cabriolet_(carriage)

## Charm

On earth, a synonym for spells in general. In *Master of the Five Magics* and its sequels, a sorcerer's spell in particular.

Wikipedia: http://en.wikipedia.org/wiki/Charm

## Clarence

A four-wheeled, horse-drawn carriage. Room for seating four, with a driver sitting in front on the outside.

Wikipedia:
https://en.wikipedia.org/wiki/Clarence_(carriage)

## Compressed air amplifier

Not an outlandish concept at all.

YouTube: https://www.youtube.com/watch?v=J7SV65DFNy8

## Demon

Resident of another realm different from that of the universe containing the earth and the world of *Master of the Five Magics*. With the exception of djinns, of limited physical power in our realm. Synonymous with devil.

Wikipedia: http://en.wikipedia.org/wiki/Demon

http://en.wikipedia.org/wiki/Devil

http://en.wikipedia.org/wiki/List_of_fictional_demons

## Devil

A synonym for demon in *Master of the Five Magics* and its sequels.

Wikipedia: http://en.wikipedia.org/wiki/Devil

http://en.wikipedia.org/wiki/Demon

http://en.wikipedia.org/wiki/List_of_fictional_demons

## Dooking

A sound made by a ferret.

Reference: https://petfriendlypdx.com/ferret-sounds/

## Eclipses and primitive societies

Evidently, the historical record states that this actually happened with Columbus. The change in the tagline is my own invention.

Wikipedia:
https://en.wikipedia.org/wiki/March_1504_lunar_eclipse

## Epicycle

The epicycle is a milestone along the march of science in its quest to explain all the phenomena in the universe by what is predicted by physical laws.

In the geocentric view of the universe, the sun, the moon, and all the planets revolved around the earth. It explained things fairly well, but as measurement accuracy improved, there was one gnawing problem. When tracked against the fixed star background, the planets sometimes seemed to reverse direction.

This was caused by the fact that the earth, as well as the planets, orbited the sun. The earth, being closer, orbited faster and 'overtook' its companions from time to time.

No problem, the astronomers of the time declared. The planets did not move in a simple circle around the sun, but around a smaller circle that in turn orbited the bigger circle as it orbited the sun. So, sometimes planets actually did reverse direction.

This one correction by itself, however, still did not explain all the observations. So, a still smaller circle was postulated to rotate around the second one. More and more corrections were added to the model, but nothing could be found that agreed with observations.

Finally, the center of the universe was moved from the earth to the sun, and theory and experiment agreed much better.

Newton's postulation of the law of gravity sealed the deal. All the observations were as predicted. Well, not entirely. There still was a problem with the orbit of Mercury. It did not behave quite as it should.

The solution to this final discrepancy came about when

Einstein's model for gravitation was used instead.

Wikipedia:
https://en.wikipedia.org/wiki/Deferent_and_epicycle

**Ergosphere**

Albert Einstein's theory of general relativity was published in 1915. A year later, Karl Schwarzchild obtained the solution to Einstein's field equations for how gravity behaved outside of spherically symmetric, non-rotating body. This solution could not be extended any smaller than to a critical radius around the mass — what became to be known as the Schwarzchild radius.

Nothing inside could escape, and such objects became known as black holes. Did such objects actually exist was debated for many years.

Scientists now believe that there is a black hole in the center of every (most?) galaxies in our entire universe. One problem is that the matter infalling into a black hole most likely was previously rotating around it outside of the event horizon.

Even though black holes are weird, no one believes that the conservation of angular momentum is violated, so that the black hole itself must most likely be rotating itself. The influx of rotation has to go somewhere.

One possibility is that jets of matter exploding perpendicular to a galactic plane might be a mechanism for getting rid of some of the angular momentum. Or the matter inside of the blackhole could be speeding up.

It wasn't until 1963, almost 50 years after Einstein's original publication, that the equations were solved for a black hole that was rotating. Its behavior was even more bizarre than a non-rotating one. There was not a single event horizon, but two, and an additional region named the ergosphere.

Wikipedia:

https://en.wikipedia.org/wiki/Rotating_black_hole

and

https://en.wikipedia.org/wiki/Ergosphere

See also in this glossary: Penrose Process

## Fundamental Forces

At present, physicists think that there are four fundamental forces:

Gravity, Weak, Electromagnetic, and Strong

At high energies, it is thought that all but gravity behave the same.

See also in this glossary: Reductionism

Albert, the magician, thought there were three fundamental forces:

Gravity, Electricity, and Magnetism

He knew nothing of the strong and weak forces. It is also a stretch of my imagination for him not to have not seen the equivalence of electricity and magnetism into one basic force. Reasoning about the speed of light to have the same value universally would logically have led him to combine the two into one. But then, who knows why he didn't. We all have blind spots.

The strong, electromagnetic and weak forces all deal with things on the small scale where quantum mechanics plays a big part. At high enough energies, they merge into what can be regarded as a single type of force. The effects of gravity are seen in very large objects, some so massive that they create a black hole.

As of 2020, no one has been able to combine the two into a unified whole that holds sway over the colossal range from the very small to the very large.

Wikipedia:

https://en.wikipedia.org/wiki/Fundamental_interaction

**The Knapsack Problem**

A problem popular in mathematics for quite some time. It also appears in other works such as Neal Stephenson's Cryptonomicon.

Wikipedia:
https://en.wikipedia.org/wiki/Knapsack_problem

## Magic

The use of means outside of those normally available to affect change. On earth, the terms magic, sorcery, thaumaturgy, and wizardry are roughly synonymous.

In *Master of the Five Magics* and its sequels, each, along with alchemy, have distinct meanings. Magic is performed by the exercise of rituals, the steps of which are derived from extensions of rituals deduced previously.

The goal of these exercises is the production of magical objects, things that are perfect in what they do, such as mirrors, daggers, swords, and shields. Once created, with few exceptions, they last forever.

The power of magic is limited by the time and expense involved in performing magic rituals. Some take several generations and the involvement of many participants. Because of the effort involved, magical objects are quite expensive.

On earth, the most similar craft is that of a mathematician.

Wikipedia: http://en.wikipedia.org/wiki/Magic

## Mandrake

According to legend, when a mandrake plant is pulled from its roots, it emits a horrible shriek. Whoever hears it dies. The facts as described in *Double Magic* are a little less potent.

Wikipedia: https://en.wikipedia.org/wiki/Mandrake

Click on the link above and scroll down to the section titled *Magic and Witchcraft*.

## Maxwell's Demon

Originally conceived by the physicist James Clerk Maxwell as a thought experiment about the validity of the second law of thermodynamics. Little did he know that he was channeling a being from the realm of demons.

Wikipedia:
https://en.wikipedia.org/wiki/Maxwell%27s_demon

## Metalaws

Metalaws are laws about laws. The laws about the laws of magic is the central theme of *Secret of the Sixth Magic*. I had wanted *Metalaws* to be the title of my second book, but my editor, Lester del Rey, insisted that it would not be understood as a sequel by readers.

He proposed instead, *Secret of the Sixth Magic*.

"Sixth Magic?" I protested. "There is no sixth magic mentioned in the book at all."

Del Rey approximately countered with, "Here's what you do. Part way through the book, you have your protagonist say something like, 'Hmm, maybe there is a sixth undiscovered magic operating here … No, on second thought, that's can't be right. Something else is going on.' The term 'sixth magic' is mentioned, so the title is 'justified'. All is well."

## Master of the Five Magics

The first book in the *Magic by the Numbers* series.

## Magic Times Three

Fifth book in the *Magic by the Numbers* series.

## Murdina

Home world for *Double Magic, Master of the Five Magics*, and *Secret of the Sixth Magic*.

## Paradoxes

The consequences of the physical laws of relativity being true are bizarre. Here are links with some explanations to some famous seeming paradoxes.

### The twin paradox

One of two twins blasts off in a spaceship to a distant star and then returns. His twin stays on the earth. They stay in contact during the journey, and, because of the time dilation predicted by relativity, both observe that the other's clock is running slower than their own. Each one surmises that the other is aging slower.

But, both of them cannot be younger than the other. What is going on here?

The correct answer is that the twin who left the earth and returned is the younger one.

Many explanations have been published on why this is so. For me, perhaps the clearest one is the following YouTube video. You might have to play it a few times to wrap your head around what is happening, but it has the advantage of not requiring any general relativity or math equations in the explanation.

The key concept: W,hat is happening to the two twins is not the same.

YouTube:

https://www.youtube.com/watch?v=noaGNuQCW8A

**The ladder and the garage**

One of your neighbors has a garage that is 10 meters wide. He buys an extension ladder that gets jammed in its fullest extension of 15 meters. It will no longer fit in the garage. (Well, yes, he could try storing it lengthwise, but someone who works with ladders that are that long and can't figure that out ...)

No problem the neighbor says. "I will have a pal run past the garage at a relativistic speed. Just like the theory of relativity predicting that moving clocks run slower, lengths are contracted. So, if my pal races fast enough, the ladder length can contract to be under 15 meters, and a sideward push at precisely the right time will fit it into the garage."

What really happens?

There are many references that address this problem. Most that I could find were quite heady. Perhaps for me, the best is the following:

Wikipedia:

https://en.wikipedia.org/wiki/Ladder_paradox

This reference also discusses the paradox of the relativistically speeding train approaching a bridge with its center span missing. To the engineer, the open gap in the bridge is contracted to be a fraction of a centimeter. He will pass over it and hardly notice. An observer on the ground, however, will see this tiny, tiny train that surely will fall in the gap.

Had your fill, yet? There are other paradoxes than these more famous ones. Here are references to a couple of them to puzzle your friends with:

**The rotating disk ( the Ehrenfest paradox)**

Wikipedia:

https://en.wikipedia.org/wiki/Ehrenfest_paradox

**The snapping string**

Wikipedia:

https://en.wikipedia.org/wiki/Bell%27s_spaceship_paradox

**Penrose Process**

A mechanism devised by Roger Penrose that theoretically would allow an advanced civilization to extract energy from a rotating black hole.

Wikipedia: https://en.wikipedia.org/wiki/Penrose_process

## Reductionism

One of the central tenets of modern physics is *Reductionism* — boiling down the number of things that must just "be" in our universe. In principle, *everything else*, all the things that we see and measure in our universe can be derived from them.

### The First Reduction

The first reduction in our concept about the forces of nature was that electricity and magnetism were merely different aspects of the same fundamental law.

Electricity is based on the concept of *charge*. There are two types, positive and negative. Like charges repel and unlike charges attract.

Magnetism is based upon *currents* — moving charges. Coil a wire around an iron core. Run electricity through it, and, bingo, you get a magnet, a device that interacts quite differently with other things than did isolated charges.

But one person's charge is another person's current. Traveling past a stationary charge is the same as standing still and having the charge move past in the opposite direction instead. A moving charge is a current. So, like a magician, you can transform electricity into magnetism just by walking around a bit. The term *electromagnetism* was coined to show that what were originally thought to be quite different forces were merely different aspects of a single one.

## The Second Reduction

At the turn of the nineteenth century into the twentieth, the periodic table of around 100 different elements was explained by the concept of an *atom*. All atoms were composed of three kinds of more elementary particles: positively charged protons, neutral neutrons and negatively charged electrons. The protons and neutrons were held together in a nucleus while electrons whirled around it. Different combinations of these three more fundamental particles explained all different kinds of elements.

## Reductionism Loses Ground

But wait! The by then firmly established law of electromagnetism stated that like charges repelled one another. What was holding all of the protons together in the nucleus? Never to be slow on their feet, physicists deduced that another force existed, one so strong it could resist the electromagnetic repulsion.

So now we had three forces again: gravity, electromagnetism, and ... Evidently the more poetic physicists were on holiday, and so the down-to-earth types came up with the name for this new stronger force. It was called, tada, *the strong force*.

But wait again! Not everything in the realm of nuclei was

explained by the strong force. An isolated neutron away from any other particles was not stable. It decayed into a proton, electron, and a third particle dubbed the neutrino — Italian for "little nothing."

Another type of force was needed, and the more poetic physicists went on holiday again. The fourth force, drum roll please, was named *the weak force*.

### Reductionism Rises Again

For a while it looked as if the reductionists were losing ground, but more experiments and head scratching were used to show that at high enough energies, the strong, weak, and electromagnetic forces became more and more alike. In that limit, we are back to just two types of forces, gravity and the other guy. As of late 2020, no one has come up with a way to reduce these remaining two forces into just one.

### Robe

Practitioners of each of the five magics are distinguished by the capes and robes they wear.

Thaumaturges wear brown covered with what is on earth the mathematical symbol of similarity.

Alchemists wear white covered with triangles with a single vertex bottom-most symbolizing the delicate balance between success and failure when performing a formula.

Magicians wear blue with the palest for a neophyte and the darkest for the master and covered by circular rings symbolizing the perfect mathematical object.

Sorcerers wear gray covered with the logo of the staring eye symbolizing the ability to see far in time and place and into another's inner being.

Wizards wear black covered with wisps of flame symbolizing the portal by which the realm of demons and the realm of men are connected.

## Riddle of the Seven Realms

Third book in the *Magic by the Numbers* series.

## Scissor lift

Used even with the old magic, especially thaumaturgy. Provides a stable and strong platform that has an adjustable height. Much better than a ladder. Look at the reference to get an idea of what one looks like.

Wikipedia:
https://en.wikipedia.org/wiki/Scissors_mechanism

## The Speed of Light

In 1905, Albert Einstein published his theory of *Special Relativity*. It boils down to two simple fundamental laws of science:

The laws of physics are the same everywhere in our entire universe

The speed of light in vacuum is the same for all observers in our entire universe

It is probably easy for all of us to accept the first law as being true. It sounds quite reasonable. The second, however, is a little harder to take because it is so antithetical to our day to day encounters with moving objects. If this second law is true — and it has been proven to be true by experiment, millions of time — then there are some unexpected consequences.

Suppose a light ray heads out of the nose of my spaceship. I fire my thrusters and pursue. I have a very hot ship. It can go ninety percent the speed of light itself. So, wouldn't it look like the light ray is only going ten percent of the speed of light to me?

The answer is no. No matter how fast you pursue the light ray, it will still recede from you at the speed of light in vacuum.

Wait a minute, we say. Things have to add and subtract correctly. That law can't be right. For example, suppose I am on the freeway going 65 miles per hour and someone passes me doing 66. it looks to me like he is slowly creeping away at 1 mile per hour. The basic equation is:

deltaV = V2 - V1

In this example, 66 - 65 = 1, right?

Okay then, suppose I am going at 90 percent of the speed of light pursing the light beam. The equation would say that to me, the light beam was receding at:

1c - .9c = .1c,

where c represents the speed of light. What's wrong with that reasoning?

Well, what is wrong is the equation. It is not deltaV = V2 - V1. Instead it is:

$$deltaV = (V2 - V1)/(1 + (V1 \text{ times } V2/c^2))$$

Yeah, this looks more complicated, but it is not too much baggage. Plug in c for V2 and .9c for V1 and see what you get. Even though you are going 90 percent the speed of light, the beam is still receding from you at c! And for cars on a freeway, there is an extremely tiny effect, so small that no speedometer could measure it.

Please understand that this velocity formula was not invented in a scramble. Something that magically works for both familiar speeds and relativistic ones, too. It was not invented out of whole cloth like the explanations that come out of the flying saucer abduction conventions that have an answer for everything if the speaker is fast enough on his feet.

No, the correct velocity formula is *derivable* from just asserting that the second law of special relativity is in fact truth. Modifications also had to be derived for other formulas from Newton's time as well. All have the characteristic of working for both slow and relativistic fast motions.

The classic formulas that one learns in high school physics are Newtonian. They have to be modified when dealing with relativistic speeds. And at first, a lot of physicists resisted doing so. To make conservation of momentum still be true, for example, the concept of 'moving mass' was invented

I remember as a college freshman trying to grapple with what the mechanism could possibly be for mass increasing merely because it was moving. With perfect hindsight, that concept didn't even have to be introduced. Mass was an intrinsic property that was measured in the rest frame of the object in question. It is denoted by $m_0$. It never had to change. The formulas it was involved in could be changed instead. In fact, even Einstein could have been a little more clear if he had written $E = m_0{}^2$ for the energy inherent in mass, instead of $E = m^2$ that includes things like kinetic energy as well.

Wikipedia:

https://en.wikipedia.org/wiki/Special_relativity

https://en.wikipedia.org/wiki/Speed_of_light#Faster-than-light_observations_and_experiments

## Spell

On earth the terms cantrip, charm, enchantment, glamour, incantation, and spell are synonymous — the performance of an act of magic.

In *Master of the Five Magics* and its sequels, except for the word spell itself, each of the others have particular meanings. The word spell is a generic umbrella for any of them.

Thaumaturgy — incantation

Alchemist — formula performance

Magician — ritual exercise

Sorcerer — charm recitation

Wizard — invocation

## Secret of the Sixth Magic

Second book in the *Magic by the Numbers* series.

## Subordinate

The first four crafts have named subordinates in *Master of the Five Magics* and its sequels.

Thaumaturgy — Journeyman, Apprentice

Alchemist — Novice

Magician — Neophyte, Initiate, Acolyte

Sorcerer — Tyro

## Tambour

A word with several meanings. In *Double Magic*, it refers to the frame over which a fine net is stretched and into which lace is embroidered.

Wikipedia: https://en.wikipedia.org/wiki/Tambour_lace

## Thaumaturgy

The use of means outside of normal availability to affect change. On earth, the terms magic, sorcery, thaumaturgy, and wizardry are roughly synonymous.

In *Master of the Five Magics* and its sequels, each, along with alchemy, have distinct meanings. Thaumaturgy is performed by the reciting incantations that bind together objects at a distance that once had physically been together and with a source of energy that can perform work.

The power of thaumaturgy is limited by the fact that all incantations must conserve energy or, as sometimes stated, the first law of thermodynamics.

On earth, the term derives from the Greek for miracle and the most similar craft is that of a physicist.

Wikipedia: http://en.wikipedia.org/wiki/Thaumaturgy

## TNT

Red-tinted water is a tell-tale for the production of trinitrotoluene.

TNT's popularity is due primarily to how it can be safely handled. It takes a powerful jolt from a more volatile explosive, the primer, to set it off. Primers can be quite small and are shipped and stored separately from the TNT itself.

Definitely, an example of what can be produced by the new magic.

Wikipedia: https://en.wikipedia.org/wiki/TNT

## Toque

In *Double Magic*, a brimless hat that indicated the wearer was a baker.

Wikipedia: https://en.wikipedia.org/wiki/Toque

## Tricorn Hat

A three-sided hat popular in the 1700's.

Wikipedia: https://en.wikipedia.org/wiki/Tricorne

## Using False Color

A display technique in which electromagnetic radiation not in the visible light spectrum is transformed so that it is.

An example is the accretion disk around the black hole image published in 2019. The light around the black hole is actually X-rays and totally invisible to our eyes.

For the gnomes in *Double Magic*, the controversy of whether or not to do this is a big one that divided them into two factions.

Wikipedia:

https://en.wikipedia.org/wiki/False_color

## Wizardry

The use of means outside of normal availability to affect change. On earth, the terms magic, sorcery, thaumaturgy, and wizardry are roughly synonymous.

In *Master of the Five Magics* and its sequels, each have distinct meanings. Wizardry is performed by the invocation of demons from another realm from that of the earth.

The potency of a wizard is limited by the power of the demons that he can dominate.

On earth, there is no such craft as such, although one could argue that the practices of witches and warlocks are similar.

Wikipedia: http://en.wikipedia.org/wiki/Witchcraft

## Ytterby

A town in Sweden noted for the number of new elements in the periodic table discovered there. By an amazing coincidence, Ytterby is also the name of the village in the kingdom of Procolon in which many alchemists practicing the new magic had their shops and labs.

Wikipedia: https://en.wikipedia.org/wiki/Ytterby

## Zany Ferrets

The mention in the text about using ferrets to clean out pipes might not be as far fetched as it sounds.

https://www.atlasobscura.com/articles/felicia-ferret-particle-accelerator-fermilab

Made in the USA
Coppell, TX
22 December 2021

69916611R00215